SPARKS FLY

BIRDIE LYNN

BIRDIE LYNN

COUNTERPOISE
PRESS

SPARKS FLY

Text copyright © 2023 by Birdie Lynn

All rights reserved. No part of this book may be reproduced in any form or by any electronic or mechanical means, including information storage and retrieval systems, without written permission from the author, except for the use of brief quotations in a book review.

This is a work of fiction. Any names, places, characters and incidents are the products of the author's imagination and are fictitious. Any resemblance to actual persons, living or dead, events or establishments is solely coincidental.

First published in the United States in August 2023 by Counterpoise Press

Identifiers:

Library of Congress Control Number: 2023909468

ISBN 978-1-7367414-6-7 (paperback) | ISBN 978-1-7367414-7-4 (ebook)

10 9 8 7 6 5 4 3 2 1

To find out more about Counterpoise Press visit www.counterpoisepress.com

To find out more about Birdie Lynn visit www.birdielynn.com

To anyone who could fill a bingo card with their most beloved romance tropes.

And for those who've searched for queer spaces in a magical world and been left wanting.

1

"Hit me with your best shot, Pham."

Mika Rivera aimed a devastating smile at Arthur as they circled the middle of the classroom, wands aloft. Their professor heaved a long-suffering sigh, drowned in the catcalls and whistles from the crowd of green blazers and cream sweaters around them. Arthur stifled a smirk and rolled his eyes. Enough was enough.

"Oh, no. You're not going to break out into song, are you?" Arthur swiped his wand up in an arc, commanding the oxygen atoms in the air around him into a razor-sharp whip and snapping it in Mika's direction.

Without blinking an eye, Mika shot his wand arm out to the side, cupping his palm. A small ball of flame materialized there, dropping the temperature in the room several degrees, consuming Arthur's whip before it could strike true, sending the flame into a blaze.

"Not unless you go all-out *Dirty Dancing* on me." Mika grinned, embers alight in his hazel eyes. "Come on, let's do the lift. I promise I *definitely* won't drop you."

He cocked his arm back, swinging it in a couple circles for show before pitching the fireball back at Arthur. His showmanship cost him the element of surprise; Arthur had already gathered the moisture from the air to send a small tidal wave hurtling forward along the ground from behind him. It sluiced through the space between them.

"Sorry, am I in the right room? I'm here for the magic duel, not the dance battle." Arthur's eyes watered, bone-dry, but he couldn't complain as the wave doused Mika—and half the class—in its wake. He smirked at how closely his rival resembled a wet puppy, carefully mussed brown curls dripping down over his eyes as he pouted.

"Nobody puts me in the corner."

Only further confirming the resemblance, Mika gave a great shake, dispelling the moisture back into the air as their classmates burst into a fresh round of cheers.

Professor Hirst, soaked to the bone, blinked his eyes with great patience. "So who can summarize for us what Mr. Pham and Mr. Rivera have demonstrated here, regarding how the four elements can be harnessed in our world at any given time—"

But someone's voice in the crowd rose above the others: "Autograph my ass, Mika!" and Professor Hirst's plea for order was lost to the din for the third time in as many minutes. Arthur had half a mind to feel guilty, but he could Sense the vibrations in the air around their professor. He was already going to give them outstanding marks—as always.

No longer under Arthur's influence, the remaining water in the classroom excused itself, evaporating into the air. He rolled up his sleeves. "Is that really the best you can do, Rivera?"

Mika gave a derisive "ha" and leaned over. For a split second, Arthur thought he had dived into an elaborate curtsy, but then he saw Mika's wand touch the floor. He braced himself as Mika rose, pulling up his wand slowly, meeting resistance as the floor started to rumble.

Professor Hirst grabbed his desk to steady it. "I swear, if you open up a hole in the ground again—"

But he was silenced as the entire desk seemed to deconstruct itself in double time, collapsing into wooden planks and then into logs which coalesced to form an entire tree, spontaneously sprouting up from the floor. Much of the same was happening to all the desks pushed back against the wall and soon the room more closely resembled a forest clearing than a classroom, save for the fluorescent lighting.

Their classmates roared and stomped their approval. Several students in the back clambered up into the trees to get a better view of the duel, but Arthur merely shifted his weight onto his left leg and crossed his arms, eyebrows raised.

Mika was grinning, devouring the praise. Arthur waited.

Finally, Mika's smile faltered. Arthur pursed his lips thoughtfully and looked up at the canopy of leaves above them, which were starting to shake. The students perched there hastily abandoned their posts as Arthur glanced at his watch, then back up at Mika.

"Ten seconds. Impressive. However, I do think Newton's about to have his say here."

Sure enough, the trees began to shake violently, and in the span of a single second they cycled through their construction all over again, de-materializing into logs, shaping themselves into planks, and constructing themselves back into desks with the nuts and bolts they'd abandoned on the floor.

Mika breathed hard, and Arthur sucked his teeth sympathetically. "I hear magical stamina is indicative of your stamina in bed. I wonder if that's true?"

Professor Hirst didn't even attempt to protest as the students launched into a chorus of jeers, louder than ever.

Undeterred, Mika shot Arthur a grin through the sweat. "Like you could last any longer."

Wordlessly, Arthur tapped his wand to an antique cherrywood chair beside one of the desks, closing his eyes as he pulled up his wand, bringing a blossoming cherry tree along with it.

Keeping his eyes closed, he willed some of his own energy into the tree, aiding it in its genesis. He extended his awareness to the breeze outside and invited it into the classroom. Cherry blossom petals drifted in the air.

Someone started counting. Arthur felt the chair's fatigue, felt its creaking, stubborn tendency to want to be a chair. He siphoned off a little more of his energy into it, encouraging it as the chorus of voices crescendoed to a climax. Just a little longer...

"Fifty-five, fifty-six—"

He was going to need a long nap after this spell, but after opening one eye to see the look on Mika's face...it was worth it.

"Fifty-eight, fifty-nine, *sixty!*"

Arthur lowered his wand as his classmates yelled, staunchly fighting the desire to lie face down on the floor. He winked at Mika.

"Newton's First Law: 'An object at rest will remain at rest unless *continuously* acted upon by an external force.' Read a book once in a while; you might learn a few things. Although..." Arthur pocketed his wand and gave Mika a sympathetic look, relishing in how his jaw clenched. "Can't really help you with the stamina thing."

And even after three years of divination classes at Stonebury's Conservatory for Young Mages, Arthur couldn't possibly have predicted the impeccable timing of the class bell, chiming to signal the end of class in that precise moment.

★

"Fun show today. I think you might have topped the one on Monday."

Arthur turned to find his coworker, Tan Fernando, calling up to him from the library floor. He twisted away from the bookshelf ladder to perch back against it, squinting against the sunlight streaming through the nearest floor-to-ceiling window.

"I'll admit, I can't turn down an opportunity to put Rivera in his place."

"Never a dull moment with you two around." Tan smirked.

Arthur lowered his wand, lowering the books he'd been re-shelving along with it. He'd used up enough energy for the day.

"He loves to put on a show, I'll give you that."

"Oh, please. You're as into it as he is."

Arthur narrowed his eyes at the condescending glint in Tan's gaze. "Excuse me?"

"Just saying." They shrugged. "I'd love to actually learn something in Evocation for once."

Arthur rolled his eyes. "Take it up with Professor Hirst. He just can't let the practical demonstrations go."

Tan chuckled, and Arthur bristled. "Professor Lottie wanted me to tell you to head out after you're done with that stack. Everyone's hoarding their books for midterms, so there isn't much left to do for today."

"Aye-aye, captain." Arthur saluted his classmate dryly as they walked away, turning back to the shelf to levitate his stack of books back up to eye level.

"Sweet, I'd been looking for that one."

Mika had materialized, seemingly out of nowhere, to climb a

neighboring ladder and roll at high-speed to where Arthur stood. He snatched one of the floating books out of the air.

"Oh, would you look at the time." Arthur glanced at his watch without looking at it. "We're closing in...five minutes ago."

"This is a twenty-four-hour library, ass."

"Not sure if you were aware—" Arthur busied himself with returning a book to its proper place on the shelf— "but the library is for people who are, you know, literate."

"I read," Mika protested, cracking open the book he'd stolen as if to prove his point. It probably would have been a more emphatic argument if he hadn't opened *Feminismagic: Everything We Learn Today is Thanks to Women* upside down.

"And I work." Arthur returned the last book in his collection to the shelf. "Not all of our parents are employed by the biggest tech company in the magical world. Some of us have to innovate and work for our tuition, you privileged piece of shit."

"You mean the frou-frou phone charms you've been handing out?" Mika adopted the Lithuanian flavor that so often wormed its way into Arthur's speech. He started throwing the book up and down. "No offense hon', but I think your side hustle would have more luck at Featherwood's."

"First of all, it's called Auratech. Second of all, heteronormative much? And third of all, congratulations on proving my point that you don't understand the value of hard work." Arthur raised his eyebrows. "Pray tell, what did you do this summer? Catch a tan in *Miami?*" He tried his best approximation of Mika's grating American accent in retaliation.

Mika tossed his book up extra high. "Nah, this brown beauty's all natural."

He offered a rakish grin that made his hazel eyes sparkle, honey skin gleaming in the sunlight, bare forearm flexing under a rolled-up shirtsleeve as he hung lazily from the ladder.

A spark of ire flashed hot in Arthur's gut. He flicked his wand, and the book fell on Mika's head; Mika tumbled down the ladder and onto the floor.

He rubbed his elbow where he'd banged it on the way down. "Fuck—"

"—off, I quite agree. Bye." Arthur effortlessly slid down his ladder and stepped over Mika to make his way over to the time-punch pad, leaving his mortal enemy grumbling swear words under his breath.

Arthur wasn't usually a competitive person.

Well, that wasn't true.

Arthur had learned to be competitive. After all, he'd had good reason for it: scholarships were hard to come by at Stonebury, and he'd secured every single one he could get his hands on. God forbid his GPA fall below a 4.0—his tireless hard work leading up to his last year at university would be all for naught. Mika's insufferable insistence on effortless achievement kept Arthur on his toes, fueling his fire to come out on top of someone who had so little regard for his wealth and social status.

Needless to say, Arthur relished leaving Mika behind in the dust. He tapped his wand to the crystal pad next to the time-punch machine, clocking himself out of his shift before doubling back to step right over Mika—still working his way up from the floor—on his way out of the library.

★

"Well, everyone," Professor Silverton announced as she passed out tests down the rows of students, "if these exams are anything to go by, you all have a lot of work ahead of you for midterms...except for a select few, who got *perfect* scores. Congratulations, and treat yourselves while everyone else studies their asses off."

Arthur's Sense pricked the hairs on the back of his neck, and he looked up to find Mika making a face at him from a few seats down the live-edge wood table spanning their row. He was holding up his test; Arthur seethed at the sight of the large 100 circled in red at the top.

He flashed his own 100 back at Mika alongside a careless, raised eyebrow before dismissing him in favor of gazing out the long windows behind Professor Silverton's desk, framed by seamless wallpaper featuring an abstract splotch of forest green watercolor. From this south-facing window, he could see where the island on which Stonebury stood gave way to the lake surrounding it. In his mind's eye, he walked down the cobblestone-paved pathway stretching over the water, bridging the school to the mainland across gentle waves and leading into *Watergraafsmeer*—into the hip and upcoming block where he'd spotted the *'For Rent'* sign in the shopfront on weekend trips into the city. While Professor Silverton rattled off areas of focus in Transmutation and engineering enchantments to work on for the midterm, Arthur lost himself in daydreams of buying the shop with meager savings to house Auratech, upholstering it in sleek metallics and sparkling lights designed to help his inventions throw light, drawing oohs and aahs from eager customers—

"Mr. Pham?"

Arthur was wrenched from his reverie.

"Sorry, Professor?"

"I was hoping you could demonstrate the wandwork required for number seven on the exam? About how kinetic patterns harness the energy of atoms for us to create magic?"

Arthur blushed, burying his nose in his exam, scanning the paper quickly. "Right, of course, I—"

"Please, Professor," came an all-too-familiar voice, and Arthur knew he'd been half a second too late. "If I may?"

Instead of walking all the way around the long table, Mika sat on it and pivoted around to jump off, straightening at the front of the class. Arthur flushed deeper. *Showoff.*

"Like this?"

Mika pulled out his wand and arced it in a perfect Fibonacci spiral. The atoms in the air around his wand locked into place, glowing in a complex, intertwining pattern before dissipating harmlessly, unable to maintain the energy without organic material to cling to.

Mika shot a surreptitious wink at Arthur.

As Mrs. Silverton applauded, Arthur fumed. Engineering was his! *How dare he!*

Once Mika leapt over the table to return to the squashy armchair that was his seat, Mrs. Silverton began her lecture, and Arthur straightened. He wouldn't be caught off guard again. Having gone all out in the class before was no excuse.

"It is widely known that bismuth is the best conduit for Crystal-technology, but can anyone tell me why? Yes, Mr. Pham, go ahead."

Arthur's hand had shot up before she finished the question, and he knew even before he heard his name it had been a fraction of a second ahead of Mika's. "The circuitry of man-made crystals allows us to more finely manipulate the massive amounts of energy required to run Crystaltech, like catching the energy with a funnel and channeling it into very specific areas where it needs to go."

"Well said, Mr. Pham. I expected no less from our resident crystal engineering tycoon."

Arthur's heart swelled.

"But Professor—" Mika's hand was still up, and heat spiked in Arthur's gut. He treated himself to a fantasy about launching down the table to strangle Mika. "What other crystals have been experimented with for Crystaltech use? Wouldn't crystals with a higher capacity for storing energy—say, the versatile Clear Quartz—be better suited to handle such energy levels?"

Arthur couldn't contain the contemptuous snort. "Right, if you want your laptop to blow up every time you turn on your Wi-Fi, sure."

"I'm not saying we would use crystals straight from the damn forest, only that maybe there's an opportunity for even more sustainable—"

"If it ain't broke—"

"The only thing that's broke in here is the broken record, and it's you—"

"Why don't you stay in your own lane—"

"Boys!" Professor Silverton lifted her hands, and the electricity of their debate fizzled out into silence. "I appreciate the passion, but why don't we save discussion time for Seminar? And give Mr. Rivera more credit, Mr. Pham. We can never be so arrogant as to think the first right answer we find is the only one. We're always learning and expanding our knowledge. If there's one thing you should take away from your time at Stonebury, it's that."

She leveled Arthur with a stare before continuing her lecture.

Heat creeping up his collar notified him of Mika making another face his way from two artist stools and a shell-backed accent chair away, but he sank down further into his chintz armchair and kept his gaze resolutely forward.

God, he could not wait until Year Four was over. He'd outgrown the classroom setting.

And he'd give anything to outgrow his rivalry with Mika Rivera.

The bell couldn't come soon enough. Arthur packed his bag and stood to leave before it even ended its trill, shooting past Mika to speed out the classroom door. He retrieved his phone from his pocket as he ran through a mental checklist of things to do once he got back to his room: *Transmutation homework, hang new poster, call Ma, walk to town with Clarke and Jonathan to pick up Samhain ingredients—*

And speak of the devil: his friends were already in the group chat.

> CLARKE
> When are we meeting
> Where are we meeting
>
> JONATHAN
> Why are we meeting
> What are we meeting
>
> CLARKE
> PLEASE
>
> JONATHAN
> Lmao
> See you back at the room
>
> CLARKE
> AAAAA

"Happy Halloween, Pham!"

Arthur raised his gaze to glare at Mika, who had that insufferable grin donned once more as he threw Arthur a salute, practically skipping past him.

"Fuck off," Arthur called, returning his attention to his phone.

Clarke had sent several more panicked texts while he'd looked away. Arthur smiled and managed to shoot off a quick *'I need a nap, my room in an hour'* before his phone lit up with an incoming call. Arthur frowned. It was a Stonebury area code.

"Hello?"

There was a cough and some rustling papers on the other line. The hairs on the back of Arthur's neck stood up.

His intuition didn't disappoint.

"Mr. Pham, I'm afraid I have some bad news."

2

Arthur froze in his tracks, rooted to the spot in the middle of the courtyard.

Ms. Wells from the financial aid office cleared her throat on the other end of the line. "Mr. Pham?"

"Y-yes, sorry. What's happened?"

"I'm calling because of an issue with your tuition check from this semester."

His palms started to sweat.

"What kind of issue?"

"Well..." She hesitated. "We were unable to process it."

"What does that mean, 'unable to process it?'"

"It bounced," Ms. Wells admitted.

Arthur's heart skipped a beat. Two.

"Mr. Pham?"

"I'm here," Arthur croaked.

"Right, well." Ms. Wells cleared her throat. "We were a bit late in processing all the checks this semester, so you have some time to resolve the issue. We'll need your payment by the end of next week."

"Next week," Arthur repeated, numb.

"Right," Ms. Wells confirmed. "Shall I contact the sender of the check? A Ms....ah, your mother, Ms. Anh Pham?"

"No," Arthur interrupted. "No, I'll handle it myself. Thank you."

"You're sure?"

"Yes."

"Alright then, Mr. Pham. You have a good day."

"You too," Arthur muttered before hanging up.

He stood, staring. Students done with class for the day—clad in greens and creams and ties and shimmering crystal lapel pins—now flooded the circular pavement of the courtyard laid into the expanse of succulents planted in the ground, spiraling out from where a bronze statue of the original Headmaster Elias Stonebury stood, wand aloft. Arthur was seized with the impression of glittering insects flitting to and fro in a garden, dancing in interwoven patterns as he tried to count his breathing. In-one, out-two, in-three, out-four...

Once he got to ten, he forced his legs to keep moving, raising his phone once more to call his mother.

He wasn't sure what he'd expected, but he still felt a flash of frustration when the phone rang five times, then went to voicemail. He shot off a text:

> Call me back, financial aid said something's up with your check?

Think. Arthur paused on the east side of the courtyard to settle on a bench under a willow and tried to count his breaths again. *Think, think, think. How can I fix this?*

He called his mom three or four more times, to no avail. *How can I fix this?*

He shot off a text to his sister.

> Where's Ma?

ANNABELLE
> Annabelle: Work, picked up an extra shift. Why?

> Just school stuff, no worries.

Arthur leaned his elbows on his knees and stared at his phone. *Think.*

It buzzed again.

> **MA**
> At work. I meant to tell you, the car needed work.........
>
> But I thought the tuition checks got processed last month?

> They're running behind this semester.
>
> When should I tell them the check will go through?

> **MA**
> Well.........I saved up that money over summer to pay.
>
> Will save up more, have it ready in a few months, could you pick up another work study shift......

Arthur closed his eyes tight. How hadn't she realized the money had never been deposited? How had she forgotten his work study limit? How was this happening, why was this happening, what was he going to *do*?

> I'm already doing the max amount; they need it by end of next week.
>
> Maybe I could ask for an extension but not that long probably

It was five minutes before the reply came.

> **MA**
> I could pick up more shifts.........

Guilt roiled in Arthur's gut.

> It's fine. I'll figure it out.

> **MA**
> I know you will son.........I love you

Arthur rested his elbows on his knees again, toying with the crystal charm on his phone, right leg bouncing. *Think.* His vision started to go fuzzy around the edges, and he could feel the warning signs of an anxiety attack settling in, so he reminded himself to count his breaths, but he only got to five before his brain found more pressing things to think about—if his mom's check had bounced, and his mom couldn't make the payment in time *and* was already picking up extra shifts, he had to come up with the money himself, and *how was he going to come up with the money himself?* The cash he'd made selling the Auratech stock he created over the summer was only enough for spending money—not nearly close enough to how much was owed for tuition this semester—and there was no way he'd find the time to create enough charms to have the money ready by next week or even by the end of the semester. More financial aid was likely out of the question, too, because the incredibly stingy scholarship board had made exceptions for his outstanding performance the past three years to award him with a fifty-percent tuition credit, and he was already allotted the maximum amount of hours of work study students were allowed, but maybe he could find a part-time position in town on the weekends or after school. But then how would he have the time to study, to maintain his scholarship—

"Coming to the party tonight, Pham?"

Arthur's runaway thoughts came to a grinding halt, stomach lurching at the sound of the very last voice he wanted to hear.

He shut his eyes resolutely, refusing to spare Mika a parting glance. "In your dreams, Rivera."

"Don't have a costume?" Mika didn't seem to be getting the memo that Arthur wanted him as far away as humanly possible, because he strode to Arthur's bench and flopped down next to him gracelessly.

"Don't have a life?" Arthur shot back, staring at the blank screen of his phone.

Mika didn't seem to have a comeback for this, and Arthur glanced up to find Mika's eyes also on Arthur's phone. He caught the tail end of an odd look on Mika's face, accompanied by the uncomfortable pressure of Mika's Sense attempting to extend into his personal space.

Arthur hurriedly siphoned off energy from his already-buzzing entirety to block him out.

It was over as soon as it began, and Mika course corrected into one of the seventeen shit-eating grins he had in his expression Rolodex.

"Don't have a date?" Mika smirked, picking up where they'd left off. "You know, staring at your phone won't make them text back any faster."

"Leave me alone before I reenact a different scene from *Dirty Dancing* with you," Arthur snapped, fist clenching.

"Bye," Mika said brightly, wiggling his fingers before finally, blessedly, making his exit.

"Jesus." Arthur shook his head as a new wave of exhaustion washed over him from the emergency shutout. His phone vibrated once more in his hands, and his eyes flew to the screen.

He deflated. Just an email.

Stonebury Conservatory for Young Mages: Class Rankings Updated

Students,

The Year Four class rankings have been updated on the Stonebury student portal. Please note that the first in class, automatically awarded the title of Electi Magi, will be featured prominently during the graduation ceremony and will be eligible for the exceptional Elias Stonebury Grant, an exclusive, prestigious post-graduate fellowship. Those in the top ten slots will...

Arthur sighed, scrolling down to the end of the email and opening the link automatically. He already knew what he'd find.

He entered his student credentials to log in, and sure enough:

1. Michael Rivera 4.025
2. Arthur Pham 4.025

Mika's full name—'*Mee-kai-yel*'—burned too bright on his phone screen, taunted him in his mind, and left a bitter taste in the back of his throat. He tossed his phone onto his bag beside him, resting his head in his hands.

He'd been neck and neck with Mika for years—practically since the day they entered their first year of Stonebury at age thirteen. Inexplicably, despite getting identical scores on tests, assignments, and practical exams, Mika remained first in their class. Arthur knew it had to be purely bureaucratic—that the class ranking system probably didn't allow for two students to share the number one spot. But it was almost worse that the rote, automatic, absolutely neutral filing system had put Mika first. Hell, it wasn't even alphabetical—what kind of system was this? If only he could manage to secure the number one spot of Electi Magi, it would rocket-launch his post-graduation plans to success, especially if his mom would no longer be able to support him financially—

Arthur's eyes flew open.

He checked his phone. *Excellent.* A whole half-hour until office hours closed.

He propelled himself off the bench, hitching his bag over one shoulder and walking back through in the direction of the academic building, bypassing it for the administration hall.

He was going to fix this.

3

Arthur rolled his shoulders back and swallowed hard, staring intently at the double doors in the highest tower of the castle. His heart beat a tattoo against his chest, much faster than he would have liked.

He closed his eyes and took a deep breath—two, three—before knocking.

A distant voice from within greeted him, and he pushed open the doors to Professor Stonebury's office.

The headmaster—Elias Stonebury the Third, as it were—tended to a variegated monstera near the southernmost of the floor-to-ceiling windows encapsulating the circular room. It was one of dozens and dozens of houseplants—some floating—placed around the office in increasingly quirky pots; Arthur spotted one by the raw edge desk that looked like the derrière of Michelangelo's David. Stonebury looked sharp in his signature forest green suit, and he beamed when he saw Arthur in the doorway.

"Mr. Pham! Office hours have been terribly slow today. Please sit. Sit."

He set the elegant, golden, elephant-shaped watering can on the desk and pulled out the velvet high-backed chair behind it, gesturing for Arthur to join him.

Arthur stepped into the room and closed the door behind him, careful not to disturb the zebra bust emerging from the other side of it. He sat down in one of the mid-century armchairs in front of the desk.

Stonebury placed his elbows on the desk, resting his chin on interlaced fingers. Arthur admired all the thin, mismatched golden rings displayed across them, the grey lining the brunette hair at his temples.

"So. How have you been enjoying the first months of your last year at Stonebury?"

Arthur forced himself to meet the headmaster's gaze and forced a smile on his face. "Just fine, Professor."

"Getting along well in your classes?"

Arthur couldn't help but examine the herringbone hardwood, his smile turning bashful. "Just fine, Professor."

"Fuck humility, Arthur. You're top of your class."

Arthur's eyes snapped back up, heart sinking impossibly lower. "Almost."

Stonebury leaned in conspiratorially. "So you saw the updated rankings? It really is uncanny how you've always been neck and neck with that Rivera boy. Have been since Year One, in fact. Funny thing."

"Right. Funny thing. Well, Professor, that's actually what I came here to talk to you about."

"Oh?"

"I have...a proposal for you."

Stonebury's eyebrows met his hairline. He leaned back and crossed his leather wingtip-clad feet on the desk. "Lay it on me."

"Sir." Arthur straightened in his chair. He forced himself to maintain eye contact, palms sweating on the arms of the chair, and let the words tumble out as he'd rehearsed them on the walk over:

"I got some bad news today and, um—" he cursed himself for slipping— "apparently my mom's tuition check bounced. She's not able to provide her portion, even with the generous scholarship money I've been granted and my work study money. I'm in a bit of a tight spot."

"Oh, Arthur." The pity etched into Stonebury's features made Arthur sick to his stomach. "I'm sure we can figure something out. Let me get the financial aid office on the phone, surely there are loan options, or we can arrange a payment plan—"

"No, Professor. Please," Arthur ground out. "I can't accept charity. No more than I've already been given."

"But—"

"Please." Arthur closed his eyes. "I can't. I want to start a business after school, which won't make me money for a while. I can't do that if I'm already in debt."

"Surely—"

"Sir, please. I have a proposal, remember?"

Stonebury looked pained. "Mr. Pham—"

"Delay my tuition for this year. If I win Electi Magi, I'll use the fellowship money to pay for it."

Stonebury stared at him. The seconds ticked by, and Arthur's heart beat in double-time.

"Well..." Stonebury's mouth twisted. "Mr. Pham, I would really rather...are you *sure* you won't take out a loan? Or finance your payment?"

"If I don't get Electi Magi," Arthur conceded, "I'll put off my business plans after school and find a job to pay you off. With interest."

"Without interest," Stonebury amended.

"Sir—"

"Without."

Begrudgingly, Arthur nodded and offered his hand.

Stonebury looked at it, brows furrowed.

"Are you sure?"

"Please, sir." Arthur managed a smile. "For my pride."

Stonebury watched him a moment longer, no doubt Sensing Arthur's determination. Arthur hoped he couldn't detect the sheer panic swelling underneath the guise.

"I'll talk to the donors," he said slowly, "but given your excellent academic track record, I think that should be fine."

Stonebury finally shook his hand.

"Deal."

After sitting through the myriad phone calls required to get their agreement approved, Arthur trudged down the spiral stairs from the administrative wing, past the statue of Stonebury the First in the courtyard where students were in equal parts lounging, Casting, and chatting. The fatigue from the show he'd put on in Evocation earlier, combined with the adrenaline from the mental gymnastics of the past hour, was finally getting to him. As he opened the heavy door to the dormitory building, he was more desperate than ever for his bed.

Back in Year One, the high ceiling of the lobby enchanted him daily, its midnight blue color adorned with slowly revolving golden constellations, its hanging golden chandelier made of nested golden hoops and hemispheres. Now, all he wanted to do was fast-forward to his dorm room for blessed, much-needed unconsciousness.

The adrenaline was wearing off, and doubt started to creep back in. Should he have accepted the headmaster's offers to make exceptions on the strict tuition payment for him? Wasn't his proposal just *another* exception for him? What made him so special?

It's an exception on your *terms,* he told himself sternly. He took the golden pneumatic lift at the end of the room, watching the trees separating the school grounds and the lake shrink on his trip up to the fourth floor. As he passed the floors housing the wings for Year One, Year Two, Year Three, his brain conjured futures where he had to delay his plans, spend the first two years of his post-graduate life in debt to school instead of fulfilling his potential and living out his dreams. He imagined his mother, working day in and day out to make rent, a fraction of his tuition, without support and without time spent for herself. He imagined Annabelle, forced to settle for a lesser conservatory next year for money's sake, or worse, putting off her own schooling to help their mom at home.

Arthur swallowed.

This was how it had to be.

His cream sneakers were silent atop the birch hardwood of the top floor Year Four wing. He autopiloted past the black walls, decorated here and there with bright neon signage and animal busts and geometric wall planters, to Room 419.

He was finally tapping his wand on the crystal reader on the wall when the door to Room 420 across from him swung open, revealing raucous laughter and chatter as Mika emerged. He was taking snack orders over his shoulder from his guests, and *what cosmic entity had decided to make Arthur's life a living hell today?*

Mika turned as the telltale smell of cannabis wafted over Arthur, and he was exhausted at the irony of it.

"Ah, if it isn't Wham, Pham, Thank You Ma'am, my age-old rival."

"Can you *please* tell your people to keep it down? Some of us actually study in this godforsaken school."

He knew Mika didn't need to extend his Sense to tell that Arthur was beat. "Aw, widdle baby Arfur needs his beauty rest?"

"Jesus, are there people from Featherwood in there?" Arthur glanced into the room where Mika's company were snickering at the exchange. "It isn't even the weekend yet. Hell, it isn't even five yet."

"It's five o'clock somewhere." Mika grinned.

"Except here, where it's always 4:20," Arthur deadpanned, but it didn't have the desired effect; Mika and his guests hollered in approval, and one of the Featherwood students passed a joint along to the boy next to her.

Arthur raised an eyebrow. "I'll remember this next time you try to insult me with my dedication to nonmagic culture."

"I'll remember this next time I bang your mom," Mika retorted.

"Right," Arthur said. "Bye."

"Good night." Mika beamed.

Arthur flipped him the bird as he closed the door to his own room.

He'd just kicked his shoes off and was draping his forest green peacoat over the desk chair when a knock sounded at the door.

"What now?" he snapped as he opened it, but he immediately softened. "Oh, sorry."

"Why does it smell like a nonmagic college dorm in here?" Clarke asked, wrinkling his nose. The movement scooched his wire-frame glasses up.

"And how can I get in on it?" Jonathan's imposing frame took up most of the doorway.

"Take a wild guess," Arthur sighed, ushering his friends inside. "Quick, before the smell permeates my entire life."

Clarke and Jonathan moved to occupy the far end of the suite, dumping their schoolbags to claim the black leather couch. Despite the bone-deep exhaustion, Arthur couldn't bring himself to kick them out—he'd used his time to douse his hellfire of an afternoon. He snapped his fingers and flame erupted from the friction; he lit a stick of incense before shaking his hand out to dispel it. At least now the room would smell like *ritual* herbs.

He strode across the black and white thick-striped rug that stretched across the expansive concrete floor. He thought, not for the first time, that despite the nepotistic donors and their tight-fingered grip on the scholarships, being top of his class (almost) had some perks —namely, the spacious and personally designed dorm. In the week before class started, a team of interior designers had arrived to his new suite with catalogs in hand, waving their wands this way and that at Arthur's discretion to design the beauty in which he now resided: the walls were cream save for the exposed stone, the farthest from the door housing his double bed (dressed in piles of comfortable cream and dark green linens) nestled in between two floor-to-ceiling windows, and the right housing his desk and bookcases. The door to the room was built into the exposed stone wall, and to the left of the door was the corner seating area where Clarke and Jonathan now sprawled under a spartan, geometric golden chandelier. The suite even came equipped with a private bathroom, off the left wall and next to the closet.

Arthur hadn't previously been a partaker in baths, but how could he *not* when there was an honest-to-god clawfoot tub in there?

Now, he perched on the ottoman for the Eames chair across from the couch. "Make yourselves at home." He smiled wryly at his friends, already setting up camp on the couch.

"Thanks Dad," Clarke said dryly, scrolling through his phone. Arthur felt a surge of pride at the crystal charm hanging there—one of his own creation.

"You're stressed." Jonathan trained a shrewd gaze on Arthur, propping up his feet on the raw wood coffee table.

"Your enormous feet are going to crush the poor table." Clarke batted Jonathan's legs, which begrudgingly left the tabletop. "But on a more pressing note..." Clarke returned to his phone. He'd exchanged his pressed school blazer for a cozy-looking grandpa cardigan before arriving, and was drowning in it. "Arthur is stressed."

"How's the Auratech working? Still good?" Arthur reached out to brush the charm with a fingertip.

"Fucking lifesaver." Clarke looked up and clutched the crystal charm reverently. It shone iridescent in the fading light. "It's hard to believe that after a whole summer of engineering it's actually *here*."

"No bugs? I wasn't sure about the spread of the the Wi-Fi enchantment."

"Lightning speed. Everywhere," Clarke reassured him. "I never thought I'd be able to use a nonmagic phone here—my parents are *never* gonna buy me Crystaltech. Honestly, I don't think I've seen a single nonmagic phone here without Auratech on it."

"I've already started inventory to make the next round over the winter holiday. Jonathan, how's the graphic design coming along?"

Jonathan was frowning. "He's deflecting."

"Ugh!" Clarke put down his phone, crossing both his arms and legs. "You're right."

"What's up?" Jonathan leveled a look at Arthur, who hesitated.

The deal he'd made with the headmaster felt like something dirty—something he'd discovered under a rock, something he wanted to keep hidden away lest it see the light of day and speak to his weakness. It wasn't his friends' job to take care of him. He wasn't high maintenance; there was no need to burden them, and the last thing he needed on top of the pressure was their pity.

He felt their Sense tickling his own, and for the umpteenth time that day found the very bottom of his energy reserves to block them, projecting what he prayed was a more positive aura.

"Nothing out of the ordinary." He stared at the ceiling to avoid their gaze. "Midterms are coming up."

Clarke rolled his eyes. "Of course the genius is stressed about school during Year Four."

"Clarke was hoping it would be boy problems." Jonathan grinned.

"When have I *ever* had time for boys?" Arthur scoffed.

Clarke was pouting now. "For your information, one *makes* time for boys," he huffed, nose held high in the air.

"I'll tell that to your alleged boyfriend in New York," Arthur scoffed.

"He *does* exist!"

"Right," Jonathan added, "you definitely have the stereotypical long-distance nonmagic theater-school boyfriend, who we've mysteriously never met even over the phone, and who doesn't believe in social media—"

"Who doesn't 'get' magic, which is why he can never visit." Arthur made air quotes, holding back laughter at the shades of red that Clarke's face was currently achieving.

"I am literally texting him *right now—*"

"Anyway." Jonathan patted Clarke on the arm to simmer him down, refusing to acknowledge the phone screen thrust into his face. "Since you refuse to talk about your stress or your love life, we have Plan B."

"Therapy?" Clarke piped up, at the same time as Arthur muttered, "Gay people don't need Plan B."

Jonathan ignored Arthur. "No, that's Plan C."

"Don't we already have a Plan A? To go pick up Samhain ingredients?" Arthur sighed. He was really fighting sleep now.

"Halloween Party in 405," Jonathan corrected him.

Arthur groaned, his very life essence protesting the thought of staying awake that late, let alone socializing with ingrates at *any* time of day.

"I thought we were just going to do a ritual here," he protested. Mika's taunting voice echoed in the halls of his mind. "Quiet? Intimate? Low key?"

"Your whole life is quiet-intimate-low-key," Clarke groused.

Jonathan leaned forward. "We hear some Featherwood people are bringing Homebrew potions."

"Why can't you people ever just walk into town to pick up a handle of liquor at the corner store?" Clarke groaned.

"I think said Featherwood people are pregaming across the hall as we speak," Arthur noted. "And Clarke, you *are* aware that Homebrews contain liquor from said handles from said corner store, right?"

Clarke scoffed. "Yeah, but y'all put all those herbs and flowers and shit in it. Sometimes a guy just wants some plain old *vodka*, please, for the love of god."

"Why do you go to magic school again?"

"Beats me." Clarke leaned back with his phone again. "But hell, what I wouldn't do for just a god-damned wine cooler."

"Come with us?" Jonathan pleaded.

"No." Arthur shook his head.

"Please?"

"No."

"You need to let loose a little."

"No."

Clarke cut in, "I heard they're also bringing advanced books from the Featherwood restricted section."

Arthur bit his lip, considering. "Fine."

"Huzzah!" Jonathan leapt from the couch, nearly knocking over the table.

"Yes, excellent." Arthur rubbed his eyes. "Now vacate my home so I can take a disco nap."

"Arthur's gonna party with us, Arthur's gonna party with us," Clarke sing-songed as Jonathan steered him out the door.

"As if I don't concede every single time you both want to go to a party." Arthur rolled his eyes, pushing them out the door.

"Every tenth time, more like it," Jonathan revised.

"Let's text about costumes!" Clarke called back to him from down the hall, holding up his phone.

"See you at dinner," Arthur yelled back before shutting the door.

He was unconscious before he hit the bed.

4

Four hours later found Arthur trapped in his desk chair as Clarke pasted his eyebrows down with a glue stick.

"Why can't you just do it with magic?" he sighed. "You did the ears with magic."

"Because, like I keep telling you buffoons, magic isn't always the answer," Clarke murmured, intensely focused. "Also, this morning Jonathan had the audacity to imply that I'm not cut out for drag, and I need to put him in his place."

"I never doubted your makeup skills," Jonathan protested from where he sat on a white fur cushion stolen from the couch, tugging at the black turtleneck under his yellow long-sleeved tee. "I'm more concerned about the thickness of your skin. Or the lack thereof."

Pointedly ignoring Jonathan, Clarke set aside the glue stick, fanning Arthur's eyebrows before taking a stick of concealer and an eyebrow pencil to his face. After several minutes of silence, he leaned back.

"There." He leaned down to retrieve a silver pin from his bag for Arthur, who took it to the mirror to affix it to his blue shirt over his heart.

"Convincing," he conceded, tentatively flicking the pointed ears, "although I don't think he has an undercut. Or freckles. And I don't think he's Asian, let alone half."

"Everyone's a critic," Clarke muttered.

"Wow." Jonathan looked up to assess. "You're giving Leonard Nimoy a run for his money."

"God, I should hope so." Arthur leaned forward to inspect further. "Considering the man is *dead.*"

The next half an hour was spent first convincing Jonathan that *yes,* Leonard Nimoy was in fact dead ("How did you miss that?"), then convincing Clarke that no, he was not dressed as the most boring character of the trio ("But I'm not even pre-med"), and, finally, convincing Arthur that absolutely not, they could not Charm the pants to be bigger, because the last pair Arthur borrowed from Clarke hadn't been the same since.

By the time they finally made their way to Room 405, Arthur was upholding his running tradition of grousing over being dragged to a party.

"I want to be in bed by midnight," Arthur reminded them as they knocked. "And could these jeans be any tighter?"

Clarke waved him off. "Beggars can't be choosers. How do you not have a single pair of black pants in your wardrobe? You could fill a closet the length of a city block with your damn clothes—"

"I could have just Charmed my joggers."

"And—" Clarke ignored him, stabbing a finger into his chest— "you're twenty-one god-damned years old with thighs any man would feel lucky to be strangled with. Be a slut for once in your life."

"If you want, I've got Plan B in my room." Jonathan nudged him.

"I swear to *god—*"

The door opened before Arthur could finish protesting, revealing a soundscape that closely resembled a chaotic remix of "The Monster Mash." Benjamin Lasher, one of the residents of the 405 triple-suite, greeted them in a particularly uninspired white bedsheet as a toga. If the way Benjamin toppled over in hiccupping laughter was any indicator, they had arrived fashionably late.

"It gets better every time!" he choked. "Trekkies for *life!*"

"Every time?" Arthur frowned as he stepped into the room. Immediately, he spotted Mika near the beer pong table, sporting the same black-turtleneck-yellow-shirt combo as Jonathan. The girl next to him —donned in a short red dress, coarse hair teased into a beehive—was adjusting a silver pin on his chest.

"Nope." Arthur turned on his heel to leave, but Clarke and Arthur hooked his elbows in theirs, dragging him in.

"Just ignore him," Jonathan leaned down to murmur in his ear once the door shut behind them. Arthur mourned for his own Samhain ritual kit in the back of his closet. And for his ritual pajamas. And ritual bed. And ritual sleep.

"Besides—" Clarke nudged him, turning him to face forward— "your makeup is *way* better than his."

Mika caught sight of them, and Arthur looked on in horror as a grin creeping into Cheshire territory spread across his features.

"Well, well, *well*, if it isn't my trusty second officer!" Mika held his arms aloft, beer sloshing over the arm of his yellow sleeve. The girl— Arthur could have sworn he'd seen her before—smiled bemusedly, a flash of white against dark skin, and generously relieved Mika of his drink.

"If it isn't the last person I wanted to see for the eightieth time today," Arthur sneered as they passed.

"You've met Cherry, the illustrious and decorated girlfriend?" Mika gestured to the woman next to him, and Cherry took a polite little bow.

"I prefer communications officer, actually." Her American accent matched Mika's.

"I don't know why you associate yourself intimately with this imbecile," Arthur sympathized.

"Honestly?" She rolled her eyes fondly. "Me neither."

"Live long and prosper," Mika beamed at Arthur, "to your ass in those jeans." He held up a hand with fingers spread, blissfully oblivious.

"Can we be done here?" Clarke pleaded with the ceiling.

"Gladly," Arthur agreed, cheeks aflame, towing his friends along to the punch table tucked into a corner of the kitchen. Maybe, if he was lucky, the party would end up being a bust, and he could be in bed by *eleven—*

"Pham!"

Tan Fernando had devil horns growing out of their head and an enormous bottle of Fireball in tow. "Nice eyebrows, doll."

"Thanks," Clarke supplied on his behalf.

Arthur frowned as Tan hefted the carafe onto the counter and procured ten shot glasses with their wand. Out of thin air, six other classmates materialized around them. "Hey, wait a minute—"

"Double, double!"

A shot glass full of sickly-sticky-cinnamon booze was thrust into his chest. "Oh no, I don't think—"

"*Toil and trouble!*" everyone chorused, downing their glasses.

"Fire burn and cauldron bubble," Arthur muttered, begrudgingly imbibing in his shot.

So much for getting to bed by midnight.

★

An hour and a half later, Arthur wasn't minding the party so much anymore. At least the music had improved; now a song with a driving bassline and topical spooky lyrics blasted from the stereo system. He nodded his head to the beat and took a swig of his third Homebrew cider, struggling to focus on what one of the three Featherwood girls in front of him was saying.

"The walls at our school are too thin." She shook her head and her long blonde pigtails trailed along with it. She tugged on the blue shift dress and took a big swig of beer. "Doesn't make for good parties. And, you know, the enchantments against boys unless you get a registered exception."

"It's a feminism thing," the curvy one, donning a green dress, chimed in. "Safe spaces for women."

"How does it work for trans women?" Clarke chimed in.

The one with pigtails (Beatrice?) tilted her head. "Well, the Enchantments just...I don't know. They just *know*."

"So the walls are thin," the curvy one in the green dress continued, "and there are some people there that are *really* not into the party scene. Lane hated it last year. Right, Sam?"

Sam, with a red bow in her long, dark, wavy hair, sat on the arm of the black leather couch in her pink dress, legs crossed, typing quickly on the Crystaltech phone she was occupied with. "Yeah, my girlfriend usually stays home." She looked up. "Even now I don't understand her sometimes. I swear she, like, prefers to read."

Arthur couldn't help but think that this girlfriend sounded more like the type of company he preferred to keep.

"We'll have to get a weekend team together." Jonathan gestured vaguely back toward the window. "There's this one dive bar near *Oosterpark* that just opened earlier this year."

"*Spelbalk?*" the curvy one said. (Molly?) "Hell yeah, I'm a champion at darts!"

"I think that's the one—"

But suddenly, the music cut out.

"People, people. Hey, *people.*" A girl in a frothy pink princess dress and a tall silver crown stood on the beer pong table. (Julia? Arthur talked to her at a party last year.) As members of the crowd started jeering, attempting a disjointed chorus of "Ding, Dong! The Witch is Dead," another Featherwood student passed her a thick, mustylooking book with royal purple binding and runes etched in gold leaf. She held it up to silence the crowd.

"I have, in my hands, *Divining the Unknown*, the only copy of which is in none other than Mrs. Featherwood's restricted collection," Julia announced emphatically, crown bobbing up and down with her head.

The crowd let out a long chorus of "ooh." A voice rose above the din. "What does it do?"

"Nothing, dumbass," Julia shot back, "unless you use the rituals in it. And we've been brewing the potion for the most difficult one all summer."

Most of the crowd had already dispersed and returned to quiet conversation around the room, but maybe a dozen or so people still surrounded Julia. Arthur dragged Clarke and Jonathan to the front of the crowd as she flipped through the large tome. There was no way he was missing magic this big.

"You are *not* ready," Julia gushed, holding the book open. Only after everyone protested for the requisite anticipatory moment did she turn the book outward. Arthur leaned over Clarke's shoulder to read:

'*Stars Align: Discovering the Identity of Your Soulmate.*'

"But this is crazy advanced!" Tan had ended up next to them. "Finding your soulmate with magic is next to impossible. That was, like, day one in Year One Divination."

"Not up for it?" Cherry teased. She'd dragged Mika into the circle, and he stuck out his tongue at Arthur, who flipped him the bird in return.

"It's not that it's impossible," Julia corrected, "it's just inconvenient, and finicky, with unreliable results." She started to count on her fingers. "We can only perform the ritual for two people at a time, they need to have near-perfect command of their magic, and we need two circles of six and seven around them. *And* it has to start precisely one minute before midnight on a night ripe with huge amounts of natural energy. Performing it as a Samhain ritual is perfect."

People started to protest at the amount of work required, and Arthur cut in hastily.

"Come on, this is super-cool magic. When else are we going to get to try something like this? There are no copies of this book in circulation."

"I think Arthur should be one of the two," piped up a short girl dressed as a pumpkin.

"What?" Arthur whipped his head around. She looked embarrassed, but nearly every other Featherwood student, and just as many from Stonebury, was agreeing enthusiastically.

There were far too many giggles going around the circle for Arthur's liking, and he placed a hand over his forehead to stave off the attention. *Jesus Christ.*

"Well it's obvious who should be the second," Cherry beamed, and she thrust Mika in front of her. "The two best at Stonebury!"

"Live long and prosper!" The group chanted, and before he knew it, Arthur found himself in the middle of two concentric Circles, sitting cross-legged across from his so-called captain on the filthy living room floor of Room 405.

"You have *got* to be kidding me," Arthur grumbled, downing the last of his cider.

"Be a good sport," Mika chided him, leaning back on his hands, dark curls starting to come undone over his forehead. He'd abandoned the yellow overshirt an hour ago and was now wearing it tied around his waist, black turtleneck sleeves rolled up to the elbow. Arthur felt a strange jolt in his stomach and wondered if the shots from before were threatening to come back up.

A warm, chipped mug that proclaimed "World's Best Daddy" was thrust into his hands. He took a cautious sniff.

"You've been brewing *hot chocolate* for six months?" He turned to Julia, who was busy drawing perfect chalk Circles on the concrete floor and a variety of complicated runes in between the Circle members.

"The best damn hot chocolate you'll ever taste," she corrected him. Tan was passing out more of the potion in mugs of varying shapes and sizes to everyone in the circle. Bestowed upon Mika was one that resembled an eerily accurate ceramic likeness of a penis.

"Charming," he said, and turned to Cherry to mime giving it a blowjob, sending her into a fit of giggles so intense that she had to put down her mug for fear of it spilling.

Arthur stared resolutely into his own mug. He was suddenly feeling very warm.

"Don't worry." Clarke leaned over his shoulder from where he sat behind Arthur's left, glasses askew. "If your soulmate is Jonathan, I'll forgive you."

"And if your soulmate is Clarke—" Jonathan rolled his eyes from where he sat behind Arthur's right— "I'll steal his phone and call his boyfriend."

"I thought you didn't believe he existed," Clarke hissed.

"Well then, I guess you're having *very* convoluted masturbation sessions in our bathroom at two in the morning."

"Okay, we're starting!" Julia stood atop the circular coffee table once more, now in the center of the room between Arthur and Mika. She was attending to a record player adorned with an Auratech charm beside her on the table, adjusting the vinyl inside it. The mismatched rugs previously spread out over the room were now pushed up against the walls, and the classmates once uninterested in the ritual now hovered around the Circle, murmuring to each other and watching intently.

"Think of this like the guided meditations we did in Year One. It's really important that everyone focus and follow my instructions within the half-second."

"Why didn't we do this at the beginning of the party when everyone was still sober?" Arthur grumbled.

"Shut up, nerd." Mika grinned. "Do you wanna do the 'super-cool' magic or not?"

Arthur shot him a loathsome glare and gripped the moonstone he'd been gifted for the ritual like a dagger, holding it like a threat. Mika pretended to look scared.

"Everyone ready?" Julia looked around.

The other fifteen people in the Circle assented.

"Okay. Breathe in..."

There was a collective breath.

"...and breathe out."

As everyone exhaled, Julia touched the tip of her wand to the innermost Circle. Arthur could feel the energy activate, a static-charged balloon to his entire being. The runes closest to him, Julia, and Mika glowed a blinding white that housed every color of the rainbow, even colors Arthur couldn't name. The glow rippled out to the outermost Circle and an opalescent sheet of atmosphere sprang up from the floor, shimmering *pink-purple-turquoise-indigo* and encasing all sixteen of them in otherworldly light.

"One more time. In...and out."

This time, Julia touched her wand to the hot pink candle in her hand. Spontaneously, the pink candles in front of Arthur and Mika ignited, and one by one, the white candles spaced in between every person in the Circle lit themselves, spiraling out until all sixteen candles were aflame. Warm candlelight mingled with the colors of the Circle; the effect was that of being underwater at night in a pool with multi-colored lights inlaid into the walls. The heady scent of rose and jasmine filled the enclosed space, and Arthur's eyes closed of their own accord. Maybe it was good that he was a little drunk for this—he found it easier than usual to get into the mood of the magic.

"Close your eyes. I'm going to make sure everyone is breathing in time," Julia said softly. Arthur didn't see her move her wand, but he felt the air around him shift subtly, encouraging him to breathe in and out according to its will rather than his own. He felt a sense of deep calm wash over him, similar to his nightly breathing exercises.

After nearly a minute, she continued. "Good. Now we'll work our way through the senses, starting with the Sixth Sense. Extend your Awareness out to everyone in this Circle."

Arthur did, slowly. In the closed circuit of the ritual, his Sense was amplified; he could vividly make out Clarke and Jonathan, the three girls they'd been talking to earlier, Julia and Cherry and Mika. Despite the murderous instincts the latter tended to inspire, he reminded himself to observe curiously, objectively, and without attachment.

"Smell the candles, infused with rose and jasmine."

There was a particularly audible communal breath in and out.
"Hear..." There was a sound of the needle hitting the record. "Our Lord and Savior, Louis Armstrong."
After some gentle, dusty feedback, the trilling piano introduction to "La Vie en Rose" tumbled from the middle of the Circle, the sound quality akin to that of an amphitheater designed intentionally for acoustics.
"Touch the Moonstone," Julia instructed. "Understand its form with your hands."
Arthur gripped his crystal and studied its bumps, sharp bits, and smooth expanses. He felt certain spots where its energy vibrated more resonantly, where he knew it shone brightest in an iridescent, alien blue.
"Open your eyes."
Arthur did, and he found his gaze magnetized to the way the luminescence of the Circle played across Mika's features, his rumpled hair, tan skin, the face that was usually split wide in a grotesque grin was eerily calm—an expression Arthur had never seen there before.
Mika opened his eyes too, and Arthur barely looked up at Julia in time to avoid meeting them.
"See..." She Conjured a pink rose from midair, and Arthur could feel the atmosphere shift as she blew. Petals scattered and slowly revolved around the circumference of the Circle.
"And we save the best part for last." Julia smiled. "Look into your mugs."
Arthur did. The magic in the Circle was palpable now, leaking into the hot chocolate in his cup. It rippled in crystalline patterns on the surface, steam rising in a perfect spiral upward, colors and candlelight shimmering in his cup.
He wasn't sure if it was the sleepy jasmine sapping his focus, or the alcohol slipping his resolve, or the energy in the Circle rattling in his bones, but something tugged up his eyes once more. His gaze caught Mika's, and a funny sensation clicked in his gut—like the feeling right before he Cast a spell, elements and energies lining up in precisely the right order.
"And now...Taste."
Julia's voice tore Arthur's attention away and back to the "World's Best Daddy" mug in front of him.

He picked it up and took a cautious sip. Though it was hot to the touch, the hot chocolate was the perfect sipping temperature. The taste was complex; Arthur distinguished at least three types of cocoa—dark, white, and maybe ruby chocolate—as well as the same floral essence infused into the candles. It was undoubtedly boozy, with something darker and headier than Kahlua, and there was a sparkly sort of taste to it; he thought it might have been brewed with rose quartz. It was so sweet and thick that Arthur wondered if whipped cream was melted into it.

True to her word, Julia had made the best damn hot chocolate he'd ever tasted.

"Everyone in the Circles," she went on, "continue visualizing as you drink. Remember to keep breathing. My two soul-searchers—" she glanced at Arthur and Mika to make sure they were listening— "you're on your path now. Surrender yourself to destiny—be at ease in your predetermined fate."

Arthur was halfway done with his hot chocolate now, and with every sip he felt as if he were sucking the magic in the room through a curly straw.

They were getting close to the *pièce de résistance.*

"Your perfect match is closer now than they've ever been. Reach out with your Sense, your energy, your soul..."

Arthur took his last sip.

"...and catch them."

Suddenly Arthur's empty mug burned hot, and he fought the urge to drop it. But that wasn't quite right—it wasn't the mug that was burning, it was the skin on the palm of his left hand, just along the love line.

"Mother Earth." Julia no longer addressed them, but the ceiling. "Guide our lost lovers in the night, so they may find their final destination. By your design, allow the stars to align."

The energy in the Circle spiraled upward, rose petals revolving faster and faster. Arthur's hand started to smart rather badly, and he tried to realign his focus with his breath.

"Mother Earth, we beseech thee. *Omne quod factum est, quod sit omne id sit, est quia omnia erunt.*"

As was tradition in ritual spellwork, the members of the Circle parroted the parting line after her. Arthur's voice sounded startlingly loud in his ears.

"*Omne quod factum est—*"

His hand burned as if he'd actually caught a fallen star.

"*Quod sit omne id sit, est quia omnia erunt—*"

The vortex of energy coalesced at the ceiling and Arthur, to his surprise, felt half of it funnel down into his empty mug.

"*Est quia omnia erunt.*"

Julia reached down to touch the tip of her wand to the inner Circle. The energy collected in his mug radiated out into Arthur's hands, soothing the burning on his left one like a salve. He felt the magic make its way up his arms, down to his stomach and into his legs, and back up through his heart and throat.

On his next exhale, it escaped him. As Julia released the Circle, it flew up and away into the night, disappearing along with the final, crackling notes of Louis' trumpet.

5

No one moved.

The record player snap-crackle-popped, and Arthur felt as if he'd just awoken from a too-long midafternoon nap.

"So?" Tan's voice broke the silence. "Did it work?"

Arthur flexed his left hand, placing his mug on the table so he could massage it with his right.

"It did *something*," he decided, glancing up at Mika to see if he'd been similarly affected.

He expected to be met with a stupid smile, or at the very least an insult at the ready, but Mika was staring intently at his own hand, dark brow furrowed. Cherry was tugging at his arm, trying to see what held him in such rapt attention, but he remained resolute. His eyes scanned back and forth, back and forth—

Until suddenly, Mika burst out laughing.

He laughed so hard he fell over onto his side, disturbing the classmates in the circle behind him.

Arthur frowned. "What—"

He didn't even register Clarke sidling up beside him to grab his hand.

"Holy shit." Clarke breathed out a laugh.

"What?" Jonathan and Arthur asked at once. Jonathan leaned over Arthur's shoulder as he repossessed his arm, observing his palm as Mika had done. Electricity danced along his spine at the sight of

letters along his love line, pink and a little raw, closely resembling a month-old burn:
Michael Rivera.
Arthur blinked.
It played out in his head, familiar yet foreign in his mind: *Mee-kai-yel.*
"Oh my fucking god," Jonathan guffawed, clutching Arthur's forearm, but Arthur wasn't paying attention. He must have been far more intoxicated than he thought—he kept reading the words on his palm, knowing what he saw was of extreme importance, but unable to comprehend its meaning. How many drinks had he had? He tried to count but kept losing track. Maybe the hot chocolate was stronger than he thought—did rose quartz have hallucinatory effects? He scrolled through the rolodex of potion ingredients in his head, trying to remember—
Michael Rivera.
Michael Rivera.
Michael Rivera.
Suddenly, a different hand closed around his wrist.
Mika had crawled halfway across the table between them, record player be damned, snatching Arthur's hand away to see for himself.
The shock of skin on skin was what finally did it. Arthur snatched his hand back—*revolting*—but it was too late; Mika had seen.
Arthur clutched his hand with white knuckles, eyes wide, mouth clamped shut.
Cherry finally got ahold of Mika for long enough to take his hand, twisting it so she could read, grinning—but as she did, her smile faded to a blank facade. She raised her eyes to stare at Arthur with an owlish gaze.
"What's happening?" Pumpkin Girl shouted over the crowd's confused murmuring.
Julia clambered down off the table to kneel in front of Arthur, next to Mika. "Are you both okay? Fuck, I knew I should have practiced more—"
"It's okay," Arthur tried to say, but it came out more like, "gluurk."
"We're just peachy, haven't you heard?" Mika beamed. He launched himself over the table and threw his arms around Arthur. "We're in *love!*"

Alarm bells echoed off the walls of Arthur's brain as he struggled madly to free himself. Mika smelled like a winning combo of cheap beer, Old Spice, and jasmine.

"Don't fucking touch me," he snarled.

Mika acquiesced, releasing Arthur so he could thrust his hand in front of Julia's face.

"Oh!" She squinted. "Palmwriting? That's *so* old school."

But Mika shoved it closer. She caught it with her hands to avoid getting slapped in the face.

"Oh. *Oh.*"

Her eyes went wide and—Arthur wished he was surprised—swiveled directly over to him.

"What the *fuck* is going on here?" Arthur finally found his voice.

Mika changed course, pivoting to thrust his hand in Arthur's face. Arthur squinted to read:

Arthur Pham.

Arthur frowned, eyes trained on the same spot even as Mika's hand disappeared from his field of vision—even as Clarke took possession of his arm once again to show Julia.

"No." Julia gasped. "What are the chances?"

"It's true love!" Mika sang, swaying dangerously.

"Touch me again, I fucking dare you," Arthur hissed, backing away.

"They're...it's them. They're soulmates." Julia covered her mouth with her hand.

"*What?*" someone in the surrounding crowd yelled.

"They're soulmates!" Tan, to the left of Clarke, stood up. "Arthur and Mika! *They're each other's soulmate!*"

Chaos ensued. Everyone who'd been in the Circle surged forward to get a closer look, and everyone in the crowd around them broke out in uproarious activity—a dizzying combination of catcalls, jeers, and applause. Arthur found himself in a daze, still frowning, getting jostled into Mika's shoulder, Clarke's voice just behind him at a register previously only known to canines, his hand being passed from onlooker to onlooker—

Suddenly, it clicked.

"Oh, *ha-ha.* Yes. Yes, very funny everyone!" His voice shook. "Very good joke."

"It's not a joke," said a soft voice near him. He was surprised he'd heard it at all.

Mika was now showing his palm off to everyone in sight, leaving Cherry sitting beside Arthur.

"You felt the energy in the Circle." She swallowed. "You can't fake ancient magic like that."

Arthur stared at her.

And then his heart took off at a million miles a minute.

"Okay," Clarke cut in, getting a surprisingly solid arm around Arthur's shoulders and hauling him up. "I think that's enough fun for tonight."

Jonathan immediately followed suit, using his imposing frame to force a pathway through the crowd of drunken, wildly enthusiastic students. Arthur thought he might be sick. He was breaking out in a sweat, throat swallowing convulsively.

After what felt like hours—finally, blessedly—they found the door to the suite's bathroom. Jonathan swung it open and ushered Clarke and Arthur in, but just before he could close it behind them, Arthur glanced back into the middle of the room where Mika was soaking up the adoration, now standing up on the table and yelling-more-than-singing the lyrics of "La Vie en Rose."

As the crowd applauded raucously, he caught Arthur's eye, his smile faltering just an inch—

And then the door swung closed.

The sound in the main room was swallowed up, merely a dim throb in the candlelight of the bathroom. Clarke immediately released Arthur, lowering the toilet seat. He sat gratefully.

"Try to breathe, babe," Clarke said in a low voice, and Arthur realized he was hyperventilating. He closed his eyes and tried to steady his gasps.

"Is this real?" he heard Jonathan mutter to Clarke.

"I don't fuckin' know," Clarke squeaked. "Ancient ritual magic is powerful, but—I dunno, the concept of soulmates is *really* complicated."

"This is why that book was locked up," Jonathan said darkly.

Arthur finally managed to get his breathing under control, but his heart still pounded against his ribs.

"This—" he grit his teeth— "is why I don't go to parties."

"Are you okay?" Clarke leaned down in front of him. "Do you want a Calming Charm?"

"I'll be fine," he ground out, forcing his eyes to open. *Don't be such a drama queen.*

"Well," Jonathan sighed, "if you're destined for a life with Mika Rivera, then maybe we better put you out of your misery now."

"Yup, here we go." Arthur got up, sending Clarke scrambling backward, and lifted the toilet lid. He leaned down, took a deep breath, and promptly vomited.

"Shame," he croaked when it was over, flushing the toilet. "That was really good hot chocolate."

"Here." Jonathan rummaged for his wand and drew a counterclockwise circle, free hand cupping an invisible object. A moment later, a bottle of mouthwash popped into existence within it.

"Thanks." Arthur took a swig and spat in the sink as Jonathan Sent it back to his room.

"Better?" Clarke's nose wrinkled.

"Yeah," Arthur said, half-truthfully. His heart was returning to normal, but he was trembling. He closed the toilet lid and sat, resting his elbows on his knees, and stared at his hand.

Michael Rivera.

"You've gotta be shitting me." He put his head in his hands, then dropped them quickly, holding out his left hand gingerly so it wouldn't touch anything. It tingled unhelpfully.

"Listen," Clarke reassured him, "we can't necessarily understand this kind of magic. There's a reason they don't teach it in school."

"Exactly," Jonathan agreed. "It's imprecise."

"And what, pray tell, is imprecise about *this?*" Arthur flashed his hand where Mika's name was now etched across his palm.

Jonathan started laughing to himself, shaking his head.

"This is funny to you?" Arthur's voice reached a hysterical octave. "Go on out and laugh along with that asshole then, why don't you."

"No, no! I just—" Jonathan met his eyes. "It *is* funny. You asked the universe for your soulmate, and the universe picked up on the first ring just to say 'fuck you.'"

Arthur considered this. "Yeah...yeah. Well. Fine. Then I say 'fuck you' right back."

"Hell yeah." Jonathan raised his hand in praise.

"I make my own goddamn destiny!" Arthur pounded his fist on the sink.

"Hell yeah!" Clarke rallied, glasses askew on his nose.

"This..." Arthur spread out his left fingers, then clenched them into a fist. "This is just a reminder of what I have to do."

His fingernails dug into his palm.

I will get Electi Magi.

"Wait. What do you have to do?" Clarke deflated, squinting.

"Nothing," Arthur corrected too quickly. "I mean—finish strong at Stonebury, and then start our business. Start Auratech. Mika is a...a metaphor."

"A metaphor!" Clarke and Jonathan chorused, definitely drunk, pumping their fists in the air.

"Now." Arthur stood from the toilet, businesslike, burying the last of his anxiety. "Time to show him who's boss."

"You're the boss!"

"I'm the boss!"

Arthur mustered everything—confusion, frustration, anxiety, anger—and barged out of the bathroom, making a beeline for where Mika stood showboating on the coffee table. His audience now shouted the lyrics of "L-O-V-E" by Nat King Cole as he swayed, conducting them jovially.

Clarke and Jonathan lagged behind, exchanging looks in the doorway of the bathroom.

"What if..." Clarke shook his head once. "What if it's true?"

Jonathan's mouth set in a grim line. "Let's just hope you've been reading too much fanfiction."

As Clarke punched him in the arm, to no avail, Arthur pushed his way through the crowd and stepped up onto the table to join Mika.

"May I have this dance?"

He held out his hand, channeling all the vitriol he could muster through his smile. The crowd went wild.

Mika's grin froze—but without missing a beat, he took his hand. Arthur pulled him close, much rougher than necessary, placing his other hand around Mika's waist to lead him in a simple two-step. Everyone around them screamed, falling back into their caroling.

Mika swallowed, smile fading. "Hey, are you—"

"Let's get three things straight, Rivera," Arthur interrupted as they circled the table. His left palm tingled where it grasped Mika's right.

"One." He spun Mika out, and then back in. "This means nothing."

Mika blinked and donned a pout. "You mean you *don't* wanna get married and have my babies?"

"Two." He twirled Mika around on his finger. "I wear the pants in this relationship."

"How heteronormative of you."

"And three—" Arthur twisted Mika to lower him into a drop as their classmates finished their chorus, devolving into wild screams. He leaned in close, to be sure only Mika could hear—

"Two can play at this game."

—before dumping him unceremoniously on the floor.

As the crowd swelled with applause and laughter, Arthur hopped off the table to make his way to the door of the suite. Clarke and Jonathan fell into step behind him, and he left Mika on his ass without sparing him a parting glance.

6

Arthur woke up the next morning with a headache that he suspected had very little to do with how much he drank the night before.

Please let it be a dream, he squeezed his eyes shut. *Please let it not be real.*

He squinted one eye open to examine his left palm, curled up in front of his pillow:

Michael Rivera.

Well.

That would have been too easy.

He launched himself out of bed, made his way to the bathroom, filled up the glass there with water from the tap, and downed it. He downed one more for good measure, although he never got hungover anyway.

He retrieved his phone from where it was Charging—via the Auratech charm—in the sunlight streaming onto his desk. Seven notifications:

> **CLARKE**
>
> text us when u wake up ok
>
> we'll debrief over brunch
>
> dress cute let's go into town
>
> hello?? u never sleep in this late

> pls don't tell me u threw urself over the balcony in a fit of melodrama
>
> JONATHAN
>
> Please text Clarke back.
>
> I'm going to throttle him if he doesn't stop pacing the room
>
> CLARKE
>
> jonathan is threatening to strangle me help

The last text had come in only five minutes ago. Arthur replied:

> As if I ever dress any less than cute. I'll be by in fifteen.

True to his word, fifteen minutes later found Arthur freshly showered, teeth brushed, donned in a tan-and-cream kimono-over-sweater combo topped off with his beloved special-edition sneakers. He threw his phone, wallet, and wand into his back pockets, swung open the door, and came face to face with none other than Michael Rivera himself.

Arthur stiffened, and then made to close the door.

"Well, well, well." Mika got his arm in the way of the door lightning fast, faster than should have been fair. "If it isn't my beloved. Care for a romantic stroll in the village?"

Arthur resisted the urge to slam the door into the hand that now rested on the door frame.

"Sorry," Arthur clenched his teeth, not even trying to make it look like a smile. "I've got a date."

Mika scoffed. "As if. With who?"

"Your mom." Arthur glared. "Let me go."

"Not until you give me a kiss." Mika jutted out his jaw, putting his head within range of the door. Arthur did try to slam it this time, but Mika gripped it open with his hand.

"Wasn't the concussion you got when I dropped you enough?" Arthur demanded. "Move."

"*You, shall, not, pass.*" Mika lifted an imaginary staff.

"And *I'm* the nerd?" Arthur rolled his eyes and shifted his weight to one hip so he could fish out his wand. He pointed it at Mika, who immediately raised a hand to meet the other in surrender. He stepped aside into the hall.

"Thanks, *beloved*," Arthur sneered, closing the door behind him and stalking past Mika and down the hall.

"Hey, wait," Mika called out to him.

"Leave me alone," Arthur called back.

"Pham."

"Fuck off."

"Arthur."

He stopped in his tracks and turned slowly, eyebrows raised expectantly.

There was a strange look on Mika's face, something that Arthur couldn't quite place.

His hand tingled.

The silenced stretched on, and when Mika still didn't say anything, Arthur gestured impatiently.

Mika looked down and away. By the time he met Arthur's eyes again, he had the signature shit-eating grin plastered on his face. He wiggled his eyebrows.

"Did you pack a condom?"

Arthur glared and whipped his wand down in an aggressive curlicue. A shower of Conjured condom packets rained down over Mika.

"It's Christmas!" Mika cried, jumping to catch as many as he could. Arthur swallowed a surge of irritation and turned on his heel to walk down the hall and around the corner to Room 430. He decidedly banished that incomprehensible look on Mika's face—and the tingling of his left palm—from his mind.

Resolve fortified, he clenched said left hand and used it to knock on Clarke and Jonathan's door.

"Finally," Jonathan huffed, stepping out into the hall to join Arthur. "He thought you'd choked on your own vomit in your sleep."

"Arthur has been through a major shock." Clarke lifted his nose in the air as he closed the door behind him. "The body acts in unpredictable ways when that happens."

They walked through the halls to the elevator, passing by Arthur's room on the way. The atoms of the Conjured condoms had dispersed back into the atmosphere—both they and Mika were nowhere to be seen.

"I thought you wanted us to dress cute." Arthur assessed Clarke, adorned in an outfit straight out of the wrong side of the century.

Clarke straightened his bowtie defensively as they got into the elevator and started their descent. "Just because not all of us are sneaker-obsessed—"

"I'm sorry," Arthur retorted, "but who's been voted best dressed for the yearbook three, coming on four, years in a row?"

Clarke scoffed. "Winning a majority vote from a student body that's half stoners doesn't make you fashionable."

They made their way across the courtyard, peaceful for all the students nursing hangovers in their rooms. This was the ideal time for weekend brunch—beating the rush of students who would finally stumble out of bed at noon, desperate for sustenance.

"Maybe not, but following trends does," Arthur pointed out.

"If you insist, Anna Wintour," Clarke returned haughtily.

They continued their back-and-forth about the ins and outs of fashion all the way through the main building, out into the entrance of the school, and across the long bridge spanning the length of lake between the campus island and the mainland. They could have rented out brooms from the campus stock, but walking was a tradition of theirs; the sound of the waves was calming to Arthur, and Clarke maintained that the moisture in the air did wonders for his hair. Jonathan was only in it for the weekly cardio.

Soon they were in town, passing the *'For Rent'* sign in the shopfront they'd been eyeing for the better part of a year and then walking up to their favorite brunch spot, *Ontbijt*. There was an ongoing debate between the three of them over whether *Ontbijt* was actually its name, or if it was a nameless café with a sign outside advertising "breakfast," but that was part of the fun.

Once inside, they were greeted by a familiar scene: mismatched homey furniture, creaky hardwood floors, and walls crammed floor-to-ceiling with various vintage posters and paintings by local artists. The early hour was on their side; they were seated immediately at their favorite table by the window, attended by pink, squashy armchairs.

After giving their drink orders to the waitress, Clarke steepled his fingers together, peering at Arthur from across the table.

"So."

Arthur waited, but Clarke only gazed at him.

"Speak your mind, I'm not a Divination major."

"What are we going to do?"

"About?"

Clarke grabbed Arthur's left hand and pointed at his love line. "About *that*."

Arthur snatched his hand back, cradling it protectively. "I thought I was writing my own destiny."

"Destiny shmestiny," Jonathan said matter-of-factly, thanking the waitress who brought him his pot of *verse munt thee*. "Unfortunately, by now the whole school knows."

"What does that have to do with anything?" Arthur sulked. The waitress delivered his *koffie verkeerd*, and he warmed his hands around the glass.

"If you thought your rivalry with Rivera was bad before..." Clarke trailed off, accepting his *zwarte koffie*. He took a sip and shook his head in lieu of continuing. The trio paused to order their food, and once the waitress was gone, Arthur leaned in.

"Nothing has changed," he insisted. "I'm still me, he's still an insufferable asshole, and we're still top of our class." *For now.*

"And—" Jonathan raised a finger to interject— "the school's latest, irresistible piece of gossip."

"So?"

"So," Clarke continued, gesturing at Jonathan in acknowledgment, "now they won't just be enjoying the show."

"They'll be shipping you." Jonathan smirked.

"What is this, a fanfiction?" Arthur scoffed. "They egg us on most of the time anyway."

"And now they'll be wolf-whistling." Clarke started counting off on his fingers. "And making kissing noises, and singing annoying songs, and—"

"I'm not worried about that." Arthur waved him off. "If you ignore it, they stop caring."

"Soulmate magic is no easy feat," Jonathan warned. "Most of the time it doesn't even work. Sure, when it does it's imprecise, because of how unpredictable humans are. But it *did* work."

"They'll eat it up," Clarke agreed. "They already are. Your little stunt at the end of the night—brilliant, genius, of course," he added, because Arthur had given him a glare, "but you're giving them exactly what they want. It'll only have fueled the fire."

"So I'll get it removed," Arthur said, ignoring how his hand seemed to itch in protest at the mere thought. "I'll make an appointment with Professor Celeste."

Clarke and Jonathan exchanged glances.

"Sure." Clarke sipped his coffee. "You do that."

"I don't want to talk about it anymore," Arthur insisted. "I don't even want to think about it anymore."

"Spring Social." Jonathan raised his hand, seeking the floor.

"It is October—" Arthur shook his head. "Scratch that. November."

"Are you really that desperate to get laid?" Clarke said.

"You don't need an occasion, Jonathan," Arthur laughed as Jonathan rolled his eyes. "You're huge. Girls love that, don't they?"

"Boys love it too," Clarke crooned, batting his eyelashes and clinging to Jonathan's arm.

"I have plenty of sex," Jonathan said loudly, just as the waitress arrived with their food.

She gave him a bemused look before setting their food down, and Clarke snorted, dropping Jonathan's arm like a hot potato.

"Speaking of boys." Jonathan lowered his voice, appropriately chagrined. "Is this alleged New York boyfriend coming to Social?"

Clarke nearly choked on his *boterham*.

"Real." He punched Jonathan in the arm. *"Not* alleged!"

"Again." Arthur gestured with his fork. *"November."*

"Thanks, I got it, Neil Sedaka," Jonathan drawled. "Half the people between Stonebury and Featherwood are paired up with each other—"

"Or taken," Clarke pouted.

"—so if we want dates, we'd be better off getting a head start before people start panicking."

"Can we at least get through finals first?" Arthur picked at the *uitsmijter* on his plate. "Or midterms? One thing to panic over at a time."

"As if you have to panic." Clarke frowned at him. "Mr. Straight-A-Plus Student."

"Nice one," Jonathan said through a mouthful of *wentelteefjes*. "Is it your wit that your alleged boyfriend loves you for?"

Clarke launched a piece of ham at him and Arthur leaned back, toast in hand, to make sure it couldn't be sacrificed as fuel for the scuffle that ensued. He really couldn't give a single shit about Social—not now that he had Electi Magi to secure. There was no room to slip up and even if he didn't, he'd likely be neck and neck with Mika until the very end. Unless...

Unless he got Mika to slip up.

A piece of syrup-soaked bread came flying in his direction, and he called on the energy of the wand in his pocket to shift the air around him so it landed on the table instead. Keeping offensive food stuffs off his kimono jacket was worth the extra effort of doing magic sans wand.

"Please keep me out of this." Arthur released a long-suffering sigh. "My wardrobe can't take another hit."

"Come on, the wine stain came out of the shoes!" Clarke whined.

"Yes, but I lost at least three years of my life getting it out of the stitching," Arthur hissed. "This brand is expensive, it was a legitimate miracle I found them for so cheap, and I already had to get the preexisting stains out—"

"Snob," Clarke snapped.

"Geek." Jonathan came to Arthur's defense, flicking Clarke's bowtie.

"It's called *class*, Jonathan."

As they started bickering, Arthur leaned his chin on a hand and eyed the 'For Rent' sign across the street through the window.

Despite the hell he'd been through yesterday—the tuition and the party and the *Mika*—he couldn't help but smile.

"Just imagine," he sighed, and Clarke and Jonathan fell silent. "Brunch every weekend, rolling in the riches of our successful small business..."

"Profiting off needy, desperate students." Jonathan shook his head sadly.

"I'm trying to figure out a sliding scale model," Arthur reassured him as the waitress brought their check, clearly not nearly caffeinated enough for her shift and eager to have them off the premises as soon as possible.

"Three cards?" Clarke pulled out his wallet, and Arthur's stomach dropped. He reached for his phone to check his account balance—

"I got it." Jonathan pulled the check toward him. "We'll be rolling in riches soon enough. Maybe we'll finally be able to upgrade to Bourgeoisie Brunch."

"Who knows?" Clarke wiggled his eyebrows. "Maybe *Michael* will be sitting with us, getting handsy with Arthur under the table."

Arthur cursed the blush that flooded his face, tossing a sugar packet at him.

"I'm just preparing you." Clarke dodged the projectile. "You'll have to deal with way worse."

"I'll be fine." Arthur leaned back in his chair. "I can block anything out. Trust me."

7

But Arthur, as it turned out, was not fine.

Monday after the Halloween party, he made it as far as the courtyard.

"Damn, Pham," called Toby Morano, Arthur's neighbor in 421. "You and Rivera wasted no time—banging against the wall all morning yesterday!"

He did a lewd hip-thrusting sort of jig, and Arthur glared at him.

"I was putting up a poster," he insisted.

Clarke, who was next to him, led him away gently by the arm.

"Ignore him."

"But..." Arthur glanced back over his shoulder, where Toby was brandishing his tongue in a horrifying manner. "I really was—putting up my new poster—"

"I know, hon."

"I bought it from our favorite artist's website, I sent you a picture—"

"Let's just go."

Jonathan waited for them against the white brick wall near their favorite table by the tallest window in the dining hall, illuminated by soft morning light from the greenhouse ceiling.

He caught the look on Arthur's face and sighed sympathetically.

"Ah. It's started."

"Toby Morano." Clarke rolled his eyes.

"He's an ass anyway," Jonathan muttered, and they entered the line for quiche. "When's your appointment with Professor Celeste?"

"In half an hour," Arthur sighed. "Couldn't come soon enough."

"What business does Morano have giving anyone shit about noise anyway?" Clarke muttered. "He's gotten so many complaints about the aural tragedy he considers music that I'm shocked he hasn't been evicted from the hall."

"It's like he's going for a record," Jonathan agreed.

"I don't think the man has seen a record in his life," Clarke said darkly.

His friends fell easily into slandering Toby's name, and Arthur left them to it, lapsing into silence as they inched forward in line. He stared at the writing on his hand, summoning all his willpower to wipe it from existence—to no effect. He switched tracks to manifesting better odds for Professor Celeste.

His Sense pricked the hairs on the back of his neck, and Arthur turned to see someone at the waffle station looking away just in time.

Frowning, he faced forward once more.

By the time they reached the front of the line, he'd nearly caught five people staring.

He made it all the way through ordering, across the hall to the table, and half his quiche before he finally caught a Year Two looking his way and giggling, whispering to their friend.

"Arthur?"

He turned to find Clarke peering at him. "Hm?"

"We were asking if you wanted to split some pancakes."

The pity on both Clarke and Jonathan's faces made Arthur squirm more uncomfortably than the inconspicuous stares had.

"Nah. I'm okay," he said, standing abruptly. "I'm actually gonna go see if Professor Celeste can see me early. I need this thing gone yesterday."

Clarke and Jonathan exchanged glances.

"Do you want company?" Jonathan tried.

"Don't worry about me." Arthur forced a smile, closing himself off from their Sense, creeping closer by the second. "I'll see you later?"

"Sure." Clarke hesitated. "Text us if you need anything?"

"You got it," Arthur conceded, and turned on his heel to flee the dining room.

★

An hour later left Arthur more frustrated than he'd already been, which was quite the feat.

Once he'd managed to lie through his teeth about how he got access to such advanced and archaic magic in the first place—something about a classmate bringing it from home—Professor Celeste had proceeded to speechify about the endless meanings of the word "soulmate" before pulling a convoluted tarot spread to "guide him on his spiritual journey" and "determine the culmination of all his future life paths"—a thirty-minute endeavor in which Arthur found himself not only relieved that he'd never even considered a Divination major, but also convinced that every single one of her decks was rigged to include The Tower, The Lovers, and The World in every spread.

After a polite stretch of stomaching the proselytizing, Arthur firmly insisted that all he wanted was a way to get the damn thing off his hand—a request to which she'd blinked and merely said, "Oh. No, that thing's there for good, hon."

At least stewing over her distinct lack of help distracted him from the stares. And the whispers. And the giggles.

Until Evocation that afternoon.

As Professor Hirst reviewed the Laws of Thermodynamics, Arthur welcomed the salve to the brain that was familiar magic theory: "The First Law states that the total increase in the energy of a system is equal to the increase in thermal energy plus the work done on the system."

Arthur leaned over his notebook to jot down: *'1st law: ^ in energy of system = ^ in thermal energy + work on system.'*

THWIP.

A crumpled sheet of lined paper landed on his desk. Arthur glanced around, but no one seemed to react. He unfurled the note:

'When's the wedding?'

Arthur bit down a growl and brushed the paper onto the floor, focusing in on his notes as Professor Hirst prattled on.

"The Second Law states that heat energy cannot be transferred from a body at a lower temperature to a body at a higher temperature without the addition of energy."

'2nd law: heat energy x transferred from low temp to high temp w/o energy.'

THWIP.

"The Third Law states that the entropy of a pure crystal at absolute zero is zero."

'3rd law: entropy of crystal at A0 is 0.'

THWIP.

Forty-five minutes into class, Arthur's desk was littered with folded paper and crumpled scraps. When the next one hit him in the back of the head before falling to the floor, Arthur rubbernecked around to catch the perpetrator once and for all.

Several students were stifling laughter, but Arthur found their source of delight to be Mika. He had a collection of crumpled paper comprehensive enough to rival Arthur's, but was opting out of the lecture in favor of Evoking small flowers from each note and arranging them in his hair. He now bore a crude resemblance to a forest nymph in a school uniform. Arthur seethed and glanced at Professor Hirst, who had his back turned to the students to draw diagrams on the chalkboard.

Arthur cleared his throat loudly, and Professor Hirst looked over his shoulder. Instantaneously, Mika's notes-turned-flowers Vanished, and his audience sobered.

"Interesting note-taking strategy, Mr. Pham." Arthur startled, finding that Professor Hirst was instead keenly eyeing the litter around Arthur's desk. "I expect a wastebin for a backpack, next."

Heat crept into Arthur's face as the class chuckled collectively. He opened his mouth to protest, but someone cut in before he had the chance.

"Professor, I'm not getting it. Can we have a practical demonstration?"

Professor Hirst eyed the class warily as Arthur aggressively Vanished the notes around his desk.

"...Sure," he conceded. "Can anyone—" Professor Hirst pointedly avoided eye contact with Arthur and Mika— "demonstrate how the nature of molecules affects Heating and Cooling magic?"

Arthur swore he could hear a pin drop. It was the most reserved he'd seen his classmates all day—maybe even for the entire time he'd been in school with them.

"Alright." Mika eased up from his chair and made a show of stretching his arms, cracking his neck, and rolling up his shirtsleeves. "I got this."

"Thank you Mr. Rivera, but—"

"Pham?" Mika strode over to Arthur's desk, offering a hand. "For this trick, I'll need my devoted second officer."

Arthur shot him the dirtiest glare he could as the students around them catcalled. Professor Hirst protested in vain.

"Boys, I don't—"

"Sure." Arthur swallowed his pride and pasted a smile on his face, determined not to let even an ounce of weakness show. "Always up for an opportunity to show you how it's done, Rivera."

He dismissed Mika's hand and rose from his seat of his own accord.

The students stomped and screamed, and Professor Hirst mumbled something entirely inconsequential as he took a seat behind his desk. He scooted both himself and the table as far back into the corner as possible.

Mika led them to the front of the room where their professor once stood, and Arthur struggled to get his breathing under control. This he could handle. Standing off against Mika was never a challenge; the anxiety he felt was just excitement. That's right—excitement at the chance to best Mika again.

So then why were the catcalls making his clothes feel too tight for his body?

"There isn't really such a thing as 'hot' and 'cold.'" Mika slung an arm over Arthur's shoulders, and Arthur immediately picked it up gingerly to remove it. "There's just 'hot' and 'less hot.' That's what your *beloved* nonmagic books say, right Pham?"

Arthur seethed at the emphasis but grit his teeth against it. "Far less elegant than I'd have explained it, but sure."

Mika ignored the dig. "So that means that it should be easier to increase the heat in the room than to decrease it, because..."

He grinned at Arthur, who rolled his eyes.

"Because harnessing the natural movement of atoms all around us to transpose it into heat is a more intuitive process than the effort of both temporarily halting that movement and Sending heat away."

"Thanks, Encyclopedia Brown," Mika grinned, and the class laughed heartily.

"Get to the point, Bill Nye."

"A contest," Mika proposed, turning to Arthur. "We'll each try to manipulate the temperature of the classroom at the same time. You want hot or cold?"

Arthur bristled and blurted, "Cold, obviously."

Mika rose his eyebrows. Infuriatingly. "I expected no less."

The class voiced their approval with sound-barrier-breaking decibels of enthusiasm. Professor Hirst sighed and sank lower into his seat.

Mika raised his wand. "On three?"

Arthur raised his wand to match, closing his eyes. "One, two—"

Mika may have been arrogant, but he knew his magic theory. Before Arthur had even finished sounding off the signal, the air around him began to warm—fast. He heard rustling as students shed their blazers and loosened their ties. He could practically hear Mika's grin widen, feeling the atoms all around them grow agitated as his Sense urged them to move faster, to generate heat that compounded on itself—and they were happy to oblige.

Arthur extended his own Sense, feeling the near manic energy in the atmosphere around him. He felt giddy with the wildness of it, and he suppressed a tickle in his gut threatening to cough up to the surface in a fit of giggles. Mika was sending the small pocket of the universe around them into chaos, and he was doing it with ease.

But Arthur had asked for a challenge.

He began with the particles immediately surrounding him, taking a deep breath in and, with his exhale, inviting them to do the same. They began to calm, and so Arthur extended out as far as he could, breathing steadily.

But as he mastered the area around him and moved on to the next, Mika egged on the atoms he'd just calmed to set them off once more. Arthur's mouth twisted in frustration—atoms wanted to move. It was near impossible to keep all of them still but far too easy to get them all moving and so the temperature rose steadily, reaching a stifling ten degrees above the comfortable classroom thermostat setting.

"Whenever you're ready," Mika drawled. "We're starting to heat up in here, Pham."

Arthur's eyes snapped open to meet Mika's as the students hollered. He'd loosened his tie and undone a couple buttons while he worked. A single curl stuck to his forehead.

Arthur felt sweat slide down his temple but refused to buckle. He tried to block out the sound of his classmates' jeers, tried to focus in on the roguish, cavalier sparkle in Mika's eye—but for every degree he managed to claim, Mika raised him five. The students' roar echoed in Arthur's ears, and Mika's smile settled into something loose and arrogant, forearm glistening with sweat as he held his wand. Arthur kept finding his focus pulled by beads of sweat rolling down Mika's neck, and it was getting harder and harder to retain control over the few atoms he still had command of.

Mika took a step further, into Arthur's personal space. Their classmates' cheers rose to a fever pitch.

"Whatsamatter, Pham?" Mika let out a low chuckle as his eyes dipped down Arthur's face and back up to his eyes. "Not enough stamina?"

Something swooped low in Arthur's gut, and his control slipped further. It had to be a good thirty degrees above normal now.

"Give in, darling." Mika's voice was laced with glee, but something else too—something that gave Arthur the ludicrous idea to let his knees buckle and sink to the floor.

"Just kiss already!"

Toby Morano's voice rose above all the others, and Arthur was launched headfirst out of the heat, the haze, the—the *whatever* this was.

He broke eye contact and took two shaky steps back to distance himself, releasing what little focus he had left and turning his wand down to point at the ground—a show of surrender. Their audience groaned as students slumped in their seats, and Mika dropped his focus too, throwing back his head and laughing.

"I concede," Arthur grit out. "You've got science on your side."

"Thank god." Professor Hirst stood from his chair and raised a wand, easily and steadily lowering the temperature back down to its thermostat-regulated level now that the particles had no one to pester them. "There you have it—why cold doesn't actually exist, just the absence of heat, *et cetera.*"

He was eager to get back to his lecture, and Arthur was eager to get back to his seat—far away from Mika. He felt as if he were too big for his skin, itchy and restless everywhere despite the classroom being a comfortable temperature again. His head was pounding as thanks for his effort, and his left palm tingled uncomfortably. He could Sense Mika's eyes on him, desperate to gloat, and Arthur refused to give him the courtesy.

Before he could pick up his pen to continue taking notes, another scrap of paper landed on his desk with a *thwip*. It wasn't even folded properly, and Arthur could make out its contents:

'*Fuck/marry/kill: Mika Rivera, Mika Rivera, Mika Rivera?*'

Arthur closed his eyes and summoned all his willpower not to scream into the void.

The class proved impossible to rein in after a stunt of such magnitude, so Professor Hirst released them for lunch a good twenty minutes before the bell sounded. Arthur was going for a record for fastest route to the dining hall when Tan caught up to him.

"Arthur! Do you have a second?"

Arthur hesitated, gazing longingly at the entrance to the hall. It was Pasta Bar Monday...

"What is it?" He eyed Tan warily.

"I just need help carrying my project to my next class." Tan started to walk backward, back in the direction of the classrooms. "It'll only take a minute, I swear."

Arthur spared one last, longing glance at the dining hall—*Pasta Bar Monday!*—and followed after Tan.

"Just a minute, right?" he asked, tapping his fingers against his pants. "I'm starving—that shit Mika pulled took it out of me."

Tan shot a mischievous glance over their shoulder. "Oh, I bet it did."

Arthur narrowed his eyes. "What—"

"It's in here." Tan gestured, holding open the door across the hall from Evocation. Arthur sighed and walked in.

"Okay, where—"

The door closed abruptly behind him, and Arthur jumped at a short laugh on the other side of the room.

"Come here often?"

Arthur whipped around to find Mika perched on the professor's desk in the back of the room, backpack abandoned on the floor.

"Of course," Arthur sighed, and turned around to walk right back out of the classroom.

"They locked it," Mika warned, just as Arthur tried the handle.

Arthur pulled out his wand, ready to dismantle the lock, but Mika cleared his throat.

"And make your way through the horde of horny Year Fours with nothing but time on their hands and nothing better to do? Nah, I don't think so."

"Tan!" Arthur cried, and he heard their laugh alongside others. *Where had they been hiding?* "I thought we were friends!"

"Oh, how the mighty fall," Mika scoffed.

Arthur turned around again. He was catching a twitch under his eye.

"Okay, so what do you suggest, asshole? Because I'd rather deal with fifty of *them* than be trapped in here with one of you."

"You flatter me." Mika grinned. He jerked his head over to the window. "That's your best way out."

Arthur closed his eyes and breathed deeply.

"It's only noon—" he took great care to keep his tone even— "and you've already depleted half my energy for the day with your imbecilic, unwinnable contest. If I invest the effort to levitate down two stories—"

"I'm sorry." Mika stopped him with a hand. "Were you not the one who chose the unwinnable side? After giving *me* shit about stamina three days ago?"

"Being goaded into a contest with you is on my daily list of expected rote tasks," Arthur shot back. "Being tricked into a locked classroom with you is, admittedly, not how I thought this day would go."

"Well, then I guess you're lucky you're in the Home Ec room."

Mika slid off the desk and strode to the cabinet on the right side of the room, opening it to reveal swaths of scrap fabric in various colors and textures. "Let's hope your physical stamina is up to snuff."

Mika started tossing out the sturdiest-looking scraps.

"Please," Arthur scoffed, securing scraps together in tight knots. "I work out."

Mika paused where he was bent over in the cabinet to raise an eyebrow at him. "Yeah, right."

"Come a little closer." Arthur smiled humorlessly, showing him a fist. "I'll show you."

"As truly thrilling as a brawl with your insufferable ass sounds—" Mika moved to join him in tying— "lunch ends in half an hour."

They busied themselves securing fabric end on end until they'd created a makeshift rope long enough to safely jump to the courtyard below. Arthur threw one end out the open window and secured the other to a sturdy-looking cabinet under the window.

"Okay, you go first," he said, focused on the knot, "I'll go after you're done so it doesn't break."

"And fall to my doom when you untie it once I'm climbing?"

Arthur leveled him with a look.

Mika donned an expression to match it. "You've got murder in your eyes, Pham."

"Fine." Arthur conceded, tugging on the knot to ensure its security. "I know at least *I* could save myself if I fell."

"You know what—"

But Arthur was already out the window, bracing his feet on the wall to rappel down the side of the building.

Halfway down, his legs were aching, his arms were burning, and he was wishing he'd just Levitated himself.

Mika's head appeared at the window. "Are you done yet? Only ten minutes till class."

"Maybe if I didn't have to give you progress reports every five seconds," Arthur panted through clenched teeth, "I'd have the energy to go faster—"

"Rapunzel, Rapunzel, let down your long hair!"

Arthur froze.

Toby Morano was walking past with two cronies, and they all burst into unbearable snickers. Arthur's arms screamed, and he stifled a groan.

"Hey, why don't you go fuck yourself," Mika called down to the offenders, boldly throwing up two fingers, but they'd already disappeared into the building.

Arthur reached the end of the rope and jumped the remaining six feet with nothing hurt but aching knees, a bruised ego, and, honestly, sore everything. He wanted to go back to his room and take another long nap. He had a feeling long naps were about to become a necessary staple of his daily routine.

He started to stalk off to class, but Mika's voice stopped him in his tracks.

"Oi! Princess! Aren't you gonna spot me?"

He'd already started climbing down, and Arthur let out an exasperated sigh.

"Only because I don't want to go to jail for your murder," he called back, "because I know, somehow, from the grave, you'd still find a way to make my life harder than it has to be."

"Stop, I'm getting turned on."

Arthur shifted his weight to one hip and crossed his arms, waiting. His stomach growled. So much for Pasta Bar Monday. He Summoned a measly protein bar from the stash in his room and munched as he waited.

Finally, with three minutes to spare, Mika jumped down from the end of the rope and promptly fell over.

"You should try out for the ballet team." Arthur started walking away, not waiting for him to get to his feet. "I hear they need someone to suck so bad that they make the other dancers look good."

Mika caught up to him, breathing hard. "I'm actually very good at dancing, thank you very much."

"Don't care." Arthur sped up. "And fuck off, do you know what they'll say if we're walking together?"

"Right." Mika gasped for breath. "As you were."

Arthur sped ahead and spared him a glance over his shoulder.

"Also—" he flashed a rare grin— "you seem out of shape. You should try working out."

Trying his best to carry himself as if he weren't wretchedly, bone-deep exhausted, he continued on, leaving Mika behind in the dust once more.

8

And that was only the first four hours.

The rest of the day was an endless stream of taunts and jeers and songs, in class and out. Even the dorm was no longer safe—at the end of the school day he was greeted by a smattering of documents pinned to the bulletin board on his door comprising fanart of him and Mika in colored pencil (rather good), a construction paper valentine containing a lewd haiku (rather bad), and a ten page print-out of a smutty composition starring him and Mika (pointedly unread). Arthur opted for tearing down the bulletin board entirely before entering his room.

The next three days were even worse.

On Tuesday, someone Conjured doves to fly out of his locker. The glitter they shit everywhere, bafflingly, did not disappear when the doves did, and Arthur spent the afternoon scrubbing rainbow-hued sparkles out of his uniform—even magic couldn't get glitter out of every nook and cranny. By dinnertime, Arthur hypothesized that it was made out of particles that were clearly not of this universe.

On Wednesday, he found himself tangled in a tree with Mika, struggling to extricate his elbows from Mika's armpits as a throng of classmates down below sang, *"Arthur and Mika kissing in a tree, K-I-S-S-I-N-G!"*

On Thursday, someone Animated tiny cupid figurines to flit around their heads, singing high-pitched love songs loud enough only for the victim to hear and prodding them with minuscule arrows every several seconds. While Mika befriended his cupid, Arthur pulled his hair out trying to figure out the Counterspell. Inspired, his cupid started pulling on his hair in tandem.

And, on Friday, the first A- Arthur had ever seen in his life landed on his desk.

He knew when he took the Transmutation exam on Wednesday that it hadn't been his best work—he hadn't had time to fully revise since he'd been scrubbing glitter until at least midnight—but he hadn't realized it had been *that* bad. He stared at that tiny dash, tiny and significant and horrifying, and knew he had to be losing it now because he could have sworn it was *laughing* at him—

But no, that was just Mika two seats away. Arthur turned his exam upside down hastily, glaring at where Mika held up a paper with an A+ circled, accompanied by a smiley face.

Blood rushed to Arthur's face as he fixed his gaze resolutely forward.

He tried to tune into Professor Silverton's lecture, but his brain worried away at that minus behind his A, ominous and all-consuming. While a perfectly acceptable grade, acceptable was not enough, not if he wanted—*needed*—to win Electi Magi, not if he wanted his year's tuition paid in full upon graduation. This was only the first week of having a rival-turned-soulmate, nay, the first *five days*. If things continued the way they were...

Arthur stared at his quiz, face-down on the desk, eyes itchy with exhaustion. Dread settled in the pit of his stomach.

By the end of class he was on the brink of a panic attack for the second time in a week, and his legs carried him out of the room on autopilot as his brain occupied itself with spinning potential game plans on several plates. If he could go back to Professor Stonebury and get placed in independent study for a class or two, maybe that would ease the scrutiny—but then wouldn't that make them all even more excited, trying to figure out why he'd disappeared? And then, when he *was* in class, it would be that much worse...did he have enough credits to graduate early? He would still have to complete the Year Four seminar—but no, he still had two elective credits to fulfill, so maybe if—

"Hey Pham, can I get some help rearranging the chairs in here?"

Arthur was too distracted to notice who was asking.

"Sure," he said, allowing himself to be guided into an empty classroom.

He didn't realize his mistake until the door slammed shut behind him.

"Get a room, lovebirds!" Toby Morano sang.

Laughter echoed from behind the door, and Arthur looked up to find Mika, once again, lounging on the Home Ec professor's desk.

"Again?" Arthur groaned, pressing his face into his hands.

"Looks like you walked in willingly, at least." Mika grinned. "They hoisted me onto their shoulders and dumped me unceremoniously. I'll have a bruise on my ass for a week."

Arthur gazed warily at the open window. "I can't rappel down this building twice in one week."

"Above two workouts in a day?"

"Beneath my dignity," Arthur corrected wearily, slumping into a desk.

Mika descended from his own, stalking up and down the width of the classroom. "There's gotta be something we can do to shut them up."

Arthur eyed him as he paced back and forth, noting the dullness under his eyes, how his shirt leaned more disorganized-rumpled than effortless-rumpled. The A- flashed before his eyes, and he promptly felt like throwing up.

"Agreed," he said. His voice was muffled, having just buried his face in his arms on the desk. He was fresh out of savage remarks, his store of witty retorts scrubbed clean alongside the glitter.

"Independent study," Mika suggested.

"They'll go mad about where we've gone."

"Graduate early?"

"Not unless you've been taking secret classes I don't know about," Arthur drawled.

"Shit."

"Shit indeed."

Arthur raised his head just enough to reread the words on his palm for the hundredth time.

Michael Rivera.

"What a sick joke," Arthur muttered.

When Mika didn't answer, Arthur swiveled his head to glance up at him. He was looking out the window, eyes searching, biting his lip as he tapped his heel against the floor. Arthur scowled.

"Your foot tapping is giving me anxiety." As if his anxiety wasn't already at an all-time high even before the foot tapping.

Mika stopped tapping. "What if we're meant to work together?"

Arthur stared, then made a gesture to encourage Mika to get on with it.

"I have an idea." Mika perched up on the professor's desk again. "But I don't think you'll like it."

"Try me." Arthur crossed his arms.

Mika's eyes met the ceiling. "What if..." He shrugged. "What if we beat them at their own game?"

Arthur narrowed his eyes. "What do you mean?"

"I mean..." Mika picked at a little knot of wood with his finger. "It won't be as fun for them to make fun of us if we go along with it."

He looked back up at Arthur.

"Go along with it." Arthur shook his head, brows knitted together.

Mika rolled his eyes. "For a so-called genius you really are dense, aren't you?" He started talking at a snail's pace, making large gestures between them. "You, me, go out, together, as boyfriends."

Panic lurched in Arthur's gut.

"What! Jesus, *eugh—god—what?*"

"You'd get to cut in front of at least three people in line." Mika shot him a rakish grin.

"As if—I would never—how could you even—*bastard—*" Arthur's brain-to-mouth connection seemed to be irreparably severed. His heart-to-face connection, however, seemed well-wired—he felt his cheeks flush hot as his anxiety conjured up its second intrusive memory of the day: Mika up close, taunting him, beads of sweat at his temple, smile slow and easy—

"Not for real, genius." Mika scoffed. "Have you even heard of fanfiction?"

Arthur shook himself. "Have *you*? *Star Trek* was home to the first *ever* fandom revolving around a same-sex—"

"We can pretend," Mika interrupted, hopping off the table. "We can pretend to go out. They get everything their sick little hearts desire, and we get them off our asses."

"That's..." Arthur closed his eyes and shook his head, holding his hands up. "No. That would never work."

"Why? You doubt my acting skills?" Mika grinned, holding a hand up theatrically. "To be or not to be—"

"Because I'm getting acid reflux just being in the same room with you, let alone getting within a foot of you, or holding hands with you, or *kissing* you, Christ, my whole lunch is coming up just thinking about it—"

"Okay, okay," Mika placated him. "We don't have to go full boyfriend. But Pham—" he donned a simpering expression— "if you were embarrassed about being a bad kisser, you could have just *told* me."

Arthur shot him an acerbic glare. "This is ludicrous."

"Thousands of clichéd stories beg to differ," Mika retorted.

"You're only proving my point," Arthur said.

"Better ideas?"

Arthur ground his teeth and stared at Mika but, for once, his brain had no solution to the problem, which had demonstrated an uncanny knack for spiraling further and further out of control: *no tuition, make Electi Magi, beat Mika, Mika's name, classmates laughing, losing sleep, worse grades, won't beat Mika, no Electi Magi, no tuition...*Arthur was dizzy with it, pressure building in the base of his skull, vision going blurry at the edges, hatred for Mika pounding in his veins—

But then something occurred to him.

An agreement like this would require them to spend a lot more time together by design, and as distasteful as that sounded, he'd be remiss if he didn't acknowledge the chance to get to know Mika better, to take inventory of the insecurities—potential avenues to inch past him—under that cocksure facade...

Wouldn't that be worth it? Wouldn't that truly be the solution to cut straight through the never-ending cycle?

What better way to beat Mika than from the inside?

Arthur felt like a villain in a bad superhero movie.

Mika raised his eyebrows expectantly.

"We'll need rules," Arthur said, almost inaudibly. He thought he might actually be close to throwing up, now.

"What was that?"

"Rules," he ground out.

"Ah, we have our first one." Mika made an X over his heart. "No kissing. But we might have to be more convincing than that—how about kissing with no tongue?"

"I've entered an inferior, cursed timeline," Arthur whined, closing his eyes and fighting off the impending migraine. "You can kiss...god, gross. I don't know. My forehead?"

"Okay, Jane Austen."

"Please," Arthur scoffed. "Jane Austen's prose would have you blushing at the mere touch of the fingertips."

"What about cheek—"

"Fine."

"—with tongue."

"What?"

"Final offer."

"Cheek, fine; no tongue, ever, *anywhere*." Arthur clapped to emphasize the words.

"Great," Mika consented. He dug for his wand, then drew a clockwise circle with it. A piece of paper appeared out of thin air. "I'm writing this down."

"That paper is going to disappear within the hour." Arthur squinted at him. "Summon one from your room instead."

"As if I just have stacks of paper lying around in my room?" Mika protested.

"You are so—" Arthur pulled out his wand and Vanished the Conjured paper, then drew a counterclockwise circle. The leather-bound notebook from the desk in his room popped into existence over the table, clattering onto the desktop.

"And I'm the one taking this too seriously." Mika rolled his eyes.

"I refuse to get conned by you." Arthur glared, retrieving a fountain pen from his bag.

"Why would you think I'm trying to con you?"

"Because I don't trust you further than I could throw you," Arthur muttered, etching out their contract in his neat script:

Falsified Romantic Relations Between Arthur Pham and Michael Rivera

Terms and Conditions

1. PDA

Kissing on the cheek is permitted.
No tongue permitted, EVER.
No other kissing permitted, EVER.

"I dunno, Pham." Mika pulled up a chair in front of the desk Arthur was writing on, straddling it backwards. "Put your money where your mouth is. I'm sure you could throw me at least a foot."

"Don't push me, Rivera."

"We're talking about throwing, not pushing." Mika jabbed a finger into the notebook. "Hey, why does your name go first?"

"Alphabetical."

"Age before beauty, more like it."

Arthur retrieved his wand to point it at Mika's neck. "You're asking for it."

"You're no fun." But Mika stood down, hanging over the back of the chair.

Arthur placed his wand on the desk so he could keep writing.

2. Permitted Touching
Hand holding.
Arm around the shoulder.

"And waist," Mika interjected, reading upside-down. Arthur sighed and added,

Arm around the waist.

"And butt spanking," Mika suggested. Arthur reached for his wand again.

"Kidding, kidding. Hey, wait."

Mika peered at Arthur's wand on the desk. "You have a Rainbow Fluorite core?"

Arthur raised his eyebrows and studied his wand. The purple crystal handle was laced with hints of green, embedded in walnut wood carved to taper smoothly out at forty-five centimeters. There were some nicks in the wood here and there; he remembered trading in his starter wand for this one the summer before starting at Stonebury.

Arthur placed a hand over his wand protectively. "You've been dodging my spells for four years and never noticed?"

Mika sucked on his teeth impatiently and pulled out his own wand, placing it on the desk next to Arthur's. The juniper wood was raw, curving here and there with the natural knots of the wood, and it was shorter than his, closer to thirty centimeters. But at its handle—smudged from where Mika had clearly handled it without cleaning it in some time—was a Rainbow Fluorite core, a murky green laced with purple, as if they were cut from different sides of the same crystal—the perfect complement to one another.

"That's weird," Mika said brightly.

The love line on Arthur's left hand tingled.

"Yeah." He frowned, clenching his hand under the desk. "Weird."

"Social obligations," Mika said.

"Huh?"

He pointed to the notebook. "Next on the list."

"Oh." Arthur picked up his pen again. "Right."

"We'll have to sit next to each other in class," Mika decided.

"So you can cheat off me." Arthur shot him a look.

"As if I need to." Mika rolled his eyes. "Write it down."

"Fine."

3. *Social Obligations*
Sitting next to each other in class.
No cheating on tests or assignments.

"Also," Mika added, "you have to come to parties with me."

"Oh, come *on*."

"*You* come on."

"Only Fridays or Saturdays," Arthur conceded. "And only once every other weekend."

"Killjoy." Mika grinned.

Arthur leaned down to write, but paused. "What about your girlfriend?"

"Cherry?" Mika blinked. "What about her?"

"What do you *mean*, what about—is she gonna be cool with this? What about when your Featherwood friends come over, you're just going to ignore her?"

Mika dismissed this with a wave of his hand. "Cherry's cool, don't worry. I'll talk to her tonight."

Arthur narrowed his eyes.

"Seriously. We've been friends forever. She's not the jealous type. Trust me."

"Jealous type or not—" Arthur raised his eyebrows— "you have to admit this is unconventional."

"Why don't you let me worry about my relationship—" Mika placed a hand on his chest, then pointed at the notebook— "and you worry about your precious rules."

Arthur shook his head, but leaned down to write once more. "Fine."

"Are you gonna tell your friends?"

Arthur looked up quickly. "Clarke and Jonathan?"

"Yeah."

"Are you gonna tell yours?" Arthur deflected.

Mika scoffed. "Are you kidding me? I'm friends with the whole school. That defeats the purpose, obviously."

Arthur just barely resisted strangling him for his arrogance to consider Clarke and Jonathan, to consider telling them about a fake-dating arrangement with his rival, to consider the questions they'd ask:

'Why don't you just ignore them?'

'Because my grades will slip, and I won't beat Mika, I won't make Electi Magi. I'll have to go into debt to pay my tuition for the year, we can't start our business—'

Their looks of pity haunted Arthur, making him sicker than the dreaded A-. If he pulled this off…

He shook his head. "They don't need to know. I can handle you alone."

Mika shrugged, and fifteen minutes later, the rest of their contract was complete:

> *4. Attending Parties Together*
> *Once every two weeks maximum.*
> *Fridays OR Saturdays only.*
>
> *5. Pact of Secrecy*
> *The only parties who may remain privy to the arrangement are those directly involved, plus Cherry.*
> *Involved parties (plus Cherry) may not intentionally divulge the arrangement to anyone, and must do their utmost not to unintentionally divulge the arrangement to anyone.*
>
> *6. Amendments to the Arrangement*
> *Amendments may be made as needed, and will be initialed by both involved parties before they are signed into action.*
>
> *7. Ending the Arrangement*
> *The arrangement may be terminated by either party for any reason at any time as long as the other party is given notice.*

Arthur let out a long-suffering sigh. "Are we really doing this?"

"Oh, we're doing this." Mika pasted a roguish grin on his face and stuck out his hand.

Arthur made a face, loath to make any more physical contact than necessary—but then again, maybe it was time to get used to it.

He clasped Mika's hand. It was warm, and dry.

They shook once, and Arthur released him immediately, wiping his hand on his trousers.

Mika huffed out a laugh and grabbed the notebook to sign his name, then pushed it back to Arthur, who did the same.

"We're in business, baby." Mika clapped Arthur on the shoulder.

"Hold on, we did *not* include pet names in the contract—"

But Mika had already vacated his seat, unlocked the door with his wand, and was halfway out of the classroom in a matter of seconds. "What's that, beloved? I couldn't hear you, love. See you in Transmutation, darling!"

And then he was gone, vanishing into the crowd of students waiting for them in the hall, leaving them thunderstruck in his wake.

Arthur stared down at the notebook in front of him, at the ink drying where they'd signed their names.

"What have I done?" he whispered.

9

As mages, we cannot be so arrogant as to assume that magic is the solution to all our problems. In fact, there is much we can learn from non-mages, as they have made leaps and bounds in technology, medicine, and physical production that would have left mages behind decades ago had we not piggy-backed on the efforts of our non-magic allies. Crystaltechnology, green eco-manipulations, and herbalogical medicine are just a few examples of the collaborations between mages and non-magic folk. It is because of this that incorporating the study of non-magic physics and chemistry is crucial to a deeper and more nuanced understanding of how magic works. Consider this excerpt from our sister company, Pearson Education:

"Science consists of the theories and laws that are general truths of nature as well as the body of knowledge they encompass. Scientists are continually trying to expand this body of knowledge and to perfect the expression of the laws that describe it. Physics is concerned with describing the interactions of energy, matter, space, and time, and it is especially interested in Physics is concerned with describing the interactions of energy, matter, space, and time, and it is especially interested in Physics is concerned with describing the interactions of energy, matter, space, and time, and it is especially interested in

Arthur blinked blearily. He'd been reading the same line for the past ten minutes.

He thrust an errant sprig of lavender from his ritual kit into *Real World Magic* to mark his place before coaxing it shut and pushing it away from him, leaning his elbows on the desk to massage his temples. Midterms were in a week, and he couldn't get through study sessions more than fifteen minutes at a time.

His mind kept returning to Mika's wide, unapologetic grin. *'We can pretend.'*

Arthur dragged his hands down his face.

Mika making an X over his heart. *'No kissing.'*

Arthur sighed and slumped in his chair, staring at the ceiling.

Mika peering at their matching wand cores. *'That's weird.'*

Arthur's left hand tingled, and he balled it into a fist before standing abruptly. Maybe he'd clean his room. For the third time that weekend.

But no sooner had he stood than there was a knock on the door: *shave-and-a-haircut!*

Arthur moved to get to his feet, realized he was already on his feet, and finally gained his bearings to cross the room and answer the door, only to find none other than Mika himself.

Arthur glanced down at his own palm suspiciously.

"Good." Mika started to push past Arthur through the doorway. "You're home."

Arthur refused to budge. "It's a school night."

"Thanks, Mom," Mika sneered. "Let me in."

"Why?"

"Because I'm your boyfriend, that's why."

"Only in public, asshole." Arthur was starting to get a headache.

"Yeah, starting tomorrow," Mika said, as if Arthur was only proving his point—one which Arthur had yet to be made privy to. "We need to practice."

"Practice," Arthur repeated.

"Practice," Mika confirmed.

"I think I can handle *pretending* to be your boyfriend," Arthur scoffed.

Mika reached out without warning, but before his hand could make contact Arthur smacked it away, recoiling instinctively.

"See?" Mika grinned. "Hence, practice."

And with that, he pushed past Arthur into the room.

"You surprised me," Arthur protested, but Mika wasn't listening.

"Wow." He was turning in a circle, taking in Arthur's room. "I wouldn't have pegged you for a mid-century modern kind of guy."

"Pegging isn't in the contract," Arthur shot back resentfully.

Mika gave him a surprised grin, lopsided, then cocked an eyebrow. "Correct me if I'm wrong, but I don't think pegging is relevant between the both of us."

Arthur blushed, and hated it, and hated Mika, *so fucking much.* "I don't have time to make sex jokes and hold hands with you all night, so can we just get this over with?"

His voice cracking at the end of his sentence also made the list of things Arthur hated.

Mika seemed content to let it slide. "We have to be convincing," he reasoned, falling easily onto Arthur's couch. "Otherwise they'll think we're fucking with them, and they'll only double down on the shit-giving."

"Sure," Arthur conceded. "But why couldn't this have happened, say, seven hours ago? When I wasn't dead tired and fighting off a migraine?"

Mika shrugged, spreading his arms across the back of the couch and crossing an ankle over one knee. "Something told me you needed a distraction."

Arthur glanced at Mika's left hand. Maybe premonition *was* part and parcel of the soulmate thing, a sort of enhanced Sense. He remembered an old wives' tale of soulmates reading each other's minds with enough time and magical resonance—if that was anywhere near possible, well. There went the whole reason he'd agreed to this harebrained scheme in the first place.

Schemes notwithstanding, the idea of Mika thinking at him all day made him shudder, and—to his horror—blush even further.

"Half an hour," Arthur grit through his teeth, making his way over to the couch to sit as far away from Mika as possible. "That's all you get."

"Then you better work hard." Mika grinned.

"I know no other way." Arthur rolled up the sleeves of the green fisherman's sweater he'd been lounging in.

Mika's quippy retort didn't clock in at its usual speed. Arthur chanced a glance over at him, startled to find him staring and—

Was he redder than usual?

Arthur raised an eyebrow. "Like what you see?"

"Sorry, spaced out." Mika fell quickly into the easy, arrogant grin that so often stole across his stupid, stupid face. "Contrary to popular belief, I *do* study, you know."

"You can read?"

"Whatever it takes to keep up with you, Pham." Mika smiled crookedly, and Arthur took note of the dullness just under his eyes again, despite the way his eyebrows wiggled.

Arthur looked away pointedly, unsure of how many more innuendos he could withstand on a school night. "Your timer is down to twenty-five."

Mika sat up straighter on the couch. "Alright. For starters, you should probably sit closer."

"I can reach you just fine from here," Arthur insisted.

Mika shrugged and held out his hand between them.

Arthur summoned every ounce of courage he could muster before reaching out his own hand to meet it, fighting off the reflex to retract immediately and giving in to a deeper, unsettling instinct to intertwine their fingers. Mika's grip was warm in Arthur's perpetually icy hand. Mika gave a squeeze, sending something thoroughly unexpected down Arthur's spine—

And then Mika pulled *hard*, throwing Arthur off balance and nearly sending his face into Mika's lap.

He caught himself with his other hand just in time, pushing himself up as Mika chuckled.

"Fine," he muttered, begrudgingly scooting closer.

"You made it through Round One," Mika congratulated him. Arthur rolled his eyes. "Ready for Round Two?"

"I'm waiting with bated breath."

And so, Mika—unbothered and casual as anything—placed a hand on Arthur's thigh.

Arthur side-eyed him severely, pulling out his wand to Summon the contract and pen from where they lay on his desk.

2. *Permitted Touching*
Hand holding.
Arm around the shoulder.

Arm around the waist.

Still side-eying Mika, Arthur added:

Hand on thigh, no higher than three inches below finger-line.

And he initialed it before handing it to Mika, still glaring.

Mika chuckled and took it to sign, effectively removing his hand from Arthur's thigh, much to his relief.

Mika Sent the contract and pen back to Arthur's desk and leaned back. "Your turn."

"You're kidding."

"And wipe that look of disgust off your face before you seriously offend me. No one's going to buy it if it's one sided."

"You seriously offend me," Arthur muttered.

"Thanks, honey," Mika simpered. "Now put your hand on my fucking thigh."

And so on and so forth for the next twenty minutes, Mika dragging Arthur through a crash course of socially-expected physical intimacy, insults flying back and forth the whole way there. Mika seemed to be extremely at ease with his own body, a feat which Arthur, who'd never been a touchy-feely person even with boyfriends of the past, found utterly befuddling. They finally reached an immovable roadblock when Arthur consistently froze under Mika's arm every time it got slung around his shoulders, no matter how many insults Mika threw his way to loosen him up. After their third attempt Mika released him breezily, suggesting they work up to it later.

"You're making progress," he said brightly as they walked to the door.

"I don't appreciate the condescension." Arthur glared at him.

"No, I'm serious." Mika turned to look him in the eye. "Listen, I don't want to make you uncomfortable. It just has to be convincing enough for them to buy it."

Arthur reeled back at the unfamiliar earnestness and paused, searching Mika's face. A split second too late, he realized he was staring.

"Yeah," he said, dropping his gaze quickly. "Whatever. Thanks."

Mika opened the door, looking back over his shoulder. His insufferable affection was back. *"Enchanté,* you awkward fuck."

"Charmed, I'm sure." Arthur couldn't stifle the yawn, which somewhat lessened the impact of his sarcasm.

Mika rested his hand on the doorframe, hesitating. Arthur inhaled to tell him to get lost already but found that he couldn't bring himself to speak—nor could he seem to remember how to exhale.

After a moment of staring at the floor, Mika looked back up at Arthur from beneath unfairly thick eyelashes.

"One last lesson." His voice was quiet, lips quirking up at one corner.

Arthur froze, heart picking up a pace.

Mika leaned in slowly, bringing his face next to Arthur's, so close that Arthur could smell his shampoo.

"May I?" Mika said, low, next to his ear.

Arthur's heart skipped a beat.

"Sure," he tried to say, but it came out in a whisper.

Agonizingly slow, blink-and-you-miss-it, barely there—Mika kissed him on the cheek.

Arthur's left hand twitched, eyes sliding closed—

And then it was over.

"Night, darling." Mika's arrogant grin was back, and he was already halfway across the hall, gone as soon as he'd come. "Walk to breakfast tomorrow?"

Voice lost to the ether, Arthur merely nodded.

Mika gave an irritating little wiggle of a wave before closing his own door behind him.

Arthur stood in the hall for several moments longer, trying to calm his heart.

'May I?'

He closed the door, walked to the bathroom, and brushed his teeth.

Agonizingly slow, barely there.

He turned out the lights, set his phone to Charge under the moonlight stretching across his desk, and got into bed.

His left hand was warm, as if he'd held it to a campfire moments before, as if his love line was alit with gentle embers. And as Arthur drifted off to sleep, he finally got a finger on what made him so uneasy about their farewell:

If he didn't know any better, he'd think he was almost disappointed to see Mika go.

10

Arthur woke up the next morning with a start.

"Shit," he hissed as he launched himself out of bed and into his morning workout routine—push ups, crunches, squats, yoga—all the while wracking his brain for a way to explain via text that *'Hey, I know you're my best friends and I tend to update you with important life changes, other than things that involve financial concerns probably because of trauma from my divorced parents but anyway, I have a boyfriend now, and also, that boyfriend is my sworn rival of the last three and a half years.'*

"Shit," he muttered as he climbed into the shower.

Ten minutes later and still he had nothing.

He wrapped the towel around his waist, staring at his phone screen. Finally, he settled for:

> Please don't hate me.

He tossed the phone in alongside the books in his bag and tore a set of uniform shirt and slacks from his closet with shaky fingers, stumbling into them and back into the bathroom to brush his teeth.

Mika, close, smiling 'May I?'

Arthur shook his head, forcing his imagination through Clarke and Jonathan seeing right through his lie, eyebrows raised, mouths twisted in disdain. He spit into the sink and scrambled to make sure his Sense was permanently on guard, ensuring none of the above parties would be able to see through the ruse.

Arthur stared at his reflection in the mirror, reconsidering his choices.

Somewhere in the liminal space between too fast and too soon, a knock sounded at the door.

"Housekeeping!" Clarke's voice sang out.

Shit.

He strode to the door, messenger bag in hand, and flung it open.

"Ready to go?" Jonathan asked.

"Can we hurry it up?" Clarke looked cagey. "The omelet station always has a long line on Mondays."

"Okay, so—" Arthur tried to interrupt.

"Daddy needs his omelet," Clarke insisted.

"Just let me—" Arthur tried again.

"What was up with your text?" Jonathan looked at him quizzically.

"That's what I'm trying to—"

"Hey," Mika piped up.

Clarke and Jonathan leaped back as if electrocuted. Mika closed his door behind him and stepped between them.

"You both joining us for breakfast?" He grinned, looking between them.

"Joining—"

"—Us?"

"I have—" *a boyfriend!* "—plans," Arthur finished pathetically.

Clarke and Jonathan stared, wide-eyed, from Mika, to Arthur, to each other.

"Ah." Mika looked bemused. "You haven't told them."

"Told us what?" Clarke demanded.

Arthur eyed Mika, who gave him a look. *'Be convincing,'* he was sure it said.

He looked back at his friends. Clarke's eyes looked like they were about to pop out of his head. Jonathan was failing to stifle a grin.

Arthur steeled himself, gathering the anxiety about his arrangement with Mika, the fear of his ability to secure his future, and the guilt of lying to his friends for the sake of said future—he put all those things in a box, and put the box up on a shelf in the back corner of his brain.

Arthur was going to have to get good at compartmentalizing. And acting. Fast.

He let his embarrassment play out, let himself blush, let his discomfort show—he raised a hand to rub at the back of his neck, avoiding eye contact.

"Well, I didn't know how to tell you. I feel kind of stupid, honestly."

"Tell, us, *what?!*" Clarke practically screamed.

Mika came to his defense. "We're dating."

He held out his hand in offering. Clarke and Jonathan froze, waiting for Arthur's reaction.

Arthur took a deep breath...

...and accepted Mika's hand.

Clarke squeaked.

"Turns out that soulmate magic has some legitimacy to it," Arthur said sheepishly, closing his door.

Mika squeezed his hand. *'Convincing,'* it said.

"You're shitting me," Jonathan exclaimed.

"You hate each other," Clarke insisted.

"Love and hate." Mika shrugged. "Two sides, same coin."

Clarke and Jonathan stared daggers at Arthur. He tried desperately to arrange his facial features in a way that meant, *'I'll explain later.'*

Clarke looked like he wanted an explanation ten minutes ago, but Jonathan seemed to have read Arthur's meaning. He put a hand on Clarke's arm.

"So." He smiled brightly at all of them. "Breakfast?"

The walk down to the food hall was...surreal, if Arthur had to name it. He was preoccupied with trying not to look like he was on the verge of violently relieving Mika's hand of his own, and Clarke was preoccupied with staring at Arthur as if he'd sprouted an extra arm from his forehead, so Jonathan and Mika carried most of the conversation.

Despite the revulsion of prolonged contact with Mika—even after all the practice last night—Arthur couldn't help but note the shift in energy of the students passing.

It was almost quiet, for lack of pointing and singing and jeering. There were stares still, to be sure—whispering, maybe—but the endless assault had vanished into thin air. In the courtyard, a couple classmates clapped Mika on the back as they passed, and a couple more fist-bumped his unoccupied hand. Arthur caught Tan's eye in the entrance to the dining hall, where they made a face of approval and nodded with a thumbs-up.

Was it...was it actually *working?*

In the dining hall, Mika broke off with a grin and a promise to find them upon acquiring food. The instant he was out of earshot, Clarke and Jonathan turned on Arthur.

"What the *fuck—*"

"It's been less than twenty-four hours since we last saw you—"

"What business do you have—"

"The *audacity—*"

"Let's get Clarke an omelet, shall we?" Arthur muttered through his teeth, steering them toward the station, where two cooks were gathering omelet accoutrements and Sending them into levitating pans swirling in time with the eggs.

"Well?" Clarke demanded as soon as they secured their spot in line.

Arthur bit his lip and swallowed hard, wondering where in the hell he was supposed to uncover the strength to lie to his favorite people in the world.

"I know it's crazy," he started. "I know what I said. I know I look like an idiot right now—god knows I feel like one."

Well. At least none of *that* was untrue.

"But last night..." He watched his friends' faces light up with shock and absolute captivation. "He came over and asked to study—"

"The bastard!"

"Obviously a ploy to use you to get ahead—"

"Please," Arthur begged, stamping down the guilt at the irony, "do you want me to explain or not?"

Clarke and Jonathan zipped their mouths shut, eyes bugging out of their heads.

"I know what it sounds like. But we started working, and it was a lot of the usual at first." Was this even vaguely convincing? "Insults and competition, or whatever. But after a while..." He struggled to find the words as they moved up a couple spaces in line. "We actually started to..." He cringed. "Get along."

"Get along *how?*"

Jonathan elbowed Clarke, who bit his lip and positively shook with excitement.

"Just get along—oh my god, *chill.*" Arthur couldn't help but smile.
"But—"
"But?" Clarke squealed, taking Jonathan's hand and giving it a white-knuckled squeeze.
Arthur rolled his eyes and looked away. "At the end of the night..."
"Yeah?"
"I can't explain how it happened, but..."
"But?"
"...he kissed me."
Also not technically a lie.
Clarke threatened to collapse and Jonathan caught him, hauling him forward in line.
"I wish I could justify it, or explain my logic," Arthur said, again, truthfully. "But..."
And just in time, a stroke of inspiration: he raised his left hand, showing off the words there. "I don't think it can be explained."
"Damn," Jonathan said quietly, and Clarke looked as if he might cry. "So it is real."
Arthur nodded, and shrugged. "I guess you were right."
"You have to tell us everything." Clarke recovered all at once, leaning his face very close to Arthur's, gaze intense. "Take us through the conversation, line by line. Is he a good kisser? How long did it go on? What—"
"You know," Arthur interrupted him, winking, "what they say about kissing and telling."

Clarke bit on his fist to keep from screaming, and Arthur turned around to order his omelet, swallowing the bitter taste at the back of his throat.

This is temporary, he reassured himself. *Once it's all over and we've started up Auratech, I'll tell them everything, and we'll all laugh.*

This is temporary.

It had become a mantra by the time they got their omelets and took their preferred table. He recited it with renewed vigor as Mika eased onto the bench beside him, sidling up and promptly placing a hand on his thigh.

"So y'all are an omelet crowd." Mika raised an eyebrow, utterly unbothered. "I'm more of a hashbrown guy myself."

Arthur tried very hard to look like he very much wanted Mika in his personal bubble. He had a feeling it was probably looking more like he had gas.

"No accounting for taste." Clarke sported a wry grin, taking a bite of his breakfast.

"So—" Mika stuffed some hashbrowns and pancakes in his mouth, continuing without pause, repulsively— "embarrassing stories about Arthur, go! *Ow—*"

Arthur kneed Mika's leg and Mika stomped on his foot in retaliation, making Arthur's eyes water.

They both snapped their attention to Clarke and Jonathan, who watched curiously from across the table. Arthur and Mika smiled widely.

"This guy." Mika turned his fake smile at Arthur, who fake-smiled back.

"I'm still teaching him about boundaries," Arthur cooed.

"And I'm teaching him how to get that stick out of his ass," Mika preened.

"It's hard to forget just two days ago we were rivals." Arthur felt manic. "To the bitter end."

"To the happy end, more like it," Mika said through clenched teeth.

"So true," Arthur simpered. He dug into his omelet aggressively, determined to ignore Mika's hand on his thigh.

Clarke and Jonathan exchanged looks.

"I won't lie, friends." Jonathan shook his head. "This is gonna take some getting used to."

"You're telling me," Arthur muttered.

11

Day 1

By the last class of the day, Arthur's nerves were shot to hell.

Despite his best efforts, Mika reaching for his hand in the hall sent a jolt of panic down his spine, and as he summoned every ounce of willpower not to flinch away at the hand unceremoniously placed on his thigh *(no higher than three inches below finger-line)* in the middle of class, he wondered if this was better than the teasing after all.

Convinced his brain was rattling nervously in his skull, Arthur gave up on the lecture in front of them and wrote on the edge of the paper in his notebook:

Ease up on the PDA, Rivera.

He scooted the notebook a few inches over. Mika peered at it, and took his hand from Arthur's leg to write back on his own notebook:

Why, getting hot and bothered?

It was accompanied by a winky face. Arthur's cheeks flamed.

If by hot and bothered you mean ready to vomit, sure. Trying to concentrate.

Mika replied: *You flatter me, Pham.*

But he didn't touch Arthur again the entire rest of the period, and by the time the bell rang, Arthur had taken more notes than he had all day.

But out in the hallway, Mika took hold of his hand once more.

"Over here." He jerked his head over at an alcove in the wall and tugged Arthur along.

Safely tucked away from the flow of students, Mika released Arthur's hand and then held out his own. Hesitantly, Arthur hit it for something in between a handshake and a high five.

"Quittin' time." Mika smirked. "We killed it today."

"I don't know if I'd go that far," Arthur said. "But at least they stopped making fun of us."

"Suckers," Mika agreed, and they ducked deeper into the shadows to avoid a group of Year Fours passing by.

"No PDA in class," Arthur hissed.

"Aw, you're no fun."

"I have a GPA to maintain."

Mika grinned roguishly. "I guess I'll take it as a compliment that you find my touch so distracting."

"Fuck off." Arthur spun on his heel to take his leave from the alcove, hiding his blush in the process.

"We'll work on it," Mika called after him, and Arthur made sure there were no other classmates around before flipping him the bird as he walked away.

Day 9

"Bring it on, Pham."

"Oh, now darling," Arthur simpered, "I thought we'd grown out of the whole last name thing."

"You're right," Mika grinned. "Although I prefer 'baby'."

"I think we've exhausted the *Dirty Dancing* references, *Baby*."

"The lift offer still stands." Mika held his arms out in welcome.

Arthur smirked and swooped his wand up, urging the air molecules around Mika to follow his lead. They did, and Mika was thrust into the air where he levitated and spun, limbs akimbo.

"I promise I definitely won't drop you." Arthur beamed.

Their classmates went wild, stomping and wolf-whistling. Professor Hirst sat on a stool beside his desk, head resting wearily in his hand.

It was hard to believe anything had changed in the past ten days.

Arthur took his time in wandering to where Mika levitated, carefully positioning himself directly under him, and placing his feet in a steady stance.

"Ready?" He looked up.

He caught a flash of panic on Mika's face, but it was quickly smoothed over with a smile. "I think I need a Band-Aid."

Arthur swished his wand down and caught Mika bridal-style with a *woomph*, air dissipating back into its preferred activity.

"Why?" Arthur projected over the screams of their classmates, unable to contain a smile.

Mika placed a chaste kiss (*no tongue*) on Arthur's cheek. "Because I think I'm falling for you."

The crowd lost all semblance of composure and, in the hullaballoo, Mika was able to mutter into his ear.

"Genius, Pham."

"I hate you," Arthur muttered through his stage smile.

He carried Mika through the crowd and out the classroom door, and Professor Hirst dismissed class early. He couldn't even remember what the assignment had been.

Day 12

> **ANNABELLE**
> Heads up, Ma's in a mood again. Brace yourself.

Arthur glanced up from his phone to the lunch table, where Mika was instigating a debate between Clarke and Jonathan—something about the sartorial repercussions of pairing black and brown together.

"Be right back." He ducked out from under Mika's arm, trying to look regretful. "Bathroom."

Sure enough, he'd just found his way into the quiet corridor beyond the dining hall when his phone rang.

"Hi Ma," he sighed.

"Thank goodness." His mom sounded harried. "How are you, son? Are you free to talk?"

"I've got twenty minutes left for lunch."

"Can I vent?"

Arthur's heart lurched. "Sure, Ma."

The remainder of his lunch period was spent listening to his mom go on and on—from her boss to her stress about making enough money for rent to Annabelle's conservatory application process. She had her heart set on Featherwood, and Ma didn't know how she was going to save up the enrollment fee if she got in.

Arthur listened attentively the whole time, pacing up and down the empty Academic Hall, heart beating hard.

I need to fix this.

When his mom finally paused to breathe, Arthur spoke up.

"Don't worry, Ma." He summoned all the conviction he could muster. "It's just for a little bit longer. Once Auratech gets going, I'll be able to help you and Bella. End of next year, max."

His mom sighed. "Son, I don't want you to—"

Arthur hushed her. "I've got this. I want to."

She paused. "Thank you. Thank you—that helps."

The bell rang, and Arthur swallowed. "I have to go to class now, Ma."

"Okay. I love you."

"Love you, too."

He hung up and began walking to Transmutation with the uncanny feeling that the weight on his shoulders had just doubled in size.

Day 18

After three weeks, Arthur was starting to get the hang of this whole fake boyfriend thing.

Mika joined them for breakfast every other day and walked him back to the dorm every alternating one, making occasional appearances at their lunch table. True to his word, he hadn't laid a finger on Arthur in class—but in the hall and at mealtimes, Mika remained sidled up close, hand in Arthur's or linking their arms together (not technically in the contract, but benign enough to let slide). That morning he'd even let Mika sling an arm over his shoulder without looking like he'd prefer decapitation.

Their classmates had left them alone for two weeks straight—even the occasional fist bump or nod of approval had died out after the first. Arthur was sleeping better, taking quality notes in during class, and hadn't seen a single minus behind his As since before this whole mess started. In fact, he'd gotten perfect marks on all his midterms last week.

He was loath to admit it, but Mika had made his life easier for once.

They'd gotten through yet another day of successful fake-boyfriendhood, and the shutting doors were still echoing in the empty dormitory lobby when Mika ripped his hand out of Arthur's.

"Eugh." He made a face, shaking out his hand. "Your hand gets so clammy."

"If I have to deal with your Old Spice all over my clothes at the end of the day, you can deal with my sweaty hands." Arthur rolled his eyes, pressing the elevator call button.

"Old Spice is a classic." Mika frowned as they made their way up.

"It's plebeian." Arthur held his chin high.

Mika put on a goofy voice. "Sorry, not all of us care to ball out on *Jo Malone*."

Arthur stared at him as the elevator dinged open. "How did you know?"

Mika shrugged and threw him a grin over his shoulder as he exited. "Cherry takes me perfume shopping."

Arthur rolled his eyes. "I buy it on eBay. People sell the tiny little samples you get with rewards points at department stores for dirt cheap. I don't pay full price for *anything*."

"Even sneakers?"

Arthur paused in the hallway. "What?"

"Your shoes." Mika stopped and turned, glancing down at the floral pair Arthur was wearing today. "You've always got the coolest stuff."

"You're—" Arthur frowned, starting to walk again. "You like sneakers?"

"Hell yeah," Mika enthused. "You haven't seen me in street clothes?"

They'd reached Rooms 419 and 420. Arthur's brow furrowed further. "I guess I haven't."

"Maybe we can go stand in line for the new collaboration release this season." Mika's mouth turned down contemplatively.

A peace offering.

Arthur snapped back into himself. "I'd rather gouge my eyes out."

"That's a visual," Mika chuckled. "I'm almost offended, Pham."

"I'll try harder next time," Arthur retorted, entering his room and closing the door in Mika's face.

Arthur's heart pounded, face hot as he crossed the room to his desk and pulled out his materials to begin his Transmutation revision. What the hell was he doing, making *small talk* with his one obstacle to victory?

I'm just getting to know him. He opened his Transmutation book. *Like I said I would. It's just a transition period.*

As he started their assigned reading, Arthur looked down at his shoes and fought a smile.

He'd start plotting Rivera's demise soon.

Next week. At the latest.

12

"I can't believe I let you put this in the contract."

"Parties are supposed to be fun, genius."

"Parties are time that would be better spent studying." Arthur sighed and tugged at his spoils from the thrift store hunt last weekend, a designer tee that plainly stated, *'boyfriends are temporary.'* It had been too good to pass up.

"Bullshit." Mika rolled his eyes. They were once again standing outside door 405. "If you have time to go shopping, you have time to go to a party. That shirt's new. And honestly, inspired."

"I thought so."

Mika bit his lip, considering. "The eyeliner is cool, too."

Arthur narrowed his black-lined eyes. "If you think flattery is going to convince me this isn't about to be a total waste of my time—"

"Loosen up, darling." Mika grinned and hooked his arm in Arthur's. "Two hours. And if you still aren't having fun, we can leave."

"I'm holding you to that." Arthur glared, and Mika knocked on the door.

Benjamin Lasher greeted them, releasing a flood of music and booze and weed from the room behind him.

"Hey!" He threw his hands up. "Phamvera is here!"

Beyond Benjamin in the doorway, Arthur saw the majority of the crowd beyond him throw up their hands and yell in unison, "Phamvera!"

Mika threw up his hands too, taking one of Arthur's along with him.

"I can't believe we have a ship name," Arthur muttered as they went inside.

"Oh, I can," Mika muttered back. "We're Stonebury's most popular couple."

"Mika!"

Arthur turned them around—Mika had linked their arms again—and spied Cherry making her way through the crowd toward them, hair pulled into two spritely poms. The vintage red dress looked stunning on her slight frame, and Arthur marveled at her sparkly designer sneakers.

"I neglected to ask." Arthur side-eyed Mika. "What did Cherry say when you told her?"

"Uh."

"Mika." Cherry was breathless from wrestling through the sweaty crowd of students. "You've been monosyllabic for weeks, is everything okay?"

"Hey, Cher." Mika threw one arm around her and squeezed briefly.

"What's..." Her eyes lighted upon Arthur, and their linked arms. "...Up?"

She looked amused. Arthur snatched his arm away.

"I'm gonna..." He searched the room desperately, avoiding both of their gazes. "...Go pee. I'll catch up with you later."

And without a backward glance, he made his way into the crowd, pulling out his phone as he went.

> Please tell me you're both at Ben Lasher's right now.

JONATHAN
> Window by the kitchen

Arthur doubled back through the crowd, finally finding his friends, who were each nursing a bottle of Homebrew beer.

"I thought you were here with Mr. Wrong," Clarke quipped, swigging his drink.

"Ha-ha," Arthur intoned. "I was. I am."

"Trouble in paradise?" Jonathan smirked.

"Paradise is a strong word," Arthur muttered and paused, choosing his next words carefully. "Mika never told his girlfriend we got together."

"His ex-girlfriend, you mean?" Clarke asked.

Arthur stared at him.

"Oh, shit." Jonathan's eyes went wide as he took an incredulous sip of his beer.

"Wait. You're telling me he never broke up with Cherry?" Clarke looked murderous.

"I don't know what their...situation is," Arthur said honestly. "All I know is she looked clueless, and Mika looked like he'd forgotten to take the meat out of the freezer before Mom got home."

"Relatable," Jonathan sighed.

"How can we help? What do you need?" Clarke demanded.

"I never thought I'd say it, but..." Arthur said grimly, "a drink."

"Aye-aye, captain." Jonathan reached over the cut-out bar in the kitchen and plucked him a Homebrew from the ice bucket.

"Cheers." Arthur raised it and took a swig.

And four beers later, Arthur was thinking maybe his situation wasn't so bad.

No one made fun of them anymore. If they were a source of gossip, it was all behind closed doors, and Arthur (not to mention his GPA) was grateful for it. He knew he'd find a weakness soon—he'd learned tonight alone that Mika had trouble with attention to detail, to say the least, and it surely wouldn't be that hard to find more intel now that they spent so much time together.

So what if Mika hadn't handled his own business? It wasn't Arthur's problem. If anything, the ensuing drama could knock Mika off his game. All he needed was one misstep on Mika's part to pull ahead and secure Electi Magi.

Watching his friends laughing beside him, Arthur only wished he didn't have to do it all alone.

Clarke wheezed—Arthur had missed whatever they were laughing about. "Hey, Artie."

"Nope."

"Artie—ugh—fine, fine—Arthur," Clarke amended, stumbling, "I wanna go dance."

"Great idea." Arthur smiled. "Take Jonathan."

"Aww," Clarke whined, "you're no fun."

"You're right," Arthur agreed. "Jonathan is, though. He likes grinding more than me."

"I have a *boyfriend*," Clarke gasped.

"And you're drunk." Jonathan patted his head affectionately. "Come on, let's get it out of your system."

"Hooray!" Clarke cheered as they made their way through the crowd, where twenty-something people were writhing together in time to a highly inappropriate song with a highly addictive hook and driving bassline.

Arthur sighed and perched on the windowsill, sipping the last of his beer. He figured he'd better go look for Mika; Cherry or no, they were supposed to be at this party together, and Arthur didn't want to be roped into another one next week by means of a loophole.

He got up off the sill and was about to make his way around the bartop to find cocktail fixings when he heard voices from inside the kitchen.

"Come on, Cherry. You know it's not like that."

Arthur managed to duck back behind the wall just in time before slowly peering around the cut-out bar into the kitchen. Mika was sitting on the kitchen counter next to the sink and Cherry stood in front of him, arms crossed resolutely.

Arthur's heart picked up a pace. *I should leave.* His body didn't seem to get the message, staying rooted to the spot. *I should definitely leave.*

"You've had this little rivalry with Arthur for years, Meeks." Her voice dipped down into an undertone, and Arthur strained to hear: "Allegedly, at least."

"What the hell is that supposed to mean?" Mika's expression was stormy.

The intense and undeniable curiosity of hearing one's name in a private conversation had Arthur in a death grip, and he latched onto the kitchen bar with a sweaty palm. The angle made it hard to see Cherry's face, but Arthur could practically hear her rolling her eyes.

"I doubt your lizard brain could handle it."

"Try me," Mika challenged.

Cherry seemed to deflate, looking away and mashing her lips together. "Love and hate are two sides of the same coin, Mika."

Arthur's heart skipped a beat.

Mika stared at her for several seconds. Cherry raised her gaze to meet his, and finally, it clicked.

"Jesus, Cher." He laughed, bringing a palm up to his forehead. "You can't be serious."

She put her hands on her hips. "Told you so."

"Told you so, my ass." Mika's voice was laced with laughter. "This soulmate stuff is bullshit. We had to shut everyone up—people at this school are assholes. We're just fucking with them, babe."

"Don't *babe* me, Mika." Cherry sounded exasperated, if not angry. "I've known you practically since we were in the womb. Don't you think I *get* you? Don't you think I understand how you think—why you act the way you do? You really won't even *consider* what I'm saying?"

"What you're saying is a joke." Mika wasn't smiling anymore. "You're taking this too seriously."

"And you're not taking it seriously enough." Cherry turned on her heel to leave.

"Wait." There was urgency in Mika's voice now. "Cher. Cherry."

She turned back around slowly.

"I want to go home, Mika."

His eyebrows turned up with an emotion Arthur had never seen there before. "You're not..." He swallowed. "This isn't. We aren't...?"

Cherry heaved a deep sigh and stepped forward to take Mika's hand.

"I love you, Mika. Of course not. Just—promise me you'll think about this."

Mika shrank back, avoiding her eyes. "Yeah, sure, whatever."

Cherry sighed again and dropped his hand. "I'll text you tomorrow, okay?"

"Sounds good." Mika leaned back on the counter, eyes still trained on the floor.

And with that, Cherry made her exit.

Arthur straightened and flattened his back against the wall, brain whirring through the slosh of alcohol to understand what he'd just overheard. Cherry didn't seem angry so much as concerned with Mika's feelings about it all. *But that doesn't make sense.* Arthur frowned. *Assholes don't have feelings.*

That wasn't fair, Arthur realized, remembering Mika's face when he'd thought Cherry was breaking up with him.

He chanced a glance back into the kitchen.

Mika was gone.

"Hey, boyfriend!"

Arthur's heart nearly leaped out of his mouth (or maybe that was the beer) as he whipped back around to see Mika grinning at him, drink in hand.

"Where have you been all night?" Mika slung an arm around him, and Arthur found it hard to believe he'd ever witnessed an expression other than "shit-eating grin" on his face, much less moments before.

"I could ask you the same thing," Arthur returned. He hesitated before adding, "How's Cherry?"

Mika made a dismissive gesture. "Bah, she's fine. I told you she'd be cool."

"Right." Arthur checked his watch. "Well, you've got half an hour left until we go home."

"Great." Mika Summoned a Homebrew for Arthur with his wand. "Just enough time for a game of beer pong."

Arthur groaned, and as Mika led him back into the crowd of sweaty bodies, he tried very hard to dismiss the scene he'd witnessed in the kitchen from his mind.

13

"Hey, Arthur?"

"Hm."

Clarke and Jonathan sat beside him in front of the coveted future home of Auratech in *Watergraafsmeer*, sporting the *'For Rent'* sign in the window and providing shelter from the first snow of the year as they sipped coffee from *Koffie*—similarly vague as to whether it was a café named "Coffee" or merely an unnamed storefront advertising the stuff. They'd gotten out of Transmutation early, and Arthur *loved* snow. He cherished the warm *koffie verkeerd* in his hands, the cold on his cheeks, unprotected by his school coat or thick scarf and beanie. He shifted his feet, relishing the crunch of snow underneath.

"How are you here right now?" Clarke continued.

Arthur made a face. "What?"

"Don't you have a boyfriend or something?" Clarke huffed. "I mean, I guess it's cool to be independent or whatever, but..."

"We're together constantly," Arthur said, faster than he'd have liked.

"Not outside of school," Clarke retorted. "It's weird."

"We have our own lives." Arthur's cheeks grew hot against the cold. Clarke was inspecting him a little too closely, and Arthur made certain his Sense was a solid wall around him. "What's wrong with that?"

"Nothing." Jonathan eyed Clarke. "We think that's great."

Clarke didn't catch the hint. "But like. When do you have sex?"

Arthur choked on his coffee. Jonathan patted him on the back, sighing.

"I'm sorry?"

"You heard me," Clarke pressed.

"We have sex," Arthur said, strangled, gesticulating wildly. "We have tons of sex."

"Oh, yeah?" Clarke narrowed his eyes at him. "So what's it like?"

Arthur's coffee threatened to enter his windpipe once more.

"What ever happened to kissing and telling? Or, more importantly, the lack thereof?"

"Just answer the question."

"Clarke." Jonathan gave him a look. "Come on."

"I don't buy it." Clarke stood to place himself in front of Arthur so as to better confront him. "I don't know what it is, but there's something you're not telling us. I can Sense it."

Arthur struggled to keep all those things—anxiety, guilt, fear—compartmentalized in the little box on the shelf in his mind, far away from where they could escape through his aura, where they could be discovered. He closed his eyes and took a deep breath, trying to level his whirling thoughts—tuition and schoolwork and Electi Magi and Mika and his infuriatingly uncrackable facade of jovial carelessness and the resulting lack of a plan—

Arthur released his breath, suppressing the exhausted whine that threatened to escape along with it.

What if he just. Told them?

Clarke watched Arthur expectantly. Jonathan pretended to be fascinated by his shoes.

Once he came up with a plan to undermine Mika, he'd tell them. Once he had the situation under control, he'd tell them everything.

"That's not fair." Jonathan finally broke the silence, nudging Clarke's arm. "Arthur doesn't have to tell us everything, he's entitled to his privacy—"

"Rough." Arthur steeled himself. "It's rough. Super, *super* kinky."

Clarke squealed, and Arthur continued, waving his hand dismissively. "BDSM-adjacent. Biting, spanking, the whole nine yards."

"I knew it! What did I tell you, Jonathan?"

Arthur stifled his sigh of relief. Clarke couldn't resist gossip.

Jonathan's eyes met the sky, stifling a smile. "I'll be totally honest—I pictured you as more of a gentle lover."

"You could try not picturing me as a lover at all," Arthur drawled.

Clarke grabbed his arm and shook vigorously. "You can't just drop knowledge like this and not elaborate!"

Arthur took a deep breath and prayed for the best. "I think it started as hate sex, really."

Clarke squeaked.

"He's just begging for it, you know? With that dumb face of his." Arthur allowed a bemused grin to grace his lips. He could almost picture it. "I couldn't be gentle with him even if I wanted to."

Clarke looked about ready to swoon. "Who tops?" he managed.

Arthur gave him a look of pity. "Please."

Clarke nearly did collapse that time, spilling some of his *zwarte koffie*. Jonathan hauled him up, shaking his head.

"You know what this does to him," Jonathan scolded Arthur.

"He loves it." Arthur's grin was brittle. "What about you, Clarke? How often do you and that alleged boyfriend of yours have phone sex?"

Clarke straightened his pink beanie and blushed. "I'd rather not say."

"At least twice a week by the sound of it," Jonathan supplied.

Clarke screeched, and Jonathan chuckled, and Arthur kept taking steady breaths as his heart slowly returned to its standard-issue pace.

He pulled out his phone as Clarke started punching Jonathan, to no avail, as per usual.

> What are you up to this weekend?

MIKA
> party at tan's, wanna come?

> Nice try, I fulfilled my party quota for the fortnight last week.

> I think C and J are starting to catch on.

> They say we never hang outside of school.

MIKA
hmm

wanna come over on sunday?

> We could just say we hung out and not, I just want to get our stories matched up.

MIKA
nah dude just come over it's cool

we'll do whatever u want

> I study on Sundays.

MIKA
so we'll study

> You say that as if you read.

MIKA
come over at 1

> If I must.

MIKA
see u then, genius <3

Sunday found Arthur lurking outside Mika's door across the hall, wearing track pants and his favorite cream fisherman's sweater, messenger bag in hand, shifting his weight from one foot to the other.

This was stupid.

Yeah. This was stupid, because there was no need to spend any more time with someone so insufferable than strictly necessary—*it wasn't even in the contract!*—and he was going to turn right back around and go back into his room.

He'd just pulled out his phone to cancel when he heard Mika's voice through the door.

"Your stress is deafening, Pham. Door's unlocked."

Arthur felt heat rise to his cheeks. *Shit.*

Bracing for the worst, he opened the door.

He hadn't ever really taken a good look inside Mika's room—only glances. Arthur's side of the building got all the natural light, so Mika's room was darker. He'd leaned into the den-like shadow; the room was smaller than Arthur's, lined with black walls and a hardwood floor covered in intentionally placed gatherings of floor pillows, futons, and blankets, all in shades of turquoise, mustard, and hot pink. His bed was a lofted double in the left corner next to the window, hastily made linens of dark teal strewn upon it. Next to it, against the left wall, was a blackwood desk, which looked like it hadn't been touched in ages. Its accompanying chair was hard to make out for all the white shirts and charcoal trousers and forest green ties draped over the back of it. The bathroom in this room was off to the right, and in the corner, nestled between its door and the window, were a happy-looking bamboo palm and a hot pink neon sign that read 'Let's Get Weird' in a loopy font. The wall behind Arthur was plastered with deep blue wallpaper scattered with zebras.

Next to the bed, under the window, was a mustard velvet sofa. This is where Mika now lounged in grey sweatpants and a black vintage cartoon tee, with...

...a book.

"Welcome, officially, to my humble abode." Mika held his place in the book—*Twelfth Night*, Arthur read sideways—with a finger and gestured with the other arm.

Arthur glanced to the right, finding a fully stocked bar cart, an assortment of bongs, and a hookah jammed into the corner.

"Charming." He raised his eyebrows, closing the door behind him. He'd expected the smell of weed to have seeped into every nook and cranny of the room, but to his surprise, it smelled like jasmine incense.

"Help yourself." Mika dog-eared his book—Arthur cringed—and leaned forward to rifle through the backpack at the foot of the couch.

"No, thanks," Arthur declined, oh-so-politely. "Um, where...?"

"Anywhere." Mika gestured vaguely. Arthur strode to the desk and started to relieve it and its chair of laundry—whether dirty or clean, Arthur refused to contemplate—to make room to sit.

"Business first," Mika continued, "a loose end in our agreement has been brought to my attention."

"And that is...?" Arthur plucked clothing items one by one, minimizing direct contact so as to avoid developing some sort of rash.

"We're not leaving a paper trail." Mika beckoned with a lazy finger. "Gimme the contract."

Arthur unceremoniously dumped the last of the various accoutrements crammed on the desk to the floor and Summoned the notebook from his room, walking over to watch Mika cram his untidy scrawl under Arthur's neat lines of handwriting:

Bi-weekly social media posts.

"You're shitting me," Arthur whined. "I barely have enough time to study as it is, let alone time to *post* about you."

"Don't worry, Princess," Mika said in an utterly patronizing tone, "I'll handle it."

He pulled out the latest model of Crystaltech's phone from his pocket and spread his legs, patting the empty space on the floor between them. "C'mere."

Arthur glared, cheeks flaring. "Ew."

Mika rolled his eyes. "God, you are so—ten seconds. Max."

Arthur eyed him suspiciously as he turned and lowered himself onto the floor, framed between Mika's legs. He started counting. "One, two."

Mika leaned down and rested his arm on Arthur's head and his own head on his arm. He held out the phone in his other hand.

"Act like you don't hate my guts for the next eight."

Arthur made his best attempt at a face that disguised his contempt, and Mika snapped several photos before shoving Arthur's back with his socked foot.

"Now begone." He started tapping on his phone screen, and Arthur muttered to himself as he retreated to the desk.

He was a quarter of the way into his Transmutation reading when he heard Mika rise from the couch. Before he knew it, there was a phone in front of his face.

"There," Mika announced.

Arthur peered at the photo and fought a smile. Mika donned an overdone grin as he rested on Arthur's head, and Arthur had actually managed to look as if he was enjoying the attention: a wry smile on his face, his eyes directed up to where Mika rested atop him. The caption under the photo read: *'Study date with the genius.'* The likes were already pouring in.

It was—god, Arthur was loath to admit it, but—it was *cute*.

An incoming call lit up Mika's phone, from a so-called *'Mom.'* Arthur swallowed, blinking. The picture was seared behind his eyelids.

He waved Mika's arm away. "Your mother is calling."

"Admit it, Pham." Mika dismissed the call without missing a beat. "It's good, and you know it."

Arthur's mouth twisted as he turned to watch Mika fall back down onto the couch with a *flump*.

"It's a good photo," he admitted. He ground his teeth. "It's a good idea, too."

"See? Not so hard, is it?" Mika donned that rakish grin that Arthur hated so much.

"Harder than you know," Arthur muttered, leaning his head in his hand.

"And now that *that's* taken care of." Mika pulled out a bedraggled notebook from his bag. "I was hoping you could help me study for the Transmutation final."

Arthur's hand slipped from his head.

"You—you *what?*" he spluttered.

"I've got everything else down," Mika continued, as if it wasn't utter blasphemy to be asking his academic rival of four years for *help*, of all things, "but I can't seem to get the hang of how the physics plays out in tech."

Arthur righted himself and blinked. His brain was still rebooting. "You...want my help?"

"Yeah. That's like, your thing, right?"

"What, being smart?"

"Helping people, Mister Closing-the-Wage-Gap-or-Whatever. Are you down or not?"

Arthur found it hard to remember this was the man he was trying to beat when faced with a smile so dazzlingly bright aimed directly at him. Still, that ever-present voice in the back of his mind, the one constantly assessing his goals and future prospects—and launching him into anxiety attacks at the prospect of his life going in any direction other than the one he'd carefully planned—was whispering insidiously that this would be the *perfect* opportunity. One concept explained poorly, one wandwork demonstration just a hair off...

But Arthur took in that smile, open and honest and—when had it evolved from sarcastic and condescending?

Arthur dismissed the voice. He wasn't in the mood for plotting today, that was all.

"What are you struggling with?"

Over the next few hours, they worked on practical magic, which mostly looked like Arthur walking Mika through a nonmagic physics textbook and Mika scoffing until Arthur bullied him into listening. He didn't seem incapable of grasping the concepts so much as he stubbornly insisted upon questioning every teaching point Arthur tended to make—especially the finicky, detail-oriented bits.

"But what about pulling off huge amounts of energy?" Mika sulked.

Arthur had lost his patience three complaints ago. "By huge amounts of energy, do you mean turning the desks into trees?"

Mika threw his head back, laughing. "You have to admit, that was pretty cool."

Arthur pressed his lips into a line, trying to conjure a retort and failing. "It *was*, but—"

"But nothing." Mika grinned proudly. "Go big or go home."

"This is your problem," Arthur deduced. "No subtlety. None whatsoever."

"Subtle is boring," Mika retorted.

Arthur shrugged. "Pretty sure I won that day with the cherry tree."

Mika made a dismissive gesture. "Agree to disagree."

"Do you want to get better at practical magic or not?"

And so on.

Eventually, "practicing" devolved into sending the book flying across the room, which devolved further still into sending it flying into each other's heads, and Arthur called it there, returning the book to the safety of his bag and bidding his fake boyfriend farewell.

"I've got dinner with Clarke and Jonathan tonight," Arthur said, hefting his bag over his shoulder, "but breakfast tomorrow?"

"Yeah."

Mika didn't move from the couch, so Arthur turned on his heel and began to walk himself out.

"Wait."

Arthur paused in the doorway, looking over his shoulder.

"Yes?"

A small, crooked smile lit up Mika's face, one Arthur wasn't sure he'd seen before.

"Thanks for helping today," he said, picking up *Twelfth Night* once more. "Maybe you've got a point about all that nonmagic stuff."

Something did a backflip in Arthur's stomach, and his left hand warmed around the strap of his bag. He blinked, and couldn't help but smile as he said, "See? Not so hard, is it?"

He closed the door and paused, shaking his head to dispel the—the *whatever* it was that was buzzing around, making his head fuzzy and his chest hot.

Focus, he scolded himself as he returned to his room. *Next time. Next time, he's going down.*

14

It killed Arthur to admit it, but the posts really were a good idea.

The photo of them in Mika's room received hundreds of likes. Arthur wasn't sure how, as there weren't nearly that many students in their class, let alone the whole school. The one Mika snapped on Wednesday in the dining hall of Arthur on his way to a bite of omelet (simply captioned: *'yum'*) reached that many in less than an hour. Now that their classmates had something tangible to salivate over, they'd stopped acknowledging Mika and Arthur as a couple entirely—almost as if their relationship had become routine, something of a new norm.

Despite the curveballs he'd been thrown over the course of the semester thus far, and how blatantly *not* normal the outcome had been, this was the first week that had felt...well, normal.

Until Saturday, when Arthur woke up to a flurry of texts.

> **JONATHAN**
> Gotta skip brunch today, Mom called and wants help moving a sofa
>
> **CLARKE**
> brunch is sacred!!!!!!!!
>
> **JONATHAN**
> So is my mom

> **CLARKE**
> tell your mom she can fuck off
>
> oh shit
>
> I'M SORRY I WAS KIDDING
>
> ARTHUR JONATHAN'S GONNA KILL ME
>
> ow
>
> **JONATHAN**
> As if you're not too hungover to move anyway
>
> **CLARKE**
> last night I learned that weed and homebrew don't mix as well as I thought they would
>
> **JONATHAN**
> let's just skip this week, Arthur's not even awake yet
>
> **CLARKE**
> i saw him at Tan's last night!! maybe HE'S hungover too

Arthur was surprised to find he was more relieved than disappointed about brunch being canceled—a reprieve from the mental gymnastics required to keep up the act sounded welcome.

Also welcome, that movie-villain monologuer in the back of his mind piped up, *is that plan to undermine Rivera.*

Arthur typed out a reply:

> Not hungover. But fine to skip, let's just meet at dinner.

He locked his phone and stared at the ceiling for two minutes before opening it again.

> I know it's last minute, but is there any chance you're awake right now?

To his surprise, the dancing ellipses started up almost immediately.

> **MIKA**
> woah
>
> i'm convinced this soulmate thing comes with a sense enhancer
>
> i literally JUST woke up

> I know the feeling.
>
> Do you want to get brunch in town?
>
> We could get a head start on next week's photo.

> **MIKA**
> sure

Arthur locked his phone and stared at the ceiling again, fighting a smile.

You're happy because this is your chance to find out his weakness, the movie villain said. *Look sharp, Pham.*

Determined to make the most of this morning, Arthur promptly got out of bed to get ready for his date—with sabotage.

"You weren't lying," Arthur said, closing his door behind him.

"What?" Mika closed his own door.

"Your shoes." Arthur pointed. They were olive, cream, and baby pink—a brand he'd been admiring for a while now.

"Aw, thanks babe," Mika crooned, and Arthur shoved his arm as they started to walk down the hall.

"But won't you be cold?"

"Are you a wizard or not?" Mika sneered. "I Insulated them."

"God, I'm just making conversation."

"And doing a shit job. Here, let me show you how it's done: did you see the new designer collaboration that dropped last night?"

Arthur shot him a look but played along. "With the dark green everything?"

"It's like they were *made* for our uniforms."

"What about the high-tops with the tan suede? With our winter coats?"

"Ugh, *high-tops* though?"

Sneaker talk carried them all the way to the elevator, out of the dorm, and across the bridge. Mika finally interrupted Arthur's monologue about the superiority of lace-up styles over Velcro when they reached the heart of *Watergraafsmeer*.

"Hey uh, where are we going?"

Arthur paused. He'd been so invested in the conversation that he'd automatically led them to *Ontbijt*.

"Oh." He shook his head. "Sorry. My friends like this place."

He pointed ahead to the sign, and Mika frowned. "Is that the name of the restaurant? Or is it just advertising 'breakfast'?"

"We're all dying to know," Arthur said wryly as they began walking again. The *'For Rent'* sign flashed tantalizingly in Arthur's peripheral vision. "Clarke is very much in a New York state of mind and thinks it's being trendy. Jonathan's from here; he insists it's the latter."

"I think I'd trust the native, but looks good either way," Mika concluded. The bells by the door rang as they stepped through the threshold.

Arthur led him to a table for two accompanied by dining chairs upholstered with mismatched brocades. It was on the opposite side of the room from the one Arthur usually shared with his friends. As Clarke would have said, some things were *sacred*.

"Where are the other two?" the waitress asked Arthur after taking their drink orders.

Arthur smiled wryly. "Hungover."

"Aren't we all," she drawled. "Be back soon."

"Wow." Mika leaned back in his chair and grinned. "So I'm a pity invite, huh?"

"Well sure, I tend to prefer to hang out with people who don't make me want to puke." Arthur sneered.

"You must have a strong stomach," Mika returned. "We've been dating for almost a month and you haven't puked once."

"Fake-dating," Arthur corrected.

"Right." Mika's smile faded, and he picked up the menu to inspect it thoroughly. "What's good here?"

"What do you like?"

Mika eyed him. The grin was back, in peak shit-eating form. "Everything."

Arthur raised his eyebrows. "A human trash compactor?"

Mika turned his nose up and donned a piss-poor British accent to correct him. "An avid consumer of fine dining."

"I hate you." Arthur dismissed him. He scanned Mika's menu upside down, pointing. "My go-to is the *uitsmijter*. But the *wentelteefjes* is to die for."

"I've never actually had any local dishes here."

Arthur stared. "You've been going to school here for three and a half years, you filthy American."

Mika had the decency to look vaguely chagrined. "The usual crew only ever wants to go out for binge drinking and burgers, what do you want from me?"

"Well." Arthur tapped the menu insistently. "Your education starts now."

"Do you want to get two and split?" Mika suggested. "So I can try both?"

Arthur peered at him. It had never occurred to him to share that way.

"Sure," he acquiesced. "Why not."

The waitress came back with Arthur's *koffie verkeerd* and Mika's highly syruped frappé. It appeared to be mostly whipped cream.

"It's freezing outside." Arthur frowned after she left to put in their food orders. "How can you stomach a cold drink right now?"

"I'm a glutton for punishment."

"I repeat: filthy American."

Mika shrugged and sucked his straw slowly. Arthur knew it was an attempt at being irritating, but the way his eyelashes fluttered, hazel eyes sparkling, one unruly curl escaping its confines onto his forehead as his cheeks hollowed—

Arthur cleared his throat, ignoring the way his face warmed, looking resolutely out the window. "You're insufferable."

"Yet you were the one who asked me out."

"To fulfill our contract requirements."

"Speaking of which—" Mika took out his phone— "let's take a video."

Dutifully, Arthur lifted his mug to tap it against Mika's glass, rolling his eyes.

Mika looked down to post, and Arthur sipped his coffee, watching. An incoming call came through on Mika's phone and he made a face before dismissing it. The bright, snowy light cast a flattering light over Mika's cheekbones, his hair mussed from the hood of his coat, his mouth so rarely at ease, with no trace of his trademark grin.

Something flipped in Arthur's midsection, and he found his mouth twitching up at the corner. He pulled out his phone and positioned it.

"Hey."

"Wha—?" Mika looked up and Arthur snapped the photo, inspecting it before turning it toward Mika.

"Well, look at you." Mika's grin was back, and Arthur almost regretted ending the peaceful moment. "Post it."

"Please." Arthur reclaimed his phone. "I haven't posted in a year. I can't break my streak now."

"Come on, fuel my inner narcissist."

"Inner, outer, all around—"

"Pleeeeease?"

Arthur groaned but sank in his chair to open the app. He imagined his phone dusting off cobwebs to do so.

"I don't remember my login info," Arthur whined.

"Don't be a baby," Mika dismissed him. "I've been doing the lion's share of the work in this relationship. Chip in for once in your life."

"Fake-relationship," Arthur supplied.

"Just post the damn picture."

Fifteen agonizing minutes later, Arthur finally managed to post the picture, sans caption. He wouldn't be caught dead doing any more work than necessary on such an endeavor.

"There," he said, showing Mika. "Happy?"

"You have to tag me, dingus. God, are you sixty?"

Arthur let out a long groan just as their waitress brought their food, and he was grateful for the excuse to put his phone away.

"Wow," Mika exclaimed when he took his first bite of *wentelteefjes*. "It's like French toast but *better*. The flavor is insane. It's more than just cinnamon—is that clove? Or cardamom? It's like...chai spice or something. Damn." He raised a hand in reverence, closing his eyes and shaking his head as he chewed.

"Your first *wentelteefjes* and you're already a connoisseur," Arthur said once he was finished with his first bite of *uitsmijter*.

Mika shook his head and finished his bite. "My dad is head chef at a restaurant," he explained, preparing another forkful. "I grew up in the kitchen."

Arthur raised his eyebrows. "That's cool."

"Yeah," Mika replied. "Probably why I'm such a foodie now."

"Foodie my ass." Arthur huffed out a chuckle. "Mister binge drinking and burgers."

"Foodie-in-training," Mika allowed. "If our dorm had a more robust kitchen—damn, game over."

"I did a lot of cooking for me and my sister when I was a kid," Arthur confessed, "so yeah, seconded."

Arthur froze. Where had *that* come from?

"What do you like to cook?" Mika didn't seem at all thrown by the blatant overshare, so Arthur continued.

"At home I make a mean pho."

"God, I love a good pho. You'll have to make it for me sometime."

"Don't count on it." Arthur glanced up at him and couldn't help but smile to himself. "What about you?"

"Spaghetti. Hands down." Mika gesticulated with his fork as he spoke. "My dad has this recipe where you simmer the sauce for like three hours. Sometimes we even make the pasta from scratch, and then it's *really* mind-blowing."

"Damn." Arthur pursed his lips, considering. "You'll have to make it for me sometime."

"Don't count on it." Mika donned a devilish grin, and Arthur shook his head, rolling his eyes.

"Here," Mika continued, "switch."

Arthur peered down at the ham and egg and cheese and toast on his plate, half-consumed.

Sabotage—poison it!

Arthur blinked.

No, he scolded the voice in the back of his mind. *Jesus. Not like that.*

"What." Mika watched him pause. "Changed your mind?"

Arthur snapped his eyes up and quickly shook his head. "No, no. I'm...I'm just imagining you in a chef's hat with an Italian accent."

"Well, I *am* a quarter Italian. I think." Mika didn't miss a beat, pinching his fingers together and donning an over-the-top accent, even less passable than his British. "Spicy meat-a-ball-a!"

Arthur snorted and promptly clapped his hand to his mouth, much to Mika's delight.

"Oh my god. Did I just make stick-up-his-ass Arthur Pham *laugh?*"

"You did no such thing—"

"This is our new inside joke—"

"I'd rather jump in the literally freezing lake."

"Spicy meat-a-ball-a!"

Fighting traitorous giggles, Arthur swapped their plates. "Eat your damn *uitsmijter*, Rivera."

"Stop thinking up here—" Mika rapped on Arthur's skull— "and start thinking down here." He pointed to Arthur's hands in his lap.

They were sitting cross-legged on the floor of Arthur's room on Thursday after class and had already posted their picture—matching wands strewn amongst study materials—an hour ago.

Arthur batted his finger away. "With my dick?"

Mika rolled his eyes. "Ass."

"No, that doesn't sound right either—"

"Here." Mika picked up one of Arthur's hands. "With these."

Arthur let out a long-suffering sigh. "I don't know what you're talking about, Rivera. My brain is in my head, not my hands."

"Maybe try thinking creatively, for once in your life?" Mika pressed.

"I've gotten along just fine thinking logically," Arthur returned, wrenching his hand from Mika's grip. "With my brain. Where's yours?"

"And I've managed to keep up with you all the while," Mika pointed out, ignoring the insult. "Just trust me?"

"Not as far as I could throw you."

"Not this again." Mika shoved his shoulder. Arthur shoved his back. "Close your eyes."

"Not until I confiscate all the Sharpies in my room. And your room, for good measure." Arthur raised his wand threateningly. "I won't be caught off guard again."

He wiped at his lip self-consciously; he'd managed to remove the illustrated mustache from Monday, but one could never be too careful after Sleep spell mishaps.

"Okay, okay. Pinky-promise." Mika hastily held out a little finger.

Begrudgingly, Arthur linked his with Mika's to shake, closing his eyes.

"Now hold out your hands."

Arthur obliged. "I feel stupid."

"Probably because you are."

"Rivera, I swear to *god*—"

"Eyes closed!"

Arthur grumbled but obeyed, holding out his hands in front of him once more.

"Now. Tell me what spell I'm casting," Mika instructed.

"How am I supposed to—"

"Just think," Mika said, "with your hands."

Mika rustled for his wand, and greater than Arthur's desire to protest again was his inability to turn down a challenge.

At first, he felt nothing. He was about to say as much when, suddenly, he Sensed the particles around his fingers shift, guided away by a force beyond them.

"No peeking," Mika warned, but Arthur found he didn't have to. The direction in which the energy was being pulled, the speed at which they were being gathered, combined with knowing Mika's dominant wand arm—

"You're Summoning," Arthur concluded, and opened his eyes.

Sure enough, Mika was now holding a Sharpie. Arthur eyed the pencil cup on his desk to confirm he hadn't just Conjured it.

"See?" Mika sing-songed.

"I don't see how this is relevant," Arthur insisted.

"You get too cerebral about magic, Pham." Mika circled the Sharpie harmlessly, tapping Arthur's head with it. "Sometimes you gotta just...feel it."

"Why would I feel it if I could just think it?" Arthur demanded.

"Fine, then think fast."

Mika launched his wand up in an arc, and a slice of air hurtled across the short space toward Arthur. Reflexively, he called upon the energy of the crystal in his wand on the floor next to him to swirl his hand in a perfect circle, urging the particles around him to solidify and absorb the razor-sharp atoms of the spell.

"Feeling is more practical," Mika concluded, setting his wand aside. "Contrary to what your precious books say, it's a more intuitive way to use magic. Especially because *we—*" he gestured between them— "know our shit."

Arthur mashed his lips together, but couldn't come up with a retort.

"Say it." Mika smiled, and it lit up the room.

Arthur glared at him.

Mika leaned forward, leaned in closer. "Say it."

Arthur was resolute.

Mika's grin faded to something lazier, something more mischievous, and he leaned in further, close enough to whisper in Arthur's ear:

"Say it."

A shiver ran down Arthur's spine, breath catching in his throat. Mika lingered, breath ghosting down Arthur's neck. He swallowed hard, closing his eyes, willing his brain-to-mouth connection to reboot faster.

"This one, singular, *fluke* of a time," Arthur said, voice low, "you were right."

"What was that?" Mika murmured in his ear, and Arthur heard him smile even wider.

"You were right, ass." Arthur shoved Mika out of his personal space. Mika retaliated immediately, and soon the shoving devolved into tussling, laughing and spitting insults until Mika lost his balance and toppled backward, taking Arthur with him.

Arthur quickly got his hands on Mika's wrists, pinning them to the floor to keep them from shoving at him again.

"*Ha!*" He beamed, reveling in his victory.

Mika's smile faded. He wasn't fighting back. His eyes flicked down a few inches from Arthur's, then quickly back up, and then—was he *blushing?*

Mika's voice was low—an octave lower than where it belonged.

"Was that so hard, genius?"

With a start, Arthur realized the compromising position they'd found themselves in.

He released Mika at once, launching off him and back onto his own ass. He found himself sporting a flush to match Mika's and deep down, *way* deep down in some abandoned crevice somewhere between his appendix and his intestines, he was...

...pleased.

Embarrassed, he corrected himself.

Embarrassed. He pulled out his Transmutation book.

"Now let's get back to everything else that I'm right about." He flipped to where they'd left off on Sunday.

"As you wish, Princess." Mika leaned back against the couch, smile turned lazy, hair tousled from their roughhousing. Arthur forced himself to keep his eyes on the textbook.

Later that night as he washed his face, Arthur caught a glimpse of something on his hand. Grumbling at how on earth Mika had snuck in a Sharpie doodle *again* despite constant vigilance, Arthur moved to scrub it—but paused, inspecting further.

With a start, he realized it was Mika's name.

He hadn't looked at it too closely since the first few weeks after it appeared. He'd admittedly gotten used to it by now, save for the occasional tingles that lit it up. But tonight, he realized the faint white words had darkened to something closer to the color of a coffee stain. He rubbed a finger over them to no avail. Had the water been too hot? Were his hands too cold?

As his heart skipped, he forced himself to put it out of his mind, continuing with his nighttime routine.

It wasn't until he was in bed twenty minutes later, drifting off to sleep, that he realized:

He hadn't once remembered his plan to thwart Mika that night.

15

Arthur was surprised at how easily they fell into a rhythm. It was getting harder and harder to remember that Mika was supposed to be his rival—let alone to remember his underbaked plan to undermine him—and when they were talking alone, away from the prying eyes of their classmates and friends, Arthur was surprised to have Mika's attention on him, undivided and curious, albeit irritating as all hell. He was even more surprised to find that he was starting to enjoy it.

Still more surprising was that Mika, attention-whore-arrogant-ass-loves-the-sound-of-his-own-voice-extraordinaire, managed to get Arthur to talk so damn much.

"There's just something about finding a fantastic deal on an expensive designer item that's so satisfying," Arthur was saying as they stood in front of the one unassuming sneaker store in town. They'd been in line for the new collection for hours, Mika having abruptly stood from their Sunday study session to announce that if they kept at it the way they had, their brains would resemble over-hard fried eggs before they even had the chance to sit for their first final in a week and a half.

"Buying shoes full price just doesn't give me the same satisfaction," Arthur continued as Mika listened intently. Arthur had never seen him as still and quiet as when Arthur was talking; there was something extremely gratifying about shutting him up for once. "It's just...it feels like cheating somehow. Like I didn't work for it at all."

"I don't know," Mika mused, once Arthur fell quiet for the first time in fifteen minutes. "You have to work hard to make enough money to buy it full price, right?"

Arthur narrowed his eyes. "I worked in the financial aid office in Year One. I know your family is paying full price for school."

Mika rolled his eyes. "I don't mean me specifically, I mean generally. In theory, right?"

Arthur leaned against the wall, folding his hands into his puffer jacket to keep them warm. "Since when are you so obsessed with the theory of things?"

"I learned from the best." Mika leaned in to knock his shoulder against Arthur's, shit-eating grin plastered on his face.

Arthur huddled further into himself and shoved Mika away with his own shoulder. "Get away from me, bourgeois scum."

Mika's smile turned genuine—something easier and softer that Arthur could distinguish, now—as he obliged, leaning against the wall and taking out his phone. Arthur couldn't help but catch the first notification there:

> MOM
> You can't avoid my calls forever.

Ignoring this, Mika opened his phone to compose a text to Cherry:

> MIKA
> chat later? mom. AGAIN.

Arthur watched Cherry respond before he forced himself to look away.

> CHER
> Ugh Auntie Michelle I swear to god...

> CHER
> free at 7

Arthur busied himself by watching a group of girls laugh at the cafe across the street. He realized he recognized them from the parties he'd been frequenting.

"Hey, I wanted to ask you something."

Arthur's heart stuttered, and he brought his attention back to Mika. "What?"

Mika put his phone away, and then held his left hand out for Arthur to see.

Arthur Pham.

It was the color of English Breakfast. Just like Arthur's.

"It's been getting darker," Mika confirmed, and he looked up to meet Arthur's eyes. "Has yours been, too?"

Arthur unearthed his own hand and placed it next to Mika's. They were a perfect match.

"I wondered about that," Arthur said quietly. "Last week I scrubbed at it so hard my hand was red for days."

Mika smiled. "'Out, damned spot!'"

Arthur stared at him.

Mika persisted. "'What, will these hands ne'er be clean?'"

Arthur shook his head, bemused.

"Seriously? Where's your obsession with non-mages now, Pham?"

"No." Arthur blinked, shaking himself. "No, I know MacBeth, I just —wouldn't have pegged you as a Shakespeare guy. Like a memorizing soliloquies kind of guy."

"Not the pegging again."

"Rivera—"

"I'll admit I'm more a fan of the comedies," Mika allowed. A small smile played on the edge of his mouth, and he rolled his eyes at himself. "The romance."

Arthur's gut gave a nasty lurch that he ignored heartily, elbowing Mika instead.

"Don't get all soft on me now," he warned, but there wasn't as much animosity behind it as he would have liked.

They cleared their throats and went back to staring at their hands.

Mika made a face. "No chance it's a reaction to the cold, right?"

Arthur gave a wry smile. "My hands have been cold since the beginning of time."

"As if I don't have firsthand experience," Mika teased, putting his glove back on. "Pun intended. Do you dunk them in ice water every time I'm about to hold your hand?"

"You'd have noticed me carrying around the bucket, don't you think?"

"Yeah, but they're *sweaty* too. How is that possible—hands that are both cold *and* sweaty?"

Arthur made to punch him in the chest, but he doubted it had much effect for all the layers Mika had on. Mika punched him back, to a similarly dulled effect, and they tussled for a few seconds before someone cleared their throat behind them—the line had started to move.

Arthur withdrew and straightened his beanie righteously. "Bourgeois scum."

Mika grinned. "Sweaty hands."

Two hours later and they were back in Mika's room, several degrees warmer and, in Mika's case, several hundred dollars lighter in exchange for a pair of sparkling white leather low-tops. Mika worked on posting a photo depicting the two of them giving the new shoes reverent looks, and as Arthur got back to his revision for the Transmutation final, he idly wondered if he could find a way to Jinx the new kicks to sprain Mika's ankle—just bad enough to distract him from answering every question correctly on their exams.

Arthur snapped his Evocation textbook shut and slumped back onto the futon in Clarke and Jonathan's room. Its interior design was much more rudimentary than his and Mika's—signature Stonebury creams and greens, and plastered with posters of old Hollywood stars (Clarke's) and gritty reboot movies (Jonathan's).

"I think my eyeballs are about to shrivel up and implode in my skull," Arthur groaned, closing his eyes and placing his cold fingers there to soothe them.

"Same," Clarke sighed, staring at Arthur's Conjuration notes. "How do you write all this shit *down*? I swear your brain functions at a higher speed than mine."

"Sounds like you need to get less bad at stuff," Jonathan said without looking up from the laptop at his desk, where he was tip-tapping away at his final essay for Illusions, titled *'Prestidigitation: Not Just for Amateur Non-Mages.'*

"Sounds like you need to get your mom," Clarke pouted.

"One day we'll collectively allow 'your mom' jokes to die," Arthur sighed, as Jonathan, without looking up from his essay, tossed a stress ball over his shoulder to bounce off Clarke's head.

After re-opening his book and attempting to read the same sentence over and over for the next ten minutes, Arthur gave up for good and stood to stretch. "I think I need a break. Can we walk into town or something?"

Jonathan looked away from his essay for the first time in hours to peer at Arthur, as if *he'd* just been the one to insult his mother. Clarke abandoned the Conjuration notes to do much of the same.

Arthur's eyes darted side to side under their scrutiny. "What?"

Clarke narrowed his gaze and brandished a fountain pen menacingly, wand lost somewhere in the chaos of notebooks surrounding him. "Who are you, and what have you done with Arthur Pham?"

"You?" Jonathan added, widening his eyes further. "Take a break? From studying?"

Arthur rolled his eyes and packed his things, scoffing. "It's a beautiful day outside! The snow is finally gone! And I take breaks."

"Since *when?*"

Jonathan shot an amused look at Clarke. "Since he's been getting laid."

As Clarke snapped his fingers appreciatively, Arthur tensed, cheeks flaring.

"Offer canceled," he said, strangled. "I'm going alone."

"If you wanted to go fuck your boyfriend you could have just told us." Jonathan beamed at him.

"That's! I'm not—I—" Arthur spluttered and, sensing this was not a battle he would be able to win, turned on his heel to leave.

"Congrats on the sex!" Jonathan called to him, and Arthur closed the door on Clarke collapsing on the floor in hysterical giggles.

He stood still for a moment, shaking his head, and pulled out his phone to check the notifications he'd missed while studying all morning.

His heart skipped a beat. The most recent one was from none other than Mika himself, fifteen minutes earlier.

> MIKA
>
> what are you up to today
>
> it feels physically impossible to study when the sun is shining for the first time in a month

Arthur's left palm tingled, and he marveled at the timing: not for the first time since Mika's name had appeared on his hand, he wondered at the validity of the whole Soulmate Sense theory.

Arthur shot back, 'On my way back to the room, meet me there,' and pocketed his phone, heart and feet picking up a pace.

When he turned the corner of his own hallway Mika was already in front of his door, sporting casual outdoor gear, and speaking into his phone.

"Yeah, I know babe. I'm sorry—finals are in a week, I just think I gotta focus in. Is that okay? ...I'll make it up to you. ...Yeah. Movie marathon when we're home?"

Arthur's eyebrows rose.

Mika chuckled at something on the other line. "Yeah, I'll tell him. Love you, too."

Arthur finally reached Mika's side.

"Cherry says you're a good influence on me."

Arthur found himself unsure of how to respond to such a ludicrous suggestion.

"You look like a Patagonia ad," he settled on, tapping his wand on the crystal pad to unlock the door.

"I thought we could go on a hike." Mika followed Arthur in, closing the door behind him. "If you're up for a *physical* challenge, for a change of pace."

Arthur turned to find a suggestive grin on Mika's face and scoffed, pivoting to his closet to hide his blush.

"You have good timing." He pulled out an outfit similar to Mika's. "I was just thinking about what a nice day it is."

"I'm telling you." Mika tapped his head as Arthur took his clothes to the bathroom. "Soulmate Sense."

"God, don't remind me." Arthur elected not to share that this was *also* what he'd just been thinking, stripping his current tee to replace it with one more suitable for outdoor activity.

Mika didn't seem to have the usual quippy response to this, and Arthur glanced over through the open bathroom door to make sure he wasn't getting into something he shouldn't.

He was startled to catch Mika staring—for only a split second before he pointedly looked away, aimlessly, at the collection of posters above the couch. Something warm and satisfied settled low in Arthur's stomach as he pulled on the new tee and he couldn't help himself—

"Like what you see?"

Mika turned to face him again as he exited the bathroom. "Just making sure you're not exaggerating about your workout schedule."

Arthur paused as he donned his jacket, looking back at Mika. He was lounging easily on the couch, an alarmingly frank expression on his face. He shared a small smile with Arthur, one at a dimmer wattage than usual, before looking down at his phone.

Arthur raised his eyebrows and removed the schoolbooks from his backpack, replacing them with a water bottle and protein bars before zipping it. "I don't know how your girlfriend would feel about blowing her off so you can blatantly check me out."

"Cherry's not the jealous type," Mika dismissed him. Arthur took note of how he chose not to protest at the second half of the statement.

"You keep saying that," he said as Mika stood to join him, "but I still find it hard to believe she'd willingly give up all her free time with you so you can fake-date me."

"I've known her forever," Mika said while they exited Arthur's room and made their way down the hall, "and she goes to school halfway across the city. We video chat."

"And hang out on the weekends?" Arthur gave him a pointed look.

Mika hesitated. "We have all of winter break to hang out together."

Arthur appraised him once they were in the elevator, cautiously extending his Sense. He observed a tense grid of particles around Mika before he shot Arthur a look and steeled his defenses.

"Stop snooping, asshole."

"Trouble in paradise?" Arthur smirked.

"Everything is fine," Mika insisted. "Let's stop by the dining hall. We can eat sandwiches on the trail."

"Soulmate Sense," Arthur insisted, wiggling his fingers in Mika's face. Mika batted his hand away.

"It's been..." He rolled his eyes. "I mean, yeah, it's been *weird*, dating someone when your alleged soulmate's name is on your hand, and it's not the person you're actually dating. Not to mention having to fake-date said soulmate publicly while real-dating someone in private."

"Sounds complicated," Arthur said with bemusement, taking pleasure in watching Mika squirm—and on a rare subject that wasn't shoes, magic theory, or messing with Arthur.

"But she's my best friend." Mika inspected the to-go sandwich packages and picked one. "I love her. So."

He didn't seem keen to elaborate, so Arthur focused on selecting his own sandwich.

"Alright." He shrugged. "Your problem, not mine."

Mika's shoulders lowered ever so slightly as he changed the subject. "So I was thinking we could find our way to *Naardermeer*."

Arthur pointedly avoided all topics related to Cherry, or their fake relationship, or his workout routine as they crossed the bridge and veered right, away from town and off toward the peatland, until they happened upon a tourist trap establishment advertising overpriced bike rentals. Despite Arthur's vehement protests that they could save money on foot, Mika thrust a credit card into the shopkeeper's face, and by noon they were cycling side by side on purple and green bicycles. An hour later, they paused along the expansive waterfront to scarf down their sandwiches, taking turns Conjuring nuts for wild squirrels and laughing when the nuts disappeared before they could eat them. Mika captured their photo for the day as Arthur threw back his head and laughed at a particularly quizzical squirrel they'd tricked five times in a row, and before they got back to the hike, Arthur made sure to like the photo on his feed, commenting *'Squirrel torture really tickles me.'*

Two hours later—comprising mostly of a conversation about whether squirrels liked spaghetti or not, and Arthur once again laughing so hard at Mika's terrible "meat-a-ball-a" impression that he nearly fell off his bike—they happened across a bench overlooking a mire overrun by flowerless lily pads that hadn't yet succumbed to the cold of winter. The sun, which had been in and out of the clouds all afternoon, shone down in the golden hour, throwing light across the dazzling wetlands, glittering in the breeze.

"Wow," Arthur breathed, taking in the scene.

"Yeah," Mika agreed. "Let's stop here."

"I haven't experienced nature in so long," Arthur admitted, rubbing the back of his neck. "I'm usually stuck inside. Studying."

Mika propped his bike against one side of the bench and plopped down onto it, removing his helmet and jacket despite the cold. "What changed today?"

Arthur did the same—running a hand through his helmet-hair—and settled beside him, remembering how Clarke and Jonathan had gaped outside *Ontbijt*.

"I don't know." He glanced cautiously at Mika. "I guess I've been realizing I do better work when I take breaks."

He looked away before Mika could catch his gaze, but he heard him smile. "I'm glad our friendship's been a good influence on you, too."

Arthur reeled back. "Sorry, our *what?*"

Mika looked at him strangely. "Are we not friends?"

Arthur gaped at him. "Since *when?*"

Mika started counting off on his fingers. "We sit next to each other in class, at lunch. We have inside jokes. We stand in line together for sneaker releases. We go on hikes together. We go to brunch—"

"But—"

"I repeat: we go to *brunch.*"

"Our arrangement, though—"

"Please." Mika grinned and leaned his hands back on the rock. "Our arrangement is about the fake boyfriend shit. When was the last time we had an honest-to-god duel in class? Or outside of class, for that matter?"

Arthur bit his lip. He'd been so preoccupied with his determination to keep his grades higher than Mika's that he hadn't noticed their relationship changing in the process. Mika was still his rival, at least in the most literal sense—his only competition for Electi Magi. He'd kept it a secret for so long at this point that it had turned in on itself, manifesting into a mantra.

But when was the last time he'd felt actual animosity toward his so-called rival? In fact—if he was honest with himself—most days he even *enjoyed* Mika's company.

Arthur gave a shudder that had very little to do with the cold.

"I mean," Mika offered, "don't get me wrong. I still think you're an insufferable smartass. But I'm not complaining if we don't have to put on a performance every other day in class to prove our loathing for each other."

"But," Arthur frowned, "aren't we still putting on a performance?"

"Hm." Mika looked away. "I guess so."

They fell into a comfortable silence, and Arthur wasn't sure how to feel about this development—about how the situation had so unassumingly grown beyond his control, beyond his scope of understanding. When was the last time he'd seriously thought about sabotaging Mika, outside of idle daydreams?

He looked over to study Mika's utterly unreadable face.

How had he let himself start to *like* his so-called nemesis?

That box in his mind, holding everything he'd striven to contain for the past couple months, gave a hearty shake.

Emerging from his reverie, he realized Mika was smiling again.

"Hey." He turned to face Arthur. "What do you want to do after graduation? I mean. If you've thought about it."

Arthur looked out at the silent, sparkling water across from them. They'd finally reached a topic that felt a little too close to Arthur's ulterior motives.

But that wasn't quite it. Things had changed, and he realized—not without some horror—that something new was at stake. Something that sounded like this companionable silence in a quiet waterland, this whip-smart banter back and forth, this teaching each other new ways of thinking about magic, this not-so-secretly checking each other out, this pretending-to-hate-spending-time-together-but-secretly-finding-ways-to-spend-more, this...

...Whatever this was.

And if they were friends (and Arthur found it was getting easier not to cringe at the word), couldn't he at least reveal his dream, without mentioning what he'd have to do to make it happen, and the crucial role Mika played in it?

Arthur swallowed.

"I've thought about it." His voice came out quiet. He glanced at Mika, but his face was impassable, trained on the lily pads before them. Just a little bit of the truth couldn't hurt, right?

"I want to start my own business," he confessed, "with Clarke and Jonathan. Auratech has been such a hit at school that we decided to do it for a living." He looked up to the sky, painted a crisp golden-hour blue. "Making non-magic technology widely available to the magical public."

If I can use the Electi Magi fellowship and leave school debt-free to even start said business. If I can beat you to make Electi Magi in the first place.

"So you're telling me when you graduate college, you want to work to close the poverty gap by making elite technology more accessible to the less privileged?"

Arthur started to regret revealing so much of his hand. He whipped around, expecting a haughty, patronizing expression aimed directly at him as he shot back, "Yeah, that's about right."

But to his surprise, Mika had that soft, genuine smile on his face.

"I'd expect nothing less, genius."

It might have been the most earnest phrase out of his mouth to date. As Mika turned to catch his gaze, Arthur looked away, back at the peat. He hoped Mika would assume he was flushed from the cold.

"It's just been hard—" Arthur found he was speaking despite himself, as he often did around Mika nowadays— "growing up with magic as someone worse off. I want to make it better for other people like me."

"That's. That's...cool, Pham." Mika's voice was quiet. "I like that."

They sat in silence for a few more minutes. After a while, Arthur felt Mika's gaze boring into the side of his face. But when he turned to look at him, Mika was gazing out at the lily pads again.

Arthur looked out, too, and told himself he was imagining things.

"I'm cold," he lied. "Let's go home."

Mika finally caught his eye and looked as if he was on the verge of saying something.

Arthur waited with bated breath.

But the hesitation evolved effortlessly into an easy smile and Mika stood, offering a hand down to Arthur.

Despite himself, Arthur accepted it.

16

The Monday before their first final, Clarke and Jonathan were in a state of panic, claiming they needed one hundred percent of their focus for their final projects in Evocation. Arthur had offered to help, but they avidly denounced it as an opportunity to gloat, as he'd already finished his several days prior. He'd had to calm his mom over the phone for the third time that month, and the pressure was starting to weigh on him once more; no matter how prepared he felt for finals, his brain wouldn't allow him to breathe, let alone feel confident in his own abilities. He needed to find a way to focus—for his sake, and Clarke's, and Jonathan's, and Auratech's. For his mom's sake.

Leaving his friends to their manic predispositions, Arthur decided to seek out alternative study companionship. Before dinner, Arthur gathered his things and crossed the hall to Mika's room, formulae and theories swarming his mind as he placed his hand on the doorknob and twisted—

Alarm bells sounded in his head.

He retracted his hand and paused. At first, nothing...

And then he Sensed a spike of frustration—hot and anxious from behind the door—accompanied by Mika's voice.

"Mom, come *on.*"

Arthur couldn't help but strain to hear.

He contemplated tiptoeing back to his room and coming back in half an hour, but countless dismissed calls on Mika's phone in the past month kept him rooted to the spot.

"He's already invited me," Mika was saying.

Arthur frowned. *Who?*

Whatever his mom said on the other end of the line sent a spark of irritation rushing through Mika, its shade rushing through Arthur. "I don't get why this is such a big deal. I'm twenty-one. I'm an adult now, and I can decide who I want to spend my time with, whether or not you *approve*. You have me for the whole winter holiday, it's only one weekend—"

Silence again, and Mika's tension built within it for five seconds...ten...

"Just because you hate Dad doesn't mean I do. Keep your mess to yourself. I'm going to enjoy a weekend helping him open the restaurant because, like I keep saying, I'm an adult, and you don't get to tell me what to do anymore."

Arthur's eyes went wide. For all his battles with Mika over the years, for all the arrogance he'd witnessed in the classroom, he'd never heard him take a tone like this.

"No. I can't do this right now. Whatever, Mom. Bye."

Arthur remained frozen in shock. Despite his own parents' divorce, despite being forced to become the man of the house at a young age and the occasional gnawing resentment that accompanied it, he'd sooner donate his entire sneaker collection than show anything but the utmost respect for his mom, who'd raised them alone. His duties to the family, as well as hers, were mutually understood—an unspoken agreement.

He wondered now, though, what kind of pressure would cause him to snap.

Carefully, he eased away from the door, not wanting to pry any deeper than he already had.

"Stop creeping, Pham."

Arthur jumped a foot in the air.

"No more dramatic phone calls," Mika continued from behind the door, "promise."

Arthur grimaced, but opened the door to peek in.

"Sorry," he mumbled.

"Nah." Mika made a dismissive gesture from the couch. "It's all good. Family drama—you know."

Arthur hovered in the doorway. "Sure."

The silence lingered.

"Do...you want to—" Arthur swallowed hard— "talk about it?"

Mika's eyes snapped up to his. "You're not going soft on me now, Pham."

Arthur felt his cheeks heat furiously. "Look, you're the one who said we were..." Arthur shaped his mouth around the unfamiliar word, "friends."

He was surprised to find that Mika didn't have a witty retort to this. He only sighed, leaning against the back of the couch. "I don't want to bore you."

Arthur closed the door behind him and crossed the room to sit next to Mika, dragging over a pink velvet pouf so he could prop up his feet.

"You've got fifteen minutes—" he interlaced his fingers on his lap sagely— "before I cut you off to start working."

"How generous of you." Mika rolled his eyes.

"Finals start tomorrow," Arthur shot back, "and with that brilliant retort, you're at fourteen minutes, fifty-five seconds."

"I swear to god, Pham." Mika sighed. "Fine. My parents are in the middle of a divorce."

Arthur's heart lurched. "Shit."

"Yeah." Mika's eyes hit the ceiling. "It's a long story, but the short version is my dad is bored of being a part of our family, and his big dreams don't match up with my mom's."

Arthur tried very hard not to look taken aback at his flippancy, instead trying for something similar to sympathy. "Big dreams?"

A small smile graced Mika's lips—the genuine one. "He wants to open his own restaurant."

"Wow." Arthur lifted an eyebrow, contemplating. "Ambitious."

"My mom doesn't seem to think so." Shade colored Mika's tone. "Which is less than ideal, because—between my dad's dream and hers—I don't know. She wants me to follow in her footsteps and join the company when I graduate...but, well..."

His eyes sparkled with a passion that Arthur didn't think he'd ever seen before. Mirth, yes, humor, yes, but...

"I want to work with my dad," Mika continued. "I don't want to work my way up some stupid corporate ladder to make a six-figure salary. I want to spend my time—hell—*feeling, doing...*" He trailed off thoughtfully.

Arthur remained still, listening with rapt attention.

"I love food. And sometimes it feels like the only thing I do love," Mika finished.

Arthur mulled this over, frowning. "But you're good at so many things." He hesitated. "We're tied for top of our class. You don't love any of what we're learning?"

Mika shot him a wry smile. "You sound just like my mom."

Arthur swallowed a biting retort, switching tactics. "So what are her big dreams, then?"

"Oh you know, the usual." Mika gestured carelessly to illustrate his point. "Climb the ladder to become CEO of Crystaltech—she's already COO, so, you know, it's not out of the question. Make millions of dollars more than she's already making. Land some fancy 'most influential persons' list on some fancy tech site. *Et cetera, et cetera.*"

Arthur's heart leapt into his throat. "Your mom is Michelle Wrigley?"

Mika grinned. Arthur stared, trying to make sense of it.

"Yeah. Why? That impress you, genius?"

"Um." Arthur frowned. "Yeah?"

"I told her about the little tchotchke you made."

Arthur's heart promptly made its way back down to his stomach.

"You...you—what?"

"Yeah, I mentioned it over the phone back in October. On account of how mega popular they are?"

Arthur's heart was beating. Fast.

"You told your mom, Michelle Wrigley, COO of the magical world's leading tech company, about my product—a product that directly interferes with the sanctity of her brand?"

Mika's eyes slid sideways. "Well, when you put it like that..."

"Rivera." Arthur leaned forward, emphatic. "I could get sued."

"I don't think—"

"Wait, wait. Hold on." Arthur stood from the couch, anger bursting into flame in his chest. "I told you my dream after graduation was to make Auratech a reality. Two days ago."

"Pham—"

"And you just—" Arthur made an incredulous gesture— "didn't think it was worth mentioning that the biggest name in magic technology—one of my potential biggest competitors, if it makes it off the ground—is practically *run* by your mother?"

"Listen—"

Something clicked in Arthur's hindbrain, and his anxiety took off without him. "Were you going to go tattle to her about my business plan, too?"

"She was impressed," Mika finally managed. "She thought it was inventive."

If he'd meant for his words to placate Arthur, they were having the opposite effect. Alarm bells rang in Arthur's mind, and that voice in the back of his head screamed at him: *You see? You see what happens when you let your guard slip for even a moment, when you get cozy instead of getting even, when you don't best your enemy before he bests you—*

Before Arthur knew it, his mouth was speaking without his consent. "You have the audacity to call us friends, and then you pull something like this? Was there ever a time you weren't trying to screw me over?"

"Where is this even coming from—"

"And you want to go cook with your *dad?*" Arthur was running out of breath for how quickly the tables had turned. All the pent-up tension from the past month—from lying to his friends to keeping his grades stellar to procrastinating his sabotage plans to whatever *this* was with Mika—it was all for naught, now that the rug was getting swept out from underneath him before he even had a chance to—before he could—

"Here I am," Arthur said, cutting over whatever Mika was going to say next, "giving my all, hauling ass to graduate top of my class, and you're just coasting—getting easy As and living off Mommy's money until you decide what low-stakes non-magic career will be *worthy* of your attention—"

"Stop." Mika stood abruptly, face stony.

His tone shut Arthur right up, heart pounding as he glared.

"That's not fair and you know it, Pham," Mika continued, the ubiquitous light in his eyes snuffed out. "I don't know what shit you've been going through, but don't pile your baggage on me."

Arthur felt Mika's Sense all around him and his breath caught in his throat, panic rising to an all-time high. Arthur avoided his eye and counted his breaths quietly: in-one, out-two, in-three, out-four...

Slowly, his heart calmed. Carefully, he picked it all back up—*guilt-frustration-anxiety-fear*—and packed it away in the neat box on the shelf of his mind. He rebuilt his walls brick by brick, shutting Mika out.

He was good at compartmentalizing now.

"I'm sorry," he ground out. "You're right, I..." He swallowed. "That was uncalled for."

Mika donned a sardonic smile. "So sorry that my dreams aren't as ambitious as the esteemed Arthur Pham's."

"No." Arthur dragged a hand down his face. "No, please. That was stupid."

"I know, genius."

Arthur snapped his eyes up to Mika, who had that rakish grin plastered on again.

"I'm fucking with you," Mika said.

Arthur groaned and covered his face again. He needed to leave five minutes ago. Scratch that—he needed to have never come over at all. He needed to sink into the ground and cease to exist, in a place where his problems didn't exist, his stress didn't exist, Mika didn't exist, *he* didn't exist—

"Hey." Mika's grip on his wrist was firm, but his tone was gentler than Arthur would have expected. He lowered Arthur's hand from his face and didn't let go. Arthur eyed him warily.

"Don't disappear on me." Light danced once more in Mika's eyes.

Arthur's heart jolted.

"I'm sorry for telling my mom." Mika's tone was serious, rare earnestness written into his features. He slid his hand from Arthur's wrist into his hand, a now-familiar warmth. He gripped it firmly. "It was before we were friends. And I swear she didn't take major note of it. She's had other things on her mind—namely, you know, a divorce."

Arthur searched Mika's eyes, tried to Sense deception...but there was none.

"I know. Thanks." Arthur sighed. "I've just been under a lot of pressure. I was dumping it on you. You're right—not okay."

Mika watched him for a moment more, and Arthur let out a breath of relief when he released his hand and threw him that careless grin. "Look at us, dueling again. It's just like old times."

Arthur reluctantly allowed the last of the tension to leave his body. "Going soft on me now?"

Mika only smiled and threw himself back on the couch, looking as if he hadn't been subject to the rantings of a raving lunatic mere minutes ago. "You're just jealous that I'll be getting paid to make-a da spicy meat-a-ball-a."

Arthur huffed a single laugh, and Mika beamed.

"So are you ready to get schooled in Evocation or what?"

Arthur's smile crept up on him as he leaned down to retrieve his textbook from his messenger bag.

"Stop smoking so much, Rivera." He took up residence on his favorite floor pillow by the couch. "It's making you forget how much better I am than you at everything."

17

Throughout all of December, Arthur and Mika had studied Transmutation, Evocation, and everything in between, so despite his stress getting the best of him in Mika's room on Monday, Arthur found himself breezing easily through every final—whether it be essay or multiple choice or practical demonstration. Mika's kinesthetic techniques had him thinking about subjects in ways he'd never considered, and with an auxiliary skillset at his disposal, he'd never had an easier time with his exams. And he was already *really* good at exams.

Ironic, that for all the obsession with sabotaging Mika, he'd actually set Arthur up for success.

With finals securely behind them, Arthur was in Mika's room on the last Sunday before winter holiday, Clarke and Jonathan having bid them farewell after walking them up to the dorm from lunch, shooting them suggestive looks, and glancing at each other mischievously.

"See you at dinner, Arthur," Clarke had sing-songed, and Arthur rolled his eyes heartily.

He now had sketchbook and pencil in hand, doodling new Auratech designs, allowing himself a break—at Mika's insistence—before cracking open the books for the next semester. Mika had *Romeo and Juliet* open upside down on his chest, lounging across the couch as he scrolled his phone.

Arthur stretched, working out the kinks elicited from being hunched over for the past hour.

"Hey, what are the dinner hours today?" He blinked the last of focus mode from his eyes. "I might have to meet Clarke and Jonathan soon."

Mika didn't answer. From his angle on the floor, Arthur could see his screen.

> BEN
> finally ordered weed, see you in 5 at toby's?

Arthur's heart lurched despite himself. Course-correcting, he drew breath to reassure Mika he didn't mind calling it for the day—especially since it was the last day before break—but Mika was already typing out a response:

> MIKA
> hangin with the bf ;) i'll catch y'all later!

Arthur flushed, averting his eyes.

"Sorry." Mika tossed his phone further into the couch and out of sight. "What'd you say?"

Arthur peered up at him curiously. Mika made a face. "What?"

Arthur looked down, stifling a smile. "Nothing."

"Pham."

"It's just that you're so stupid," Arthur simpered, recovering enough to reach up and pinch Mika's cheek. "And I fucking hate you."

"Jesus." Mika slapped his hand away, and Arthur laughed. "Dinner's at six."

Arthur blinked, then squinted, calculating, and scoffed. "Ugh. Americans."

"I never did learn how to count past twelve," Mika admitted with a wistful sigh.

Arthur turned back to his sketchbook, ready to dive in and re-emerge when it was time for dinner, but Mika sat up abruptly.

"Hey, I've been meaning to ask." He plucked Arthur's sketchbook from his hands and repositioned himself on the other side of the couch, flipping through it idly. "What got Thing One and Thing Two in a bunch about our after-school hours in the first place?"

"What do you mean?" Arthur reached over to tug the sketchbook back, closing it and tucking it safely back into his bag.

"Pre-study-dates," Mika prompted, as Arthur's heart traitorously skipped at the word, "pre-friends, pre-social-media-addendum?"

Arthur squinted. He adjusted the hot pink floor pillow so he could lean his head back against the couch. "God, that feels like forever ago. I don't know. They're very...nosy. Well, Clarke is, anyway. I think they must have realized that if I wasn't at school or at a party with you, I was either with them or in my room studying."

"Independence in relationships really needs to be destigmatized," Mika scoffed, picking up his book once more.

"I swear to you I said the same fucking thing, but Clarke insisted on knowing when we have sex."

Arthur froze, staring at a zebra on the wallpaper across the room and feeling his face burn. *Shit. Shit, shit, shit—*

But Mika, who gave a short laugh, didn't seem fazed in the least. "What did you tell them?"

Arthur's brain seemed to have disconnected from his mouth, because while his brain was screaming at him to *shut up, shut up, shut up*, his mouth was saying: "Well, Clarke loses his mind when I kiss and tell, so I told him we have tons of really rough sex, and that shut him up."

"Hm." Mika pondered while Arthur contemplated throwing himself out the window. "I would have imagined you as a gentle lover."

Arthur grinned lazily, and the words were out of his mouth before he had a chance to weigh in. "I guess you don't know me very well."

Shut up, shut up, shut up—

Mika didn't seem to have a response to this, and Arthur chanced a glance up at him. He just barely caught a flush and a look of incredulity on Mika's face before he shook his head and disappeared behind his book.

Arthur whipped his head forward again and pinched the bridge of his nose between his fingers. "Agh. I was just fucking with them. It was a while ago. I shouldn't have said that shit, I'm sor—"

"Pham." Mika chuckled, and the sound sent a spark up Arthur's neck. "Chill. God. It's fine."

Arthur chanced a glance up over his fingers. Mika was frowning thoughtfully.

"What?"

Mika's eyes cut over to his. "When you say rough, what do you mean, exactly?"

Arthur glared at him, resentful for having to spend more time than absolutely necessary on this topic in the first place—resentful toward himself for having brought it up at all. "I believe the exact words I used were BDSM, biting, and spanking," he ground out.

Mika stared at him. "You're kidding."

Arthur reeled back. "What?"

Mika let out a long-suffering sigh and lowered *Romeo and Juliet* dramatically. "We'll have to prove it now, genius."

Arthur blinked. "Excuse me?"

"You can't just go around saying you have rough sex with nothing to show for it." Mika leveled him with a look. "Especially after a *month* of hanging out for extended periods of time since they asked."

"You're going to have to elaborate here." Arthur stared at him, bewildered.

"Rough sex—" Mika sat up, leaning forward emphatically— "leaves marks."

"Marks," Arthur repeated. "Marks..."

Mika raised his eyebrows expectantly. Suddenly, it clicked.

"*Marks?* You want to give me a *hickey?*"

"Or you me, either way works," Mika said without a trace of humor, ignorant to Arthur's blatant alarm.

"I'm pretty sure there's a *no-tongue* stipulation in our contract," Arthur spluttered too-fast, voice several octaves higher than he would've liked it to be.

Mika rolled his eyes and Summoned their leather-bound notebook, all too familiar now, and grabbed a pen from the windowsill to start scribbling. Arthur desperately willed his brain to catch up with what he was hearing. He wanted to magic his mouth shut permanently. He wanted to gouge his eyes out, to bang his head against the wall—

Mika handed him the contract and pen, and Arthur read, with horror:

Hickeys, as needed, in private, with explicit consent

Arthur thrust the notebook back at him. "No fucking way. I cannot believe I *ever* considered you my friend for one *iota* of a second, you disgusting, neanderthalistic—"

"Do you want them to start asking questions again?" Mika interrupted. "Guaranteed—if you have proof, you won't have to keep blatantly lying to them."

Arthur's retort got lost in his throat. The guilt, carefully locked away on the shelf, rattled the box noisily.

He closed his eyes and took a shaky breath. He'd done this before. It was just temporary closeness. And a lot of sucking, and some spit. It was no big deal. It was no big deal whatsoever.

So why did it feel like one?

"Okay," he sighed, willing his heart to slow. It paid him no mind. "Okay," he repeated, as if speaking the word into existence would make it feel as such. He initialed the addition and passed the contract back to Mika. "Fine. But we should both have one. And I want to go first."

"Be more specific, Pham."

"What?"

"Give or receive?"

"*Give.* Jesus—give, Rivera. Fuck."

"Peachy." Mika initialed the contract and Sent it back to Arthur's room. He patted the couch next to him. "Come on up."

And just as Arthur's heart rate had started to slow.

"Wait." He felt dangerously short of breath. *"Now?"*

"Yes, now, genius." Mika had a face screaming *what-the-hell-is-wrong-with-you* aimed his way. "Was I just imagining the very unsubtle looks they were throwing you before they left? What do you imagine Clarke thinks you're doing with me, in my room, alone, right now, the weekend before holiday break?"

Arthur stared at him. "Studying?" he tried weakly.

Mika gave him a pointed look and patted the seat next to him again.

Numbly, Arthur eased up onto the couch, staring alternately between Mika's face and his neck. His *neck*, which he was going to have to put his *mouth* on and how the *hell* was this happening?

"You're not gonna logic your way through this one, Pham." Mika smirked.

"Watch me," Arthur muttered, scooting closer. Mika smelled like Old Spice.

"You *have* done this before, right?" Mika asked, not without a hint of condescension.

"Yes, asshole," Arthur hissed, meeting his sparkling eyes to glare at him—*nope, no way*—and then down at his neck. Where he was supposed to give Michael Rivera a hickey. Right now. With tongue. Without any prior warning whatsoever. He could see the tendon there, could see his blood pulsing—it made Arthur's own pulse race even faster, and he was suddenly struck with a horrifying realization.

He wasn't nervous.

He was excited.

Carefully, he extended his Sense...and found the feeling was reciprocated.

Some sick, evil, visceral corridor of his brain—parallel to the movie villain's but on the opposite side of the compound—was thrilled at this discovery, and leaned him in to feel that pulse for himself.

Mika inhaled sharply. It sent something electric and powerful down Arthur's spine, urging him to reach his left hand up to touch Mika's chin, guiding it farther aside with his thumb for a better angle. He opened his mouth and tasted skin-sweat-boy, thrilled at how Mika's pulse thrummed faster under his ministrations. He mouthed there again and sucked, moving his hand down to Mika's collarbone to brace there, and his love line lit up, a hot-bright sensation that he could swear Mika's heart rose up to meet, beating hard under his hand.

Arthur came up for air with a start, falling back on the couch and breathing harder than he thought appropriate. He stared at the wet, red spot on Mika's neck—already bruising—then met his eyes, dark and languid. He didn't dare extend his Sense again...not that he needed it to read the reaction he'd elicited.

Arthur's eyes darted to Mika's parted lips and felt something in his gut unravel entirely.

"Your turn," he breathed.

He'd barely gotten the words out before Mika was just *there*.

Arthur liked to think he had a precise, finessed skill when it came to this business, but Mika gave hickeys like it was all he did day in and day out. His left side pressed in to align seamlessly with Arthur's right, and his hand slipped up his chest, his collarbone, fingers reaching through the short hair at the nape of his neck. Mika's lips met his skin and Arthur couldn't help but stretch to give him better access as his mouth languished, licking and sucking and *biting*, and Arthur couldn't have held that sound in if he'd tried—

And at that, Mika lazily traveled up, lips grazing Arthur's ear as his thumb brushed against the other side of his neck, touching at his pulse there. He murmured: "If that's what you meant when you said I didn't know you very well..."

Arthur thought he might melt straight into the couch. In all his years of studying magic, he'd never experienced this—this closeness and heat and *spark*—

Lips at his ear, Mika continued, "I think I'd like to get to know you better."

It was involuntary, really—the growl in Arthur's throat, the way his head swiveled to face Mika nose-to-nose, his left hand coming up to grip Mika's right where it lay at the base of his neck. He was overcome with the sudden, intense urge to climb into Mika's lap, to run his hands through his messy hair, to finish what they'd started—and by the look on Mika's face, hazel eyes nearly black, mouth open and wet from where he'd worked at Arthur's neck, he was thinking the same.

Mika twisted his right hand to catch Arthur's left, bringing it in between them, leaning their foreheads together. He lay Arthur's palm open, tracing his love line.

"Arthur..."

Arthur opened his eyes, not remembering when he'd closed them, and caught sight of his hand, heart in his throat. The words were blood red, like henna freshly tattooed, more intensely there than they'd ever been:

Michael Rivera.

Arthur was on his feet in a fraction of a second, heart thudding hard against his ribcage, pins and needles erupting in his left hand, blood rushing in his ears. The box on the shelf in his mind toppled and out came everything—guilt and fear and anxiety mingling with the thrill and the terror of what had just happened. He stared at Mika, and Mika stared back, flushed and obviously hungry and—to Arthur's combined horror and inexplicably soaring triumph—hard.

Arthur's protests along with his scorching and undeniable desire to collapse back down onto the couch and pull Mika on top of him all got stuck in his throat somewhere around his spasming heart, but Mika was nothing if not quick on his feet.

He crossed his legs easily and leaned back on the sofa, tossing Arthur that now-familiar lopsided grin.

"Wow, Pham." His voice was an octave lower than usual. "You sure know how to woo a man."

"When I do a job I do it right," Arthur blurted, despite the loud, persistent buzzing in his ears.

"Go big or go home," Mika agreed, grin absolutely incorrigible as his gaze traveled down to the front of Arthur's pants.

"Well." Arthur hastily picked up his messenger bag and draped it across his body pointedly, pulling at his collar to show off his new badge of honor. "If you think that will do the trick?"

Mika raised his eyebrows, dark satisfaction in his gaze. "That'll do," he agreed softly, hooking a finger into his collar to show off his own.

Arthur stifled the noise that threatened to surface from deep within his throat and nodded, swallowing hard.

"Great," he said. His voice sounded strangled, so he cleared his throat. "Awesome. Well, thanks...for the hickey. I guess."

Mika saluted him lazily. "Back atcha."

"See you tomorrow. I mean—next year?" Arthur wrenched his eyes away from the sight of Mika—pleased as punch and draped carelessly on the sofa—and turned on his heel for the exit.

He'd gotten the door open and was halfway out of it when Mika called from across the room.

"Arthur."

He startled, and turned.

The expression on Mika's face was utterly unreadable. He looked on the precipice of something—something of grave importance, something that gave Arthur the uncanny feeling of *déjà vu*.

Whatever that something was, Mika seemed to take a purposeful step back from it. An arrogant grin stretched across his face, and he winked at Arthur.

"Don't be so gentle next time."

Arthur let out an exasperated noise, eyes wide as he slammed the door shut. He could hear Mika cackling from the other side of it.

He strode across the hallway to his own door, fishing for his wand

and tapping it to the pad on the wall—but he paused, unable to help himself.

He lifted his hand to gaze at where the name was emblazoned, blood red, into his palm.

Without turning back, he extended his Sense—*carefully*—back to Mika's room.

He was overwhelmed with a burst of color and sensation, pink and yellow and turquoise, the chaos of glee and lust and frustration and the flavor of something else—something somehow both more subtle and more huge, unfathomable but undeniable—a blooming warmth viscerally deep in the gut, something on the tip of his tongue and something terribly exciting and terribly frightening.

He snapped his Sense back into himself and reeled, head spinning with the whiplash.

Well. *That* was new.

Hand tingling so hard it smarted, desperately hoping Mika hadn't Sensed him lingering, Arthur opened the door to his room and slipped in quietly, determined to lock up what he'd Sensed in that box on the shelf in his mind along with what just happened, a noteworthy addition to his growing collection of unspeakable, uncontrollable things.

18

Arthur wasn't sure how he'd gotten here.

Ben Lasher's kitchen was dark and sweaty and loud; rib-rattling bass through the speakers in the living room rumbled in his chest and every inhale was a lungful of cheap vodka and Homebrew beer and incense and weed. He could see the crowd of people through the cut-out bar—the room was packed full to bursting, but the kitchen was empty.

Save for him, of course, sitting on the counter—and Mika, nestled between his legs.

Arthur could have sworn he hadn't taken a single drink but he must have, because there was no way that Sober Arthur would have his arms around Mika's shoulders, his legs around Mika's waist—no way he'd be letting Mika close enough to be stroking up and down his back with warm, dry fingers, breathing into his chest—

And when the hell had he taken his shirt off?

Mika's hands disappeared from Arthur's back to pin one of Arthur's hands down on the counter, the other reaching up to lace fingers in his hair. Arthur leaned into the touch, drunk and lazy, until Mika tugged hard to tilt his head to the side, exposing Arthur's neck—a strangled noise escaped Arthur's throat and then Mika was just *there*, mouthing and biting and sucking.

He shifted his grip to tilt Arthur's head back so he could gain access to more of his neck, licking up a tendon and sucking to bite at the other side and Arthur let out a moan from deep in his chest—Mika's lips spread into a smile against his neck, his ear, with just the barest hint of teeth at his earlobe. Arthur inhaled sharply and Mika made a noise that was downright unfair before murmuring:

"I think I'd like to get to know you better."

Electrified, Arthur pushed off the counter to press Mika up against the wall beside it, one hand at the front of his shirt and one on his neck as he buried his face there, returning the favor and savoring the noises every kiss-suck-bite elicited. Mika managed to slot their legs together, moving lazily against him, hands slung low on his hips and neck straining to give Arthur more access.

"You want this," Arthur growled, the realization spurring him on. "You've *been* wanting this."

Mika didn't respond, instead using his grip on Arthur's hips to spin them around, reversing their positions. Arthur looked into dark eyes before they sank down, down, down...

A jolt in Arthur's chest—they were in public, anyone could see—

But then Mika's mouth was on him, around him, and a soft whimper sounded from deep within and suddenly he didn't care if they saw, didn't care what they thought, *wanted* them to see—to shut them up, to prove that he was in control, that Mika was his—

Mine.

He slid a hand into soft brown curls and met the wet-soft-tight-friction with every bob of Mika's head, reaching deeper than he'd thought possible. Clarke and Jonathan were pointing and whispering, and Cherry was rolling her eyes, and people were pointing and staring, but Arthur didn't care. Let them see; all that mattered was Mika, and Mika's mouth, and Mika's hair and Mika's hands and Mika's eyes which had flickered open to meet Arthur's, desperate and open, and Arthur keened loudly, tipping over the edge—

His eyes flew open, greeted by the dizzying, breathtaking reality of his dawn-lit dorm room, the end of the noise turning to a strangled groan in his throat...

And sticky wetness in the sheets around him.

"Fuck," Arthur whispered, rubbing his face with his hands. "Fuck!" he said more forcefully, launching himself out of bed, ripping the soiled bedding off the mattress.

'I think I'd like to get to know you better.'

"Fuck, fuck, fuck—" Arthur dumped the bedding in the Crystaltech washer in the bathroom and leaned his hands on the machine.
Mine.
"Fuck."
Arthur bowed his head. It was cold in the bathroom, but he welcomed it; he hated that he was still hard and relished the way his body protested the chill.
Mika's eyes, flickering open to meet Arthur's—
This was bad.
This was *really* bad.
Despite the cold, Arthur turned on the shower and got in before the heated water kicked in. He felt viscerally unclean, reveling cruelly in how his body shivered to refocus the direction of blood flow.

Spring semester started in two days, and Arthur had spent the majority of holiday in his room at home, alternately creating a new batch of Auratech charms to sell, fighting off anxiety attacks, and actively not thinking about Mika. Or his hickey-giving skills. Or Clarke and Jonathan's faces when they'd caught a glimpse of it under his collar during dinner before the break. The change of environment had done him good, even despite witnessing his mom's stress firsthand and noting how it was already shaping his sister's ideas about what her future would look like. If anything it had cleared Arthur's head, realigning his perspective and bringing him back in touch with the reason he'd gotten caught up in this fake-boyfriend business in the first place.

But spring semester started in two days, and he was back at school, and he was realizing now that it was all just as complicated as it had been before—

If not more.

The water finally started to warm. Sans erection, Arthur finished out the remainder of his shower determined.

After toweling off, he got dressed for the day, not trusting himself to go back to sleep. He pulled out the chair at his desk and sat grimly, picking up his phone to compose a text.

> We have to talk.

He put down the phone and rested his head in his hands, settling in for a long wait.

But to his surprise—and alarm, and anxiety and anticipation and apprehension—Mika's text popped up less than a minute later.

> MIKA
>
> weird
>
> i just woke up from a dream about you
>
> soulmate sense is real

Arthur's heart skipped several beats before he snapped himself out of it, willing his numb fingers to respond.

> Go back to sleep, isn't it almost midnight in Chicago?
>
> MIKA
>
> well now you've instilled the fear of god in me with those words, sir
>
> is this an in person kind of talk?

Arthur hesitated. He considered the possibility of crossing the hall to Mika's room after a full day of class within inches of him—Mika's hand on his thigh, Mika's arm slung around his shoulder, Mika's laugh breathless in his ear—opening the door to find him lounging on the couch, grinning with dark eyes trained on Arthur, sliding to his knees...

Nope. *Nope*, definitely not.

Arthur crossed his legs firmly and started to type.

> Text is fine. I just wanted to check in. People seem to be done making fun of us. Maybe we can "fake break up" soon?

Arthur gripped the phone with sweaty hands, heart beating, staring at the *dot-dot-dot* wiggling on Mika's side of the screen. It danced for a moment, then disappeared. It danced again for an entire minute, then disappeared again. Finally, after five minutes, his response came:

> MIKA
>
> i'm not sure we should drop the act just yet

> we're soulmates, if we break up after only 3 months people will ask questions
>
> which honestly may be even worse than the teasing

Arthur's heart stuttered in his chest as flashes of *bass, fingers, wet-tight-hot* flickered in his minds-eye, an instant replay without his consent.

Fake boyfriends he could handle. Sex dreams...well. He hadn't signed up for sex dreams, nor what sex dreams might mean.

Panicked, he began to type, but Mika beat him to it.

> **MIKA**
>
> i think it makes more sense to keep it up for now.
>
> thoughts?

Arthur stared at the screen, deleting his half-baked protest.

You need to end it, his brain urged him.

The audacity of his brain to urge such a thing and replay the dream within the same breathing space did not sit well with Arthur. He closed his eyes and inhaled deeply.

It wasn't just the dream. It wasn't just the irreparably blurred lines. It wasn't even a deep-seated desire to return to two months ago, before the hickeys and the dates and the lying and the contract and the tuition—it was so much more than that now.

Something unfathomable but undeniable. Something on the tip of his tongue and something terribly exciting and terribly frightening.

Something that told him not to end it. Not just yet.

His left hand tingled intensely, pins and needles erupting along his love line. Arthur's fingers were typing before he'd given them permission to.

> Fine. But I have my limits.

> **MIKA**
>
> what do you mean

> I want to cross hickeys off the list.

Dot-dot-dot, dancing across the screen again.

MIKA

you got it boss

no tongue above all ;)

Thanks.

MIKA

leaving for the airport in the morning, need a full night's sleep to deal with a drive with mom for an uninterrupted 45 mins

seeya monday at breakfast?

Sounds good.

Arthur put his phone down and stared out the window at the brightening sky, willing his mind to release its grip on the dream, still as vivid as it had been while he was living it: the sticky tile of the counter under his hand, fingers tugging sharp at his hair, mouth on his neck, growling in his ear, against the wall, Mika sliding onto his knees, soft brown curls under his fingers—

And Arthur was hard again.

He let out a helpless noise and let his head fall to the desk with a thud.

Things had, irrevocably and nonconsensually, gotten so much worse.

19

It was different after that.

Despite his best efforts, Arthur couldn't cram the dream into the box. Impressions haunted his consciousness daily, intrusive flashes of hands and mouths and more nefarious things. He was convinced it was ultra-dimensional, defying the rules of time and space, ever-present, ever-taunting.

They came back from the holiday break and Arthur was wound up, an instrument strung too tight, a creature stuck in between fight or flight. Mika would sling an arm around his shoulder and he'd tense, blood rushing unceremoniously to his face. Mika would kiss him on the cheek after class and Arthur would inhale sharply, eyes fluttering closed at *boy-sweat-Old Spice*. Mika would place a hand on his thigh at lunch and Arthur would fight against the sudden, wild, untameable hope that he'd hike it up above the previously agreed-upon three inches below finger-line, to keep going, and going—

Arthur would gulp, take a shaky breath, give a brief excuse, and retreat shamefully to the bathroom for the remainder of the break.

And the worst part was Mika knew what he was doing. Arthur had no idea how, but he *knew*—he'd bet his secondhand designer tee drawer on it.

Mika would feel Arthur tense under his arm and loosen his grip, drawing light lines up and down his back before retreating.

He would feel Arthur breathe him in up close, and Arthur would hear him smile, breath grazing out in a laugh at his ear.

He would feel Arthur undeniably magnetized toward him at lunch, watching him jump from the table, and Arthur would catch a glance of darkened eyes—a smile sparkling with mirth—before fleeing.

And as if Mika wasn't enough to contend with, Spring Social season was already in full swing.

The student committee hit the ground running after they returned from break in February. Apparently three months wasn't even close to too early, because the halls of Stonebury were now draped in swaths of frothy turquoise and coral and Conjured soap bubbles and seafoam above their heads, advertising this year's theme: *Under the Sea!*

The first weekend back, Jonathan dragged Arthur and Clarke to a sister school event in the ballroom at Featherwood to find a Social date among the straggling singles. Arthur was grateful for the distraction—he didn't want to even *begin* contemplating what his arrangement with Mika might mean for his Social plans, and as Jonathan chatted up every available girl from here to Timbuktu, Arthur and Clarke made small talk, spinning grandiose tall tales and directing young ingenues over to their tall, well-muscled friend, who went on a run every single morning, rain or shine, didn't you know?

The second week of February, Arthur did his best to ignore the Social antics in favor of moving the last of the Auratech inventory. Despite selling out his entire supply the previous semester, the demand was still high for those who hadn't managed to get in on the first round. Arthur, Clarke, and Jonathan managed to sell the majority of what Arthur made over winter holiday via word of mouth, and the rest quickly disappeared when they set up shop at the Valentine's Day party in Benjamin Lasher's room that Friday.

When Arthur sold his last charm around midnight, Mika, drunk as ever, picked him up around the middle to spin him around, singing, *"My Valentine is a successful small business owner!"*

"Put me down," Arthur insisted, flushed and buzzing from the sudden and unexpected press of Mika's body against his own. Mika obliged, but only so he could Conjure bouquets of roses and chocolates and stuffed animals until Arthur was buried entirely.

He was grateful for how they hid the tightness in his white selvage jeans, which were...unforgiving, to say the least.

Spring Social Court votes took place the third week, and Arthur was only mildly surprised to get a nomination for Rex Magus. He knew he should have expected it, given the notoriety of his rivalry-turned-(fake)-relationship with Mika, but it was overwhelming nonetheless. He found himself standing on a table in the dining hall at lunch when the nominees were announced, next to Ben Lasher and Mika himself. He watched the crowd disjointedly chant their names and wondered bemusedly just how many parallel universes he'd skipped over to land in this one.

By the final week of February, Social proposals were cropping up left and right. In the dining hall at lunch, in class, in the courtyard—students from Years Three and Four were proposing to their past, present, or future Stonebury beaus. During parties and weekends in town, their peers Social-proposed to Featherwood students—*a cappella* arrangements, flowers, magical fireworks indoors, skywriting—all the pomp and circumstance was starting to be a bit much, if Arthur was being completely honest. But at least it was a welcome change from the undivided attention he and Mika had received for most of last semester.

It was a miracle he kept his grades up at all in February. His nerves were shot, he barely paid attention during lecture, and he knew if he hadn't read ahead for his classes over the break, his hopes of winning Electi Magi would have been past dashed by now—not to mention the seafoam and bubbles and sparkles he kept walking headfirst into on his way to class.

But true to Mika's tutelage, and despite his brain misfiring at every turn, Arthur managed to keep up his streak through instinctive spell-work by following his gut. He had to give Mika credit for that, at least.

By some streak of good luck—for once—his fake boyfriend was too busy with his social life to reinstate their study dates, and Arthur was grateful for it. They met at weekly parties, took their pictures, and Mika posted them, all under the supervision of Clarke and Jonathan or their peers at large. He wasn't sure how long he'd be able to make excuses before he'd have to explain himself—to confess why he'd been acting like a ticking time bomb since they'd been back. He just had to find a way to move past the memory of *sweat-skin-boy* and go back to the way things used to be.

But for now, exactly one month and two days after the dream, it was as close to the front of his consciousness as ever. He and Mika were in the courtyard for mid-morning break at a picnic table with Clarke and Jonathan, who were having a heated debate about Nutella versus cookie butter, and Arthur rolled up his shirtsleeves to search for a snack in his bag.

Blessedly, Mika was sitting across from him—nowhere near thigh-touching distance. But to Arthur's acute horror, he wasn't even trying to hide his stare, open and shameless, gaze hot within Arthur's keen awareness.

He made it through half his apple before he broke.

Tossing the rest in the trash, he mumbled something about seeing everyone in class and gathered up his things, staunchly avoiding eye contact with Mika and evacuating the table as quickly as possible.

He hadn't even made it to lunch this time.

In the private handicap bathroom near the classrooms, Arthur splashed cold water on his face for the third time that week. Shaking the shiver from his spine, he banished Mika's eyes—dark and insistent, quiet and confident. He turned off the tap, leaning over the sink and gazing at his palm.

Michael Rivera.

The words were still dark and lush, and Arthur could have sworn they pulsed lightly in time with his heart, hot just under his skin.

He let out a little whimper and leaned his head into his hands.

What the hell is happening to me?

The bathroom door opened and Arthur straightened hastily.

Of course—*of course*—none other than Mika himself leaned against the doorway. Arthur's heart took off at a sprint.

"You know, the handicap bathroom is reserved for people who actually need it. Is this where you've been running off to all the time?"

He *knew*, the bastard. His face was lit up with pride and sanctimonious good humor. And Arthur hated it.

"Using the *single-use* bathroom—" Arthur tried his best to gather up his pride and look haughty— "is a human right, especially when the hall is empty, and especially when you stay properly hydrated. Don't tell me you want to extend the contract to include joint bathroom visits, too?"

But oh, that had been the *wrong* thing to say because at that, Mika sauntered into the room, locking the door behind him and leaning back on the sink instead, too close and looking up at Arthur from underneath his eyelashes.

He *knew*, goddammit.

"Only if there's something interesting happening in here." He grinned.

Arthur's eyes slid closed. In-one, out-two...

But before he could conjure up a witty response, Mika chuckled. Arthur opened his eyes in time to see him looking away, letting him off the hook.

"Get that stick out of your ass, Pham. Clarke was doing that high-pitched thing he does, so I was desperate for a reprieve."

"He can get like that when cookie butter's reputation is at stake," Arthur offered, hoping his voice sounded stronger than he felt. Mika was *so close*.

"You know," Mika said thoughtfully, picking idly at a hangnail, "when you texted me right before break ended?"

'I think I'd like to get to know you better.'

Arthur gulped audibly, clearing his throat to try and disguise it. "Sure."

Mika frowned, still observing his nail. "It was weird timing, you know."

Arthur couldn't find his heartbeat. "Oh?"

"Yeah." Mika pouted his lips contemplatively, looking up at Arthur. "I was dreaming about you, and then I woke up to your message."

Arthur found his heartbeat, as his heart was now threatening to leap out of his throat.

"So you said," he managed. "I'm torn between flattered and insulted."

"We were at a party." Mika frowned, eyes drifting toward the ceiling, and Arthur's stomach swooped low in his gut.

"It was dark," he continued.

Arthur swallowed convulsively.

"There was way too much bass," Mika said, a smirk quirking at the corner of his mouth. "The kind you feel in your chest."

Arthur's palm gave a particularly impassioned throb.

Mika's gaze shifted and Arthur didn't think to look away fast enough, because their eyes met and Arthur was absolutely positive—

one-hundred percent sure—that Mika knew, that he could tell *exactly* what kept motivating Arthur to disappear from mixed company.

And worse, Mika was enjoying it.

But stronger even than embarrassment—and shame and self-hatred—was an intense, full-body-experience desire to lean in, to close the gap between them, to push him up against the wall, to slide down to his knees, to open his mouth and to taste and to savor and to swallow around—

Arthur came to with a start, blinking, heart hammering in his chest. It hit him like a ton of bricks: the realization that it wasn't just another impression, that this was new—a reversal projected into his consciousness, vivid and too-real. The perfect match to his own dream, the other side of the same coin.

He'd been Sensing.

And that meant...

The temperature of the bathroom rose a good ten degrees.

"Huh." Mika grinned, breaking eye contact to lean further back on the sink.

Arthur raked sweaty, shaky fingers through his hair. "I think I might be having an aneurysm."

Mika seemed much less—unfairly less—affected than Arthur did at the confirmation that they had *shared the same sexual dreamspace from across an entire ocean.*

Mika pondered his hand, entirely too casually. "Soulmate Sense. Wild."

"I cannot believe—"

"No wonder you wanted to cross hickeys off the list."

"Rivera—"

"I'll take it as a compliment," Mika boasted, "that I'm *that* good at giving them."

"You had the dream, too," Arthur shot back.

To his horror, Mika didn't look abashed—not one bit.

"Yeah," he agreed, scooting closer to Arthur to lean up close to his ear. "And it was a *really* good one."

"Please." Arthur crossed his legs surreptitiously. "Spare me the theatrics."

"Oh, Pham." Mika grinned and stepped back out of Arthur's

personal space, clapping his hands once with absolute delight. "You're so fun to tease, it isn't even fair!"

"Sex dreams are *not* in the contract," Arthur complained.

"Come on." Mika cuffed him on the shoulder, and Arthur flinched at the jolt it sent down his body. "Use that brain of yours, genius. It's totally natural: hormones, proximity, the hickeys—hm. Yeah. The hickeys were probably pushing it."

"You think?" Arthur despised the way his voice broke.

"I know it," Mika said, voice low, and Arthur couldn't help but catch his gaze, devilish and arrogant as anything. He felt his knees go weak, and the retort he'd been searching for fizzled on his tongue, which suddenly felt too big for his mouth.

The bell rang, and he let out a breath he hadn't realized he'd been holding in.

"Don't worry." Mika turned, breaking the spell, gesturing at him dismissively as he made his way to the door, unaffected as ever. "Lean into it. It'll get worse if you push against it."

"Lean into—*god*, you are the most odious human alive, I *despise* you—"

"Love you too, honeybun." Mika unlocked the door to the bathroom and winked over his shoulder. "Meet me in class. I've got a surprise."

Arthur sputtered out half a protest, but he was already alone.

He took a deep breath in and a deep breath out, steeling himself to reemerge.

Suddenly the bathroom door opened, and Mika peeked his head in once more.

"Oh, and Pham—" he had a devilish grin on his face— "you might wanna do something about the boner. We've been gone a while, and I don't want people to think I'd leave the love of my life unsatisfied—"

"*Rivera!*" Arthur roared and dove for him, but Mika slipped out of his grasp, leaving him furious and pushed up against the bathroom door.

And hard.

Arthur let out an existential groan and banged his head against the wall.

The sobering thought of having to ace an Evocation quiz without having studied was enough to kill Arthur's erection by the time he'd settled in his seat, pointedly avoiding eye contact with Mika next to him.

Professor Hirst looked even more harried than usual, and his voice was laced with the distinct tone of being completely done with the day at only eleven.

"For today's quiz," he sighed, eyeing Arthur and Mika with great exasperation, "I'll need you to partner up."

The class burst immediately into a flurry of activity, students pairing up all around them. Arthur desperately searched the room for someone *other* than the person with whom he'd shared a sex dream to partner with, but alas. His eyes finally fell upon Mika, standing expectantly beside him, brows waggling.

Arthur suddenly remembered his ominous parting words:

'Meet me in class. I've got a surprise.'

Arthur wanted to lie down on the floor and go to sleep for a very, very long time. He shoved aside a particularly horrifying scenario in which Mika Conjured condoms to rain down over his head and then gripped Mika's arm, hard.

"No funny business," he muttered as their classmates pushed all the tables to the walls of the room.

Mika donned a serious expression, but the sparkle in his eyes was a dead, resolute giveaway. "I've never had a sense of humor. Not a single day in my life."

Arthur's heart sank.

"Do we have a pair of volunteers to go first?" Professor Hirst looked as though he could use a lie down on the floor, too.

Mika's hand shot up immediately. "Me and Pham."

Their classmates erupted in cheers, and Arthur could have laughed at how familiar the scene was if not for the gnawing feeling of being dragged, kicking and screaming, to the depths of hell.

"We don't even know what the quiz is yet," Arthur protested as Mika dragged him into the center of the room. He thought he might be sick.

"Since when has thinking on your feet been a problem for you, Pham?" Mika murmured in his ear, and Arthur shuddered at the closeness of it.

But just like that, Mika left his side, crossing to stand opposite him in the makeshift circle. The audience—*classmates*, Arthur corrected himself, *Jesus*—murmured in anticipation.

"For this practical demonstration—" Professor Hirst made eye contact with Mika and looked like he immediately regretted it— "you need to demonstrate how movement and entropy affect the foundational principles of Evocation. Do you need a moment to confer?"

Arthur looked dubiously at Mika. He raised an eyebrow and offered him a rakish grin.

"It seems like Mika has a plan." Arthur's look of uncertainty was rivaled only by Professor Hirst's.

"That it does." Their teacher sighed, leaning back against the chalkboard. "Do your worst."

Arthur made eye contact with Mika and they walked toward each other, wands up—a well-rehearsed opening to a duel. When they were only a foot away, tradition dictated the way they crossed wands, nodding politely. The smile playing on Mika's lips worried Arthur more than it reassured him.

He made to turn and walk back to his spot—the next movement in the practiced sequence—but Mika grabbed a hold of his hand to stop him.

Arthur watched, bemused, as Mika brought his hand to his shoulder.

Arthur blushed, horrified, as Mika brought his own hand around to Arthur's back, drawing him closer.

Their classmates screamed their approval.

"I hate you," Arthur whispered with all the vitriol he could muster as the smell of Old Spice filled his *everything*.

Mika's smile spread into his full signature grin before he leaned in closer so Arthur could hear over the cheers:

"Do you?"

It was a good thing Mika had chosen to lead, because Arthur's legs nearly gave out entirely. It was a good distraction, because in all the closeness and the sound of Mika's smile in his ear and the hullabaloo of the students, he didn't notice Mika gesturing to Tan—didn't notice Tan touching their wand to a speaker adorned with one of the Auratech charms from the new batch.

Music filled the room, just barely loud enough to reach Arthur's ears over the students' roar, and before he could protest, Mika was guiding him in a dance.

An all-too-familiar song filled the room.

Their classmates started singing along, and Arthur's groan went unheard. He had a terrible feeling he knew where this was going.

As Nat King Cole crooned "L-O-V-E" once more, Arthur allowed himself to be led. Just when he was wondering what this had to do with the objective of the quiz, Mika moved his wand where it was still crossed with Arthur's.

Arthur followed and, as was second nature to him now, allowed himself to Sense Mika's intent in the way the particles gathered around their wands.

Together, they drew moisture out of the air, out of the breath of their friends' voices, out of Professor Hirst's long-suffering sigh, and cast it into a fine mist through the air. The kinetic energy of their dancing amplified the magic in their wands and when Mika moved to spin Arthur out, he used the centrifugal force to harness the weak sunlight coming through the window, magnifying the light rays and bending them to create swirling rainbows in the air above them.

Mika spun him back in and Arthur couldn't contain a smile.

This was *cool.*

They continued dancing and making magic together throughout the dance break of the song, swooping their arms up together to levitate for a moment, waving their wands to and fro in tandem to turn the mist into dancing clouds, throwing rainbows and sparkles of light over the heads of their delighted classmates. Arthur didn't know where Ben Lasher had acquired a single pink rose, but he threw it into the circle, and Mika managed to catch it and place it in his teeth. As they spun, petals fell, accumulating in the air until they were dancing in a whirlwind of them. The students chanted the last chorus of the song at a reckless decibel, and Mika beamed through the rose stem and Arthur was breathless with laughter.

Mika brought the dance to a close by suddenly dropping Arthur low in a dip, revolving petals falling slowly to the ground around them with nothing left to direct them. Mika leaned in close, *too* close, until they were nose to nose and their classmates were yelling and stomping and pounding the floor and Arthur's heart was up in his throat and Mika's eyes were sparkling with mirth and his breath was dancing over Arthur's lips and Arthur's eyes fluttered shut, completely wrapped up in the moment—

And then Mika bypassed his mouth, leaning in to kiss Arthur's cheek instead.

Without tongue.

The song ended and students broke out in raucous applause and suddenly, hollers of approval.

Arthur's eyes snapped open as Mika lifted him to his feet, and he looked down.

The rose petals had all cascaded down to the floor, spelling out the letters:

'SOCIAL?'

Arthur whipped his head to look back at Mika—who had the biggest shit-eating grin on his face to date—and then to his classmates, where Ben Lasher and Tan were holding the speaker with a bouquet of pink roses and giving an enthusiastic thumbs up, and then to Professor Hirst, who'd crossed his arms and still looked weary but was smiling fondly despite himself. He didn't look the least bit surprised.

Arthur tried to glare at Mika, but his face refused to stop smiling.

"Bastard," he whispered.

"Is that a yes, genius?" Mika was still smiling shamelessly.

"Spring Social isn't in the contract," Arthur muttered.

"We'll iron out the details later," Mika returned, and he threw an arm over Arthur to crush him in a side hug as their classmates surged forward to lift them both on their shoulders and carry them out the classroom door.

Professor Hirst let them all go. It was only fifteen minutes into the class period.

20

The weeks leading up to Spring Social finally, blessedly, started to fly by.

Arthur had expected that he'd eventually be able to put the dream behind him, that the vivid memory of *lick-suck-bite-'I'd like to get to know you better'* would fade with time. But if anything, knowing Mika had shared almost exactly the same experience had instilled the exact opposite effect. Every look exchanged was laced with the communal knowledge of what their mouths felt like at each other's throats, and even the accidental brush of a hand came with the inextricable Sense of electricity. When they were in a room together atoms buzzed at a high frequency and Arthur's left palm twitched and, more often than he cared to admit, his pants became uncomfortably, embarrassingly tight.

But it was easier to recover from these high-octane encounters with an event to plan for.

With *clothes* to shop for.

Avoiding alone time with Mika was easy now that he had an endless stream of excuses:

"I can't; Clarke needs help planning a virtual Social proposal for his alleged boyfriend."

"I wish I could, but we're measuring Jonathan so he can get a suit made!"

"I know my friends wanted to order their boutonnieres, so let's invite them, too."

As crystal clear as the dream remained in his mind's eye, Arthur found it easier and easier to concentrate on his schoolwork again. Though he begrudgingly missed the company of Mika's study sessions, he stubbornly refocused on the fun of being in Clarke and Jonathan's room, quizzing each other back and forth. Or the deep focus he could attain when he was alone in his room at night, nose buried in a book, absorbing knowledge and taking notes at the speed of light.

But Arthur would be lying if, on those nights alone in his room, he claimed not to be overcome with frequent, sudden urges to run across the hall and demand to be let into Mika's room for less-than-studious reasons.

Mika's breath on his neck haunted his days and nights; the sound of his smile in Arthur's ear resided in the back of his mind rent-free. It was maddening, dizzying—but he needed to stay focused. Mika was a challenge, a distraction from his goal, and being a little more tight in the pants than usual was *not* going to derail Arthur from his plans.

One day Arthur woke up on the first gloomy day of March, and the next day woke up in the second week of April to sunshine and crisp air. During the weeks in between, Arthur had found himself with, as per usual, perfect scores on quizzes (real ones), exams, and finally, midterms. He also found himself sneaking glances at Mika's scores, also infuriatingly perfect. But there was no time to plot, not with the flurry of activities and obligations leading up to Spring Social. There was nothing for it; Arthur had to hope he'd think of something before finals rolled around.

The first weekend after midterms—and the last Saturday before the Social—Clarke and Jonathan were in Arthur's room, commandeering a pair of console controllers they'd rigged to Arthur's laptop with the assistance of Auratech charms.

Clarke, predictably, was losing. "God, *stop fucking doing that.*"

"What—playing the game the way it's meant to be played?" Jonathan beamed.

"No," Clarke snapped. "Pushing me off the damn edge of the damn thing—"

Arthur had tucked himself into the couch as his friends leaned back against it on the floor. He stretched to prop up his feet on the coffee table beside the laptop.

"Have either of you followed up on the boutonniere order?" Arthur winced as Jonathan's character combo-punch-kick-special Clarke's. "It's been a month."

"No Mom, I thought you were gonna do it." Clarke's fingers on the controller were clicking madly—seemingly at random, and likely hoping for the best.

"Do I have to do everything around here?" Arthur grumbled.

"Ask the group chat." Jonathan waved him off before letting out a victory cry.

"Again," Clarke snarled as their scores tallied on the screen, and Jonathan obliged, starting a new game.

Arthur pulled up the group chat that Tan—who'd asked Clarke to Social platonically (read: out of pity) after Clarke's boyfriend said he couldn't make the trip—had started for their Spring Social party.

> Has anyone checked in on the boutonnieres?

> And Julia's corsage

Several people started typing immediately.

TAN
> I called yesterday! They'll be ready to pick up Saturday afternoon

JULIA
> Thank youuu

> Thank god, someone competent in this group.

Arthur's heart leapt once he saw Mika come online. He scolded it sternly.

MIKA
> excuse me, who was the one who thought to order them ahead of time in the first place???

> Were you expecting a gold medal or...?

MIKA
don't make me take back my social proposal

I wish you would <3

JULIA
I'm still in disbelief I made you two soulmates

Sometimes I wonder if I made a terrible mistake

I think the same every day <3

TAN
Y'all are too much!!

MIKA
that's what pham said last night

Bye.

Arthur, feeling far more pleased than was appropriate, was about to put down his phone and ask for a turn at the game, but it buzzed once before he could.

MIKA
oh my lord the shoes!!!!!!

how much???

And if he thought he'd been too pleased *before*.

He couldn't help but smile. He'd sent a picture of the designer dress shoes he found at the consignment store in *Watergraafsmeer* the day before. They were exactly what he'd been looking for to complete the fabled all-discounted Social outfit.

Guess.

MIKA
200?

Less.

MIKA
150?

> Less.

MIKA
?? 100??

> Less.

MIKA
what the fuck!

> €50.

MIKA
OH MY GOD

MIKA
i am CONVINCED you have a literal magical gift for bargain hunting

> I call it my Shopping Sense.

MIKA
related or unrelated to soulmate sense?

"Look how cute I am," Clarke crooned, maneuvering his player into a frilly, sparkly spin-kick.

"Maybe if you spent less time on the outfits and more time on the actual gameplay you wouldn't lose so often," Jonathan pointed out. His player knocked Clarke's off the platform again.

"My queen!" Clarke cried. "You killed her, you bastard!"

His character used her last life to revive herself and he hunched over his controller with renewed vigor. Arthur smiled and returned to his phone.

> Speaking of soulmates...
>
> How does Cherry feel about Social?

MIKA
we're gonna meet there

> She's cool with you taking me?

MIKA

why is it that i'm always reassuring YOU about MY girlfriend?

I'm just checking! Jesus, you're an ass.

MIKA

You LOVE my ass, more like it

Arthur's cheeks flamed and he side-eyed his friends warily. They were still entirely enthralled, now arguing about who'd chosen the best outfit for their player.

I'd love to kick it to the curb, more like it

MIKA

that's not what my soulmate sense says

at midnight

when you're up late studying

i wish you WOULD come to my door

Arthur's heart launched into overdrive. The bastard *knew*, god dammit, he *always* knew and he just *had* to lord it over Arthur's head. He composed several retorts one after the other, unhappy with all of them. Mika put him out of his misery before he could settle on a comeback:

MIKA

i told you it was only natural

Arthur couldn't stop the memories, too close to the surface of his mind, from flooding back in—Mika pressed up against his side, fingers at his neck, lounging on the couch, hair mussed, straining against his pants. He struggled to catch his breath, as if the air had been gut-punched out of him.

Blinking, he came back to himself and raised his defenses in place immediately, locking his Sense around him. He had a new notification.

MIKA

god, you're too easy!!!

> You need to get your Soulmate Sense recalibrated.
>
> And stop snooping, perv.

MIKA
> I'm the perv??

> Some of us have the maturity to leave well enough alone.

MIKA
> sounds like y'all need to get laid

> Sounds like you need to mind your own business.

MIKA
> i would, but the guy right across the hall from me is literally so tangibly horny that it's impossible for me to do so

Arthur wanted to melt into the bed, through to the floor, and then *into* the floor, and then die.

> I hate you.

MIKA
> do you?

> ugh mom's calling again. seeya tomorrow

Arthur lowered his phone face-down to the couch and stared up at his ceiling, willing his face to cool. Now he had to guard his defenses in the comfort and privacy of *his own room?* He dragged a hand down his face, then held it out to stare at it.

Michael Rivera. Dark as night, stark against the cold white of his palm.

This had gotten so, *so* far beyond his control.

He started as Jonathan gave an uncharacteristic scream.

"What the fuck?" He stared at the scores tallying on the screen. Arthur was surprised to see that—

"*Ha!*" Clarke shoved Jonathan. "Proof! Femme aesthetic supremacy!"

"Cute outfit nothing, you got lucky."

"Sore loser."

"Sore winner."

Jonathan wrestled Clarke back and Clarke screeched. "Stop fucking around, you're gonna mess up the laptop."

As if on cue, the dropped controller disconnected from the makeshift TV and jerked it dangerously close to the edge of the coffee table. The screen went black.

Clarke turned to Arthur. "Stop sexting your boyfriend and reassure our poor, naive friend while I fix the laptop."

Arthur swallowed hard, put on a brave face, and nudged Jonathan's leg with a socked foot.

"When will you stop playing video games together?" he scolded. "It never ends well."

"He's the one who wanted to play," Jonathan hissed, seizing the controller back into his possession.

"Stop fucking with the wires!" Clarke protested, holding onto the laptop for dear life.

Jonathan put his hands up in surrender as Clarke secured their delicate wiring system, then put up his own hands in deference to the security of the setup. Once the main menu of the game reappeared, they both settled back against the pillows, as Clarke picked up his controller once more.

Arthur scooted across the couch to steal the controller out of Jonathan's hands and chuckled at the betrayal in his expression. As he scrolled down the start screen to select his character, he resolved to set up a spell jar to protect against Mika's nosy Sense.

Maybe one of these days he *would* go knock on Mika's door at midnight.

Just to see what would happen.

21

"Arthur, where's your blow dryer?"

"Under the sink," Arthur called out to Clarke from where he sat in front of the full-length mirror behind the door, lining his eyes with kohl. "But I don't have a diffuser."

"Not for me." Clarke's voice was muffled as he rifled through the cabinets in Arthur's bathroom. "For Tan."

"Still not clear on how your boyfriend is fine with you taking someone else to Social." Jonathan appeared in the mirror behind Arthur, adjusting the knot of his velvet smoking jacket.

"Alleged boyfriend," Mika called out from where he was struggling to untangle his bolo tie at Arthur's desk.

"Not you too." Clarke heaved a long-suffering sigh. "And it's not my fault he's broke. Ah! Here it is—Tan?"

Tan clicked over to the bathroom in their heeled boots. "Thanks, darling."

The sound of the blow dryer swallowed all other competing sound in the room. Arthur capped his eyeliner and looked up.

Mika was staring at him through the mirror and Arthur's heart lurched as they made eye contact, watching as one moment turned into two. Finally, Mika's face sank into something mournful as he held up the tangle of tie. Arthur rolled his eyes, swiveling to get up off the floor.

"Amateur," he muttered, swiping the tie from Mika's incompetent fingers, stomping down rabid curiosity at just how competent those fingers might be in favor of pulling his wand out of his back pocket. He closed his eyes and tapped it to the tangle, slowly deciphering the pattern of its atoms and coaxing them to unravel themselves.

"Are you a wizard or not?" Arthur thrust it back at Mika, but he was smiling.

Mika looked down so he could arrange the bolo tie under the collar of his white shirt. "Will you do my makeup, too?"

Arthur raised his eyebrows.

Mika grinned up at him from beneath thick eyelashes, tone sardonic. "You make it look so pretty."

I'd like to get to know you better.

Arthur blushed and broke eye contact. "Clarke is the master. He taught me."

"Did somebody say 'makeup master'?" Clarke sidled up to them out of thin air, now donning his tux—a pale pink brocade number. He was halfway through his own face, blush highlights high up on his cheekbones, a couple shades of shimmering pink eyeshadow on his lids.

"Nothing too crazy." Mika fingered the shimmering suit jacket hanging on the back of Arthur's desk chair. "Maybe a little gold? Here and there. Or something."

He looked away, blushing. It was cute.

Arthur shook his head. *Dumb.* It was dumb.

"I'll leave you to it." He clapped Clarke—already digging through his makeup kit—on the shoulder, retreating to the bathroom where Tan and Jonathan were jointly working on their hair.

"Where is Julia meeting us again?" he asked Jonathan, scooping a finger of product from a jar and running it through his own hair. He coaxed one strand to fall artfully over his forehead.

"At the venue." Jonathan was teasing his hair up with a small comb. "That'll be easier. She's getting a limo with some of her Featherwood friends."

"Smart," Tan agreed, before Arthur deemed his hair *utterly perfect* and retreated from the bathroom.

Clarke was still working on Mika, so Arthur relinquished his suit jacket from its hanger, standing in front of the mirror once it was on to make sure all was in order: black mandarin-collared shirt, black jacquard suit with gold fleur-de-lises, and black brogue dress shoes.

All thrifted or purchased on sale, for under €150. Just as planned.

"Alright hon', you're good to go," Clarke announced with a flourish where he stood in front of Mika. "Do *not* touch your face for the rest of the night. Arthur?" He gestured over at him. "Your approval?"

Arthur obliged, crossing to the desk to replace Clarke, who hurried back to the bathroom to harass Jonathan.

"Just a little blush," Clarke bargained.

"Fuck off," Jonathan protested.

"Mascara?"

"No."

"Highlighter?"

"Only if it's gold. Yellow undertones, remember?"

Arthur chuckled, making sure Tan had a handle on breaking up their tussle before returning his gaze to Mika.

His breath caught in his throat, and Arthur wished he'd been given some kind of warning.

Clarke had studded the outer corners of Mika's browbone with scattered gold rhinestones, and the sparkle caught in Mika's hazel eyes as he looked up at Arthur. His face was swept with subtle, shimmering gold: at his cheekbones, just under his thick brows, down his nose, and at the cupid's bow above his lips.

Arthur's hand tingled. His whole body tingled.

Those lips, at his throat, at his ear, smiling, whispering—

"What do you think?" A grin stole across Mika's lips and with a jolt, Arthur realized he'd been staring at his mouth.

He blinked a couple times.

"Like what you see?" Mika's voice was low, the shit-eating grin easing into something lopsided, easier, lazy. Arrogant.

"Yeah, I mean. You, um—"

'I wish you would come to my door.'

Arthur blinked slowly, shaking his head. "Clarke is a makeup genius. He did you well."

"He's not the only one." Mika winked.

Arthur's heart skipped in his chest. "In your dreams."

"Literally."

Clarke's yelp startled them; Jonathan had won the tussle.

"Ass," he muttered at Mika's grinning face.

"Boutonniere time!" Clarke announced, steering all of them to the coffee table. "Jonathan is on picture duty, since Julia's putting his on when we get there."

He handed Jonathan a clunky-looking Polaroid camera with an Auratech charm attached.

"Old-school," Tan remarked.

"It's my dad's," Clarke bragged. "I Enchanted it to use perfect exposure, every time."

"Impressive." Arthur took the camera from Jonathan, turning it upside down to look for the battery cartridge. "Can I see—"

Clarke snatched the camera and handed it back to Jonathan. "We're on a schedule here, nerd. You can study the Enchanted camera tomorrow."

Arthur pouted, but accepted defeat and turned his attention to the coffee table to locate the case containing two simple burgundy camellia boutonnieres. He watched as Clarke pinned a pink boutonniere to Tan's long fur coat. Jonathan leaned down, trying a couple angles, before snapping a picture.

"Well?" Mika said expectantly.

Arthur turned. He tried to look somewhere right between his eyebrows, finding it difficult to look directly into his eyes, maddeningly dark and bright at the same time.

"Well, what?" Arthur frowned.

"Aren't you going to put mine on?"

"Put your own on," Arthur muttered.

"That's not very *boyfriendly* of you," Mika said from behind clenched teeth.

"You first, then," Arthur hissed, hoping his blush didn't betray the way his heart stuttered.

Mika gave him a patronizing look but relieved Arthur of the plastic case pointedly, opening it to retrieve one of the boutonnieres and moving close to take hold of Arthur's coat.

Arthur's body flinched of its own accord.

Against all odds, he'd managed to avoid being trapped alone with Mika since that day in the bathroom. But here and now, in the intimacy of his own room and with Mika in that cream and gold brocade suit...even with friends to act as a buffer, he was not capable of being within five feet of Mika, let alone within inches of him, not after—

Mika's mouth languishing at his neck, licking and sucking and biting—

Inexplicably—irresistibly—still as vivid as ever.

"You good?" Mika said in a hushed tone as Tan worked on Clarke's boutonniere. "You've been acting cagey all night. More so than usual, sweaty-hands."

"Stress," Arthur lied, swallowing hard. "Midterms took it out of me."

"Well relax, genius," Mika smiled wickedly. "I don't bite."

Oh, yes you do. Arthur's mouth went dry.

Mika's face couldn't have been more than five inches from Arthur's as he took his lapel, working to get the pin through it. Every brush of fingers against his chest through the shirt, the breath between them, those brows furrowed over eyelashes too long and too thick, his mouth full and accented gold, relaxed out of the grin Arthur had become so accustomed to—Arthur was spellbound, unable to wrench his eyes away or think about anything but—

The words on his palm tingled, a too-familiar sensation now.

Michael Rivera.

And then Mika was gone, leaning down to pick up the remaining boutonniere.

"Your turn," he said softly, and Arthur could have sworn he caught a knowing glint in Mika's eyes. It sent blood rushing to his face—and to other much less convenient places.

Willing his fingers to stop shaking, Arthur took the pin from Mika.

Static sparked where their fingers met.

Mika retracted his hand, clenching it, and Arthur's heart was off to the races as he moved in closer to reach for his lapel.

Mika was warm under the jacket. Arthur could feel Mika's breath on his own cheek as he tried to ease the pin in gently, and he cursed his damned fingers and their numbness. He reached his other hand in further to brace the jacket more solidly and found that he could feel Mika's heart, beating a steady rhythm hard against his chest.

Though he hadn't dared since the night before winter holiday, Arthur's Sense reached out of its own volition, searching.

Mika's heart was thrumming, heady as a drum, and Arthur's heart raced to match it as he saw a burst of colors again, this time black and gold and deep red, swelling and swirling and that too-big feeling latched in Arthur's gut once more, unfathomable but undeniable, terribly exciting and terribly frightening—

But above all that, in bold overtones: bone-deep, gut-wrenching, heart-clenching *need*.

Arthur's eyes snapped to Mika's, bright and dark, and he felt him Sensing right back. He was powerless to block him, flooded with Mika's *want-want-want* and unable to distinguish it from his own. He'd been convinced that Mika had been messing with him, utterly unbothered and holding the dream over Arthur's head to torment him. But now...

Now, he realized that with one hundred percent certainty, *Mika wanted him, too.*

He forgot himself in their shared Sense, one indistinguishable from the other. He only knew the soaring triumph of a desire requited, finding himself magnetized, eyes latched onto those lips, parted and shimmering just there, and he couldn't help the way he started to lean in—

The loud clack of the camera cut through the spell, and he jumped and dropped the boutonniere.

"Nice," Jonathan smirked as the Polaroid worked its way out. "This one's gonna be good."

He threw it face-down on the table with the others as Arthur scrambled to pick up the boutonniere. He hastily attached it to Mika's lapel.

"Sorry," he muttered. His pulse felt deafening in his ears. He wasn't sure exactly what he was sorry for.

"Don't be."

That grin was back, dimmed down to soft and lazy—one that was quickly becoming Arthur's favorite.

He stifled a noise that threatened to climb its way out of his traitorous mouth.

"Everyone ready?" Tan was looking at their phone. "The car gets here in ten."

"Perfect timing." Clarke reached into his bag on the couch and pulled out a fourth of cinnamon whiskey, Summoning five shot glasses.

Mika whooped, raising a fist in the air as he moved to help Clarke fill the glasses and pass them out. Arthur took his numbly, still in shock from their exchange.

"Bottoms up," Clarke announced, and everyone downed their shot.

The spicy liquor bloomed warm in Arthur's stomach, loosening the tension in his limbs. He glanced at Mika, who met his eye as he wiped his mouth with a thumb.

Arthur looked down quickly.

"One with all of us." Jonathan picked up the camera once more, turning it toward himself and stepping up onto the couch. Arthur had half a mind to protest—that was *real* leather—but then Clarke was scooting in front of him, arm linked with Tan's, and Mika had sidled in out of nowhere, snaking an arm around Arthur's waist. He pulled him in close, and Arthur had just enough time to compose his face into what he hoped was the smile of a totally sane person before Jonathan clicked the shutter.

"Five minutes," Tan called, checking their phone again as Jonathan added the new photo to the others on the table.

Everyone chorused their approval before making their way toward the door. Arthur and Mika walked in silence down the hall as the others laughed and shared a flask amongst themselves, and when they got in the elevator, Mika slung an arm over Arthur's shoulders. Without thinking—seduced by the closeness, egged on by liquid courage—Arthur eased his arm around Mika's waist and snuck a hand into his back pocket.

He heard Mika smile.

"We'll have to add that to the contract," he murmured close to Arthur's ear, sending a chill down his spine.

Arthur swallowed, hard.

This was going to be a long night.

22

After a fifteen-minute rideshare comprising passing of the flask, flashes of the Polaroid, ribbing Clarke about his alleged boyfriend, and more stolen glances at Mika—radiant and flushed and laughing—than he cared to admit, their disgruntled driver brought the car to a stop. Arthur found himself ushered out of the vehicle and through a line full of formalwear-clad classmates to flash his ticket (purchased by Mika) and into a nondescript building painted in a festive shade of blue.

It was anything but nondescript on the inside.

Through the door to the venue was a vast room; a bar stood directly to the right on the back wall, housing a suspiciously innocent bowl of punch and various tiered stands of appetizers and treats. Before him was an industrial warehouse filled to the brim with plants, arching up toward the sky in planters surrounding the walls of the room. Above was a vast greenhouse ceiling, open to let in the fresh night air through which bubbles and seafoam and sequins and glistening, glimmering streamers of turquoise and coral and cream floated, glittering in their movement.

Already there was a group of Stonebury and Featherwood students at the head of the courtyard, dancing under the stars to something with a funky beat that Arthur was confident he'd heard more than once in Ben Lasher's room. On the right wall was a keyhole-shaped entryway to a large room scattered with square tables and chairs, painted 3D plaster on the walls depicting the rolling waves of a sunset scene.

"Come on!" Clarke wrenched Arthur out of his reverie, grabbing his wrist with one hand as the other steadied the Polaroid camera around his neck. "Snacks!"

"Wait—there's Julia!" Jonathan waved as they all made their way to the crowd around the bar. Clarke busied himself with taking dutiful pictures of Jonathan and Julia as they exchanged corsage and boutonniere. Tan took it upon themself to art direct the photoshoot, and suddenly, Arthur found himself very much alone with Mika.

"Punch?" Mika smirked at him, taking a sturdy, plastic margarita glass from the stack beside the bowl. Arthur peered suspiciously into the foamy, pink, fruity-smelling concoction.

"Why not." He shook his head as Mika ladled what Arthur was beginning to believe was liquid, radioactive cotton candy into the glass. He took a sip and nearly choked.

"Holy shit." He braced the glass on the table, coughing. "Spiked."

"Excellent," Mika said in a low voice, pouring himself a glass and downing half of it in one go.

Arthur watched his Adam's apple bob and, already feeling tipsy, took a large sip of his own Pink Monstrosity.

"Pour me one, will you?" Clarke returned with Jonathan and Tan in tow.

Between Arthur and Mika serving, everyone had their drinks in only a minute, and Clarke dropped several canapés onto a pale pink plate.

"Let's go," he said through a mini chocolate cupcake, which Arthur had no idea how he'd managed to sneak in, considering how full his hands were with camera, drink, and canapés. "Let's drop our stuff off so we can dance."

Arthur blanched. "I don't know if I want to dance just yet," he protested as the group towed him along across the courtyard and through the keyhole entrance to the other room. He chanced a glance at Mika, who'd already removed his jacket and was starting to push his shirtsleeves up to expose very shapely, very nice-to-look-at forearms.

He suddenly, *viscerally* understood why Mika was always staring when Arthur rolled up his own sleeves.

"Sure you do." Jonathan grinned as they reached the table, politely extracting Julia from her coat to drape it over a chair. "What the hell else is there to do at Spring Social?"

"I can think of at least one thing." Mika's smile was downright sinful as he made eye contact with Arthur across the table. Arthur glared daggers at him, clasping the chair in front of him in a death grip.

"Save it for the afterparty, Fabio." Tan rolled their eyes with a smirk, elbowing Mika.

"Fine." Arthur cleared his throat, willing his heart to climb back down out of it. "But I'll need at least another drink. If not seven."

"That can be arranged," Clarke encouraged, gently placing one hand at Arthur's back and the other under his elbow, encouraging him to partake in the margarita glass he already held. "There you go," he cooed soothingly.

Arthur stomached the last sip and made a face. He hated vodka.

"You take this one." Clarke handed him his own glass. "I don't need help to boogie down."

And that's how—three minutes later—Arthur was three drinks in and packed, sardine-like, into the dance floor, swaying to an electronic beat and desperately trying to keep Clarke, Jonathan, Tan, and as many other errant bodies as possible in between him and Mika.

Clarke took his hand and twirled Arthur around so his back was against Clarke's front. Arthur stumbled and laughed, grinding down with his ass and effecting a loud cheer from Jonathan and Tan and other Stonebury students directly surrounding them. Clarke lassoed one hand in the air and grabbed Arthur's hip, letting out a whoop himself and gyrating wildly on Arthur, who laughed even harder.

He glanced over as he dipped down especially low and caught a glimpse of Mika, who was staring from several feet away and dancing side to side, mouth parted. He recovered quickly, smiling and sticking his tongue out between his teeth as he turned to dance next to Tan.

Arthur straightened, blushing, and turned around to face Clarke, taking his hands and moving them to and fro in a strictly PG-13 manner. Clarke didn't miss a beat, squealing with delight and allowing Arthur to spin him round and round.

Over the next ten songs or so, Arthur was passed from partner to partner—from Clarke to Jonathan to Julia to Tan—and their circle expanded exponentially. Arthur found himself dancing with one of the

Featherwood girls who frequented the parties (Molly?) and then even with Cherry, who'd made her way in and had been dancing with Mika for the past twenty minutes. Her hair was big and wild, a fun contrast to her vintage-looking champagne silk dress with a high neck that left most of her skin exposed. She beamed at Arthur from several inches higher than he remembered; a quick glance told him she was wearing bright red stilettos.

He smiled back, happy to find his presence was welcome. He put a chivalrous arm around her waist and took her hand, leading them in a waltz that was laughably inappropriate for both the time signature and theme of the bump-and-grind hip-hop number blaring throughout the room. Their dance ended with Cherry throwing her head back with laughter, yelling into Arthur's ear that she was going to be rid of her shoes, and imploring him to let Mika know where she'd gone.

And then he turned to find himself face-to-face with none other than Mika himself.

"Cherry went to go take her shoes off," he blurted. He was forgetting why exactly he'd been avoiding Mika in the first place.

"Tracks." Mika nodded.

Arthur seemed to have lost his grasp on the English language. A new song pulsed through the speakers, bassline dark and beat thrumming low. Mika wiggled his eyebrows suggestively.

Schooling his features into a neutral expression, Arthur huffed a determined exhale and started to move, taking Mika's hand but staying a safe, sensible one-to-two feet away from him. The beat was infectious; Arthur frowned his approval and dipped a little lower, digging down into the groove of it and pointedly avoiding Mika's gaze. The group around them crowded in as more people flooded the dance floor, forcing Arthur to reduce the space between him and Mika—closer to the one-foot side of the scale than the two-foot side.

An elbow appeared out of thin air to shove into Arthur's back, sending him stumbling forward into Mika. Arthur whipped his head around to tell off the offender only to find Clarke sporting a mischievous little smile and a wink.

The fingers in his own gave a tight squeeze and he turned to find Mika *far* too close—much, *much* closer than the sensible one-to-two feet he'd mentally measured so carefully—and grinning that roguish grin. He leaned in to Arthur's ear so his voice was audible over the music.

"Let's give 'em a show."

Arthur's heart kickstarted, hammering against his chest. *No no no...*

But *yes yes yes*, he realized, as Mika leaned back, hovering inches away, waiting for Arthur's response and gazing at him with eyes too-dark-too-bright, sparkling with mirth.

There was nothing for it. Arthur nodded.

Mika smiled and started to move again. Arthur felt as if his body was the tide and Mika and the music were the moon—the touches and the glances and the smirks he'd tried so hard to block out all evening, all month, all *semester*, came flooding back—the too-vivid memory of Sensing Mika, the *want-want-want*.

Against his better judgment, he was helpless against the urge to move, too.

And with that, Mika used his grip on Arthur's hand to turn himself around so his back was against Arthur's front, holding eye contact until the last possible moment.

Arthur's hand released Mika's, sliding across his stomach to rest on his hip. Arthur expected him to lean over like he'd done to ham it up with Clarke, but he found him close—closer than he'd ever had him, with Mika's back flush with his chest, knees bending to slot his ass back into Arthur's hips, making up for their mere inch of difference in height and then Mika was *moving*, hips grinding into Arthur's and maybe it was the heat of the dance floor, or the heat of Mika, or the heat of the alcohol in his veins, but something broke inside Arthur—maybe permanently, definitely for the worse, and so, *so* sweetly.

Arthur slung his other hand low on Mika's hip—anxiety and apprehension and confusion be damned—and rolled his hips forward, thrilling at how Mika met him at every thrum of the beat. Everything in his body screamed *yes!* and Arthur was drunk on it, drowning in heat and sweat and Old Spice and Mika and fuck, he *wanted* this.

Mika moved against him, moved with him, and nothing had ever felt so right. Arthur dipped low and Mika didn't miss a beat, leaning to dip down with him and something in Arthur's gut swooped dangerously—he was drunk and shamelessly hard and gripping Mika's hips probably a little too tight, but Mika didn't seem to care and, in fact, seemed to *like* it. He ground down harder, longer, slower, and Arthur was grateful for how the music drowned out the sound deep within his chest.

And—well, if Arthur thought they were close before, he was wrong. Mika slid one hand over Arthur's on his hip, snaking the other up behind Arthur's head to tangle in his hair as he dropped his head back onto Arthur's shoulder. His hand burned hot against Arthur's skin, where he knew his own name was branded.

"Fuck." Arthur's voice broke, and with it broke his willpower. His Sense got the better of him once more and it compounded Mika's want, his need, and—holy shit—*desperation* with Arthur's own, thrumming hard along with the undercurrent of the song.

Arthur couldn't help it—he buried his face in the crook of Mika's neck, high on *boy-sweat-aftershave-Mika* and his mouth moved of its own volition, seeking purchase at his collar—finding none, he lifted a hand to loosen Mika's tie and undo a button or two.

He tore aside the fabric and reveled in the taste of him, mouthing desperately, hungry for more.

"No tongue," Mika teased in his ear, but the way his voice came out breathless and low made Arthur think he didn't really mean it.

To prove it he doubled down, sucking at a tender spot and biting, lips grazing Mika's neck on the way up to his ear. He felt Mika's groan vibrating in his throat more than he heard it, and the force of it echoed around Arthur's brain, his Sense picking up and amplifying the *want-want-want*.

Teeth on Mika's ear and knowing what it would do to him, Arthur murmured:

"You want this. You've *been* wanting this."

In lieu of an answer Mika spun in Arthur's arms to face him, syncing up with a well-timed pause in the song. He latched his hands at Arthur's waist and slotted their legs together, swinging their hips to the beat as it dropped back in. That low, sweeping feeling in Arthur's gut made a startling appearance yet again when he found Mika hard against his leg. Arthur brought up an arm to sling over Mika's shoulder as the other—his left, love line burning red-hot—reached down to grip at his ass. Sense wide open, Arthur felt a coil spring loose in Mika, and then he was tilting his head to bite at Arthur's neck.

Overwhelmed by the music and Mika hard against him—*with him*—and his scent so close, heat mingling with his own, tongue on his neck, breath at his ear, Arthur ran his hands up into Mika's curls and wrenched him away, gasping for air and desperate to be closer all at once.

Mika met his gaze, sweat glistening on his forehead, rhinestones glittering at his eyes, dark and hooded. The hand at Mika's shoulder slid down to his loosened tie and Arthur tugged so Mika's forehead fell against his own. Their noses bumped, and Mika's eyes were too close to focus on now so Arthur brought his gaze down to his lips, open and golden and wet, and Arthur's left hand tingled, and his gaze fell out of focus as they slipped closer, millimeters apart, lips just barely brushing, breath mingling—

The song rapidly cut out in favor of a pop song from ten years past and the crowd around them screamed bloody murder in their approval. Arthur's Sense snapped back into him and he felt Mika's do the same as they met each other's eyes, coming back to themselves from the edge of something very, very precipitous.

"I'm gonna—" Arthur swallowed when his voice cracked— "I'm gonna get another drink."

"Right." Mika nodded, looking mildly dazed. "I'm—gonna find Cherry."

But Arthur had already pivoted. He fought through the crowd, desperate for fresh air and personal space. He finally made it to the bar and placed his hands on the cool copper of it, relieving the burning on his left palm. He sucked in a couple deep breaths, desperately grateful no one would be able to spot how hard he was in the dim light.

Let's give 'em a show.

To his horror, Arthur realized he'd been so all-consumed by Mika that he had no idea if anyone had been watching or not. It hadn't mattered.

He covered his mouth with his hand.

What was happening to him?

He pushed off the bar and stalked off to locate the bathroom and find the closest possible thing to a cold shower.

It was down a hall to the left of the dining room. Arthur splashed his face with cold water (thank god for waterproof eyeliner), slowed his breaths, calmed his racing heart, and was about to push the door open to rejoin the party when he heard voices just beyond the door in the hallway.

"Come *on*, Mika. It's getting insulting at this point."

"I don't know what to say, Cher."

Arthur eased the door closed again and banged his head back against the bathroom wall, fighting the infuriating sense of *déjà vu*.

"You're seriously telling me you feel *nothing* for him?"

"It's all for show, Cherry. We've been over this a dozen times."

"Mika, I swear, you're so—" She paused, and Arthur could imagine the exasperation on her face. The next words were hissed in an undertone, and Arthur could just barely make them out: "I can Sense it, dude. You forget the consequences of being friends for so long. You can't pull shit with me."

"You don't know what you're talking about."

"Okay, I didn't come here to get treated like I'm *crazy*—"

"I'm not—babe, I'm telling you there's nothing happening there."

"But..." Cherry paused. "Mika. I don't care if—I just want you to be happy. I'll always be in your life. But if you have a chance at something real—"

Arthur was startled to hear her voice break, lacking any semblance of jealousy.

He could hear the smile in Mika's voice when he spoke, and hated him all the more for it. *"We're* real, babe. I don't want you to worry about Pham, okay? Trust me."

"Meeks..." Her voice was muffled—Mika must have hugged her.

"Please," he said emphatically. She didn't answer, and he continued, "Let's go dance."

Footsteps, fading, fading, and finally gone.

A Year Three opened the door and Arthur opened his eyes at once, leaving the bathroom and finding himself in an empty hallway.

'There's nothing happening there.'

Something deep inside Arthur clenched uncomfortably. Cherry wasn't the only one feeling crazy.

He stalked down the hall to make his way back to the dance floor. No more looks, no more heat, no more wanting, no more Mika. He wasn't sure where his self-control had fled in his moment of weakness but it was back, and Arthur was done feeling out of control of his mind—of his body. Mika was a tool and nothing more. He couldn't allow himself to believe they were anything more.

Not even friends.

Arthur bypassed the bar. He was sobering up, and not in the mood to keep his buzz going. He worked his way through the crowd of sweaty bodies and finally spotted Clarke's pink brocade suit. He took his elbow and Clarke turned, thrilled to find Arthur on the dance floor once more.

"Everything okay?" he yelled.

"Bathroom," Arthur yelled back, and promptly started dancing next to him, putting on what he hoped was a convincing smile. It must have been, because Clarke whooped and started dancing in earnest, whipping his body from side to side.

Arthur chuckled weakly and tried to forget about Mika—tried to forget about his face *so close* and the *want-want-want*—in favor losing himself in the music, dancing next to his friends and under the stars beyond the greenhouse roof.

23

And he did manage to forget. For a total of about one hour.

"Students! Spring Socialites! The person who spiked the punch!"

Arthur turned from where he'd been dominating a line dance beside Jonathan to the DJ booth on the platform at the head of the courtyard to see Professor Stonebury, microphone in hand, clad in a sleek turquoise tuxedo and shining gold wingtips. He was accompanied by Mrs. Featherwood, at least a foot and a half shorter and wearing a coral suit and gold stilettos, strawberry blonde updo covered by a large witch's hat extravagantly decorated with seashells, starfish, and bubbles.

A hush fell over the crowd and with a start, Arthur remembered: *Spring Social Court.*

Mrs. Featherwood claimed the microphone for herself to announce the nominees for Regina Magum. Samidha DeSilva, Beatrice Olsen, and Cheryl Johnson—who turned out to be Cherry—made their way up to the platform to accept their satin sashes.

Stonebury took possession of the microphone once more. "And our nominees for Rex Magus: Benjamin Lasher!"

Ben Lasher—the man, the legend—stumbled up to the front, long hair half up in a man-bun and dressed in an unequivocally rented-looking black tux. He looked a little green, and Arthur hoped he wasn't close to throwing up. He was pretty sure whatever the punch was made of would burn holes in his beloved shoes.

"Arthur Pham!"

Dimly, he heard Clarke and Jonathan yelling at a disproportionate decibel as the crowd parted before him. He walked numbly up to the front and stepped up onto the platform to take his place next to Cherry, who gave a fleeting smile that didn't quite reach her eyes as she looked back down.

He suppressed the manic urge to apologize, instead trying for a convincing smile into the blinding spotlight before them.

"And, last but not least, Michael Rivera!"

The roar was absolutely deafening as Mika ran up to the platform, beaming and waving and bowing as if he was already jogging a victory lap. Arthur kept looking resolutely forward as Mika stepped up onto the platform in between him and Ben Lasher. Electricity thrummed, low and sparkling, in the foot of distance between them.

"And now," Mrs. Featherwood's voice rang out across the room, "the moment you've all been waiting for!" The crowd dimmed to an excited murmur as she produced a golden envelope from her suit jacket.

"Your Rex Magus is..."

Eyes all around the room darted from Mika to Arthur and back again, and Arthur wanted desperately to go home.

"...Michael Rivera!"

The crowd roared once more and Stonebury Summoned a cheap-looking plastic crown, placing it on Mika's head with great difficulty as Mika was aggressively pumping his fist and yelling along with the crowd. Suddenly Arthur found himself pulled close in an ironclad grip, and his heart gave an impassioned leap as Mika kissed him on the cheek. Autopilot kicked into gear and Arthur felt his face grin—felt his hand reach up to high five Mika.

"And your Regina Magum," Featherwood announced, "Cheryl Johnson!"

The Featherwood contingent lost their composure entirely as their headmaster Summoned a crown for Cherry, who met Mika in the middle of the stage so she could draw Mika into a hug, smile stiff and eyes stony. They shared a look when they pulled apart and turned to the audience to hold their hands in the air, drawing screams more raucous than ever before.

"And now," Mrs. Featherwood and Professor Stonebury chorused, "The Social Court takes to the floor!"

The crowd parted to form a circle at the front of the courtyard. Cherry descended the platform, bypassing both Mika and Arthur in favor of reaching up to Benjamin Lasher's arm, encouraging him to step down off the platform to join her. The blonde, Bea, met a long-tan-and-handsome guy from Arthur's class on the dance floor, and Sam pulled a small black-haired girl wearing a boutonniere matched to Sam's fuschia dress onto the dance floor from the crowd around them. They all started revolving as the opening notes of "La Vie en Rose" rang out through the speakers.

With a start, Arthur realized what he was now expected to do. He looked out of the blinding spotlight and down at Mika, who had stepped off the platform and now held a hand up to Arthur, smile full to the brim with humor.

"May I have this dance?"

The spotlight had burned stars in his vision, and Arthur cursed how his heart beat hopefully, how his love line tingled unhelpfully.

He took Mika's left hand with his right.

Mika led him to the circle where the other couples were revolving slowly. He stopped to face Arthur and clasped their hands together, sliding his right one around Arthur's waist as Arthur brought his left arm up over his shoulder, shaky legs grateful to be led.

After this, he resolved, albeit weakly, *I'm done. After this.*

"How you holding up, genius?" Mika said quietly, so only Arthur could hear.

Arthur chanced a glance up and immediately regretted it, enchanted by the warm glow of Mika's eyes, rhinestones glimmering in the spotlight.

Arthur took a deep breath and dug down deep—far deeper than expected—to find the part of him that still hated Mika with every inch of his being.

"As well as I can, being within ten feet of your sorry ass."

But he broke off near the end, breathing out a laugh.

"Hm." Mika looked thoughtful. "You didn't seem to feel that way about my ass when it was backed up on your—"

"Please." Arthur closed his eyes and held up his left hand to stop him, but he couldn't stop a smile from touching his lips. "Spare me from reliving my most shameful memory."

Mika chuckled and didn't push the issue further, allowing Louis Armstrong to serenade them in peace.

"Hey, isn't this the song Julia played when—"

"Yeah." Arthur swallowed. "It is."

It seemed so long ago, when the idea of being attached to Mika in any destined way had sent Arthur spiraling into a panic attack, when he still despised the touch of Mika's hand in his own, when he felt nothing but loathing and rage at the sight of his face. And now...

Now there was something else beside the loathing—maybe even in its place. Something blossoming warm, deep down, something terribly exciting and terribly frightening all at once.

Arthur kept his Sense locked up far away. He didn't want to know what it would find right now.

He didn't think he'd be able to bear it.

"How long is this going to go on?"

The words slipped out of Arthur's mouth—he wasn't sure he could be held accountable for anything he said under the influence of Mika's eyes, trained on his, like *that*.

"What?" Mika's voice was barely above a whisper.

"This." Arthur wet his lips. "Us."

He bit his lip. Mika looked up and blinked a couple times.

"I..." He shook his head once. "I don't know, Pham."

Arthur considered this, trying to line his feelings up in a neat row. His insides were so tangled it was an impossible task.

"Do—" Mika cleared his throat softly— "Do you...want it to stop?"

Arthur looked up quickly, surprised to find that Mika's face was gut-wrenchingly earnest—eyebrows set in place, eyes only for Arthur.

He didn't know what to make of it. He didn't know what to make of *any* of it. Of this, of tonight, of the past five months. His promises to himself, made mere moments earlier, to end it, to put a stop to it all—

They were, inexplicably, nowhere to be found.

"I don't know, Rivera," he said, truthfully.

"Well," Mika said softly, and he was much closer now, cheek hovering next to Arthur's, "then why stop?"

Arthur's eyes fluttered shut.

Why, indeed?

Mika spun Arthur out one last time and when he spun back in, they found themselves nose to nose. Mika secured his grip on Arthur's back and leaned him into a dip; the rhinestones at Mika's eyes glimmered too close in Arthur's vision and his heart swelled three times its size, left hand sparkling so intensely that it seized up, clutching at Mika's suit jacket. His right hand bloomed suddenly with warmth and Arthur realized it held Mika's left, love line heating in his grip. The song came to an end and they were so close—just as close as they'd been on the dance floor before—but this felt different somehow. This felt *more*.

Mika straightened slowly, keeping Arthur close. The crowd around them started to flood back onto the dance floor as the DJ skillfully bridged the gap between Louis Armstrong and Top 40 pop, but Mika was looking at Arthur, and Arthur was looking at Mika, and Arthur had never seen this look on his face—the pensive set of his features, eyebrows drawn up in the middle.

Although maybe he had, once or twice.

"Arthur," Mika said, and it was the fourth time Mika had ever said his name.

He could have sworn Mika's eyes started to close, that he started to lean in just that much closer...

But out of the corner of his eye, Arthur spotted Cherry, watching.

Against the flow of the tide, against the magnetism of orbiting planets, withstanding the way the words burned into his left hand screamed in protest, he took a significant step away and out of Mika's arms.

Mika stared, arms outstretched, before he realized Arthur was looking just past his shoulder. He turned to find Cherry, smiling, eyes glassy with tears. She looked beautiful in her dress, in her red heels.

"Cher—" Mika started to speak, undoubtedly to explain—but explain *what*?

What would have happened if she hadn't been there?

Mika took a step toward her but she clasped her arms behind her back, taking a step back and biting her lip, squeezing her eyes shut and shaking her head.

"Meeks..." She opened her eyes and she was still smiling, but a single tear escaped, falling down one cheek. "I'm done."

"Cherry."

Arthur wanted to scream, wanted to promise her that this was all a mistake, a farce, a comedy of errors—he didn't want Mika, and Mika didn't want him, and this was all just a show that had gone on for too long—

But he didn't.

He couldn't.

Mika surged forward to capture her face in his hands but she got there first, catching them and squeezing them tight, tears falling freely. She spoke too quietly to hear over the music, but Arthur could see, could Sense—and he watched in frozen, horror-struck shock.

"I love you." Her smile broke. "I always do. But what we have..."

She glanced at Arthur, then back to Mika.

"...it isn't *that*."

She released his hands and turned, retreating into the crowd.

"Cherry!" Mika ran after her, pushing through the throng of students. "Cherry! Wait!"

Students filled the space where he used to be, surrounding Arthur as they danced, too drunk or too oblivious to realize what happened. He stared at where Mika had been—where Cherry had disappeared.

"Shit," he whispered.

24

Arthur really, *really* wanted to go home.

So why the hell was he in Molly and Bea's suite at Featherwood, perched on the arm of a leopard-print chintz chair, feet aching in his shoes, with an abhorrent, unidentified alcoholic concoction in hand?

He hadn't touched the stuff, and he had half a mind to dump it out the window and hope that no drunk stragglers were making their way home underneath it. Hell, he had half a mind to bum a Broom off one of the Featherwood girls, or even spring the money for a rideshare. It was one in the morning, and he was dead tired, and he was only here out of obligation to his fake boyfriend, who hadn't so much as *looked* at Arthur since Cherry broke up with him at Spring Social not even two hours ago.

In fact, his only tether to anything other than his bed was currently at the kitchenette on the other side of the room, half-concealed by incense smoke, holding his cheap plastic Rex Magus crown as he tilted his head back to yet another shot with Ben Lasher and Tan. Clarke and Jonathan had bid Arthur goodbye at the venue, promising brunch the next morning and making various un-subtle winks and nudges and inappropriate hip gyrations regarding his prospects for the night. He'd ached to go with them, to drag himself home and put off the tumultuous conflict until morning, escaping for a blissful eight-or-more hours of sleep—

So why the hell was he here?

He kept replaying the night's events in his head, trying to figure out where he'd gone wrong. He had to conclude it'd been much, much earlier than tonight.

The replay always ended with Cherry's face, broken and unspeakably sad, cheeks tear-stained and mouth painted red, twisting out of its brave smile.

He really, *really*—more than *anything*—wanted to go home.

Arthur took a sip of the drink in his hand and pulled a face. He hated vodka.

He stood and took another sip, summoning the courage to tell Mika he was finding a way home with or without him as he strode through the scattered crowd of ten-or-so people to get it done.

"Well, look who it is!" Mika drawled once he caught sight of Arthur. He stumbled to him, arms wide open and throwing one over Arthur's shoulder. Arthur smiled tightly and cursed the way his body gravitated toward Mika's warmth, his touch—the way he felt his insides (and outsides) twitch with interest despite the high-speed rollercoaster they'd been subject to for the past six hours.

Scratch that—six months.

"You know," Arthur tried weakly, "I think I'm just gonna—"

"Play a drinking game with us, right?"

Arthur frowned as Mika steered him toward the center of the room. "Sorry, what drinking game am I being coerced into, exactly?"

"A *new* drinking game." Mika leaned in to emphasize the word, but over-corrected and stumbled. Arthur caught him. "We just made it up. Just now."

"It's like all the best drinking games rolled into one," Benjamin Lasher finished for him. "Plus Twister."

"That sounds...entertaining, to say the least." Arthur raised his eyebrows. "But you know, I'm pretty tired—"

"Aw," Mika whined, leaning more of his weight onto Arthur, who had to hold him with both arms now to keep them from falling over, and the last thing Arthur could handle was being tangled up with Mika, horizontally, on the floor. "Get that stick from out of your ass, Pham!"

Arthur bristled, feeling his patience creep still further past empty. "Having a proportionate level of exhaustion from dragging your drunk ass around all night does *not* mean I have a stick up my ass, Rivera," he snapped. "Get over yourself."

Benjamin Lasher and Tan snickered, exchanging looks before continuing on and leaving Mika staring at Arthur like a kicked puppy.

"Sorry," he slurred, swaying. "You're right."

Arthur blinked. "Yeah. Yeah, I am."

Mika also blinked, and forgot to open his eyes. "You can go. Shhhould I call you a rideshare?"

Arthur peered at him, suddenly wary. "How much have you had to drink?"

Mika started to count on his fingers, going slightly cross-eyed. "One at yours, some in the car, three at Social, and then, one, two, three...four. Five? Six?" He started giggling.

Arthur's heart stuck. His mind provided him with the high-definition image of Mika passed out god-knows-where, surrounded by drunken chucklefucks that didn't know left from right, choking on his own vomit—

He was tired. He was so fucking tired.

"Okay," he sighed. "I'll stay."

"Hooray!"

"*If*—" Arthur pried the Homebrew beer out of Mika's grasp— "If you switch to water for the rest of the night."

"But I'm almost done," Mika pouted, snatching the bottle back, and raising it to his lips. He gulped once, twice, three times, and downed half the bottle in one go.

"Ooookay," Arthur laughed without humor, disquieted, wrenching the bottle away again. "Water now?"

"Cherry." Mika shifted from joviality to sorrow in the blink of an eye, and Arthur's stomach dropped uncomfortably. "She...she..."

Arthur closed his eyes and swallowed. "Water now?"

Mika came back to himself. As much as was possible, ten or more drinks in. "Water now," he agreed.

Arthur steered him back to the kitchenette to fetch a water bottle, abandoning his own drink on the counter. He turned from the fridge to find it in Mika's hand.

"Ooo, what's this?"

He managed to take a large gulp before Arthur snatched it away.

"Why do you turn into a certified toddler when you're drunk?" he hissed, shoving the water bottle into Mika's chest. "If you want to drink so bad, drink this."

Mika turned his mouth down at the water bottle. "Too full."

"*Now* you're too full," Arthur muttered. "Do your best then, I guess. Or I'm leaving and dragging you with me."

Mika obediently took a small sip, and Arthur steered him over to the gathering in the middle of the room.

"Okay, okay." Ben Lasher stood on the coffee table, addressing the crowd. "Everyone ready?"

A resounding cheer traveled around the room.

"Great. Everyone needs a drink."

Mika peered closely at his water bottle. "Wait...wait. Hey. *Hey, I need a drink—*"

"Nope!" Arthur grabbed his arm to force it back down, wrestling another arm around his shoulders to quiet him. "No, no—he's got a drink. He's got a drink!"

Sufficiently convinced of Mika's beverage (or the lack thereof), Ben Lasher began to explain the rules of the game. Mika promptly latched on to Arthur's arm, linking it with his own, and leaned his head onto Arthur's shoulder to make a comfortable sound.

"I like you," he mumbled.

Arthur's exhausted heart gave a start, and he took a deep breath. *He's drunk,* he scolded himself. *He doesn't like you. He hates you. And you hate him.*

Arthur sighed. It almost sounded convincing.

"I like you, too." Arthur patted his head before tilting the water bottle up to Mika's lips. "Now drink up."

"Okay, Mom," Mika scoffed, and Arthur was relieved to see his usual infuriating sense of humor coming back.

"So!" Ben Lasher's voice rang out, and Arthur whipped his head up. "Everyone got it?"

"Wait." Arthur panicked as everyone else in the circle affirmed that yes, they had indeed heard the rules, which Arthur hadn't heard because he'd been tending to Mika. "Wait, what are we doing?"

But nobody heard him.

"*Okay!*" Benjamin Lasher screamed. "One, two, three, go!"

Everyone around Arthur held different numbers of fingers up to their foreheads, and he scrambled to do the same, holding four fingers up and looking around frantically. Everyone started making a racket, partnering off according to number, and Arthur wheeled around to find Mika also holding a four to his head.

"Christ," Arthur heaved. "You have got to be kidding me."

"We're boyfriends!" Mika slung an arm around him as Arthur let out an existential groan. *"Boyfriends!"*

For the next half hour Arthur found himself in more compromising positions than he thought he'd ever find himself in his entire life, including, but not limited to: leaping from couch to table to floor pillows (because the floor was lava, obviously), going head-to-head with Tan at a three-round game of Twister, quizzing a drunk Mika on various facts about the sex-work industry in Amsterdam, and pouring the contents of a bottle of vodka into Molly's mouth while reciting the alphabet backwards. No one seemed to mind that Arthur and Mika were nursing water bottles instead of alcohol. Mika was drunk enough that it didn't matter, and Arthur was so tired he was sure he was passing as drunk anyway.

Finally, Ben Lasher rang a gong on Bea's desk (where had that come from?) and gingerly (drunkenly) hopped across the room on pillows and chairs back to the coffee table. He brandished the Twister-spinner-turned-roulette-wheel listing various activities, one of which being a minuscule sliver—sandwiched between *'Spin the Bottle'* and *'Truth or Dare'*—with an arrow assigning to it in crammed letters: *'Everybody go the fuck home.'* Arthur was, perhaps unrealistically, holding out hope for this outcome.

"Round and round it goes!" Ben Lasher yelled, spinning the wheel aggressively.

"Where it stops, nobody knows!" chorused the rest of the crowd. Arthur felt a headache coming on.

And actually, it really did almost land on *'Everybody go the fuck home.'*

But by a fraction of an inch, the arrow passed by sweet relief in favor of *'Spin the Bottle.'*

Another cheer rose from the party-goers, and Arthur's stomach dropped.

This is fine, his frantic brain reasoned as the ten people of the group formed a circle on the ground. *It's a one-out-of-nine chance.* Ben Lasher

retrieved an empty Homebrew beer bottle from the kitchenette. *There's no way you'll have to kiss him.*
Mika caught his eye from across the circle, smiling lazily.
It's not in the contract, he thought weakly.
"Rules and regulations!" Ben Lasher called over the chatter, rattling off a list without pausing, let alone taking another breath. "One we go clockwise two no more than ten seconds per kiss let's keep it age-appropriate people three you can deny a kiss by taking a shot and four if you spin the bottle on your teammate you get seven minutes in heaven after your kiss everybody got it?"
"Got it!" the crowd chorused again as Arthur's head spun faster than the Twister-spinner-turned-roulette-wheel.
"We start with whoever pooped last!" Ben Lasher decided.
There was a tense moment as everyone tried to ascertain who could lay claim to this title, over which Molly—on Arthur's left—got close to a fistfight with her boyfriend, a Year Three from Stonebury. "It was me, dammit!" She raised a righteous fist in the air as Bea hooked her arms under Molly's to hold her back in a surprising display of strength. "I literally took a shit *at* Social, eat me!"
Idle chatter cropped up among the crowd and Ben Lasher seemed to sense his control over their collectively short attention span was fading fast. "Okay, okay, okay!" he pointed to Molly, who plopped back down next to Arthur, sweaty and disheveled in her frothy mint-green cocktail dress. "Molly goes first, mostly because I'm afraid she'll beat the living shit out of anyone who challenges her."
Molly let out a victory roar, both fists in the air this time, before leaning forward to spin the bottle. It landed on Bea, and amidst cheers and giggles from everyone in the circle, they traded a kiss with great showmanship.
No matter how desperately Arthur willed them to stretch out the process—maybe even long enough to let everyone get bored and get up to go home of their own accord—in time's cruel way of doing just the opposite of what you'd like it to do, the next four turns went by in the blink of an eye.
And so, before Arthur knew it, Mika was spinning the bottle.
Arthur closed his eyes, nerves too shot to watch. His heart beat in his throat, and he seemed to have forgotten how to breathe uncon-

sciously; every inhale was a monumental effort of will, and he had no hope of counting them, as he'd forgotten how to even count to ten.

The ambient, ubiquitous noise of the group died away into silence. Arthur opened his eyes slowly, one at a time.

The bottle was, undeniably, unwaveringly, pointed at him.

He snapped his gaze up to Mika, and even as his heart skipped a beat against his will, he schooled his features desperately into a look that read: *'Don't even think about it, Rivera. It's not in the contract, and you know it, and I think I might legitimately have a heart attack if I have to come within breathing distance of you* again *on this night.'*

Apparently, this was just too much meaning to cram into one expression, because Mika was grinning now, and he was casting aside his third empty water bottle of the night, and he was crawling across the circle *Dirty Dancing* style—they really needed to diversify their reference material—and everyone was hollering and whistling—

And then he was in Arthur's lap.

And then his hands were framing Arthur's face.

And then Mika's gold-studded eyes found his.

And then Mika was kissing him.

Arthur's heart soared and his brain, in a moment of uncharacteristically good judgment, shut the hell up. For a breathless two seconds Mika had his lips pressed ungracefully to Arthur's in that way first kisses always go because you weren't really ready for it—before you learn how your face fits with another person's.

And then Mika shifted, smiling into his mouth, and Arthur had room to part his lips, and that's when sparks *really* flew.

Mika tasted like booze but also like something deeper, closer to that *boy-sweat-skin* taste when he'd given Mika a hickey, though somehow so much more. Arthur felt as if every atom in his body was lit up, and he was sure he must be radiating light everywhere Mika touched him: the hands on his face, the knee at his thigh, the knee at his hip, the roughness of Mika's chin against his own. Mika kissed the same way he gave hickeys—like it was the only thing he did day in and day out, lazy and slow and confident, and Arthur would be lying if he said it wasn't the best damn kiss he'd ever had.

Mika's tongue brushed against his bottom lip and Arthur inhaled sharply, opening his mouth to welcome more and Mika was hard against him, giggling as he straightened the plastic crown on his head and for the second time that evening Arthur was hard, too, fully ready to give in to the *want-want-want—*

But the cheers were turning ugly in his ears as they melted seamlessly into a chant:

"...eight...nine...ten!"

And Ben Lasher's voice cut through the applause. "Okay, okay, break it up lovebirds! Good news though—seven minutes in heaven!"

Mika surfaced first, leaving Arthur dazed and dizzy, left hand throbbing in time with his heart. He met Mika's gaze for a split second before Mika looked away in favor of their audience.

Sitting there, lips kissed wet and red, heart hammering in his chest, something clicked.

'There's nothing happening there. Trust me.'

Mika hammed up a victory lap around the circle, stumbling and laughing, and Arthur watched him—watched him bask in the attention with complete disregard to Arthur and what he thought, what he might be feeling, or how Mika's actions might have affected him—

Arthur blinked his eyes closed, feeling like he might burst.

This was the final straw.

Blood rushed in his ears and shook his very limbs as he was ushered to his feet by Molly and Ben Lasher and escorted to a bedroom at the far end of the suite. Mika led the charge, stomping like a grotesque marching band leader to the beat of the crowd chanting, "Se-ven mi-nutes! Se-ven mi-nutes!"

And then they were thrust into the room, door slamming shut behind them.

25

The chanting was dimmed from behind the door:
Se-ven mi-nutes!
Se-ven mi-nutes!
"Well, you heard the people." Mika's shit-eating grin made a glorious comeback as he crossed the space between them with open arms and an arrogant stride. "Come give Daddy a kiss."

Arthur's heart roared and, when Mika got close enough, he backhanded him across the face.

"Ow! What the—"

"What the fuck is wrong with you?!" Arthur blurted—louder than he should have, but he didn't give two fucks if anyone heard anymore. From the way they continued their chant, he doubted they could.

"What's—with *me?* You're the one—"

"No." Arthur held out a hand as Mika threatened to come nearer, shaking his head. "No, I'm *done* with this bullshit. I'm done being used as a plaything, as a way for you to get attention, as a—a—" Arthur sputtered, glaring at his hands— "as a way for you to *earn points* with these people, to soak up some twisted sense of glory—"

"Arthur. No, I—"

"Don't call me that. You don't get to pull that, as if you *know* me, as if you care."

Arthur's rage whipped into a frenzy, a storm so thunderous it left no room to recognize the upward draw of Mika's eyebrows, nor the way his smile vanished.

"But I do—"

"You don't!" Arthur shouted. "The arrogance is astounding, Rivera. How entitled could you be, to explicitly violate our agreement—and not only that, but to mislead me the whole way leading up to it? Why do you think I wrote it all down in a contract? Because I *knew* this would happen."

"I—"

But Arthur was too far gone. "I knew you would traipse across lines, devil-may-care. You're so full of yourself that you think you can get away with it, you think you can just—get away with using people to get what you want because you're so charming, and handsome, and popular—"

Mika stuttered his protest and Arthur ignored him. "Well, guess what? Kissing on the mouth isn't in the contract. Period. You disregarded our agreement. Blatantly. I told you my boundaries, and you crossed them—nay, *trampled* them—"

"Now hold on a fucking second." Mika finally got a word in and Arthur paused, chest heaving, glaring. "That is *not* fair."

"It literally is," Arthur shot back. "Do you want me to Summon the contract? From halfway across town? I'll fucking do it."

"Shut up about the damn contract, Pham!" Mika's hold on his temper looked tenuous. "You have a charming habit of assuming the intentions of other people. You want to talk about misleading? Sure, let's do it. Let's talk about the *mystifying* signals I've been getting for months—where you give me a hickey like no one has given me a hickey before in my life and then a month later tell me you want it out of the agreement, only after—*oh*, and don't get me started on the fucking dream—"

"That was—"

"—which I thought we were cool about, texting constantly and buying boutonnieres and sending pictures of shoes and teasing, no, fuck—you know what? I'll say it: *flirting* and—and then you dance with me, not once but twice at Social, looking at me like you could *eat me the fuck up—*"

"That's—"

"I can *Sense* you, Pham. I can Sense you, and I know you can Sense me, and you know what?" Mika crossed his arms, features reverting to a familiar arrogance. "This act you're pulling right now? When I know, and you know, that you kissed me all the way back?"

"Don't," Arthur warned.

Mika leaned forward. "Methinks the lady doth protest. Too. Much."

Horror crept through Arthur's veins.

"How dare you." His voice was dangerous.

"I said what I said." Mika held his ground.

"How dare you assume—"

"How dare *I* assume?"

Arthur was breathless with anger and panic and the sudden, utterly unexpected sensation of fleeing for so long only to realize he'd been running in a circle. "How bold of you—how presumptuous, how *arrogant* to think that just because I—"

"Tell me I'm wrong, Pham."

"You're deluded."

"Why are you being like this? I had that dream, too. Why is it so hard for you to believe that I kissed you not because it was some fun and wild thing to do for popularity points, but because I wanted to?"

This was too much for Arthur to take in at two in the morning, trapped in a stranger's bedroom and forced into a confrontation with a denial that had been brewing for the better part of his Year Four.

"Well, if you wanted to kiss me so badly," he ground out, "you should have just asked."

Silence filled the room. Tension sparked in the air, static electricity between them. Even the chanting outside the door had stopped.

Arthur was startled to find himself on the edge of tears, buckling under the weight of the night, of the past several months...of what he'd just said.

Mika was still—so still that Arthur had to pay close attention to make sure he was breathing. His signature grin was nowhere to be found, and his eyes were fixed on Arthur's, who felt incapable of looking away. Several of the golden rhinestones at Mika's brow had disappeared throughout the night. Arthur held his breath, waiting for Mika to crack, to smile and look away and make a joke, to pretend once more like nothing of significance was happening between them —*had* been happening between them—for quite some time now.

Mika took a breath, on the edge of saying something, then mashed his lips together. He opened his mouth again, then closed it. And finally:

"Can I?"

He said it so quietly that it was barely audible, the expression on his face so open—so vulnerable—that Arthur's heart surged painfully.

He was angry—he was overwhelmed—he was so, so tired—but he rode that feeling like a wave and it carried him three steps across the room to surge forward, answering Mika's query by kissing him straight on the mouth.

And there was no ungraceful pressing this time.

Mika had been waiting for him, ready to gather Arthur up in his arms and kiss him as if he needed it—like he needed air to breathe. There was nothing arrogant in it this time, no one watching and no one to impress. There was only Mika and Arthur and the way Mika slid his tongue into Arthur's mouth, and the way Arthur drew him in all that much closer for it, sliding his hands up into Mika's hair to angle his face just so and sending the stupid plastic crown tumbling to the floor.

Mika kissed him like he was starving, and Arthur drowned in it. He let himself believe for a mere moment that Mika was being honest—that he really was struggling with the same dilemma that Arthur was, that he wouldn't just straighten and throw away a grin and a joke and pretend like nothing happened. Arthur sucked at Mika's lip and bit down and Mika made a sound into his mouth that made Arthur want to keep him forever, close, hands seeking purchase and noses bumping together—there was nothing more divine, and Arthur slid his hand down Mika's arm to claim his hand, to rub his finger over the letters branded there, his name spelled on Mika's love line the way Mika's was branded on his own.

Mine.

He broke away for air and Mika chased him as if being apart might be the end of him. Their lips lingered throughout one, two, three more kisses before Arthur leaned their foreheads together. He met Mika's eyes, desperate to convey meaning there—to make him understand what he could not yet understand himself. Desperate, he extended his Sense and that deep-down feeling latched in his gut as he found the feeling was precisely requited—that he wasn't alone.

"Arthur," Mika breathed into his mouth, and that made it six times. "You have *no* idea how long I've been waiting for that."

But Arthur could Sense it—the confusion, the heat, the want. It was as potent and all-encompassing as it was that day outside Mika's room, that night before winter holiday, and during. Something satisfied nestled itself within Arthur's chest.

"Mika."

And that made it once.

Arthur searched Mika's face, trying to read the emotion there, to match it with what he Sensed. He felt at a loss, and his heart was still beating hard, and Mika's face was close—too close—and it was warping, and Arthur's vision was swimming, heartbeat landing somewhere in between his ears.

"Arthur?"

But it was all too much—the second kiss, the first kiss, the second dance, the first dance, and Social and this agreement and this year and Arthur was so tired and his nerves were shot and he didn't remember the last time he'd felt calm—felt anything other than on edge, and how had he let things get so out of control? How had he gone from needing to come out on top of Mika to needing to be *on top* of Mika and how had he strayed so far from the goal?

He pushed away from Mika, away from the searching, sparkling eyes and the Old Spice and the kiss-bitten lips and the pressure of his Sense pressing in on his own and he tried to count his breaths, in-one-two, out-three-four, in-six-eight—

"Arthur, what—"

"How did I let this happen?" Arthur hated how breathless his voice was, how hard his heart was pounding in his throat. He buried his face in his hands "This wasn't supposed to happen and I—"

"What do you—"

"—I only signed up for this harebrained scheme because I thought it was the only way to beat you, to find a way to come out on top because I had to." He swallowed, helpless to contain the words tumbling out of his mouth, vision going fuzzy around the edges. "You've always been ahead and I need to get Electi Magi, otherwise—*I had to*, and now everything is upside down, I got way in over my head and you—and you're—"

"You..."

Something in Mika's voice halted Arthur in his tracks. He whipped his head up to look at him, clutching the bedframe next to him as the room spun dangerously.

"All of this...was because you wanted...to beat me?"

Arthur's heart picked up a pace he didn't think possible. "Wait, no. I mean, yes, at first—"

"This was about the rivalry?"

"Just, I don't—wait—"

But the door slammed open and a roar of noise came rushing in to join them and *whatever* was blossoming between them...*whatever* was wilting and dying before Arthur's eyes.

"Time's up!" Ben Lasher announced. "Also, the party is collapsing in on itself. Molly and Bea are kicking us out. We're gonna go back to mine and finish up the last of the weed, wanna come with?"

Arthur looked to Mika, who avoided his eyes. He felt so far away now, farther than the three feet that separated them. The ephemeral magic—of being together, alone, unscrutinized and free from the pressure of their classmates—had fled, leaving the atmospheric equivalent of a semicolon, a sentence established yet unfinished, complete yet unsure. Arthur wanted nothing more than to shove Ben Lasher back outside and explain to Mika, explain everything he'd kept locked up inside the box for so long—no more secrets, no more lies or schemes or anxieties. He extended his Sense desperately, yearning to convey this to him—

But there it was: that trademark grin, locking the vulnerability away deep inside once and for all, far from Arthur's grasp—as solid as a physical wall to shut out Arthur's Sense. Mika stooped to retrieve his plastic popularity prize, placing the crown back on his head at a jaunty angle.

"Yeah man, let's do it. Ready, babe?"

Mika met his eye and held out a hand but the spark was gone, hidden behind the facade once more. He was no longer speaking to Mika, the earnest equal, the vulnerable ally, the wounded...*something*. This was Mika, the Rival, the Rex Magus, the Fake Boyfriend.

Arthur reeled, and the dreadful drop of his stomach told him something was awfully wrong—had changed irrevocably. His brain kicked into autopilot as his inner world, up in the air alongside Mika not one minute ago, escaped freefall and landed sideways.

"Yeah," he said. He felt a smile place itself on his face. "Well, I'm going to bed. But I'll catch the car home."

"Great." Ben Lasher obviously remained oblivious to the intricacies of what he'd just witnessed. "Calling it now."

He pulled out his phone and turned away from them to walk back into the suite's living room, and Mika met Arthur's eye briefly before dropping his hand.

"Mika—"

Twice.

Mika shook his head as if to clear it and smiled. "Wow. Wow, I am so drunk."

Arthur's heart was falling, falling—

"Yeah," he whispered, then cleared his throat. He was more sober than he'd been in his life. "Me, too."

As he followed Mika out of the bedroom, he wondered if he'd become so tired that he'd fallen asleep and was dreaming. If this was all just a very, very vivid nightmare.

Mika kissing him as if he needed it, like he needed air to breathe—

As he followed the Stonebury crowd out of the Featherwood dorm and out onto the street, he wondered if the punch had been spiked with something more insidious—if he'd hallucinated it all.

'This was about the rivalry?'

As Arthur stared out the car window, he wondered how he'd so hopelessly lost his way.

Mika promised the other boys he'd meet them after walking Arthur to his room, and Arthur wished he'd never gotten wrapped up in this business in the first place.

'You have no idea how long I've been waiting for that.'

As he stood across from Mika in the hall between their rooms in the dim pink light of the fluorescent signs dotted along the wall, he found that those words didn't feel true, and he got the distinct feeling he was in the presence of a complete stranger.

After an immeasurable amount of time, Mika spoke up, only briefly meeting Arthur's gaze.

"Well." He raised a hand and grinned. It didn't reach his eyes. "Seeya."

He made his way down the hall, back toward Ben Lasher's room, and Arthur stood blankly, his brain lagging several steps behind him.

"Wait," he finally managed.

Mika stopped, turning slowly.

One last time, Arthur reached out his Sense and again, he was blocked by floor-to-ceiling walls. If Mika could feel him reaching out, he showed no trace of it in his face.

Arthur reeled it back in, aching. If it weren't for his racing heart—his tingling left hand, the trace of Mika's lips on his own—he'd have thought they hadn't been kissing, so close, *too close*, not half an hour ago. Something had gone terribly awry and, as always, Mika was the one dictating what happened, and when, and Arthur was left trailing in the dust, struggling to keep up.

What had he done?

Arthur took a deep breath, forcing a smile.

"My Evocation notes." He didn't recognize the sound of his own voice. "I need them back next week."

Without missing a beat, Mika returned the smile easily. "You got it."

He moved to round the corner but paused, turning and not quite meeting Arthur's eyes.

"Also." Mika swallowed, allowing the ghost of a grin to grace his face. "Don't worry about keeping up the act anymore."

He retrieved and twitched his wand, Summoning the contract from Arthur's room. He twitched twice more, tearing the page out of the book and tearing it in half in an instant before Sending it all back.

"You're off the hook, genius."

And then he was gone.

Arthur began to hurt somewhere in between his ribs.

He wrenched the door to his room open and slammed it closed behind him. He stripped down to his underwear, tossing his suit aside and the jacket hit the coffee table, upsetting the stack of Polaroids there.

Arthur stared. He picked up the one that had fallen to the floor.

It showed him and Mika, Arthur's fingers fumbling with the boutonniere at Mika's lapel. Their faces were in profile, but the expressions there were poignant. Arthur was staring at Mika's mouth, cautious, unsure.

And Mika was staring at Arthur's downcast eyes, face soft and open and *wanting*.

Arthur blinked at the photograph for a moment more, and then tossed it back to the floor.

It's not real, he thought viciously. *It was all an act.*

His breath was staggering out of control as he crossed to his bed, sitting with his head in his hands and trying to work through his breathing exercises.

In-one, out-two, in-three...

Mika kissing him like he was starving.

Out-fourteen...shit. In-one.

'This was all about the rivalry?'

Out-twelve...*fuck.*

Too exhausted to shower and brush his teeth and focus on his breathing, too wide-awake with the memory of kissing Mika—*kissing Mika!*—spinning around and around his head like a broken record, Arthur tipped sideways to lie on his pillow, praying for sleep that would never come.

26

On Sunday, Arthur woke up—well. He hadn't really fallen asleep in the first place.

On Sunday, Arthur got out of bed because he was sick of trying to fall asleep.

He spent the morning in a stupor, body aching with bone-deep exhaustion, brain overthought to shit, heart strung out and thrumming weakly and doing its best to keep it all running. He worked his way through a shower, brushing his teeth, and tidying up his room. His stomach attempted a backflip when he compiled the Polaroids into a neat stack.

Mika hard against him, giggling as he straightened the plastic crown on his head—

Arthur sliding his hand down Mika's arm to claim his hand, to rub his finger over the letters there—

'This was about the rivalry?'

Arthur felt a ghost of warmth in his gut, a ghost of a surge in his heart, a ghost of his stomach bottoming out with guilt.

You failed, his brain supplied. *You completely, utterly, distinctly fucked up.*

He reeled with loss of the Electi Magi plan—lost to shit long before last night. He reeled with the loss of his friendship with Mika—ruined, the all-encompassing, frightening and exciting potential of…of…

Of whatever *this* was.

Whatever *this* had been.

He swayed on his feet, feeling faint with it all.

He slid the photo of him and Mika under the first three.

Clarke and Jonathan picked him up for brunch at nine. He didn't even have to explain the bags under his eyes; Clarke made a squealing comment about getting lucky, took Arthur's lack of response as a coy confirmation, and continued in his debrief of the night. If his friends could Sense what was wrong, they said nothing. Arthur had a feeling he was so exhausted that his aura was diminished to practically nothing anyway.

He didn't notice his friends watching him carefully as he tucked into his *uitsmijter* at *Ontbijt*, exchanging glances.

For the rest of the day, Arthur resolutely Did Not Think About It. He read the same line in his Evocation textbook over and over, tidied his room three more times, autopiloted through a workout routine, floated ghost-like behind Clarke and Jonathan for dinner, and above all else, avoided running into Mika—at all costs.

On the way to brunch, he didn't even look at door 420. On the way back from brunch, he could have sworn he heard a lock click, and he stole away into his room so fast he forgot to say goodbye to Clarke and Jonathan. All day his weary heart gave a panicked leap every time he heard voices in the hallway, every time he heard a door open and close. Anxiety coursed through his being from dawn till dusk and it was the only thing keeping him upright, torn between desperate hope to hear a knock on his door and desperate hope that he would be left alone.

But, as it turned out, his internal debate was for naught. Not once did Mika even make a sound from behind his door, let alone emerge from it. Arthur didn't have the energy to even attempt to Sense his presence there, let alone to find out if last night was a fluke, an ephemeral meeting of ships in the night—before he'd fucked it up. Fucked it up *so* spectacularly.

He wasn't sure if he even wanted to know.

Around three he sat on the couch, staring at the name on his hand.

Michael Rivera.

He must have *really* been tired, because he could have sworn it faded three half-shades lighter under his scrutiny. How could he even begin to make things right?

Don't. Don't think about it.

Arthur survived until the sunset, when his hindbrain took over and lulled him, at last, to sleep.

On Monday, Arthur woke up with a plan.

With a full night's sleep and a fresh start, he faced the day with resigned conviction. There was no use fretting and fussing alone in his room. He and Mika had a professional agreement as a foundation and the terms of the agreement had been breached; this alone warranted a discussion to get back on the same page, to return to a state of normalcy...even if Mika had torn up the contract two days ago.

But if Arthur could just apologize and explain, he was sure Mika would address him with that careless smile and tell him to forget about it.

He practiced the speech in his head over and over as he got ready for the day.

'I wanted to apologize for Saturday.' He took a shower, scrubbing at his face. *'I've been under a lot of pressure, and after everything that happened, I snapped.'* He made his bed. *'When this first started, I hated you. I'll admit I used to think I could use this as a way to finally come out on top.'* He donned his uniform, packed his bag. *'But then we actually became friends and...more, I hope? I don't want to throw it all away.'*

Arthur closed his eyes, pinching the bridge of his nose. *And then what, moron? You ride off into the sunset together and get married and have adopted babies? In what universe?*

If he was being honest, Arthur had no idea what he wanted. But he knew he'd been in denial for a long, long time. He had to own up to his mistakes.

As if on cue, a knock came on his door: *shave-and-a-haircut.*

Arthur collected his stammering heart and locked it up in his ribcage, striding to the door to open it with a shaking hand.

Mika looked roguish as ever, a mirthful smile on his face. If it didn't quite touch his eyes, Arthur told himself he didn't notice.

Except he forgot to speak. And so did Mika.

Arthur opened his mouth, but no sound came out. The air was thick enough to slice, as if the previously buzzing particles between them had come to a sudden halt, and Arthur knew without even trying that his Sense wouldn't be able to penetrate air that solid.

After what could have been one second or one hour, Arthur broke eye contact and rushed to speak.

"Iwanttoapologizefor—"

"I've got your Evocation notes."

Arthur halted. Mika rummaged in his bag. Arthur opened his mouth to speak again, but Mika held out the notebook, silencing him.

Arthur frowned, determined. He tried again. "I don't—Mika, I want to—"

At the sound of his name, Mika's eyes snapped back to Arthur's, eyebrows drawn. He began to say something and Arthur found his heart beating desperately despite himself, found the speech fleeing from his mind, found his entire being straining to hear what Mika was going to say—

And then Clarke and Jonathan rounded the corner.

He turned to look at them and desperately back at Mika, but Mika had already stalked off, walking so fast he was already almost at the end of the hall.

Arthur closed the door behind him as Clarke and Jonathan slowed their approach.

"So," Clarke started, side-eyeing Arthur. "Y'all good, or...?"

Arthur pressed his lips tightly closed. "Disagreement," he managed. "He needs...space."

Clarke and Jonathan exchanged looks.

"Do you..." Jonathan hesitated. "Do you wanna talk about it?"

"No." The word was out of Arthur's mouth before he'd consented. "But—" He caught the shaken look on their faces. "Thanks. Thank you. I'm okay."

It was the most egregious lie he'd told all year.

"Just let us know." Clarke made a brave attempt at a smile and led the way to breakfast.

The irony of being unable to get Mika alone after spending the better part of a month avoiding it was not lost on Arthur. What he wouldn't give for the previously dreaded brushing of hands in the hallway, being shoved into a classroom together, being texted a summons for an afternoon study session.

How had so much changed over the course of a night—nay, a semester? A school year?

Mika wasn't in Evocation until just before the bell rang, so late that even the seats next to Arthur were occupied. He disappeared before Arthur could open his mouth to call his name when the bell for lunch rang, and was surrounded by friends at lunch and before Transmutation started. Arthur stood abruptly as soon as the last bell for the day sounded but Mika didn't so much as look his way, let alone give him an opening to speak. He left the classroom side by side with Ben Lasher, deep in animated and unbothered conversation.

Arthur threw his bag over his shoulder, launching himself into the crowd of students and out into the hall, power-walking out of the building and into the courtyard. If he was fast enough, he might be able to make it back to the dorm before Mika did.

He was breathless by the time he reached Room 420, but he'd done it—he heard the elevator ding down the hall as Mika and Ben Lasher's voices emerged from it.

Arthur's heart gave a powerful lurch, and he scrambled to look casual.

He heard a distant door open and close, and the voices disappeared.

His breath left him in a rush, wind stolen from beneath his sails.

But he was still determined. So an organic meeting was out of the question—no problem. As he entered his own room, Arthur pulled out his phone to compose a text.

> I was hoping we could talk.
>
> Are you free later tonight?

He placed his phone face down and opened his Transmutation book, determined to get back to his usual revision schedule. Mika had always responded promptly to his texts; there was no way he'd just flat out ignore him.

At least, that's what Arthur thought.

An hour of Evocation homework later, Mika still hadn't responded.

After half an hour of practicing wandwork for a complicated Cooling technique, Arthur still had no notifications.

After fifteen minutes of cleaning his spotless room: nothing. Twenty minutes of organizing the desktop of his laptop: nothing. Forty-five minutes of yoga: nothing.

Arthur stared at his phone, willing the text to come.

It didn't.

He tossed his phone on the bed and looked toward the door. Well. Mika couldn't stay away from his room forever.

He joined Clarke and Jonathan for dinner, hoping he'd be able to wrangle Mika into joining them on their trek back to the dorm. But Mika was nowhere to be seen, and Arthur spent the hour giving his friends monosyllabic answers to questions and letting them lead the conversation.

Back at the dorm, he could have sworn he saw a head of perfectly mussed curls loping around a corner and out of sight. But before he could catch up to see, Clarke tugged on his arm and insisted on getting ahold of Arthur's Conjuration notes from earlier that morning. Unable to come up with a good enough excuse on the spot, Arthur acquiesced, fuming in silence.

By bedtime, he was ready to give up. The energy and determination with which he'd started the day was long depleted, and the speech he'd practiced over and over spun round and round his mind, heart wrung out from a day of anticipating confrontation and meeting none.

He closed the book he'd been failing to read at the desk and stood up, resolving to get ready for bed and try again tomorrow.

But in an instant, his left hand twitched—the trace of a tingle along his palm. He barely heard it: footfalls outside his door, the slight *bong* of the crystal reader recognizing the resident of 420.

Arthur launched himself to his door, wrenching it open.

Mika was halfway through his own door, ready to close it definitively shut.

"Oh no you don't," Arthur growled, taking two long strides and closing an iron grip on Mika's arm.

"What—"

But his protest turned into a *whoof* of air as Arthur wrenched him across the hall and into his own room.

Arthur closed the door, standing protectively in front of it.

"Jesus, Pham, what's your problem?"

"*My* problem?" Arthur took a steadying breath, determined not to let his emotions get the better of him again. He had a speech to get through.

He continued, "Check your phone today?"

Mika's face was eerily neutral. "I forgot it in my room this morning."

Arthur steamrolled on, undeterred. "We need to talk."

"What about?"

"I wanted to apologize for Saturday." The words rolled off his tongue, over-practiced.

"What are you talking about?"

Arthur halted in his tracks. He hadn't been expecting...that.

"I—I'm talking about...Spring Social," he finished lamely.

That impassive expression remained. Arthur hadn't thought a face more insufferable than the shit-eating grin was possible, but he'd been proven definitively wrong. He searched Mika's face for a twitch, a frown, a glint, anything...and came up with nothing. He took Mika's silence as an invitation to continue:

"I've been under a lot of pressure, and after everything that happened, I snapped—"

"Pham, chill. It's all good."

"—When this first started, I—" Arthur blinked. He felt several steps behind. "What's all good?"

"I get it." Mika wasn't making eye contact, and he was grinning now but it looked too stiff—there was no sparkle to it. "Your post-grad dreams are your number one priority. You're right, all this...stuff...was just too much. We let it go too far." He made a vague hand gesture and Arthur's stomach fell in his horror, voice stuck, helpless to interrupt him.

"But—" he finally choked out.

"It's no big deal."

"No, but it *is*," Arthur insisted, panic bubbling up into his throat. *When this first started, I hated you, but then we actually became friends and more, I hope, when this first started, I hated you, but then we actually became friends and more, I hope!*

"Don't worry about it." Mika's face was maddeningly unreadable, tone unnervingly even.

The dust settled in Arthur, and he felt he was choking on it, unable to catch his breath.

'Why is it so hard for you to believe that I kissed you because I wanted to?'

Arthur's stomach dropped, sank like a stone.

'...Can I?'

Realization, resignation, settled into the nooks and crannies of his reeling mind.

'Arthur. You have no idea how long I've been waiting for that.'

Mika's phone rang, startling Arthur out of the downward spiral. He glanced at the caller ID when Mika retrieved it from his pocket.

"Your mom?" Arthur was desperate now. Anything to elicit a reaction—any reaction.

Mika pasted a grin on his face again as he silenced the call, and his tone was devastatingly casual. "Don't worry, I'll see if she has any internships available."

Arthur felt an arrow lodge between his shoulderblades. Pain blossomed in his sternum.

"Wow, I—"

"I should go. Evocation quiz tomorrow, ugh."

"Mika—"

Mika's eyes snapped to his once more. "Isn't this what you wanted?"

Arthur reeled back. Mika's words were edged razor-sharp, the smile never leaving his face. The cut of it left Arthur breathless, speechless, trapped under the ice-out. He couldn't find it in him to stop Mika from leaving, couldn't make his body turn as he heard his door open.

All the words he'd practiced—all the points he'd rehearsed so carefully—were spilling from the pot, spinning out of control. He couldn't *breathe* and he was falling, falling…

And the door closed, and Arthur was alone.

27

In a sick twist of fate, Mika's grades started to slip.

His demeanor revealed nothing. He still sauntered down the halls with his friends, sporting his signature grin and acting like the same old Mika—sans Arthur, of course. But in the Evocation practical quiz the next day, his wandwork was faulty; like trying to get a lighter to flame, the first few tries didn't catalyze the proper spark. In Transmutation a couple days later, Arthur saw the B+ circled on Mika's exam before he turned it upside down.

Arthur couldn't bring himself to care.

He found that holding his pride close cost too much energy and it left a gaping hole for guilt to set in, deep-seated and ever-pervasive. He was consumed with the desire to camp outside Room 420 until Mika had no choice but to let Arthur say his piece—but what good would it do, if Mika wouldn't listen? Even if he did, what then?

Arthur had fucked up. There was nothing more to it.

His anxiety got worse. He was fighting off panic attacks every few days now, spending less and less time outside his room, and spending more and more time studying. He started avoiding calls and texts from his mom, feeling helpless to even sort through his own problems, let alone hers and Bella's.

The guilt compounded on itself tenfold and Arthur threw himself back into school. He didn't know what else to do.

Any moment he wasn't in class, he was in his room reading, writing, revising—carefully channeling the betrayal he couldn't bear, the heart-rending regret he couldn't face. At first, his classmates stopped him in the halls and sent notes to him in class asking what had happened between him and Mika. But after ignoring enough of them, the queries slowed and then stopped altogether. Arthur wondered if this should have been his strategy from the start. He thought wearily about how much of this could have been avoided if it had been.

He started ignoring his friends' texts, too—their invitations to hang out or go to meals together, dining instead during off hours. He couldn't bear the thought of lying to them anymore, of finding a way to explain what had happened between him and Mika and withstanding the looks of pity on their faces. He couldn't bear the thought of pretending to be okay while they gossiped on about the latest drama within their class or daydreamed about their future business together—Arthur didn't remember the last time he'd given a spare thought to Auratech. But he knew he couldn't hide forever.

Somewhere between a couple to several days after his final confrontation with Mika, he found himself sitting alone in his room, scrolling through Mika's social media feeds from the past six months: Arthur and Mika in line for boutonnieres, Mika kissing Arthur's cheek post-Social proposal, Arthur on the hike, with Mika's new sneakers, at brunch—

Within the hour, he'd deleted the apps from his phone and taken to staring at his hand.

The letters, so vivid and insistent just a week ago, were now barely legible—a whisper of a thing, nearly indistinguishable from the rest of his skin. The irony cut sharper than a knife.

Arthur thought this might be what it felt like to have his heart break.

The box in his mind had toppled over and, one by one, his brain gathered this fresh ammunition of insecurities, hurtling them until one stuck home:

'Isn't this what you wanted?'
'Isn't this what you wanted?'
'Isn't this what you wanted?'

Over and over and over and over and over and over and—

Arthur took a shaky breath, squeezing his eyes shut and desperate to go to sleep and stay asleep for a very long time. But even there he wasn't safe, haunted by the look on Mika's face, shocked, open, broken at Arthur's confession—angry and sharp at Arthur's apology.

'Isn't this what you wanted?'

Despite having signed the contract willingly, he felt as if he'd been strung along—played with and tossed around and then tossed aside. He'd been taken on—no. He'd *put himself* on a rollercoaster ride, and for the longest time he'd wanted off—so why did freedom leave him feeling so bereft? He'd grasped on to something so huge, all-encompassing and terrifying for just the briefest moment before it slipped through his hands—and it was no one's fault but his own.

'Can I?'

Arthur fixed his eyes on a spot on the carpet, staring.

Mika kissing him like he was starving—

He stomped down on the memory as it resurfaced for the umpteenth time, struggling to reign it back in. It was done. It was over. He had to accept it. Why couldn't he just accept it?

'You have no idea how long I've been waiting for that.'

The memories leaked through the cracks, rising higher and higher until Arthur was close to drowning: dark-bright eyes on his, the blinding flash of a white smile, eyebrows pulled up at the center, the noise Mika made when Arthur bit his lip, his mouth on Arthur's neck, thick eyelashes against honey skin, the whisper of a kiss at his cheek...

He tried to collect them in the box, a Sisyphean effort. He thought of Mika turning up the heat on him in class, re-dominating the atoms Arthur had calmed. Mika wormed his way back in, refusing to be silenced, refusing to be ignored, demanding to be seen.

Arrogant as ever.

Arthur gave up on the box.

It seemed he'd created a mess too big for it to contain.

28

When Clarke and Jonathan knocked on his door two Saturday mornings after the fateful non-conversation with Mika, Arthur sensed they wouldn't be leaving without him.

"What happened to the Arthur who takes breaks?" Jonathan chided him.

"Did we do something wrong?" Clarke whined.

"You're going to burn yourself out," Jonathan added.

"You're fine," Arthur reassured them, trying for a smile. It felt unnatural on his face. "*I'm* fine. I've just been busy."

"We haven't seen you in weeks," Clarke huffed.

Arthur sighed. "What did I miss?"

It did the trick. Clarke was off, Jonathan piping in every now and then, and Arthur drifted in and out of the conversation, counting down the minutes until he could be with his books in the safety and solitude of his room. He barely even noticed the *'For Rent'* sign on their way to brunch.

He made it through their meal by half-participating and mostly staring out the window. By the time they reached the dorm halls again, he'd even managed to reduce his contributions to one-word answers.

"Hey, Arthur, I was thinking we should go to Tan's birthday party next Friday."

"Okay."

"Do you think your books would miss you for one night?"

"Nah."

"I think it's *Rocky Horror* themed. Maybe we can brainstorm costumes on Wednesday?"

"Sure."

"Also, I'm thinking of shaving off all my hair. Jonathan's gonna dye his pink."

"Mm."

"And my boyfriend has actually been fake the whole time. You were right."

It took longer than it should have for Arthur to realize he was now walking alone. He turned to find Clarke and Jonathan staring daggers at him from a few feet back.

"Sorry. What?" Arthur tried.

"Dude." Jonathan's brow softened. "What's going on?"

"What are you—"

"Come on," Clarke interrupted, tone uncharacteristically serious. "Don't fucking do that."

Arthur clamped his mouth shut.

"You barely look at us for a week, ignore us for the next two, and then when you finally deign to grace us with your presence, you treat us like you wish we'd just left you alone." Clarke pushed his glasses up, then put his hands on his hips, then crossed his arms across his chest. "Give us enough credit to know when our best friend is pushing us away. For no discernible reason, I might add."

Arthur bit his lip and looked away.

After a moment of tense silence, Jonathan stepped in again. "Is there something you want to tell us?"

The box he'd abandoned gave an uncomfortable lurch, and Arthur felt like he might be sick. The guilt, the anxiety, the pain, the fear, the everything...he shut his eyes, willing it all to go away, to just go away—

A gentle hand gripped his arm. His eyes flew open to find Clarke tilting his head in the direction of Arthur's door and pulling him along. Arthur let himself be led.

Safely hidden away in Arthur's room, Clarke guided him to the couch and sat them both down. Jonathan took the Eames chair across from them, propping his feet up on the ottoman.

Clarke squeezed Arthur's hand once, then scooted back against the arm of the couch.

He gestured his hand grandly. "Out with it."

Arthur looked at his friends—his dearest friends—watching him expectantly.

He took a deep breath and started at the beginning.

And once he started, it was hard to stop.

He confessed how his mom was no longer able to pay his tuition, explaining his deal with Stonebury to win a back-dated scholarship along with Electi Magi so they could fulfill their post-graduate dreams. He admitted how difficult the teasing got, after the soulmate ritual, and he spun the tale of his agreement with Mika. At this, his friends' eyebrows launched themselves into space.

"What is this, a fucking fanfiction?" Clarke exclaimed.

Jonathan only shook his head, chuckling softly.

"Trust me," Arthur sighed. "I know. But listen, we're still back in... god, November."

"Okay, okay. Strapped in for the ride." Clarke sat back with his hands in his lap.

Arthur continued, explaining that when they'd started to suspect something was fishy, he arranged to spend more time with Mika and that, despite himself, he and Mika had gotten closer, becoming friends, even, and—he thought sometimes—more. He explained how they'd become an unexpected team, and how even though Arthur knew it was the perfect opportunity to plant the seeds of his own victory, he couldn't bring himself to do it—couldn't help but revel in getting to know Mika.

"Wait." Clarke frowned. "When you said you two had sex, and you had the marks to prove it. You...how..."

Arthur fixed him with a look. Clarke clamped a hand to his mouth and took a shaky breath, looking dangerously close to losing consciousness.

"Oh, my lord," he breathed. Jonathan chortled.

"We're only in December." Arthur shot Clarke a wry smile as he swooned.

Arthur continued, recounting the night with the hickeys and what he'd Sensed behind Mika's door for the first time, as well as the dream at the end of the holiday break and how he discovered he'd shared the dream with Mika. Projecting over—and unable to keep from laughing a little at—Clarke's audible reaction, Arthur explained what happened at Spring Social, the truth underneath what they'd seen throughout the night, and what happened at the afterparty—

"Wait, wait, wait," Jonathan finally chimed in. "But this means it ended up being true anyway! You're both into each other, so what's..."

He took in Arthur's silence and leaned back again. "Oh, boy."

"Will it never end?" Clarke collapsed against the couch.

"We're almost caught up," Arthur promised.

And at long last, he confessed what he'd done, how it had all come tumbling out in front of Mika—the Electi Magi stress, the plot to undermine him, everything that now felt so trivial in the face of his burgeoning...*something* with Mika. He explained how Mika tore up their contract that night, how Arthur knew he fucked up, how he tried to apologize and got shut down in the same breath.

And how now he was lost and untethered, betrayed by both himself and someone he should have known was his rival all along, someone who would never care for him again. He didn't know how to fix it, and so now it was over.

"We got carried away," he sighed. "It...I don't know. It wasn't real until it was, and I—I wish I could tell you what it felt like, the enormity of the connection there. I took it for granted. I know, hell—I was in denial about it, but somehow I still got lost in it, and I don't know how this happened, and I just...I don't know what I want. I want it to never have happened at all. I want to go back to how it was six months ago. I would have...I don't know. I don't know what I could have done, but I would have done anything but this."

"I know what you could have done," Clarke interrupted him, finally. Arthur turned to look at him. He'd recovered from his faintheartedness and now sat leaning forward, meeting Arthur's eyes ferociously.

"You could have told us," Clarke finished.

"But the contract—"

"Not about that, stupid," Jonathan joined in. "Although that was stupid, too. About the money."

Arthur deflated. "What?"

"Are we not going into business together?" Clarke said. "We could have brainstormed a plan, marketed even more Auratech—hell, we could have asked our parents for money, gotten part-time jobs—"

"Why didn't you trust us?" Jonathan said softly, and the look on his face hurt Arthur deep inside—deeper than the daggers in Mika's eyes had two weeks earlier.

"It's not that," he rushed to explain. "Of course I trust you. I just..." He swallowed. "I didn't...I love you both too much." He sighed. "I had to do it myself. I've always handled things myself."

He petered off at the looks of pity on their faces. The familiar feeling of revulsion bubbled up, threatening to spill over—the impulsive urge to sit up straight and grin and bear it, to take it all back and figure it out himself...but no, that wasn't quite it.

His friends didn't pity him.

They loved him.

It was concern—an earnest desire to help.

Jonathan stepped in. "Okay. We'll cut you some slack this time."

"Thank you."

"If you promise to ask for help next time."

"Well." Arthur laughed humorlessly. "Ideally, there is no next time."

Clarke gave him a look.

"I promise," Arthur conceded. "And...I'm sorry. I'm so, so sorry."

And with that, it was done. He'd been running on fumes, and the fumes had finally run out. He slumped onto the arm of the couch, taking a shaky breath.

"I'm going to beat up that boy so bad," Jonathan grumbled.

"Beat me instead," Arthur corrected him. "I'm the one who fucked up."

"We'll find a way to make it right," Clarke reassured him. "With Mika, and with Auratech."

"I just—" Arthur shook his head— "I don't know what to do."

"You know..." Jonathan watched him carefully. "He was good for you."

Arthur raised an eyebrow.

"Yeah," Clarke agreed. "When we thought it was real—" he gestured between himself and Jonathan— "we talked about it. You looked happier. Fuck, you would take breaks from studying."

"If you want to say I had a stick up my ass, you can just say it," Arthur deadpanned.

"Shut up." Clarke smacked his arm. "I think you're right. What you two had really was real, underneath all the complicated shit y'all added on top of it. We'll fix it."

"But how?" Arthur sighed, slumping further.

"We'll figure out the Mika shit," Jonathan decided. "But for now, let's focus on the easier problem: Electi Magi."

Arthur looked up. "What?"

"Let's make a study schedule," Clarke suggested. "If Mika's already starting to slip on his exams, all you need to do is keep up your streak and you're in the clear."

"Maybe we can set up sessions with some of the professors," Jonathan said.

"Maybe we can rent the ballroom for practical magic?"

"Flash cards!"

Warmth blossomed in Arthur's chest. He was stupid to ever have kept his friends in the dark, to have gone at it alone, to have suffered in silence when instead he could have had *this:* friends defending his honor, telling him it would all be okay, talking over each other to bounce rapid-fire ideas off the wall.

"Hey," he said softly, and then louder when they didn't hear him. "Hey, wait."

They paused.

"Can the plan wait until tomorrow?" he asked. "Maybe...maybe we can watch a movie tonight?"

"Hell yeah." Jonathan leaped up and launched himself onto the bed, stealing Arthur's laptop from his desk along the way.

"Popcorn!" Clarke exclaimed, Summoning a bag of instant popcorn from their room and stealing away to the microwave on top of Arthur's mini fridge in the corner near the bathroom.

Arthur moved to switch off the main lights in the room and draw the curtains closed. "I'm thinking romcom," he said, settling on the bed against the wall, propping up the laptop on his desk chair in front of them.

"Sixteen Candles," Jonathan argued.

"Breakfast Club," Clarke offered.

"Not a romcom."

"Is too—"

"Wait. I've got it." Arthur smiled. When was the last time he smiled?

And that was how an hour later found them piled on Arthur's bed, *Dirty Dancing* playing on the laptop on a pile of pillows, popcorn kernels in the bottom of the bag abandoned on the floor as Jonathan and Clarke sang loudly along to "Cry to Me" while Arthur dozed through it all on one of his pillows.

He settled deeper into the bed, feeling more at peace than he had in the past six months.

Maybe he didn't have to do it all alone.

Maybe it was all easier to bear with good company, at the very least.

29

The next day, Arthur woke up diagonally, left arm pinned under Clarke's butt on his bed. He blinked blearily into the room. The screen of his laptop, propped up on pillows and charging in the sunlight, housed the end credits of the movie. Benignly, it queried, "Are you still watching?" Arthur craned his neck to find Jonathan passed out on the couch under one of the many soft throw blankets in Arthur's collection.

Arthur lay back down and let out a soft sigh, relishing in the ease with which he breathed. He'd missed this, and he'd learned his lesson. He needed to learn to tamp down his pride and ask for help.

He knew he *had* help now for his little Electi Magi problem. He knew Clarke and Jonathan were backing him up, every step of the way, from here on out.

But as for the other problem...Arthur heaved a less carefree sigh.

As if on cue, his phone buzzed from somewhere within the depths of the bed.

He fished his arm out from under Clarke—who emitted a sleepy grunt and snuggled closer—and dug for his phone, finding it under his own pillow. He had a message from an unknown number.

UNKNOWN

Hey, this is Cherry. Got your number from Julia.

> I know we don't know each other too well, and this may be the last thing you want to do but I'm worried about Mika. It's last minute but would you be willing to meet up sometime today to talk? Or call?

Arthur's heart did a tap dance, and his head reeled as he struggled to recall what Mika had been like for the past two weeks. He hadn't noticed anything out of the ordinary—but then again, he hadn't been noticing much of anything at all.

He took a deep breath. An opportunity for help had fallen right in his lap. All he had to do was take it.

He typed out a response.

> Hi, how have you been? I'm really sorry about everything that went down. I haven't talked to Mika in a couple weeks, but I'm down to meet.
>
> Brunch today?

He closed his phone to wait for a response and allowed Clarke to snuggle in a little closer.

Arthur walked into Koffie later that morning, dressed simply in a white tee, jeans, a kimono jacket, and sneakers. Composing a killer outfit to wear in the fresh spring air had felt like coming back home to himself. He fished the bundle of spending money provided by the winter Auratech stock, bought a *koffie verkeerd*, and searched for his date.

Cherry was already seated at a table near the window wearing a chic sweaterdress, lips red and hair in a tall updo. She smiled and waved at Arthur, and he wondered idly how Mika had ever let go of a woman so radiant.

He joined her at the table, sinking into a comfortable armchair.

"Hi," he said.

"Hi," she replied, sipping her drink. "Thanks for coming."

Arthur shifted in his seat, picking at the lid of his cup. "Yeah, I was...surprised. I was sure you weren't feeling too keen to see me."

Cherry bit her lip. Arthur noticed the concealer under her eyes. "It's complicated."

"Yeah." Arthur laughed once. "You could say that."

"So..." Cherry hesitated. "Right, um, if at any time you aren't feeling this, or you want to leave, please let me know."

Arthur looked up from his cup to meet her eye. "Okay."

Cherry sighed. "Right. Okay. Mika has been different since Spring Social. Something's wrong, and he won't tell me what."

"I mean..." Arthur wondered how to be delicate. "Are you sure it's not. You know."

Cherry waved him off. "No. I know what you're thinking, but we've been friends for a long time. Whether we're together or not, it won't change that. We both know that. I *told* him that, during Social."

"Then...what do you mean, 'off'?" Arthur tried not to seem too eager.

Cherry cupped her drink and looked out the window, thinking. "It's hard to explain, but his energy has been strange. When I text to ask him how he is, he says he's fine like always, but he doesn't elaborate. I send him pictures and he likes them but doesn't respond. I offer to video chat and he makes excuses. Again—all normal ways to act after a breakup, but it's like he *did* break up. But not with me."

She paused to peer at Arthur, who felt his face heat under her quiet scrutiny.

She continued. "And you'd think I wouldn't be able to tell from across the city, but I just *can*. It's like a Sense magnified, like a...a..."

"Soulmate Sense," Arthur finished quietly.

She smiled. "Yeah."

"I think..." Arthur remembered the inexplicable connection he'd had with Mika, the vibrating particles between them, the shared experiences, and he imagined how that might have evolved if they'd known each other a whole lifetime. "I think I get it."

"I'm worried about him," Cherry confessed, voice wavering. She took a bracing breath and looked directly at Arthur now. "What happened? After Social?"

Arthur took a bracing breath of his own. He'd already unleashed the floodgates the day before, so the words felt familiar as he relayed the saga once more: everything from 'Spin the Bottle' to aborted confessions in the bedroom to the torn contract in the dorm hallway to the aftermath—the dismissal, the cutting words, and the distinct Mika-shaped hole in his life. He found himself pausing every now and then to watch Cherry, but she didn't look uncomfortable in the slightest. She sipped her drink, shifted to prop her chin on her hand, snorted quietly, and nodded at appropriate times. Arthur realized Mika might have learned his maddening poker face from her.

To confess the way he'd had all, most, some, and then none of Mika felt different—more like confessing a secret, something even he wasn't sure he was supposed to know. Something he was beginning to feel like Cherry had known from the start.

Finally, Arthur ran out of breath, blinking hard. Cherry was silent, listening intently.

"I feel lost, I guess. I tried to take control of this soulmate bullshit, and I got hopelessly tangled in it. I don't know what's real and what's fake anymore. I don't even care. All I know is I ruined it, and I just want...I don't even know what I want, but I know it's not this—"

He cut himself off abruptly, cutting his eyes back to Cherry. She was still watching him benignly, listening. What was it about Mika and his affiliates that got him talking like this? He took a shaky breath, centering himself.

"Sorry." He closed his eyes, shaking his head. "Long story short, he hasn't looked at me, let alone talked to me, in two weeks. When I see him at school, he looks completely unbothered. So I don't know what's going on with him."

Cherry finally opened her mouth to speak. "You've just told me what's going on with him."

"I told you what's going on with me." Arthur rubbed the back of his neck. "Selfishly," he added.

"And what's going on with you—" Cherry gave him a wry smile— "is you're going through a breakup you didn't want in the first place."

Arthur stared at her.

"We were fake dating," he corrected, "and it doesn't seem like he's too bothered by the end of that, nor the end of our...friendship."

"Seems like you don't know Mika as well as you thought." She raised an eyebrow.

Arthur scoffed. "That much is clear."

"But I do." Cherry tilted her head, giving him a cheesy smile that he couldn't help but give a short, small laugh at. "He likes to play things off with good humor. He avoids difficult emotions to maintain this cool-guy, laid-back persona. When he *does* feel something, it's impossible for him to keep it hidden."

She sipped her drink. "But he's scared, to be vulnerable like that. His parents fucked him up pretty bad. I saw it myself, growing up with him. They're fucking him up to this day. He doesn't like to feel out of control, so he pretends to be in control. Does this make any sense?"

Feeling out of control about a situation he'd found himself acting more vulnerably in than he'd initially anticipated?

Yeah. Yeah, he could relate.

He remembered Mika's eyebrows pulling up in the center, the signature grin wiped from his face, his entire being vibrating with need.

He remembered Mika's eyes snapping to his after his half-assed apology—the dangerous glint there.

"So that reaction," Cherry concluded, "is pretty classic Mika, to be honest."

Arthur frowned. "So what you've been Sensing is…?"

"He's upset, Arthur," Cherry said gently. "He's upset. About you."

"Right," Arthur agreed. "Because I lied to him."

"And…?"

"…And?"

Cherry spoke very slowly. "And why would he be upset that you lied?"

"Because…lying is…bad?"

"God, you're worse than him," Cherry sighed, slumping back in her seat. She leveled him with a look, and Arthur felt a flush creep up his neck.

"You're making a lot of assumptions here," Arthur rubbed at his face.

"Please," Cherry scoffed. "Give me some credit. That boy has been obsessed with you since day one."

Arthur's heart leapt hopefully. He stomped on it. "I doubt it."

Cherry gave out a single, derisive laugh. "Are you kidding? He wouldn't shut up about you. Especially starting this year. 'Pham did this today, he's such an insufferable smartass, I can't believe I willingly spend my time with this guy,' *et cetera, et cetera.*"

At the look on Arthur's face, she hurried to continue. "That was at first. After a while, it...changed."

"Changed?" Arthur frowned.

"Yeah." Cherry frowned, too. "Maybe around finals last semester, it started to sound more like, 'Arthur was explaining it like this. I never thought about it that way. Isn't that wild?' Or, even more often, 'Arthur and I have plans today. I can't.' And then..." She smiled sadly. "And then, that's when I noticed him looking."

"Looking?"

"At you." Cherry chuckled softly. "At parties—even if you were across the room, he only had eyes for you. When we were together in town, he'd be on his phone, responding to you. At Social." She raised her eyebrows, gave him a look. "We both were there, at Social."

Arthur blushed, clearing his throat. He fought back against his first instinct to dismiss it.

He was trying to be honest now, with others and himself.

"Right," he managed, smiling humorlessly.

"So, could you believe, maybe a little bit—" Cherry squinted for emphasis— "that he's felt exactly the same way as you all along? Honestly, if not longer?"

'You have no idea how long I've been waiting for that.'

Arthur looked out the window.

He could. Of course he could, and that was the problem.

"I just want to know," Arthur sighed, "if Mika really is my soulmate, or if this was just some cruel trick of the universe—if I really do have control over my future, or not."

There it was, on the table, in between Arthur and this near stranger —what he'd never admitted to anyone, least of all himself.

Some of the pressure eased from the chokehold around his neck.

Cherry sighed, took another sip of her drink, and lifted her chin off her hand. "That's...well, yeah."

Arthur gave her a humorless grin.

She smiled and looked up at the ceiling. "From what I understand, soulmate magic is the one area of magic that's so imprecise, like...the one thing that's uncontrollable."

She looked back at Arthur and smiled. "Because, like you've just said, humans have a funny way of choosing their own destiny. And even predicting the future is easier, because it's so easy to divine the stupid mistakes we'll make to fuck everything up in a specific way. But love?" She looked out the window again, and Arthur sensed the sadness there. "Love seems too up in the air to predict."

Arthur considered this. "But what about science? Isn't there technically one person out there who's statistically your perfect match? The closest you can get?"

Cherry made a face. "Meeks was right. You are a nerd."

Arthur blushed.

They shared a moment of silence, sipping their drinks.

Arthur shook his head. "I'm honestly astounded your name didn't appear on his hand that night. You know him so well."

She smiled softly. "I think," she started, voice a little thick, "we *are* soulmates."

"So then—"

"But," she continued, "we're not meant to be together in that way— the way that puts your name on someone else's hand."

"You've lost me." Arthur sighed woefully, and Cherry let out a laugh.

"We don't know anything about this stuff, really, right? So why can't we all have multiple soulmates? Isn't it crazy to think there's just one person out there who's perfect for you? When you have family— friends, even—who just get you? Who you just click with?"

Arthur thought of Clarke and Jonathan and watching *Dirty Dancing* all night, and started to think he understood what she meant.

"Yeah," he said slowly. "Yeah, I get what you mean."

"I love Mika," she said, shaking her head, "with all my heart. But I don't think we're meant for each other. And I think maybe it's because I decided I wanted more for myself. For him. We're not meant to be together because I decided it to be so."

She swallowed. "I love Mika. But I already found him. What use would I have for his name on my hand when it's already in my heart? I think you both needed more help finding each other. You both had lessons you could teach each other."

Arthur thought he felt his love line tingle, lighting up the words there. He remembered how they'd darkened the closer he'd gotten to Mika and faded when they'd fallen apart.

He was starting to get it.

Arthur grinned, shook his head, and put it in one hand. "You could be a writer. Or a therapist."

"I'll send the bill to your room."

They laughed, and Arthur looked into the last dregs of his coffee.

"You were the one who asked me here to talk, yet I'm the one who got a philosophy lecture."

"Another potential career for me, I suppose." She winked. "But don't worry. I think I understand better now."

"I hope he feels better soon. I..." Arthur fought the words, but they came out anyway. "I care about him. I wish I could tell him that."

"I'm sure you'll find a way," she smiled.

"Thank you, Cherry. Really."

"Thank you, Arthur. I think I'd like to be friends." She tilted her head from side to side contemplatively as she gathered her purse. "One day."

"One day," he promised, and he stood to leave.

"Oh, and Arthur?"

He turned back. Cherry bit her lip.

"Tell Mika I say hi?" she said softly, eyes shining with mirth.

Arthur smiled, too. "Only if you'll tell him I do, too."

"I'll see what I can do."

They shared a parting smile and Arthur left the café, head full to the brim with soulmates, memories, personas, and Cherry's sad smile. His mind tried to piece it all together into some semblance of sense. He glanced down at his left hand and was startled to find the words there were ablaze once more, darkening slowly, steadily, confidently.

He could do this, he thought.

He could do this.

30

On Monday, Arthur hit the ground running.

Clarke and Jonathan came over to his room after class to formulate a study plan for the remaining three weeks leading up to finals. Jonathan drew out a calendar on a sheet of graph paper and color-coded it, deciding on the days they'd aim to rent the ballroom for practice, what they'd study on Tuesdays in Arthur's room, and what they'd study on Fridays in Clarke and Jonathan's room. They made lists of supplies they had on hand—notebook paper, pens, crystals—and what they needed to run into town for—index cards, mostly.

Once Arthur adhered the calendar to the wall over his desk and Duplicated it to make a copy for Clarke and Jonathan's room, he sat back down on the couch next to Clarke. All three of them took a collective breath.

"So," Jonathan finally said. "What do we do about Mika?"

They lapsed into silence once more, contemplating what Cherry said—what they'd debriefed about after Saturday's coffee date.

"Let's sleep on it," Clarke decided, and they rose to make their way to dinner.

When Arthur returned to his room to continue working at his desk alone, he couldn't help but keep his Sense half-open, waiting. Mika had been Sensing Arthur regularly only weeks ago; surely Arthur could learn to do the same?

Later that night, Arthur's left palm gave a twitch as he heard the door across the hall unlatch, open, and close. His heart beat powerfully in his chest, waiting.

But other than what he heard, Arthur could Sense nothing.

His heart fell, but he braced himself, focusing back in on his textbook.

I'll figure it out, he told himself. *We'll figure it out.*

On Transmutation Tuesday (Arthur had rolled his eyes; Clarke had insisted that alliteration was a surefire road to success), they quizzed each other on items in Professor Silverton's study guide until Arthur was giving word-for-word answers on every question and Clarke was claiming hanger.

At dinner, they settled down at their table with their *stamppot* and looked at each other.

"Well?" Clarke tried.

Jonathan shook his head.

Arthur glanced over Clarke's shoulder to where Mika was talking animatedly with Ben Lasher and Tan at a table across the room. Once more he extended his Sense, willing it to reach Mika, to scream at him to *just look at me!*

But Mika's defenses didn't budge. He didn't give so much as a sign he even knew Arthur was in the same room, let alone Sensed him.

Arthur coiled his Sense back into himself and returned his attention to his own table, where Clarke was watching him. He lay a hand on Arthur's.

"We'll figure something out," he reassured him.

Arthur put on a brave smile and convinced himself it was true.

On Wednesday, they walked into *Watergraafsmeer* to purchase a metric ton of index cards. An hour later in the library, Arthur was busying himself with copying Conjuration terms onto flashcards when Clarke cleared his throat from across the table.

He held up a card that read, *'Mika's favorite color?'*

Arthur's heart warmed. He thought about it for a moment before shrugging.

Clarke held up another: *'Mika's favorite sex position?'*

Arthur stifled a laugh, snorting. Jonathan grinned next to him and leaned down to write something on his own index card.

He held it up. *'How big is Mika's dick?'*

Arthur buried his head in his arms, shoulders shaking, trying not to make more noise than necessary.

Someone tapped on his shoulder and he looked up.

'Does Mika have a nipple ring?'

Arthur looked away and ducked under the desk, threatening to explode.

Thirty minutes later, they had done very little studying and had a pile of wasted index cards in the middle of the table. *'Is Mika a top or a bottom?' 'Mika's ideal first date?' 'Does Mika like long walks on the beach?' 'Is Mika an insufferable ass?'* Several students around them were throwing dirty looks because Arthur had been unable to contain his laughter, and once he'd gotten going, so had Jonathan, and then so had Clarke.

Finally, Arthur cleared his throat and sobered, looking down at his own cards. He picked up his pen to write and held the card up when he was done.

'How do I get Mika to talk to me again?'

Clarke and Jonathan sobered, too. They all fell, once more, into silence.

On Thursday, they rented the ballroom to throw Evocations back and forth at each other. When Arthur made his way back to his room, sweaty and exhausted, he didn't even have the energy to try and Sense Mika across the hall.

On Friday after dinner, they settled in Clarke and Jonathan's room, typing up essays for their Year Four comprehensive projects. Arthur had finished his months ago, but procrastinated on the editing process and was now faced with editing thirty pages down to twenty. He stared at a paragraph somewhere around page seven:

'So, then: why does the divide between mages and non-mages exist? Is it genetics or merely a skill that can be taught to those who are willing to learn? It is one of the few inconclusive areas of study, despite the boom of production and research over the past several decades of collaboration between mages and non-mages. Despite how much we have learned from each other, this seems to be a great divide we cannot bridge. Despite how much we have learned from each other, this seems to be a great divide we cannot bridge. Despite how much we have learned from each other, this seems to be a great divide we cannot bridge—'

Jonathan's voice startled him out of the broken record his brain was playing.

"What if we serenaded him?"

Clarke stopped typing, and Arthur looked up to stare.

"I can play guitar," Clarke supplied.

"But I can't sing," Arthur pointed out. "And I don't think that's really Mika's style, anyway."

"Bullshit," Jonathan protested. "Are we forgetting the Spring Social proposal?"

"That's different," Clarke said. "Social proposals are a whole thing."

"You've tried texting him?" Jonathan looked at Arthur.

"What about just catching him when he comes back to his room?" Clarke added.

"I need a plan first," Arthur insisted. "I tried rehearsing a whole speech when I wanted to apologize." He made a helpless gesture. "He told me it didn't matter. I at least need to know what to say to get him to engage with me."

"Maybe you need help with the Evocation paper," Clarke threw out.

Arthur wrinkled his nose. "After two weeks of silence? Too casual."

"Your mom is sick, and you need comfort," Jonathan supplied.

"Way too dramatic. And also, a lie."

"The truth!" Clarke stood up, enthusiastic.

"I tried that, and he won't listen!" Arthur insisted.

Their comps projects lay abandoned as they brainstormed into the night. Nothing seemed to be good enough. Mika was, above all, an enigma, and Arthur hadn't managed to figure him out while they were close; how was he supposed to find the right words to say now that Mika didn't want to hear any more words from Arthur? Even after they'd analyzed the intel Cherry provided a hundred times, along with every interaction Arthur and Mika had, they couldn't puzzle through what to do—what the secret to opening Mika up again was when it had happened so effortlessly before.

Around midnight, Clarke and Jonathan were arguing back and forth about what flowers would be most appropriate for Arthur to send.

"They literally had camellia boutonnieres at Social! What do you want from me?"

Jonathan shook his head resolutely. "That was before. It needs to show he's sorry. That's the point he's trying to get across."

"*Hyacinths*, though?"

"They're in season!"

Clarke recited from his phone, open to a webpage on flower meanings: "'Longing for you. You're a flame in my heart.' Are you hearing this shit? Genius. Where the hell is the passion in a hyacinth?"

Arthur closed his eyes and stood. "Can we call it?" He was starting to get a headache. "Clearly this is going to take more than a night to figure out." He sighed. "More than a week."

Clarke sighed and slumped back onto the futon, letting out a long groan.

"Now do you see why I kept you in the dark?" Arthur smiled wryly.

Jonathan spun aimlessly in his desk chair. "I don't know how the hell you did this alone for six months."

"We didn't even make it to Tan's party!" Clarke whined. "I had a costume planned and everything."

"No one's stopping you," Jonathan shot back.

"Our friend is in crisis!"

"Maybe we can come back to it tomorrow at brunch," Arthur laughed tiredly.

"Yes." Clarke sat up, reenergized, and took Arthur's hand between his own. "We'll figure out something perfect."

Arthur, in contrast, felt bone-deep weary. "Perfect."

They said their goodbyes, and Arthur dragged himself and his five-kilogram bag back to his room. His crystal touchpad lit up with a soft *bong* as he unlocked the door, and he pulled himself through to shut it behind him.

It was quiet in his room—peaceful, and still. He'd only left a warm side table lamp on, and he didn't bother with the overhead light. His bag was abandoned somewhere between the door and his desk as he made his way to the closet, where he slid off his blazer, traded his slacks for grey sweatpants, and his collared shirt for his *'boyfriends are temporary'* tee. He removed his shoes, and his socks, and put his shirt and slacks and socks in the laundry, and then he sat down at the foot of the bed, and then he put his head in his hands, and then he started to cry.

Arthur couldn't remember the last time he'd allowed himself to cry. He had nearly done it when trapped with Mika at the afterparty—but the last time he'd been wracked with uncontrollable sobs must have been when he was a kid.

Now Arthur cried because he didn't know what else to do.

He'd gone into the school year with so much hope and ambition, full to the brim with confidence in his friends and in the future of Auratech. Mika had brought it all crashing down, and his name on Mika's hand had thrown his life into a tailspin, a storm of change and casual touches and meaningful looks and heated exchanges. Mika's devil-may-care attitude, his passion, his unapologetic authenticity, had shown Arthur parts of himself he hadn't known existed—things that urged him to stop every once in a while to appreciate where he was. He didn't care about getting Electi Magi anymore. He didn't care about keeping his grades perfect or about getting Auratech started as soon as possible. He just wanted to rest.

But more than rest, he wanted Mika back.

His mind spun with the options and possibilities of what he could say to Mika and why they wouldn't work. He thought of flowers and serenades and monologues and, for the first time in his life, he didn't know what to do—he'd found a problem with no solution, a puzzle with no right answer, and it left him more lost than he'd ever thought possible.

He replayed the botched apology in his mind. He replayed the afterparty and Social itself and beyond. He replayed the dream and the hickeys and the study sessions, the contract and the shit-eating grins and the insults and the inside jokes, the parties and the pictures and the sneakers.

He cried until there were no more tears and his head hurt and he had to walk across the room to retrieve a tissue box before returning to the foot of the bed. He blew his nose and rested his elbows on his knees and stared out at the ground in front of him, feeling emptied out.

After a while, his eyes lit upon the Polaroids, which had been upset from their place on the coffee table when he'd picked up the tissues. The one of him struggling with Mika's boutonniere had slid closest to him, and Arthur gazed at it: Mika staring at Arthur's downcast eyes, face soft and open and wanting.

Without warning, his left hand gave a violent twitch, and his palm erupted into pins and needles.

He snapped his head up to his door and extended his Sense beyond it and across the hall, into Mika's room.

A burst of color and sensation, pink and yellow and turquoise, the chaos of frustration and betrayal and bone-deep sorrow and the flavor of something else, something both subtle and huge, unfathomable but undeniable—

Something on the tip of his tongue, something terribly exciting and terribly frightening.

'Stop thinking up here,' Mika rapped on Arthur's skull.

Arthur launched himself from the bed and reached his door in four strides, wrenching it open. The hall was dark, lit only by soft pinks and purples of the fluorescent lights on the walls. Arthur crossed it in two strides.

'I wish you would *come to my door.'*

And then, without giving it a second thought, without consulting the hours of brainstorming he'd just done, without replaying the conversations they'd had for the two-hundredth time, without worrying what he was going to say or what he was going to do to convince Mika to listen—

He knocked on Mika's door.

Shave-and-a-haircut.

31

On Monday, Mika almost didn't get out of bed.

He woke up disappointed to be conscious, refusing to open his eyes in defiance of it.

He willed them to stay closed—to let him fall back into the soothing oblivion of sleep—but, as bodies are wont to do, his stubbornly rebelled.

His eyes opened to the view of his room, uncharacteristically tidy, bathed in seven o'clock light and, as had been the case for the past two weeks, all he could see was Arthur.

Arthur coming through the door, hesitant. Arthur in the middle of the room, demonstrating the wandwork shortcut he'd discovered for a Transmutation spell. Arthur on the floor, eyes cutting over to Mika's, hint of a smile on his lips. Arthur on the couch, hair mussed, lips wet, eyes bright, a speckled bruise forming at his neck—

Mika sighed out a groan and pulled the covers back over his head. The thought of running into his soulmate (nemesis? friend? ex?) on the way to class made his stomach turn unpleasantly. He flipped his pillow over to the cool side and begged sleep to take him once more.

His first class wouldn't miss him too much.

He did drag himself out of bed for Evocation, though, because he'd be damned if the bastard caught wind he was bent up over him. Before Mika left, he refreshed the Protection spell jar he'd filled two weeks ago—a half-assed production involving black jade, rosemary, black salt, and lavender, but it did the trick. There was no way he was letting Arthur in again.

Mika avoided his room all day, texting friends left and right until he managed to secure plans that would take him through until late at night when he knew Arthur would be sleeping. After a study session with Tan after class and dinner with some of the Featherwood students in town and a kickback in Ben's room with enough weed to get high out of his addled mind, Mika padded back to his room around eleven. He stubbornly did not look at the door across the hall, unlocked his own door, and entered.

He crossed the room to the couch and fell back onto it, his friends' carefully schooled expressions and questions flitting through his mind:

"Haven't seen Arthur around lately," Tan had noted.

"Did you and Pham, like, break up or something?" Molly had been unashamed.

"Aren't you soulmates?" Bea added.

"Are you okay, dude?" Ben peered at him suspiciously.

Mika banned them all from his mind and ignored the incoming call from his mom, allowing the swirling haze of his high to lull him to sleep right there on the couch.

On Tuesday, Mika watched Arthur, deep in discussion with his friends, at the table by the window at dinner.

He watched the furrow of Arthur's brow, the way his freckles squished when he wrinkled his nose, the way he made deliberate hand motions to emphasize his words.

He watched all of it and tried to remember how it had felt before he realized the features he'd come to love were all a farce, an act—the eyes that had watched him so intently, so carefully, were not affectionate at all; they were calculating.

He tore his gaze away before he was caught looking and looked instead at his left palm, where Arthur's name was still inscribed, so faint he could barely make it out.

It really was over, huh?

"Hey, Mika." Ben's voice brought him back to attention. "Think fast."

Ben threw a grape his way and, without missing a beat, Mika caught it with his mouth, pasting a smile on his face, instructing his arm to raise triumphantly into the air.

The table burst out in applause as Mika returned to his meal and didn't look at Arthur again.

Please let it be over, he thought desperately, chest aching so brutally. *I don't know how much more of this I can take.*

On Wednesday, Mika woke up from an afternoon nap where he'd been walking hand in hand across the bridge into town with Arthur, talking and laughing and confessing that he was so glad that they were together again, that Arthur didn't hate him—had never hated him.

"How could I hate you, ass?" Arthur smiled, pausing and using his hand to pull Mika in, to hold him close so he could whisper: "I love you."

Mika woke with a start, golden hour sun streaming into the room, caving into himself as his heart broke all over again.

★

On Thursday, Mika ignored seven texts from Cherry.

7:15 A.M.

> **CHER**
> Hey Meeks. Thinking of you today. How are you?

10:36 A.M.

> **CHER**
> I know you think you're doing a good job of pretending like you're ok, but you know I know you're not. Can we talk?

11:25 A.M.

> **CHER**
> I'm giving you the benefit of the doubt right now by assuming you're busy with class, but I'll check in after school.

3:42 P.M.

> **CHER**
> Ok I'm back

4:02 P.M.

> **CHER**
> Hello???????

5:56 P.M.

> **CHER**
> Mika, come on. Is this what we're reduced to???

8:22 P.M.

> **CHER**
> I talked to Arthur. He told me what's going on. If you won't talk to me, then at least go talk to him.

10:33 P.M.

> **CHER**
> Please just let me know you're ok and not dead in a ditch somewhere.

The pang of guilt got the best of Mika, and he finally responded around eleven from Ben's room, stoned out of his mind.

> **MIKA**
> sorry cher, busy day. i'm definitely not dead in a ditch, i promise. i'm fine, please don't worry about me, finals just have me bent over a barrel

He pointedly did not respond to what she'd said about Arthur. In fact, he pretended he hadn't seen that message at all. Mika leaned back against the couch and closed his eyes, waiting for the joint to be passed back down in his direction.

★

On Friday, Mika went to Tan's birthday party.

He went more out of habit than anything. And because he knew it was the one place Arthur absolutely would not be.

It turned out to be one of those nights where, no matter how much he drank or smoked, he remained stubbornly and exasperatingly sober. Mostly, he thought as he finished his fourth Homebrew beer, he felt mildly sick.

As he chatted and played inane drinking game after inane drinking game, he felt the eyes of everyone there on him. He swore he could hear them whispering behind his back. He could practically Sense what they were thinking: *Where's his other half?*

My other half, he thought to himself as he spectacularly missed a cup with his ping-pong ball, *hates my guts and screwed me over to further his career.*

Around eleven, Mika could have sworn he heard a familiar laugh, seen a familiar crop of straight, black hair turn the corner. He hated how his heart surged hopefully—painfully.

Ben came up to him around midnight as he fished through the kitchen for something stronger to imbibe.

"Hey, man."

Mika turned, and hated the pity in Ben's eyes. "Hey."

"Fun party, huh?"

Not really. "Yeah."

Ben was sizing him up, gathering his courage. Mika didn't help him along, waiting with bated breath for him to say it. *Daring* him to say it.

"Be real with me," Ben continued. "What happened with you and Pham?"

And there it was. Without much effort at all, anger surged in Mika, sharp and hot. The numbness he'd been attempting—striving for, desperate for—burnt away, revealing his wounds and leaving him vulnerable—about to snap.

Fuck this shit.

"We broke up," he said loudly, and a hush fell over the room. He was more sober, more alert than he'd been in a week, and he really didn't give two shits what they thought anymore as long as they stopped fucking staring.

"Me and Pham broke up," he continued, bracing his hands on the counter of the cut-out bar, meeting the eyes of classmates who teased them mercilessly six months ago.

"Are you happy now?" He turned on Ben, who shrank under his glare.

"And just fucking calm down about all of it, okay?"

He addressed the rest of them once more, relishing in the shocked expressions of Tan, Toby, Molly and Bea—all of them—and realizing that these were the last people he wanted to be with right now.

"You're so fucking obsessed with what other people are doing. It's fucking pathetic. Get your own lives to talk shit about."

He made his way out of the kitchen and through the crowd to leave, pausing at the door.

"Fuck. Happy birthday, Tan," he ground out.

And with that, he exited Ben's room, slamming the door behind him.

He stalked down the hall to his room, unlocking it and letting the door fall shut behind him.

It was quiet in his room—peaceful, and still.

Mika burned hot, the emotions he'd ignored for the past three weeks bubbling to the surface. His breathing turned rough and then sped up, snowballing until he was hyperventilating, unable to contain the overwhelming, all-consuming ache radiating out from his chest. Helpless to channel it or process it or think about it, he reached out to the pile of clothes on his desk chair and flung them blindly. They hit the wall pathetically and slumped to the floor.

Unsatisfied, he kicked a floor pillow, letting out a broken noise. He kicked another, and shoved a pile of textbooks off his desk, and threw a cup of writing utensils across the room. He overturned his desk chair and his bamboo palm, and it still wasn't enough. He whipped out his wand and slashed it upward through the air, bringing all the errant belongings now scattered around the room up with it. He let out a yell and Commanded the atoms around him to send the objects spinning—pencils and paper and pillows speeding through his vision before slamming his wand back down, sending everything crashing to the floor.

He heard glass shattering and whipped his head over to the corner near the door.

The Protection spell jar had joined the whirling objects in the room. Its remains were now spilled out across the floor, the conserved energy of the Charm released into nothingness.

Fine, he thought viciously. *Let him see.*

Mika stormed through pencils and pillows and notebooks to make his way to the bathroom, where he tore his Charmed gold briefs off— *stupid fucking* Rocky Horror *god damn*—turned the shower all the way up to near boiling, and stepped in.

He scrubbed aggressively at his hair and his face and his body, wanting nothing more than to be rid of the poison in his veins—the sluggish pull of Arthur in his mind, the way he wormed into Mika's thoughts and set up residence there despite...despite it all, despite *everything.*

Arthur hated him.

Why couldn't Mika hate him back?

In his haste, the shampoo bottle slipped off the surface of the shower niche and fell onto the floor.

And, just like that, he was crying.

He was so fucking sad.

He'd gone into the school year so unsure, so frustrated with his parents and about his future and leaning way too heavily on Cherry. Arthur had, unexpectedly, been a light in the darkness. His name on Mika's hand had acted as an anchor, grounding him in the storm of everything changing around him. Arthur's calm demeanor, his directed questions, his moments of silence had led Mika to parts of himself he hadn't had the focus to discover—small things like what he wanted to do after graduation and bigger things like the kind of person he wanted to be. He still cared about his mom, and his dad, and his future, and Cherry...

But, more than that, he wanted Arthur back.

He replayed Arthur forcing out an apology in his mind. He replayed the afterparty, and Spring Social and beyond. He replayed the dream and the hickeys and the study sessions, the contract and the way Arthur's eyes lit up when he talked about something he was passionate about, the pensive look on his face as he'd looked out over the lily pads of the peatland, the way his mouth worked not to smile when Mika managed to infuriate and delight him all at once.

Mika cried until there were no more tears, and his head hurt, and he was pretty sure there was more snot on his face than there was water. He turned off the shower and retrieved a towel from where it had crashed against the sink. Despite himself, despite everything...he wished Arthur was with him.

Without warning, his left hand gave a violent twitch, and his palm erupted into pins and needles. He looked sharply to find the words there as dark as ever, slightly raised, a fresh tattoo where there'd only been a whisper of a name.

Arthur Pham.

And before he could even begin to fathom what it meant, there was a knock on the door.

Shave-and-a-haircut.

32

The sound of his knuckles on the door echoed in the corridors of Arthur's mind.

The seconds stretched infinitely. He could have been there for minutes or hours or days for how long that moment of silence felt.

But it wasn't minutes or hours or days. It was five seconds, and then he heard a floorboard creak under footsteps, and then the door unlatched.

And there he was.

And of *course* he was wearing only a towel.

The door opened and Arthur was met with warm, humid air, bringing with it with the scent of jasmine incense and sandalwood shampoo and Old Spice. Mika was still damp from the shower, hair wet and product-less, beads of moisture the towel had missed dotting his collarbone. And once his collarbone was brought to attention, his shoulders followed, and the space between his arms and his chest, and the space between his chest and his stomach and the space between his stomach and the towel secured by a tightened hand, the hair there traveling down and down and—

Arthur's stomach swooped low as he snapped his gaze up and found Mika Rivera making eye contact with him for the first time in two weeks.

Don't think.

"We need to talk." Arthur kept his eyes planted firmly on Mika's. They were red around the edges, puffier than usual.

"Not this again." Mika's gaze hit the ceiling.

"We need. To talk," Arthur insisted.

"It's one in the morning."

"Move." Arthur shouldered himself between Mika and the doorway, ignoring the brush of his arm against Mika's bare chest and storming into the room...

...Which was a disaster. The pile of clothes that once resided on the back of Mika's desk chair were cast across the room, and the chair itself was overturned. The bed was unmade, and books and notebooks and pencils were scattered all around the floor. The floor pillows were no longer artfully arranged in seating areas on the ground but strewn about haphazardly.

Arthur turned to where Mika had closed the door and was standing in front of it, arms crossed.

Tension swelled in the space between them. Everything Arthur had felt but never said, every memory they'd made together over the past year, every insult and every glance and every touch was laid bare in the fathomless ten feet that separated them. The atoms in the room danced frantically, and the static of their energy prickled at Arthur's skin, his hairs standing up on end, at attention for what was about to happen next.

He swallowed hard, willed his eyes to stay above Mika's neck, and opened his mouth to let the words fall out.

"I can't do this anymore, Mika."

"Do what?" The answer came too fast, and Arthur didn't know if it was out of apathy or the opposite.

He searched for the words, holding out his hands helplessly. "I— pretending, god, pretending we're boyfriends, pretending we're not attracted to each other, pretending there was nothing there, not even friendship—am I really alone here?"

Mika's impassive face cracked just a fraction, jaw clenching, mouth pressed tightly. Arthur tried to draw the thoughts out with his Sense, desperate to pull them from Mika's being and out into the open.

"Will you just talk to me?"

"I was never pretending," Mika bit out. His voice was acerbic, broken at the edges, but at least it was there. *"You* were pretending,

Arthur. You were pretending so hard that you somehow convinced yourself I was, too."

Arthur watched the mask fall apart entirely, watched Mika's eyebrows lift, watched the emotion touch his eyes. He felt it come flooding through, a powerful wave that hit Arthur's consciousness like the heat from a bonfire blaze.

"I know," Arthur said hastily, wanting to take advantage of the walls coming down, wanting so badly to make sure he wouldn't be shut out again. "And I'm sorry, Mika. When this all started, I never—and I mean never anticipated...whatever this is—"

"I already told you you're off the hook." Mika's voice cracked halfway through. Though his words were dismissive, his gaze was sharpened with poison, and Arthur knew with horror he'd said the wrong thing. "It wasn't what you signed up for. I get it. You signed up for a way to undermine me, and use me to—"

"Will you just let me finish?" Arthur interrupted. "Of course that's what I wanted. We were rivals. I hated you. What did you expect, with a stupid plan like that?"

"If it was so stupid then why did you agree to it?"

"Because I was desperate—"

"Why don't you just get to the fucking point, Pham."

Mika started a lap around the room, picking up pencils and notebooks and placing them in piles on the couch, picking up pillows and placing them into piles on the floor. The kinetic energy of it all sent the particles around them into a frenetic frenzy, and Arthur struggled to coalesce his panicked whirlwind of thoughts into cohesive phrases.

"It's late," Mika muttered, "and I'm tired, and I don't really want to stand here and listen to you explain how you hate me, how you only ever wanted to hang out with me because you were desperate—"

"I didn't—I don't—"

"—to win, for attention, you name it, I'm done. I'm done with you fucking with me—"

"Fucking with *you?*"

"—when all I ever did was help you, and placate you, and, hell, drop *everything* to spend more time with you, and to find out the whole time you hated me."

"I didn't say—"

"You literally just did." Mika was flushed with anger now, holding a notebook in his hand. His aura was hot, spiked, dangerous. It set Arthur's teeth on edge. "And you said it all along. You hated me, and wanted to use me, and you had the audacity to accuse *me* of snitching on you to my mom to undermine you?"

"I'm trying to tell you that I'm—"

"Sorry doesn't cut it," Mika fumed, steamrolling over him. "Nothing you could say would make up for stringing me along for months all because of some sociopathic little plot—"

"*Stop.*"

"You stop." Mika threw a hot pink cushion onto the floor.

The heat of his anger was causing a domino effect in the room, compounding twice and thrice and ten times over and Arthur had left his Sense wide open—he was powerless to fight the anger from seeping in.

"You have been fucking with me since Year One," Arthur fumed. "Taunting me, teasing me—it has been *ceaseless*, and you don't get to hold my reaction to that over me."

"Even when your reaction was getting me to trust you and then pulling the rug out from under me the minute I let my guard down?"

"You want to talk about trust? How about kissing me during 'Spin the Bottle' without consent, when our contract specifically—"

"Oh, do *not* get me started on the contract!" Mika roared.

"The contract and you violating it is the beginning, middle, and end of the problem."

"Where was your obsession with consent at Social?" Mika threw his hands out. "Or giving me sex eyes the entire two months leading up to it?"

The energy in the room was almost too much to bear, a balloon stretched too tightly around helium, a sneeze held in too long. "Your standards are impossible to follow, Pham. Hot one minute, cold the next—god, you're so caught up in the rules and the *thinking* of everything that you completely ignore what you're feeling and the feelings of those around you."

Arthur sputtered. "I—look, I was confused—"

"Well then, let me be perfectly clear." Mika's voice dropped dangerously low, and the temperature in the room went right along with it. "Fuck the contract. Fuck the rivalry. Fuck whatever got us into this shit. Never in my life have I felt the way I feel about you, Arthur.

Never. And you used that against me. And you broke my fucking heart."

Arthur struggled to draw breath. "Mika—"

"And I won't accept your apology just so you can feel less shitty about using me."

The raw energy of Mika's emotion was pulling at Arthur left and right, and he felt swept up in a hurricane, fighting to keep his balance. "Mika, please, *listen*. I wanted to use you. Not even that—I wanted to want to use you—"

"Nice."

"Just—" Arthur braced himself against the doorway, steadying himself in the storm. "You're right! I'm trying to tell you that you're right! You distracted me from hating you by...by...by fucking *enchanting* me."

"Oh please, like I would use magic to—"

"Lowercase 'e,' ass," Arthur snarled. "I'm being poetic, you stupid fuck."

Mika opened his mouth once, twice, shoulders still tense, eyes searching. "You..."

"You got under my skin and I *liked* it. I actually got to know you, and somewhere along the way I started wanting to spend more time with you. You were the only person I could really be my whole self around, because I was lying to my friends. And the way you think about things, about magic, it infuriates me, but it's fucking brilliant, and I wish I had half the confidence and grace you do, to surrender yourself to life and magic without worrying about anything—"

"But that's the thing, Pham," Mika interrupted. "You don't know me. I worry about things all the time. All the time."

"And how am I supposed to know that, when you're always putting on this unaffected front?"

"You fucking hypocrite." Mika smiled humorously, shaking his head and pacing a few steps back and forth. "Giving *me* shit for putting on a front."

"I thought it was *all* a front."

"And so did I."

Arthur heaved a helpless exhale. The pressure in the room was so severe, he closed his eyes and saw spots burst in the dark. "We're going in circles."

"You're the one who wanted to talk."

"God knows why, when you refuse to fucking listen."

Mika's eyes went glassy. "I'm so sick of this." His voice broke. "If you hate me so much, then just go and leave me the fuck alone."

"I don't hate you," Arthur exclaimed.

"You said you did!"

"That was before!"

"Before what?"

"Before I fell in love with you," Arthur cried.

Mika was completely, utterly still. The hurricane of energy in the room halted, the lost momentum of it causing stars to burst in the edges of Arthur's vision.

"I'm in love with you," his voice cracked, "you stupid, neanderthalistic, asshole, insufferable—"

He had a whole stream of insults lined up but he was abruptly cut off, because Mika made three long strides across the room to take his face in his hands and slotted his lips into Arthur's.

Arthur inhaled sharply and could have sworn he'd inhaled all the tension and energy in the room in one fell swoop for how much he felt, to be kissed by Mika. Finally, *finally* Mika's walls were down and his Sense enveloped Arthur, and it was like that immeasurably huge something on the tip of his tongue had finally come to him. The relief and the rush were intoxicating—Mika's thumbs stroked at Arthur's cheeks, his face nestled just right beside Arthur's and it was like running down a hill at uncontrollable speed, like that moment in a dream where he realized he could fly, just before taking off. His own Sense was an uncased wire, raw and short-tempered as it met Mika's, and for the first time Arthur thought he really understood the fireworks metaphor—Mika's entire being washed over him in that kiss and Arthur wholly and unquestionably gave himself over to the electricity surging between them, to the way he saw sparks fly behind closed eyes.

Mika broke away but only an infinitesimal amount. He leaned his forehead against Arthur's, and their lips brushed when he spoke.

"Arthur," he breathed. "You have no idea how long I've been waiting for you to say that."

Arthur smiled against Mika's mouth, laughing breathlessly. "I also have no idea how long I've been waiting for me to say that."

He felt Mika smile back. "Sorry, I kind of, uh..." He swallowed. "Sorry I jumped you there." He pulled away just enough to catch Arthur's eye. "Is it okay if—um. Can I—"

"Holy shit." Arthur slid a hand behind Mika's head and pulled him forward. "Yes," he said into his mouth. "Please, forever, yes."

That was all Mika needed.

He dove in with reckless abandon. Arthur felt his tongue at his bottom lip, pleading, and he welcomed him greedily. With their Senses intermingling, there was no more question, no more front, no more tiptoeing, no more pretending. The defenses were down and it was just Arthur and Mika, and Arthur was tilting his head to deepen the kiss, and Mika was making a noise like he was desperate for air yet perfectly content to drown.

Arthur's knees threatened to buckle and Mika braced him up against the door, sliding his hands down Arthur's shoulders, his biceps, to grip at his forearms and raise them, bracketing Arthur's head to pin them there.

Arthur gasped at the pressure and came up for air, tilting his head back. Mika used it as an opportunity to lean down to his exposed neck, mouthing at his pulse point. Arthur made a sound low in his throat, trying to escape Mika's grip on his arms so he could bring him in closer but Mika held his grip firm, smiling against his neck.

"I'm not done with you yet." His voice came out in a whisper—his breath on the wet spot he'd left, sending shivers down Arthur's spine—and then he leaned in to kiss and lick and suck and bite down, *hard*.

Arthur made a noise that frankly, under normal circumstances, he'd be ashamed of. But here and now, under Mika's mouth and feeling the pent-up energy releasing in sparks all around them, all he wished was to be closer, for *more, more, more*.

Overwhelmed by the sheer amount of Mika but unsatisfied with not enough Mika, Arthur slid a knee between his legs, thrilling to find him hard under the towel. Mika melted at the pressure, mouth falling open at Arthur's neck, grip slackening...

Arthur released his arms from Mika's hands, using his momentum to reverse their roles. He latched a hand at Mika's waist—*skin, skin, skin*—and the other up his neck, into his damp hair. He found purchase and jerked Mika's head to the side, eliciting a helpless gasp.

"I told you I work out," he murmured into Mika's ear and grazing his teeth at the lobe, chuckling as Mika made a strangled sound. He mouthed at the side of Mika's neck and slid his left hand down Mika's side, love line lit red hot until he was met with a hip to grab onto.

Arthur paused. "How is your towel still on?"

"How are your clothes still on?" Mika blurted, and Arthur raised his eyes to meet Mika's.

He stared at Mika, and Mika stared at him, and then they burst into giggles.

"Sorry." Mika was blushing.

"Don't be," Arthur smiled. He wasn't sure he remembered how to stop smiling.

"I need you to know." Mika's face looked strange. "As much as I one-hundred percent, absolutely definitely for sure want you to take your clothes off, I..." He drew out the syllable long. "Have never done this before."

"Done..." Arthur blinked and shook his head. He realized with a start that Mika's face was displaying an emotion he had never once seen there before: *embarrassment*.

"Sex," Mika clarified. "Like, all the way."

It clicked. "Wait, wait—"

"With, I mean, okay—vaginas, I'm well versed in. But you're my first..."

Arthur closed his eyes and took a step back, holding his hand up to stop him. "Oh my god. Jesus. Mika, I'm not going to put my dick inside you the literal first time we do anything!"

"Well, I don't know!"

"What is this, a fanfiction?"

"You're so suave all the time, for all I know, you—"

"I'm suave?"

"Wait." Mika narrowed his eyes and pushed Arthur's hand off his hip, pointing at him. "Who says you're the top?"

Arthur scoffed, appalled. "I'm sorry. Who's the one who's never had gay sex before?"

There was the infamous shit-eating grin, and Arthur was horrified to find that not only had he missed it, but he now adored it.

"Please, Pham. Just try and tell me I don't exude top energy."

"Power-bottom. Take it or leave it," Arthur insisted.

"We'll see," Mika acquiesced, and he pulled Arthur back in by the scruff of his shirt to kiss him once more.

And this time, he was playing dirty.

His mouth opened slowly, unhurriedly, snaking a hand up into Arthur's hair to draw him in. His tongue danced along Arthur's, and then he was pushing closer, deeper, and making a noise deep in his throat that sent blood rushing down south at a dizzying rate.

He broke away too fast, leaving Arthur's head spinning. "Maybe that would work out after all," Mika said thoughtfully, voice low, breathless. "Riding you with your arms pinned above your head, telling you how good you're being?"

Arthur was pretty sure he was having a stroke. He was pretty sure, because otherwise there was no way he'd be placing his thumb under Mika's chin, brushing it across his bottom lip, pushing it into Mika's mouth, securing his left hand at the towel, looking Mika in the eye.

"I've always thought you talk too much," he said, voice barely above a whisper. He flicked his gaze to where Mika had begun to suck, then back up to his eyes, wide and too-dark-too-bright. "I think a gag would suit you nicely."

"Fuck," Mika ground out around Arthur's thumb, and Arthur smiled and used his grip on the towel to unlatch it from Mika's hips as he made his way to his knees.

And maybe it was the late hour, or the whole soulmate thing, or the literal magic in the room all around them but all Arthur could think, face to face with Mika's *stomach-hips-cock-thighs* was that it was the most beautiful picture he'd ever seen in his whole life.

He looked up from under his eyelashes at Mika, who made a choked-off noise and said, "I've gotta say, this is very different from how I thought my night was gonna go—*oh!*"

Mika gasped as Arthur took his entire length into his mouth in one.

Maybe he wouldn't need the gag after all, Arthur mused, because this seemed a rather effective way of getting Mika to stop talking. Different techniques seemed to elicit new reactions, each thrilling Arthur more than the one before, and he was just wondering what adding a swirl of the tongue at the top would do when Mika's grip in his hair tightened.

"I—ah, fuck—hng—A-Arthur. Wait."

Arthur released him, mouth wet, hands tight at the V-cut of his hips. "Hm?"

Mika seemed to have lost his train of thought, staring. Arthur raised an eyebrow, and Mika squeezed his eyes shut with a deep breath.

"If you keep doing that," he breathed, "I'm going to come. Like, five minutes ago."

"That's kind of the point." Arthur couldn't help but grin.

"Right, yes. Yes, god. But I..." Mika licked his lips and averted his gaze. "I wanna be closer."

He blushed visibly, and Arthur's heart fluttered.

"Embarrassment looks good on you," he noted, rising to his feet. Mika reached down to meet him halfway, kissing him as they rose together.

"My cock," Mika managed between kisses, "looks good in your mouth."

Arthur laughed and shook his head, stepping over debris on the floor and leading Mika to the couch. "Come on, Casanova."

He sat and pulled Mika down beside him.

Arthur wondered if Mika's confidence came solely from this couch, because it was the night before winter holiday all over again—Mika up against his side, arm behind Arthur's neck, mouth languid against his own, deep and lazy as he ran a hand easily through Arthur's hair, down his neck, against his chest, tracing down his stomach, across his hipbone and teasing, just barely there, against the outline of him, straining against his sweatpants.

Arthur inhaled sharply and Mika broke away, arrogant smile taking up residence on his lips. "I think you're wearing too many clothes."

Arthur came in close for another long, lingering kiss. He lifted up his hips under Mika's hand as he finally responded against his lips, "So what are you gonna do about it?"

Mika made a noise that came out more like a growl as he shifted his hand to paw at the hem of Arthur's *'boyfriends are temporary'* tee, lifting it up and over Arthur's head. He shifted to the floor to get both hands on the sweatpants, and Arthur lifted his hips so Mika could slide them off.

Arthur watched Mika sit back on his heels in front of him to stare openly, and actively fought against the desire to cover up.

"God, you're so fucking hot," Mika breathed.

"Don't think I didn't notice your obsession with my forearms."

Mika blushed. "Ass."

"Come and get it," Arthur grinned.

Obeying, Mika leaned forward onto his knees, crawling so he was in between Arthur's legs. He slid his palms up Arthur's thighs, hips, waist, and ran a tongue up the underside of his cock.

A sound escaped Arthur's mouth, and he lowered a hand to the side of Mika's face. But just as Mika was about to sink down, he pulled, urging Mika's face up to his own.

"Can you just let me return the fucking favor, Pham?" Mika breathed as their foreheads touched.

"I think we can call it even." Arthur met his eye, a devilish smile on his lips.

"Dreams don't count," Mika protested.

"They do if we're both dreaming them," Arthur pointed out. "And I want you close, too."

Mika grinned. "Yeah?"

"Yeah."

They fell back against the arm of the couch, laughing, Mika grabbing a pillow from the floor to prop up against Arthur's back before he adjusted to hover over him, slotting their legs together and bringing his lips to Arthur's.

The friction of the change in angle caused them both to gasp. Arthur thought he'd known no sweeter sensation than Mika's lips on his, but he had to admit Mika's cock against his was making a run for its money. Mika kissed him and moved with him until he could no longer multi-task; he dipped his head to mouth helplessly at Arthur's shoulder and Arthur reverently cataloged the sounds spilling from Mika's mouth, everything from low and gravelly to high and mewling.

Arthur had fooled around before, but this...this was something entirely different. His usual calculations—a mouth there, just this angle here, the thinking of it all—were nowhere to be found. There was only Mika, and Arthur's hips grinding up to meet Mika's of their own accord because there was nothing for it; he was so far gone he forgot even his own name, let alone his grasp on language. It was all sensation and feeling—*friction, need, more, want-want-want*—and he was drunk on Mika, the scent of *boy-sweat-skin* and Old Spice and shampoo.

They moved together, and it was literal, actual magic. Their Senses mingled until they were indistinguishable, one living, breathing entity fed by kinetic energy and sensation. Their breathing synced and Arthur felt Mika's left hand heat up against his neck, felt his own heat up on Mika's ass, saw the words branded white-hot behind his closed eyelids.

Michael Rivera.

With every thrust the energy swelled, building in a way that was reminiscent of that unfathomable but undeniable feeling but more, an irrevocable, inevitable climax that Arthur desperately wanted to prolong but whose pull he was helpless to resist. Mika was unraveling on top of him, breath hot at his neck and losing control over the rhythm of his hips. Arthur's mouth latched at Mika's shoulder, fingers scratching up his back and chasing the friction that was everything he needed and yet still not enough.

He was getting close, almost frightened at the intensity of it when Mika's hips stuttered and he made a broken noise next to Arthur's ear, and then: *"Arthur—fuck—"*

And he was gone.

Orgasms usually came and went without much lasting sense memory attached to them. But Arthur knew this was one for the books.

The pleasure was a full-body thing, blood halting in his veins for several long seconds before rushing forward all at once from the tips of his ears to the spot directly between his eyes and all the way down to his toes. The atoms around them were ricocheting off each other madly and spinning in fractal patterns, and when Arthur's eyes flew open in time with his mouth, he saw rainbows thrown against the dim colored light in the room, his surroundings painted technicolor and beyond with hues he hadn't known existed and couldn't even name.

And then the wave broke, and Arthur willed his shaky hands to Mika's face, pulling him up to kiss him, messy and reckless.

Mika was laughing against his mouth, and Arthur let out a helpless breath.

"So," Mika breathed. "Would you like to revisit your previous misconceptions about my stamina?"

Arthur laughed weakly, seeing stars. "I stand corrected."

He shifted under Mika, flinching at the killer combination of slick and sensitivity.

"Here." Mika lifted his hand and swirled it in a counterclockwise circle, calling on the power of his wand, which must have been somewhere in the mess of the room. His towel, abandoned on the floor near the door and still damp from the shower, appeared in his hand, and he shifted to bring it between them to clean up.

"Thanks." Arthur kissed the only part of Mika that was accessible, which was his forehead.

"Pretty sure we eliminated forehead kisses from the contract." Mika crumpled up the towel strategically and tossed it across the room.

"Couple things," Arthur noted, sitting up as Mika sat back on his knees. "One, I am five-thousand percent positive that orgasms are not included in the contract, so that ship sailed a while ago, and two, the contract is null and void, on account of how you tore it up three weeks ago."

"So that means anything goes now?" Mika donned a lopsided grin, leaning forward to kiss Arthur's knee and then his thigh and then his stomach.

"I guess so."

"Including..." Mika hovered over him again to kiss his cheek, insufferably, with tongue.

"Eugh, gross!"

"Including..." he leaned in for an open, lingering kiss.

"Definitely that." Arthur felt dazzled.

"Including..." Mika leaned back, slid his eyes to the side, then back to Arthur's. "Snuggles?"

Arthur thought his heart might have legitimately de-materialized and dissolved seamlessly into his bloodstream.

"I could be convinced," he managed.

"Sick," Mika beamed, and launched himself off the couch. "Come on."

33

Arthur made his way up the loft ladder and into Mika's bed, falling back against the pillows as Mika threw the comforter over them both.

"Why is your room a fucking disaster zone?" Arthur peered down over the side of the bed.

"I threw a tantrum before you got here," Mika explained helpfully, hooking an arm around Arthur's chest and pulling him down next to him and Arthur was still in awe at this—a shock of wonder in every moment, at the feeling of Mika's skin against his side, at the way Mika maneuvered Arthur's arm around his own shoulders so he could drape an arm over Arthur's waist, nuzzling his head into the crook of Arthur's shoulder, drying curls tickling at Arthur's chin.

Shameless as ever.

Hesitantly, Arthur raised his hand to meet Mika's on his waist and thrilled to find that their fingers interlocked on instinct.

"Tantrum?" he responded finally.

"Yeah," Mika sighed, inching closer still. "About how you hate me and I love you and there's nothing I can do about it. Thank god that's not true. Huge relief."

Arthur remembered Mika's eyes when he'd opened the door, red-rimmed and tired.

And then he really heard what Mika said.

"You..." He swallowed. "You love me back?"

"Uh, what gave it away, genius?" Mika lifted the comforter and gestured to their naked bodies under the covers.

"Well, I don't know!" Arthur protested. "Maybe you were just super horny."

"Pham." Mika gave him a look. "I don't cry in the shower over just anyone."

Overcome with affection, Arthur pressed a kiss into Mika's hair.

"I'd been crying, too," he said into his curls.

"Really?" Mika leaned back to look at him.

Arthur glanced at him, then returned his gaze to the ceiling. "Yeah. And then for the first time in three weeks I was able to Sense you, feeling the same way."

"Oh, yeah." Mika pointed across the room, and Arthur strained to look. "My spell jar broke when I sent my shit spinning around the room like a fucking lunatic."

Arthur turned back to Mika. "You were blocking me out? No wonder you wouldn't listen."

Mika sighed. "I don't think I wanted to," he admitted.

Arthur's heart gave a tired sputter. It was warm here, with Mika next to him and *loving* him, and it was two in the morning, and he was more tired than he'd ever been...but for all he knew, Mika could change his mind when they woke up, and he'd lose his chance to fix this—for real.

"I won't," Mika said, and Arthur startled.

"What?"

"I won't change my mind."

"You..." Arthur swallowed and smiled. "Did you just read my mind?"

Mika stiffened. "You didn't say that out loud?"

Arthur pulled back, raising his eyebrows. "Uh, *no*, dude."

They looked at each other for a moment, and then spoke at once.

"Holy shit—"

"How is this even—"

"All it took was sex to unlock literal superpowers—"

"We're going to need to establish boundaries—"

"Imagine everything we can do now, no more texting, test answers—"

"Cheating is forbidden in the contract!"

They looked at each other again and fell back laughing.

"We were so fucking stupid, huh?" Mika breathed, settling back onto the pillows.

Arthur turned to face him. "I was stupid, Mika."

Mika looked at him, and Arthur took a deep breath to continue. "Will you let me explain?"

Mika sighed and looked up at the ceiling. The mirth was gone from his face, but he nodded.

And so Arthur did.

It was the third time he'd gone through it, but this was the most important one. He wanted Mika to understand how high the stakes were, how high he'd *made* the stakes for himself. Arthur needed him to know that he knew how badly he'd screwed up, how badly he felt, and how badly he wanted to set it right.

Mika listened, reacting appropriately when Arthur revealed his perspective of key parts in the timeline, turning to face him in order to fully focus.

And when Arthur was done, Mika put his hand in between them, open, inviting, and Arthur met it with his own.

"I didn't make it easy for you," Mika admitted. "I *was* fucking with you. But not because I hated you." He smiled, and it was a small, sheepish thing. "I liked you. And I didn't know how to express it, and with our whole nemesis thing established..." He tilted his head. "I guess it sort of followed naturally. And that's not healthy either, and I'm sorry."

"It's okay," Arthur said, and found that he meant it. "It was...an unusual set of circumstances."

"But—" Mika frowned and looked at Arthur quizzically— "if you needed to win Electi Magi, you could have just told me."

Arthur's heart skipped a beat. "What?"

"I mean—" Mika wet his lips— "Our rivalry was fun and all. Competition is literally my only motivator. But...I don't know. I get now why you hated me, but I never hated you. I thought you were brilliant, and god—have you *seen* your cheekbones?" Arthur rolled his eyes and shoved Mika's shin with his foot, and Mika smiled before continuing. "I only kept up that mortal enemies stuff because I thought it was a game. It was a fun distraction for the bullshit going on at home. I guess that's why it didn't feel like such a big deal to do the fake boyfriends thing, because for me it just felt like a different kind of show. And there were so many times I wanted to drop it."

Arthur remembered Mika calling his name, debating—in the hall with the condoms, in his room after the hickeys.

"But I didn't know where to start," Mika continued. "I didn't have the words. Especially when I started catching feelings. All the way back before winter holiday—"

"Before winter holiday?" Arthur stared at him.

"Yeah." Mika smiled, and it was a little private thing, eyes downcast, thoughtful, before sparkling up at Arthur again. "You're behind as always, Pham."

Arthur blinked.

And then he shrank back on himself, releasing Mika's hand to cover his face.

"Oh my god," he said, and it came out muffled from behind his hand. "I feel so stupid."

"Hey." Mika tried to wrench Arthur's hand from his face and, finding it wouldn't budge, settled for scooting in closer to wrap himself around Arthur's whole body, petting his hair.

"You are stupid, darling," Mika cooed, and Arthur let out a groan. "But that's why I love your oblivious ass."

Arthur said something, but it came out incoherent.

"Mm? What's that?" Mika's tone was sickly-sweet.

"You're unbearable!" Arthur exclaimed, shoving Mika away—but he was smiling, and Mika was laughing, and they soon found themselves settled back in against one another.

"How are things, though?" Arthur paused to bite his lip and watch Mika carefully. "With your family?"

Mika let out a long groan, and Arthur chuckled. "You don't have to talk about it if you don't want to."

"No," Mika sighed. "You've been really honest. And I wanna be, too."

Arthur didn't respond, waiting.

And Mika explained how all year his mom had been pressuring him, catching him off guard with calls about his future that quickly devolved into screaming matches when Mika refused to bow down to what she wanted for him, weaponizing Mika's struggle for independence against him: *You're just like your father'* and, *You two are the reason*

I can't sleep at night' and, *'Why don't you go be with him then, if you hate me so much.'* He explained how he'd turned to his dad for support, but for all his dad's creativity and passion and love, he'd always been scattered and unreliable in a time of need.

Cherry had helped him through the worst of it, but it didn't change the fact that soon, sooner than he liked, Mika was going to have to choose between his parents, no matter how hard he fought against it. His rivalry-turned-relationship-turned-study partnership with Arthur had saved him from academic failure. Without Arthur's support, his grades likely would have spiraled down the drain from the stress.

"So you're telling me," Arthur summed up once Mika finished, "the whole time I was obsessed with being your downfall because of my stress, I was actually helping you succeed *despite yours?*"

Mika smiled a roguish grin. "Looks like I bested you once again, Pham."

"The irony is a physical pain in my ass."

"Further proof that *I'm* the top."

Arthur shook his head, chuckling, lost in thought.

Cherry had been more right than he ever could have imagined.

He opened his palm to look at the words written there. They now resembled a tattoo, long since healed, ready to stand the test of time.

Mika caught him looking and placed his hand next to Arthur's: a perfect match.

"Wow," he said.

"Yeah," Arthur agreed. "Wow."

"I think," Mika said suddenly, Summoning his phone and flipping onto his stomach to peruse it, "we need a song. To really capture this moment, you know? Enemies to soulmates to fake boyfriends to best friends to enemies again to lovers...it practically writes itself."

Arthur sighed and sank back against the pillows. "What did you have in mind?"

And then he heard the opening notes of "Let's Call the Whole Thing Off," and he sighed.

"Christ," he groaned, and Mika grinned his shit-eating grin, laughing maniacally.

"It's perfect," he insisted as Arthur wrenched the pillow out from under him to place it over his own face firmly.

"I'll fucking suffocate myself."

Mika wasn't listening. He was singing Louis' part, a truly terrible impression.

"This is awful, and I'd like to throw myself off of this bed immediately."

Mika got the lyrics wrong in the second verse, and it didn't deter him for a moment.

"I think we should break up."

When it was clear that Arthur was resolutely not going to chime in for Ella's part, Mika grabbed Arthur's hand to use as a microphone while his voice cracked on an octave higher than should have been legal. Arthur wrenched his hand back and gripped the pillow over his head to slam it into Mika—who immediately grabbed hold of his own pillow, sending it into the side of Arthur's head with a pathetic *wumph*.

"It's meant to be, Pham!" Mika laughed as Arthur got up on his knees to land a more powerful blow. "It's our theme song!"

"It ends with them calling it off!"

"God, are you even *listening* to the subtext? It's never been your strong suit, clearly."

Arthur beat Mika with the pillow until he relinquished control of the phone, and Arthur immediately paused the song to search for a different one.

"L-O-V-E" started to play gently. "Spare me my dignity for once, please," Arthur insisted.

Mika wrestled the phone back from him. "No, no, that's for the part where we did the soulmate ritual."

"What?"

"It's a playlist now." Mika smiled, thumbing through the music app. "I don't make the rules."

They argued over which songs went where and played songs truncated by each other's impatience and insistence until five in the morning. The playlist was mostly done, and Arthur was warm and loose and comfortable tangled up with Mika. As music trickled out softly from the phone speaker, and as the pre-dawn light filtered through the window, and as Mika made a low, contented noise in the back of his throat, the last thought Arthur had before he drifted off to sleep was:

Maybe everything will be okay after all.

EPILOGUE

"Hit me with your best shot, Rivera."

"Oh no. I'm so scared."

"You know, I've been practicing the *Dirty Dancing* lift with Clarke. I think with a little more practice, I'll be able to lift you. Gotta account for the weight of your arrogance dragging you down."

"Fuck you, Pham."

"Maybe later, if you're lucky."

Arthur shot a devastating smile at Mika as they circled the middle of the classroom, wands aloft. Professor Hirst shook his head and smiled tiredly, albeit fondly, at the way the students stomped and whistled their approval.

It had been a long week leading up to finals, made easier by Mika joining their study group and made more difficult by having to explain to their classmates that they were back together again yet hadn't actually been together in the first place. He wasn't convinced anyone understood the gravity of the situation, nor did they even seem to really care that much.

They really had been idiots.

Between their anticlimactic reaction, the support of his friends, his own resilience, and, of course, amazing sex with Mika, Arthur had a lot less to be worried about these days.

And after finals finished the previous week, Mika and Arthur had settled down in Room 420 for the afternoon (long since straightened by a handy tidying spell of Arthur's creation) to sort through the loose ends together. With Mika's hand in his own, Arthur had called his mom to update her on what had been going on the past year—of the measures he'd taken to make sure she didn't feel any more stress than she had to, the stress he'd taken on in her stead.

"Son." Her voice was teary. "I had no idea. I didn't mean—"

"I know, I'm sor—" But at Mika's look of warning, he paused. "I know. I think, if it's okay, I need some space. For a little bit."

"Arthur—"

"I want to help you and Bella," he continued. "But I need to help me, too."

His mom took a deep breath. "I understand. I've put too much on you."

"Thanks, Mom. I think I'm going to spend the summer here, with Clarke, at Jonathan's house. But I'll be home in the fall, and we can catch up then."

"Okay," his mom conceded. "Okay. I love you."

"I love you, too."

And after, Mika called his mom.

He told her firmly that he'd be taking a year abroad in Italy to help his dad in the restaurant while applying to non-magic culinary school. Arthur heard her begin to raise her voice but Mika cut her off, insisting they hash it out with a family therapist when he came home to prepare for the move after graduation. Mika made eye contact with Arthur as her voice lowered, his eyes sparkling.

"Okay...yeah. Oh, and Mom?" He smiled, and Arthur frowned. "Remember Arthur? My friend with the phone charms?"

Arthur widened his eyes, heart beating wildly. Was he going to be introduced to the COO of Crystaltech as her son's soulmate? Despite the progress they'd both made, the traitorous voice in the back of his mind wondered if Mika really *had* been fucking with him the whole time, planning to sell him out—

"Yeah." Mika's voice interrupted his panic. "He's got a business proposal for you."

Back in Professor Hirst's classroom, Arthur cut his eyes to Clarke and Jonathan—making a cameo in the class because it was the last day of Year Four and nobody cared where anybody was at any given time

—who nodded and reached behind them to grab matching cherry-wood chairs, which they placed in front of them.

Everyone in the innermost row of the circle followed their lead, placing chairs in front of them.

Mika stopped revolving to watch the activity around them. "Um, what—"

Arthur tapped his wand to Tan's chair beside him, closing his eyes and calling on his own power and that of the Supercharging spell vial —one of Mika's creations—in his back pocket as he pulled his wand up.

The atoms in the room vibrated as cherrywood trees grew up from the chairs surrounding Arthur and Mika in hyperspeed, pausing as their blossoms bloomed.

He was going to need a nap after this stunt, but the look on Mika's face was worth it. The thought of lying beside Mika in his room, sun filtering through the window, listening to the sound of breath puffing in his ear, was worth it.

He coaxed the breeze into the classroom and cherry blossoms began to fill the circle, floating gently in the air. Thankfully, late spring was much closer to actual cherry blossom season, and the trees required much less persuasion to stay trees.

But, that being said, it was still a lot of fucking work.

Mika stared at Arthur, wand half-lowered, eyebrow raised.

The opening trill of piano from "La Vie en Rose" sounded out over the classroom, and Arthur made a mental note to thank Ben Lasher and Tan tonight at the Grad Night party.

Mika rolled his eyes and laughed, but his blush gave him away. Arthur walked forward and Mika met him halfway. This time, he let Arthur lead.

"Sap." Mika beamed.

"You bring out the worst in me." Arthur smiled.

They revolved in slow circles and the petals around them began to swirl, accompanying them in their dance. Their friends began to sing along, accompanying Louis Armstrong in a chorus of voices.

"What a difference six months makes, hm?" Arthur murmured.

"Feels like six years," Mika chuckled.

"I think I might have lost six years off my life from the stress,"

Arthur deadpanned, "and then gotten it back from how fucking happy you make me."

Mika ducked his head to rest it on Arthur's shoulder, hiding his face. "God, what have I unleashed, Pham?"

Arthur laughed, reveling in the sparkling magic around them. "I love you."

"I love you too, dingus."

In less than twenty-four hours, Arthur and Mika would be giving their joint Electi Magi speech in front of the class, cheesy robes and mage hats and all. They'd spend all night on the dance floor, taking turns dancing with Clarke, and Jonathan, and even Cherry—who would be beaming in approval—smiling and dancing and talking into the night.

In a week, Arthur would be using the direct deposit from Michelle Wrigley, COO of Crystaltech, to make his first backdated tuition payment (in a twenty-four-month, interest-free financing plan, upon Professor Stonebury's insistence) and to fund his first round of product development for Auratech with Clarke and Jonathan.

In six months he'd have made enough progress to rent the storefront in *Watergraafsmeer*, and he'd soon be making a profit, enough to take care of his mom and his sister and, eventually, partner with Crystaltech to become a business owner under their corporate umbrella of products.

And in a year, he and Mika would reunite for their anniversary after figuring out long-distance, and if everything went well...maybe they could start their life together.

If it had been anyone else, Arthur would have scoffed at the impracticality of it all. But with Mika's name tattooed on the love line of his left palm—dark, solid, *real*—he was pretty sure soulmates could make any harebrained scheme work in their favor.

"So, genius." Mika's cheek hovered next to Arthur's. "What's the occasion?"

The song was coming to an end, horns and classmates alike singing out their final notes, and the petals had settled onto the floor around them. Arthur tilted his head and gaze to the side, and Mika followed it.

The blossoms had fallen in the form of words:

'Will you be my not-fake-boyfriend?'

Arthur leaned Mika into a dip as their classmates' cheers crescendoed into a frenzy. He raised an eyebrow.
Well?
Mika donned his best shit-eating grin.
"Fuck yeah."
The students screamed and stomped and applauded, and Clarke and Jonathan exchanged fond glances, and even Professor Hirst clapped along as Arthur kissed Mika, right then and there, on the lips, with tongue.
Contract be damned.

ACKNOWLEDGMENTS

Some people came out of quarantine with a new dog, some with extensive knowledge of the ins-and-outs of sourdough starters, and I came out of it with a book. The world was forever changed over the course of three-plus years, and so was mine—due in no small part to a bunch of my favorite people.

To Hannah, who took a chance on a fanatical writer with a love of queer romance, and put in tireless work to back it up. A special shout-out to Nicole Fedan and Dana Wilkerson for sifting through a sea of em-dashes on their journey to the heart of the story.

To Christian, who is my blueprint for unconditional, lasting love. You make me so happy that I'm overflowing with it, and I used the excess to channel into this book—and into everything I do. I love you a bushel.

To my family, who are my warm, steadfast, rice-scented hearth to come home to. Wren, you are the beginning, middle, and end of the target audience for this book. Mom and Dad, thank you for doggedly supporting my passions no matter how far they may take me from the nest—you make it possible for me to soar.

To Makenna, for blessing my life with her friendship, an infatuation with writing, and the gift of queer fandom. This book wouldn't exist without you.

To Jack, for sitting with me in a Crate and Barrel reading about a wizard-detective limping around Chicago with a heart of gold and a chip on his shoulder.

To Buttons, for warning me of the dangers of italics overuse.

And finally, to Clementine, radiant joy straight to the heart in the shape of a pug.

ABOUT THE AUTHOR

Birdie is a biracial, bisexual woman from sunny Los Angeles, living in Chicago to learn how to be an art therapist. She's been an artist since birth, and she's been making fanart and fanfiction ever since she found out what fandom was. *Sparks Fly* is Birdie's first completed original work, and she is unashamed to say that it's her favorite book she's ever read. When she's not obsessing over fictional characters—a full time job, to be sure—you'd be likely to find her snuggling with her spouse and their pug, taking roleplaying too seriously in her D&D campaigns, or baking a killer batch of cupcakes.

Milton Keynes UK
Ingram Content Group UK Ltd.
UKHW041925040823
426365UK00003B/164